THe WOLF In THe WaTCHTOWer

sue wiLDer

Cover Design: Regina Wamba, ReginaWamba,com

contents

Author's Note

THIS STORY TAKES PLACE in modern Washington, Idaho, and Canada. Some geographical details are accurate, others are the product of imagination. But I can almost guarantee that there are no hidden werewolves or vampires in these areas. No evil creatures hiding beneath the Canadian glaciers—the Canadians are far too polite to allow that. As for the witches, there may be a few running around, but they shouldn't interfere with this story.

For those of you who have read my romances, you know what to expect. The romantic moments are blush-worthy and happen on the page. The violence is what you would expect from werewolves and vampires, and there are words that put money in the swear jar. This fantasy is M/F, one couple, book one in the Sentinel Falls trilogy with a mild cliffhanger, and is intended for readers over 18.

Dedication

FOR THOSE WHO FEEL like a star is missing in the heavens... for those who have dreamed and cried with no one to hear except the midnight sky... believe in hope.

CHAPTER 1

Noa

SENTINEL FALLS HAD BECOME idyllic in the storm light.

When I looked up, lavender clouds clotted the sky while golden sunlight slashed across the foothills. If my camera had been in reach, I might have photographed the scene. But I knew the deadliest predators hid behind the loveliest views, and more cruelty than kindness lived beneath those pines.

Tepid air blasted through the car vents, doing nothing to ease the chill. The fretful wind meant a storm was coming in. The light would be useless within the hour, and if I sat here much longer, I'd lose myself in those mountains. Deep in wolf territory, where the wolves were not forgiving, no matter who my grandfather was or had been.

I hated the thought of it, though. Driving into Sentinel Falls. The town was like a movie set—a façade. Years ago, I'd seen in through a child's eyes. I couldn't see it that way now. I wasn't even sure why I'd turned in this direction. Turned to where I'd once dreamed and loved and believed in fairytales instead of the real things that went bump in the night.

But I hadn't thought about food when I left Seattle, grabbing only a few clothes, my camera, laptop, and if I wanted to eat, then I had to go in, get out, and be five miles down the road before they knew I was here.

A chill drifted down my spine. The town was quiet, other than a dog barking. Aging buildings clustered like gossiping crows, and there—against a brown-shingled building—the barbers' pole was a twist of red and white. A sign in the café's window bragged about new ownership. The general store looked the same, other than the western-style overhang—it sagged a little more in the middle.

I parked in a slanted space where weeds grew, and the broken parking meter still wanted ten-cents-for-one-hour. A gusting wind caught the car door before I slammed it closed. I needed to yank my sweatshirt hood to hide my hair. The wooden entrance door squeaked as it opened, whomped and banged as it closed, and I'd forgotten how jarring the banging was. But inside...

The familiar hit like a fist. Antler chandeliers hung beneath an open beamed ceiling. The planked, yellow pine floor bumped up where the tree knots wouldn't sand away. A crate held bananas; beside it, a spinner rack offered a sale on last winter's knitted hats. Through another half-closed door, I heard a woman humming; from the spiced apple scent, I guessed she was baking a pie.

No one else was around, other than a balding man in a red plaid shirt and blue overalls. He stood behind the counter sorting fishing lures, and the soft tap-tap-tapping of his fingers never changed. I wrestled a plastic shopping basket from the stack, wincing each time I reached for an item. Pain relievers were on my list, along with the day-old bread I wanted to toast, assuming the toaster in my grandfather's kitchen still worked. Although the kitchen was mine now, just like his house was my house.

For an instant, I couldn't move. My hand shook as the pain sank in... then the pine door squeaked. Whomped and banged as it closed. A man entered.

And adrenaline spiked.

Do not react, Noa. Don't look at him. Don't let him see your face.

"Mace," the man behind the counter said. "Hell of a storm comin' in."

The other man—Mace—didn't bother to answer. Instead, he shook rain from his spiky blonde hair as if the mess didn't matter.

Like most werewolves, he looked no different from any human male, tall, muscular. But he was alpha, and the alphas radiated an arrogance that set my teeth on edge. Hard and territorial, alphas did not indulge in casual conversations. But to the pack, they were rock stars who could do no wrong. Their word was law. Boundaries were ruthlessly enforced, even with grocery stores, and knowing that, I leaned hard into the dairy section, repeating a childhood rhyme to calm my mind... *liar, liar, pants on fire.*

Because with alphas, there were always rules.

Never show them fear.

Never let them close enough to scent you.

And never invade an alpha's territory without permission, because he'd pee on your car out of spite.

Petty, Noa.

But the alpha was stalking through the store, past canned goods and bakery items... hunting... and I knocked a carton of cream into my basket. Bolted toward the checkout, forgetting what else I needed.

The balding man didn't glance up. His sagging name tag read Oscar, and I thought of Oscar the Grouch with spikey blue hair and beetled eyebrows. Only his hair was white and not blue and... *focus, Noa!*

"Road's out fifty miles ahead," he said. "Better you head back toward Priest River a-fore this storm hits. A lot can happen to a woman alone, losing herself in these mountains."

"I'll be careful."

"Then don't be complainin' when you're stuck and can't get back."

I decided he was a gatekeeper, a wolf who steered humans away from what they shouldn't see. I'd met gatekeepers before. They were friendly to strangers and wayward children. But when I'd met them, they hadn't realized what was *off* about me. I was Leo Bishop's granddaughter, the girl who came to visit every summer, and thank the gods her trashy mother hadn't come with her.

As Oscar's scanner dinged, the alpha altered his path, and I asked, "How much do I owe?"

"Twenty-six-ninety-five. Cash, no debit since the machine's down with the storm."

I dug for my wallet, and as I pulled out several crushed bills, brunette hair fanned across my cheek. For some gods-forsaken reason, the hoodie had slipped, revealing the silvered streak I'd wanted to hide. Now it was in full view.

And the alpha was behind me, silent, stealthy—no human moved that way. His long-sleeved black Henley was rain-spotted. Black jeans were tight and his boots were muddy. I doubted he cared. His goal was to identify who I was, if I belonged.

Now he knew I didn't belong. No one with hair like mine belonged in Sentinel Falls. My mother said I was lucky, and I'd said it too, that I was lucky, so many times while a restless part of me said, *no, Noa. You aren't lucky at all.*

"Noa Bishop?" A woman stood behind the counter with an apple pie in her hands. "Is that you?"

She looked older than I remembered, white hair instead of brown, but eight years had passed, and wolves aged the way humans did. She wore a white apron with blue cornflowers on the front, and as she slid the pie beneath a glass cover, I said, "Hi, Hattie."

"My goodness. It *is* you." She pressed a hand to her chest. "I wasn't sure, but here you are. How've you been?"

"Fine." I nodded. "And you?"

"Oh, we're fine. Course you remember my Oscar, although maybe you don't. Oscar wasn't around much those summers you were here. He was logging up north—but Oscar's my mate, and he didn't mean to make you feel unwelcome."

She rubbed Oscar's shoulder, and I felt dull for not realizing Oscar hadn't made eye contact with me because he was grouchy or a gatekeeper. Someone ordered him not to alarm the strange woman until the alpha arrived.

Which meant someone—some *wolf*—had watched me from the moment I parked at the edge of town. And Mace's hair and clothes were wet because he'd been the wolf watching.

I stood mute while Hattie continued, "That man lurking behind you is Mace Riggs. This is Leo Bishop's granddaughter," she said to him. "From Seattle."

Mace Riggs didn't answer. He didn't need to, since every wolf in Sentinel Falls knew my history. I might be Leo Bishop's granddaughter, but I was also the child of a *faille* and a random shifter passing through. While I'd been too young to understand the names people called my mother, I understood how upset she'd been, and when I turned five, she decided we'd go on a grand adventure. Move to Seattle. Start new lives.

No one stopped her when we left, and she refused to come back. But the one charitable thing the pack did for me was to allow summer visits with my grandfather. I spent three months pretending I belonged. They pretended Andrea Bishop Kline didn't exist. And everything was fine until the year I turned sixteen.

Then I stopped coming.

My mother never asked why, and I never told her. But she probably knew the way Hattie knew, and I glanced up to see Hattie glaring at the man behind me.

"Mace works at your grandfather's vet clinic," she said, as Mace took a step back. "The pack's taken over the responsibility. So... not to worry when you see the lights on." She tugged the empty shopping basket from my grip and set it aside. "You're staying out at the house?"

I nodded. Leo had willed his house to me, along with a trust fund, and I'd used the money to protect what he'd loved, even if I hadn't shown it all those years ago. I'd kept the utilities on so the pipes wouldn't freeze, paid the taxes, and knew I'd never live there.

"I hope you don't mind," Hattie continued. "But I checked on the house once a week, kept the supplies stocked... in case you ever dropped in. Leo would have wanted that. The water heater works fine. Oscar looked at it last month, but after your long drive, I'm sure you want to relax."

She poked through my bags, adding a bottle of luxury shampoo and hand lotion. When she reached for a box of chocolate truffles, my throat tightened. Every time I'd come in with my grandfather, she'd slip me the candy when he wasn't looking.

My fingers were unsteady as I dug for my wallet. "How much more do I owe?"

"Not a dime, Noa. Housewarming gift."

I thanked her, reaching for the bags, but stopping when she touched the back of my hand.

"If you're going out there now, Mace should go with you. Since you've been gone, things have changed in the mountains. You don't want to miss the turn."

"I'd rather be by myself." And I was only staying one night. I didn't dare stay longer, but Hattie didn't need to know why, and neither did Mace Riggs. "I remember the tree, and the reflecting disc marking the road."

"Three disks now. I had Oscar put up extras when the winter turned hard. Outside lights come on automatically. Leo put in an alarm. The control pad is beside the door. The code is your birthday."

The birthday code hurt, when I'd ignored so many of my grandfather's birthdays. I swiped at my cheek, and Hattie's expression softened until it stung. She'd always looked at me like I needed a mother. I'd always looked back, aware of the small betrayal I felt, wishing she'd been my mother... instead of the mother waiting in Seattle.

But this was Sentinel Falls.

And things had changed in the mountains.

CHAPTER 2

Noa

THROUGHOUT MY CHILDHOOD, THE only werewolves I saw were those in illustrated books. I read every story, devoured each myth. Spent hours racing through the forest with a stick in my hand, hoping I'd see a werewolf. When I was seven, I asked my grandfather if I could watch men turn into wolves. He said I was too young. I asked again when I was eight, but he still said I was too young. When I turned twelve, I argued that I'd watched enough werewolf movies to know what it looked like. But Leo said *absolutely* no.

He kept saying it until I turned sixteen.

Then I wasn't too young. And the difference between imagination and reality sickened me. It was enough to decide my mother had been right when she said I was lucky. She'd also said once I saw the wolves as the monsters they were, I would never forget it, and she was right about that, too.

With the groceries beside me, I left Sentinel Falls, speeding down the two-lane road that glistened like black obsidian in the wet. Humans called these mountains the Selkirks. Wolves called them Sanctuary. The area stretched from northeastern Washington, into western Idaho, up through the Canadian territory, and was so wild and remote, no one knew who or what lived here.

Uneasy, I pressed hard on the gas pedal, slowing only when I passed my grandfather's old vet clinic. Milky light spilled from the windows. The blue pickup truck beside the building meant someone was there, and I was glad the pack continued with my grandfather's life work.

Leo Bishop called himself *a vet* for the human world. But what he'd been was a healer. Everyone knew he would travel for days, cover hundreds of miles in a converted fire-med truck, rescuing injured werewolves stuck in their wolf forms. Wolves who were not wild and shouldn't fall into the hands of government wildlife biologists.

The summer I turned sixteen, I'd gone with Leo on a rescue. I still remembered the dull rattle of instruments against the metal walls of the med truck. The rocking thud of heavy tires on the back roads.

On that rescue, we pulled a young female out of Montana. Injured and starving, she'd been unable to shift from her wolf form into human.

My job had been to sit at her side, and each time I dug burrs from her tangled mats, she'd whimper and thrash. To keep her calm, I sang a nonsense song. And later, when I asked my grandfather, he told me she would heal, eventually. Shift eventually, with the alpha's help.

But I would never *eventually* accept the unjust tragedy of wolf life.

If I couldn't stop wolf violence, then I couldn't witness it. Stand by and do nothing without feeling anger and resentment. Perhaps that was another trait of the *faille*—which meant exactly what it sounded like. A failure of creation. I was too emotional. I'd never be *like them*, no matter who my father and grandfather were. I was like my mother, and I'd stormed away, refusing to look back because I'd known I couldn't change what that meant.

I accepted it now. Didn't fight the emptiness late at night. And the entire time that I'd driven from Seattle, I'd told myself I could do this. Go back to my grandfather's house. Time should have blunted the memories, and all I needed was a place to hide for the night. To plan, then move on before...

I pushed at my hair, hated that Mace saw it. Or that I hadn't thought about Hattie still running the general store. I'd hoped it would be some random shifter, or one of the humans who still lived in Sentinel Falls. Who knew about wolves and hadn't left when the loggers pulled out.

Maybe I'd hoped foolishly...

A glance at the odometer told me I was close to my grandfather's road. I flicked on the headlights. Leaned forward and studied each branch that moved through the lavender dusk, every eddy of yellow leaves skittering across the road. Perhaps that was why I saw the panicked deer as she raced out of the shadows and into the headlight glare.

I slammed the brake pedal, and by the time the car juddered to a stop, it was sideways on the road. The deer was back in the forest. I was listening to the thump-pause of the windshield wipers and staring hard into the rearview mirror. A red exhaust puffed, and an unnerving chill had me checking the door locks.

The red was nothing, though. Only my foot, pressing hard on the brake pedal and reflecting off the vapors. I breathed in, stared ahead. Rain streamed through the headlight beams like white moths, but beyond the moths, glinting against a dark tree, were three reflecting silver disks.

I eased off the brake, put on the blinker out of habit and turned down the dirt road. The headlights glinted off rain-filled ruts. Tires thumped on the packed mud instead of hissing on the pavement. And the sound reminded me of Leo... all the mistakes I'd made.

I never told him the truth. He thought I hated him for being wolf. Maybe I had, but I also loved being with him, trying to do the right thing, helping the injured and the weak. In the end, I wasn't wolf enough to adapt to his life, and I left with anger driving me. The burning indignation of youth. Ignorance, really, and I regretted those last minutes when Leo stood on the deck. Waiting for me to look back one last time.

To say, "I love you."

I couldn't do it.

And what I learned from that experience was that life demanded choices. I'd made mine. And there was no way I could atone for those choices now, no matter how sharp the ache in my throat.

I drove, avoiding the worst of the ruts until the road curved and floodlights illuminated my grandfather's yard. I'd always thought the house looked like a hunting lodge, with a pitched roof, peeled-log siding, and golden light shining through the windows. No light now. Not with the house empty. But I imagined the cozy warmth inside. The round table in the kitchen. A fireplace to chase the chill.

The front door was deep blue now, instead of brown. A decorative twig wreath hung from a red ribbon and offered an inviting welcome.

Wooden steps led to the deck. I'd climbed them many times, parked my battered bike with the wheel propped against the railing. My grandfather's log bench was still beside the door. He would sit and pull off his rubber boots before going inside.

I breathed in, breathed out as the memories continued to flow.

Breathed in again when I realized I was staring at the front door. Waiting for Leo to appear.

Even when I knew he wouldn't.

But the *wanting* was so intense, I could almost see him walking outside with a smile so wide, his arm raised in welcome.

Feel him...

I drew in a jerky breath, blew it out.

He's gone, Noa. But he'd be happy you were here.

I rolled down the car window, needing the chilly air now, listening to the soft ticking of the engine as it cooled. And as the rain sputtered... as the wind offered a final gust before fading... that was when I heard it.

A faint whine.

Was it pain?

Fear?

Or a trick of the rain and imagination? My sorrow?

I pushed the car door open, ready to slam it shut, but seconds passed and nothing happened.

Birds fluttered in the twilight. I heard their shadowy rustling as they hopped through the trees. The chirp of hidden crickets enlivened the tall grass. Water continued to drip from the pines with soft splats.

Sliding from the car, I squinted against the floodlights. If I kept moving, I'd be okay. Predators preferred the dark. Not that birds would be noisy if a predator was near. Nor would the crickets. They'd be the first to fall silent.

And yet, I fought a battle in my head over whether I should grab the food and clothes and go inside the house, or if I should wait.

The whine stuck with me, and I was human enough to worry about what it meant. Taking a step, then another, I edged away from my car and toward the far rimming light where the shadows grew darker. Pausing, I balanced on the balls of my feet, breathing through my nose.

The tension in waiting, in listening for the whine, kept me braced and silent. And when I heard the sound again, my immediate thought was a lost puppy.

That wasn't probable in Sentinel Falls. No wolf would abandon a puppy the way humans did, stuffed in a cardboard box like trash. Or dumped in the wilderness to fend for itself. If a pup had gone missing, the owners would have been out searching for it.

Which left one alternative. The whine came from an injured wolf, young from the sound. A juvenile like the ones my grandfather rescued.

Perhaps this injured wolf came here believing Leo Bishop was still alive. This was Leo's house, and if he'd been here, I knew he wouldn't walk away. Or go inside and wait until daylight.

He would find the animal. Evaluate, then ask for help if necessary.

An urgency gripped me, but I forced myself to think. Leo, in that gruff, kind way he had, told me to listen to my body and not my mind. To feel with gut instinct instead of the frantic argument in my head. Because what I thought was real, wasn't always right.

He'd said there were creatures who could lure an unsuspecting human—or wolf—toward the trees. Prey on their emotions. Rogue wolves from rival packs might trespass deep into Sentinel Falls territory, intent on damage or harm. He'd also talked about nymphs and other mysterious creatures, and I remembered Hattie's warning.

She said the mountains had changed during the eight years I'd been away. I didn't doubt there were dangers hidden deep in the valleys or on the steep granite ridges.

But this was my grandfather's house, a place where I'd spent summers playing in the yard, or running through the trees. I'd ridden my bike along the road. Even with the alarm system, the house had to be safe, because if it wasn't, then Mace Riggs would have insisted on his alpha duty and come with me.

None of those arguments mattered, though. Not in the end. Because while I might hate wolves for their violence, I couldn't ignore a creature in pain. I'd feel like I was betraying my grandfather's memory enough that I'd not be able to relax or sleep knowing a wounded pup was suffering somewhere outside.

I scrubbed my hands against my jeans and pushed back the hood of my sweatshirt. Standing with my back to the brightest light, I focused on the yard where the grass was short and the details were easy to see.

Nothing unusual.

Farther out, the grass grew wild, and last year's spent seed heads hung from taller stalks like teardrops after the heavy rain. A breeze added movement, and while the shadows were disorienting, I was used to finding visual patterns.

My dream was to become a wildlife photographer. I'd studied photography in college, and after a six-month internship with a mentor, I felt at home in the wilderness. Secret spaces intrigued me. I thought the little-known lives of animals balanced the energies in the city, and if given a choice, I'd always take the wilderness.

I waited for my eyes to adjust to the low light. Then I studied the patterns, the variety in the light and dark, the unnatural lumps that didn't flow from one space into the next. And as I stared, unmoving, I heard the whine again. Noticed an ear flick when the animal raised his head, then dropped.

I crept forward.

The mounded shape jerked. Grass stalks swayed as if paws raked through them. Without thinking, I dropped to my knees and hummed. The muddy ground dampened my jeans, cold, clammy, gritty. But the song I'd sung years ago to that young wolf rose in my mind. It was a children's nursery rhyme, where I made up the words as I went along.

Hush little baby... don't you cry.

The song could last for as long as the singer could find rhyming words, and it didn't matter, the nonsense. It was the melody that soothed. The repetition.

So, I sang as I crawled until I could part the grass and see for myself what was hiding there.

A young wolf, the size of a large dog. Perhaps seventy pounds.

The gray tail thumped. Golden light flashed in the wolf's eyes, tinged with green sparks. His pink tongue lolled out, and the dark spot near the tongue's edge made him look more... human.

Then I realized why the pup whined. Clamped around the wolf's right front leg was a rusty spring trap, with the saw-tooth points buried in a mess of matted fur and torn flesh. I could see pink muscle, a scrape of white bone, and a bloody, rusted chain with broken links.

That told me all I needed to know. Illegal traps meant poachers, working for the ranchers down on the flat who paid bounties for the wolf pelts. And while I understood ranchers fighting predatory wolves, leg traps were not only illegal, they were cruel.

And the wolves responsible for the killing did not live in these mountains.

Poachers had no reason to trap here... unless they were too greedy to care.

"Assholes," I bit out as I stared at the gaping wound.

The wolf thrashed, and I remembered to sing.

The first part was easy... *hush little baby, don't you cry.*

Then the words turned violent.

How once I found the asshole...

Know what I'll do?

I stopped singing because I *didn't* know what to do, what might make the wolf's injury worse. If I removed the trap, I could cause more damage. If I left it in place, every time the wolf moved, the putrid blades dug in deeper, making me worry about infection. About bleeding. About being wrong, while the wolf waited—although his breathing was harsh.

I couldn't ask him to wait much longer. Turning my attention to the trap's release mechanism, I struggled with the stiff hinges. My fingers slipped. Gouged against the bloody iron. I didn't feel the pain because I'd somehow applied enough pressure to widen the jaws and lock them open.

I eased the iron from the pup's leg, singing about how I'd tie *the asshole to a tree... kick him in the knee...*

Metal tugged, then ripped through the matted fur. Blood gushed, but I remembered Leo saying the first rush of blood helped push out debris. I whipped off my sweatshirt, binding it around the wound while the wolf shuddered.

He collapsed on the grass. His panting alarmed me, the way his ribcage rose and fell beneath the shaggy pelt, and I wasn't even sure if I was dealing with a werewolf, or a wild wolf who would turn feral, once it realized it was free.

But as I stared into the wolf's eyes, he stared back, and I saw a flash of awareness. Knew he realized I was helping him. I had no time to waste, though, since blood oozed from the wrapped leg fast enough to form a ruby-black pool.

I wiped my hands on the grass beside my knees. Pushed up and sprinted toward the car for a blanket—which I spread on the ground, then lifted the wolf, tucking the blanket beneath him in sections. First his head, then shoulders, legs, middle, more legs, working my way down his body until I'd centered his weight.

Adrenaline rushed, and each time I touched the wolf, my palms warmed. A tingle ran the length of my arms. White spots danced before my eyes—that had never happened before. I told myself I was reacting to the pup's fear and pain. A *faille* could sense wolf energy. It was our only defense. And our curse. I should have expected a reaction. Not let it spook me.

I gripped the blanket and began the slow drag to the car, singing the nonsense song.

And if he's got no knee to kick, know what I'll do?
Cut off his balls and give them to you...
And if he's got no balls to cut...

I choked on a laugh. Gods, I was getting violent with this song, but I'd only feel bad about it if I was singing to a five-year-old. This wolf had to be sixteen or he wouldn't *be* a wolf yet.

I focused on the open car doors, putting one foot in front of the other. The interior dome light illuminated the wet grass with a milkiness that reminded me of the vet clinic. The alpha—Mace Riggs—might be there, or someone else who could help.

"Almost home." I cleared a space on the rear seat for the wolf, then tried to lift him. The weight had my muscles quivering, and after five minutes I knew I was torturing him. His hind legs would push while he chuffed with the effort, but each time I stopped, the wolf raised his head. Stared at me as if urging me on.

I couldn't stop trying. My hands turned slippery with blood and bits of fur. The same muck covered the front of my tee shirt and jeans. The wolf panted. I kept singing, sliding him the rest of the way. The fur dragged across the leather seat, and the wet sound triggered a desperate memory. For an instant, I couldn't believe I was rescuing a wolf without Leo at my side.

My eyes watered. Harsh regret clogged my throat. I gripped the blanket and wrapped it tight around the wolf so he wouldn't fight and reopen the wound, then secured him with the seatbelt. When I could stand upright, I rubbed at my back... and realized the night was silent.

Not even the rain dripped.

Nerves prickled beneath my scalp. The air grew heavy and the damp closed in. I turned, searching the shadows until my eyes focused on the shape near the edge of the light. Massive shoulders. A lowered head. The black pelt was close to indistinguishable against the black wall of trees crowding close.

Wolf!

An alpha—and twice the size of a normal wolf, vibrating nightmarish energy that burned my skin. His legs were stiff. His lips curled back, revealing red gums and gleaming canines, and as he snapped at the air, flecks of white slaver collected around his jaw.

A low growl rolled from him, vicious and primal, and terror flashed before I remembered that fear would only incite violence.

I needed to be calm. Needed to breathe.

With incremental shifts of my body, I slid along the side of the wet car, wincing as the cold metal scraped against each knobby vertebra in my spine. Moisture chilled my spine, but I kept moving until I could close the back car door, taking the chance this wolf was content with watching.

He wasn't.

The wolf reacted, launching from a formidable crouch. Landing yards away from me and gathering himself.

Muscles rippled. The second growl vibrated through the ground, beneath my skin...

I lurched toward the open driver's door, my shoe slipping in the mud while my fingers clawed at the doorframe.

No time no time.

I still lost my balance, twisting back in a struggle to remain upright.

The alpha was so close I choked on the stench. His strange eyes glinted with blue lightning, tinged with a gem-sharp emerald. His canines were out, claws extended as he leapt toward me, and despite knowing his weight would be crushing, I still braced, hoping the hit would be clean. The kill sudden and complete—until the wounded wolf yipped.

The alpha wrenched away, not enough, and his haunches slammed against my chest. I careened off the car and bounced onto the muddy ground like a rag doll. The impact pummeled the air from my lungs. I curled inward, unable to breathe. I didn't think I had lungs to breathe with and I would lie there, blinking at the night sky until I couldn't blink anymore.

Then my brain kicked in and I sucked air into my throat. Gagged on the tight inhale. Nearby, the wolf snarled. He paced, and when I dared to look, I saw a ridge of bristled hair rising from his shoulders, following the length of his spine. His paws were larger than my hands, with wicked claws. He gouged inch-deep trenches through the wet grass, and when he raised his head... focused those strange eyes on me... the threat deep in his throat tore through every nerve in my body.

Because I knew he was demanding the act of submission.

He wanted me to do what every wolf did at an alpha's command.

To submit. Expose my throat to him. My stomach. All the soft, human parts of me.

Acknowledge his power.

Be vulnerable.

Be terrified.

I didn't think I could do it. Force myself to move when every muscle was paralyzed by fear. If I couldn't even breathe properly, how could I force myself to roll on my back? Straighten knees that were locked? Uncurl my hands?

Expose the bloody clothes I wore—which seemed to enrage him.

But of course. It was the blood. The little wolf's blood that he scented all over me.

My arms felt wooden, but I dragged them down far enough to expose my throat, the front of my body, the stains that covered my hands and the cotton tee, my jeans.

I arched back, feeling the sucking mud that caked in my hair and squished around my nape. My mouth opened. I fought the nausea while running through the strategies available. If the wolf moved, I'd roll beneath the car. Wait for a chance to open another door, get inside, somehow lock myself in—as foolish as that plan was, since the wolf was larger than any wolf I'd ever seen.

And the rules did not hamper him—because they were *his* rules.

I wasn't pack. I was the invader in this alpha's territory, and I had what was probably a pack member's blood all over me. A juvenile who whimpered in my car.

Regardless of my reasons, to this alpha, I was in his world and not mine. Fair game for whatever decision he made.

He could kill me, and no one would object.

They wouldn't even know. Or care.

But the wolf stood there, his breathing harsh, as if he struggled as hard as I did against the instinct to react. Neither of us moving.

Then the young wolf whined, and I pushed to my feet, scrambled into the car, slamming the doors before throwing the automatic locks.

The black wolf never moved. And when I drove down the dirt road... I drove like the devil himself was after me.

Perhaps he was.

CHAPTER 3

Noa

TREES PASSED IN A charcoaled smear. Night closed in, and the twin cones of the car's headlights defined my world, while the weakening whines from the injured wolf had me pressing harder on the accelerator.

The sweep of headlights ran from black pavement to blacker trees and reminded me of the black wolf. Had he caused the eerie chill I felt on the road? Had his energy been so potent that I'd felt it from a distance?

Between the savage frustration and the wolf energy rolling from him, I'd felt pure dread, and I wasn't sure if I was running from something or toward it. My worst memories were those with Leo, with those injured wolves who couldn't be saved. The senselessness in the suffering. And I was doing it again, listening to the whines—more human, now. Like a baby's cry.

My hands slipped on the steering wheel as I rounded another curve. Flares were a string of ruby pearls on the black road, spitting sparks and turning the rain blood-red. I wasn't sure what I was looking at... or why a pickup truck had blocked the road.

The truck was angled across both lanes with the headlights aimed in my direction. A man stood silhouetted in the light, his feet braced as he waved a flare, pointing toward the vet clinic.

And it pissed me off—how they knew I was coming. The blockade made it worse, as if I'd keep running unless they stopped me.

But where else would I run with a bleeding wolf in my car?

I was Leo's granddaughter. I'd gone with him on rescues, and it should have been obvious. That it wasn't only proved how deeply the wolves distrusted me.

I swerved as I made the turn, kicking up the gravel in a pebbled rain before skidding to a stop. Every clinic window spilled light, even the open door, but I still flinched when Mace Riggs pounded on my window.

I hit the automatic door locks. He ripped the rear door open hard enough to rock the sedan, reaching in to cradle the blanket-wrapped wolf while I sat in the car, pressing down on the brake pedal so hard that my knee shook.

The car alarm kept beeping because the engine was running, and Mace left the rear door open. I had no seatbelt fastened, so that was contributing.

Run, Noa. Run now!
Run before they stop you.

"Noa." Hattie swung open my door and leaned in. "Turn off the engine and come inside. Now."

I blinked, unable to speak or even loosen my fingers from around the steering wheel.

"You're safe."

Hattie's voice gentled. Maybe she thought I was a wolf pup.

"Come inside, Noa."

My breathing stuttered. I should refuse. Back away and drive. Hattie was old and couldn't stop me—but where would I go? To Priest River? Where I'd show up covered with blood and trying to rent a motel room so I could clean myself up? Maybe

I could find a dirty gas station bathroom, with a pitted mirror and no paper towels...

I shuddered.

The wolves knew I was coming and they would know if I ran down the mountain. They'd know where I would stop. There was only one option within a two-hour drive that also had a motel. Or a gas station, and any responsible human would take one look at me and call the police.

If I stayed, though... I thought Hattie was on my side. It wasn't in me to leave until I knew the wounded wolf would survive. For Leo's sake, I needed to know I'd done the right thing when I removed that trap, and hadn't made it worse.

My legs wobbled as I followed Hattie into the vet clinic, and an instant passed when I felt a strange time-shift. I thought I was walking beside my grandfather, the sensation so real that I turned to say something... but then an overhead fluorescent flickered, snapping me back.

Leo wasn't here.

I was alone, standing in a clinic that felt empty when it wasn't. The light fixture continued its random flickering. I felt a migraine coming on, and it surprised me I was still standing. I'd been exposed to more wolf energy in the last hour than I'd ever experienced. And that worried me, since my mother would have been curled in a ball by now—if she'd been the one here and not me.

I rubbed at my chest, staring at the scuffed linoleum floor, a gray confetti pattern. The worn-out spot in front of the reception counter was down to the subfloor now. As a child, I'd thought a giant must have stood there. Now I knew it was only people... wolves... standing there over the decades, shuffling their feet with worry.

"Sit for a moment, Noa." Hattie aimed me toward the couch, upholstered in a drab leather that creaked as I sat down. "Are you hurt?"

"No."

"You're covered in blood."

"Not mine." Thirst made me swallow. "Can I get some water?"

"You're shocky, so we'll wait on the water." She bent down, and I breathed in the sweet apple scent from the pie she'd baked, and beneath that, the scent of roses. I moistened my lips, then breathed in again. But the scents were gone.

"There was another wolf," I said. "He..."

"I know."

I shook my head, still dazed because I'd never understood how pack communication worked. I could only guess the injured wolf told Mace through their mental connection, and he would have told Hattie—who couldn't stop fussing like I was a youngling who injured herself.

"How hard did you fall?" she asked.

"Hard."

She checked my battered fingers, frowning when I flinched. "Did you hit your head?"

"A wolf wanted to kill me, Hattie. He changed his damn mind at the last minute, so I wasn't paying attention to what hit first when I fell."

She huffed, and I wasn't sure if the sound meant annoyance or amusement. "Was there anything else that seemed... off?"

"Other than the demand that I submit?"

"The wolf demanded, Noa?"

"No." A laugh cracked in my throat. "I knew enough to do it. Something Leo would have told me. And I'm fine, Hattie. Thank you."

"Don't thank me yet. Adrenaline is still in your system. You wouldn't know if you had injuries or not."

Pushing up my shirt sleeves, she *tsked* at the bruising. Her fingers pressed against my nape, then my head, moving strands of muddy hair until she satisfied herself that I wasn't bleeding.

"Can you follow me?"

I needed her help to stand.

"Remember the living quarters?"

Leo said the clinic was his second home, where he'd stay while nursing sick wolves.

"I want you to wash off every trace of mud and blood. Use the soap that's in the drawer. The wolves are already agitated. Levi's scent on you makes it worse."

"The injured wolf..."

"His name is Levi. He's pack, Noa. Mace is with him right now."

"The trap..." I gripped my wrists. "It was spring loaded, with jagged leg clamps, and when I got it off, I was so angry I threw it toward the weeds. But I'll go back and find it, because traps like that are illegal and—"

"Still in use." Her lips thinned. "The alpha will deal with it."

I shivered at the way she said that. Her hands fussed against my back as she guided me down a hall I knew as well as I'd known my apartment. "In the shower now. I'll have clothes waiting when you get out."

Thirst still dried my mouth. But as I entered Leo's old living quarters, I breathed in, hoping for the spicy scent of aftershave he always wore. It wasn't expensive, and I'd given it to him for every birthday. Every Christmas. Until I stopped.

But there was no familiar scent. Not even a trace. It was ridiculous, expecting it. Leo Bishop was gone, and once I was alone, the tears came. No one could hear me in the shower. Not even wolves. Water rushed into my mouth, down my throat. The pine tar soap burned my eyes as I scrubbed the mud and gore from my hair, my face. From my body, then my arms until vivid red marks discolored my skin.

I wanted everything off me. Every memory, every fear.

Every moment spent lying on my back in the mud... frozen in a coerced act of submission to a devil's black alpha.

My heart thrummed over what that meant.

It meant nothing, Noa. You were terrified. You knew what to do. He didn't compel you to do it with any secret alpha power.

I knew he couldn't—wasn't I the lucky one? Because I had no wolf, I had no pack bond. Which meant no wolf could talk to me telepathically. Order me to do something.

Not even an alpha.

But shock from the experience brought doubt, and that doubt kicked up the level of anxiety.

With the shower finished, I dried off and found the clothes that Hattie tracked down—blue scrubs meant for the males. The pants were long and I needed to roll the cuffs. But the oversized shirt was soft and comforting against my skin, and one look in the fogged mirror told me I was still a mess. My shoulder throbbed with a bruise along my collarbone. Another bruise was vivid on my jaw, and the right side of my head felt tender where I'd collided with the car door.

I left my wet hair loose and wandered back to the tiny kitchen that was a door away from the reception area. Hattie was pouring a fragrant berry-scented tea into mugs.

"I've added extra sugar," she said. "How's the shoulder?"

"Aching."

"Those are pain relievers on the table. If you feel up to it, I'd like to talk, catch up. It's been eight years. You were always so..."

"Awkward?"

"Sensitive. And..." She tipped her head to the side. "Quiet. I remember you coming in with Leo like a little shadow."

I swallowed the pills she'd left with tea that tasted of spiced pomegranates, reminding me of winter evenings. "You always palmed me that candy and he never knew."

Hattie chuckled. "Oh, he knew."

"He never said anything."

"He didn't want to ruin it. Leo said only a few things made you smile. Reading his books. Wandering through the forest on your adventures. And thinking you'd pulled one over on him, letting me sneak you candy right beneath his nose."

I pushed at the hair chilling my neck, and Hattie found a thick towel, smiling at my murmured, "thanks."

"How did you find Levi?" she asked as she resettled.

The towel felt soft, nubby in my hands, but the wet hair still made me shudder. "I heard a whine."

"Was Levi close to the house?"

"No. He was in the tall grass, where it grows near the trees."

"That's a distance from the security light. Could you see that pup in the dark?"

I rubbed at my hair. "I heard him. Then I saw him."

Hattie sipped her tea.

I sighed.

"In college, I studied photography and earned a six-month internship with a wildlife photographer. He taught me how to see negative spaces. To look—not at the grass—but between the blades. And I saw light reflecting in Levi's eyes. The difference in his pelt and the muddy ground."

I could see Hattie was unconvinced, and I set the towel aside and picked up the tea.

"It was luck," I said. "I wasn't using any wolfy senses. You know what I am, Hattie."

"I see the silver streak in your hair," she agreed. "When did it first appear?"

"The summer I turned sixteen. I covered it up with hair dye so Leo wouldn't know. He'd be... disappointed."

If I'd been normal, I would have shifted for the first time that summer, like all the other sixteen-year-olds. But I'd used both my mother being upset and the wolf rescue as excuses for not feeling the compulsion. Leo never pressed me about it.

"Your grandfather understood more than you think, Noa. He knew what your mother was before she did, and he knew about you, too. You never disappointed him. He worried about you, wanting to help."

"Well, now Mace knows." My voice tightened. Soon, everyone in the pack would know. No surprise to those who always said I'd turn out like my mother.

And avoiding similar conversations was why I'd watched the town before driving in. I should have turned around, found a different place to hide. But I'd always had this secret dream, how I would find a place where I belonged.

I wanted to be a photographer full time, not when I had a free hour or two. For months, I'd been uploading images to a photography site on the internet. Sales were modest, but enough to build a small nest egg. And if I could support myself. If I had nothing else to do but stand behind my camera, seeing the world through my private lens, I could be happy. Live a quiet life.

Maybe it was a dream, something to think about late at night when I couldn't sleep. But I missed the weight of a camera in my hands.

"You're still pack, Noa."

"I'm Leo's granddaughter." I tried not to snap the words. "A girl passing through. I won't be staying long."

"Are you worried about the wolf energy?"

"I'm worried about being *faille*." Rolling my shoulders, I tested the ache, then bent my head to stretch the tension from my nape. "I know how the pack feels."

"Not everyone. And Mace wants you to stay with me tonight. Make sure you have no internal injuries or a concussion."

"He's the Alpha?" He'd been arrogant enough.

"One of them. The Sentinel Falls pack has three alphas now. Mace is one of the seconds. We have a female alpha as the other second—which should tell you how much the pack has changed. But our primary alpha isn't here yet."

"Then it's better if I take Oscar's advice and leave. Not wait until morning."

I'd had enough unpleasantness for one night. I didn't need an interrogation from another arrogant alpha. But when I glanced up, Hattie's mouth had turned down.

"Don't even think about going to Priest River in the dark. You won't survive the drive."

"I'll keep the car doors locked. I won't stop."

"It won't matter. You'll be driving a car covered in Levi's blood scent, traveling through an area filled with pack wolves.

And plenty who aren't pack. Until the alphas know what happened to Levi, they've ordered you to stay here."

Ordered?

I set my cup down and stared. "I don't take orders." And I refused to be controlled by anything or anyone.

Hattie tried to refill my cup, but I put my hand in the way. "I'm not pack, Hattie."

"And you've been gone for eight years." She set the teapot aside. "Then, the day you return, out of the blue, Levi ends up bleeding out in your grandfather's yard, and *you* are the one who finds him. The alphas won't allow you to leave until they know you aren't connected to that trap."

"How could I be?" My face tightened. "If I hadn't gotten there when I did. If I hadn't *heard* him, or bothered to find him..."

"How do we know you didn't arrange for that trap? You knew the house was empty. Close enough to Sentinel Falls, yet far enough away for activity to go unnoticed. How easy for you, showing up once you knew a wolf was there."

"That isn't even logical. Why would I trap Levi and then save him? When you know poachers set traps for the bounty."

The bite of a *wolf* was in her tone when she said, "Maybe you're working with the poachers. Saving a wolf would impress the pack, a way to ingratiate yourself after the way you left."

"For what gods-awful purpose?"

"You turned your back on Leo. Refused to come back when he asked. Made it clear how disgusted you were with wolves and everything your grandfather stood for." She was hissing now. "Why should we assume your feelings have changed? You've been living with humans for eight years, pretending to *be* human—and you are *faille*. Why should we trust someone like you?"

My thoughts turned chaotic, and I hated not being coherent. But the first hard scrape of fear had me glancing at the teapot, painted with delicate green vines. Then at the cooling tea in my cup—tart and red from the raspberries and pomegranates. Maybe she was acting on behalf of the alphas, but I'd thought Hattie was the one friend I still had, and having her turn on me felt like falling into a deep lake... falling through ice I thought was solid.

But this was judgment, wolf style. How had I forgotten? Guilty until proven innocent, and even then, the wolves would still blame me for *something*.

I gripped the table's edge. "Ask Levi what happened."

"The alpha is doing that right now."

She was more of a stranger than a friend, and I couldn't look at her. She'd put into words what the pack thought about my mother, and now me. I was the outsider. The girl who was not wolf, not human, without loyalty, but filled with disgust and anger. Perhaps that made me as much their enemy as they were mine.

Rain battered the tiny kitchen window, while muted, deep-timbered voices carried from the vet clinic. I'd belonged here once, but no longer, and I wondered if I shouldn't leave, drive away and keep driving.

But when I pushed at the chair, trying to slide from the table, the legs felt anchored in place. I wasn't sure if it was the dented linoleum floor with no give, or if Hattie was using wolf energy.

I didn't know if she was because I didn't know enough about wolves. Part of me hadn't wanted to know. The other part believed I didn't need to know.

But Levi's blood was in my car. And Hattie was right about the danger. Wolves would scent it. They would be relentless, tracking me no matter how far I drove. Or how fast. They would find me, and it was better to face the interrogation while I felt the outrage.

A false courage, maybe, but it was all I had.

"I did not hate Leo," I said. "I hated what he had to do—help the hopeless. Walk onto the bloody field and pick up what was left. Put the wolves back together so they could do it all over again."

"Do you see us as savages, Noa? Monsters?"

I could never believe that of Leo. Or Hattie. Oscar. But the alphas?

Everything about that black wolf came across as monstrous. From the strange intensity in his eyes—the mix of green and blue. The savage length of his canines. The wildness. He'd been terrifying, and I'd never forget the mud squishing in my hair while my back bent beneath the black dominance radiating from him.

Even if instinct had driven me to submit. Even if it had been Leo's advice in the back of my mind, something awful had flared to life while I panted in that mud. Igniting a need inside me... a desire to rise and be wild, the way he was...

And it hadn't gone away.

But I'd be fine. I'd be okay. I knew what I was and how to protect myself.

I breathed in while Hattie poured boiling water into the teapot, as if she hadn't ripped me open, exposing my worst faults.

I'd failed Leo and my mother. I'd failed Hattie. Destroyed what she once felt for me. And although I knew I could not defend actions I'd taken, I still said, "I appreciate how wolves might see the situation. But the one regretful thing I did today was believing I could stay at Leo's house."

"You can't stay there tonight. It's not safe."

"Nothing in Sentinel Falls has ever been safe for me."

And my chance to say goodbye to Leo disappeared two years ago. I would find nothing at his house, no person or thing able to hear those words of regret except the night sky... and that truth felt close to unbearable.

I pushed at my cheek, at the dark hair clinging there. The strands of silver.

"I'd like to show you something," Hattie said. "Will you let me?"

When her warmth returned, I guessed her wolf surfaced because the alphas made her responsible for me. She was one of the few people in Sentinel Falls I knew and presumably trusted.

I wouldn't cause more trouble for her.

I followed her to the reception area. Wildlife magazines covered the tables. A wolf figurine with a pink ribbon around its neck sat on the counter—a feminine touch I hadn't noticed before. To the left, a frosted-glass door led to the examination rooms, and the sharp yip had me turning.

"He's fine," Hattie said. "And lucky. He wouldn't have lasted much longer."

She led me toward a wall-mounted bulletin board.

"This is Levi," she said, while I stared at the photo of a boy with summer-brown hair. He looked like any human teenager in a tee shirt and jeans, with a skateboard beneath his foot and a cocky grin on his face.

"I think he was twelve then. The prankster in the pack. It's amazing he's survived this long, but the alpha has a soft spot for him. We're not supposed to notice."

The way I thought Leo never noticed when Hattie slipped me the candy. I pressed my lips together and focused on the image board. "These are Leo's patients?"

"Most of them."

Beside the photo of Levi, crayon wolf drawings made me smile. Sprigs of dried leaves—I wasn't sure why those were there, other than as mementos, like the handwritten cards and scrawled messages. Hattie unpinned a folded note and handed it to me.

"You should read this one."

Puzzled, I gripped the pink paper with trembling fingers, afraid to open the note. But then I did and stared.

The prim handwriting was easy to read.

You left before I could thank you. They told me your name was Noa, and I wanted you to know... you kept me from giving up. You sang that song and never stopped. You made me believe in goodness. In being brave. You made me want to fight hard enough to find my little brother—and I did. I hope you meet him some day.

His name is Levi.

"Laura Porter," Hattie said as she pinned the note back on the wall. "That's her name. She'll be thrilled to meet you. Did Leo ever tell you about her?"

"No." I forced the bittersweet word past my lips. I'd cut off all contact with Leo, so he couldn't have told me.

But she was the wolf I'd help rescue eight years ago.

"Laura healed enough to tell the alpha about the raiders who attacked her pack. They killed everyone. Took her. But not her little brother—he'd been playing in the mountains. He was eight, always off exploring. She didn't know if he was alive or dead. The alpha found him, brought Levi back, then adopted them both into the pack."

I couldn't imagine a boy playing alone in the wilderness, then returning home to find his pack massacred.

"You were upset when you left," Hattie continued. "Your grandfather agreed with the alpha that you didn't need to know."

My mind raced as I fit pieces together. If Levi had been eight, then I was right when I guessed he was sixteen. "I knew he was young," I said. "His wolf was so small."

"In the dark, with the shadows, maybe you thought he was small. But his wolf weighs over one hundred pounds, Noa. And somehow, you dragged him to your car and got him inside."

I shuddered.

"I'm sure Levi is excited. He's always wanted to meet the girl who saved his sister."

She unpinned another photo and handed it to me. "This photo... it's my Oscar."

I traced a finger over the image. Oscar the Grouch... smiling. But his photo was on the wall, and I remembered the way his fingers tapped when he sorted fishing lures.

A lump grew heavy in my throat. "He was Leo's patient?"

"Yes."

"An... injury?"

"No. Oscar's wolf has gone silent. Leo tried everything. But it's like a human degenerative disease. As the wolf fades, so will my mate, until..."

Hattie turned and stared through the window, toward the dark night outside.

"The end will be peaceful. I'm thankful for that."

"Hattie." I refastened the photo with extra care before touching her shoulder. "I'm sorry."

Another yip echoed from the exam room, followed by a throaty, irritated growl, and Hattie chuckled when I started for the glass door.

"Don't go in there unless you want to see Gray naked."

Exhaustion made my thoughts foggy. "What is a gray naked?"

"Not a what. A who—our primary alpha. Grayson Devante. And he's naked because he arrived in wolf form, and we don't have any clothes his size."

That annoying nudity problem for werewolves—clothes never survived the shift. Werewolves travelled faster as wolves, but when they shifted back into human form, they were naked.

I thought it served them right. If they were intent on terrorizing people, then a little humiliation shouldn't bother them—which, apparently, it didn't.

For propriety's sake, wolves stored clothes in the places they frequented. But perhaps this Grayson Devante didn't frequent Sentinel Falls often enough to leave his clothes.

Which ought to be a relief. Maybe he'd leave soon, and then... so could I.

"Gray is our best healer," Hattie said. "But right now, he's giving poor Levi a lecture only the dominant alpha can give, forcing that boy to shift again and again. Painful, but necessary."

The shrill yip through the glass door proved her point, and I sensed the *wolf* in Grayson Devante, the tight emotional control. I wasn't sure if Levi's wound caused the anger. Or if I'd made it worse by removing that trap. Maybe I was the problem, because I was here without the primary alpha's permission.

Then I remembered how Levi encouraged me, kept me going when I struggled with his weight. I'd told myself it was because he knew he needed help.

But what if he'd done it because he believed in me? Because he knew who I was, when I didn't know myself?

A sixteen-year-old wolf... caught in a trap near Leo's house and asking me to help him. And his older sister, telling me I made her feel brave enough to fight.

Was it any wonder that the alphas were suspicious? If nothing else, it proved surreal things happened in the Selkirks.

The entire day felt that way.

"How long will they be in there?" I asked.

"Gray and Levi?" Hattie clicked her tongue. "For as long as it takes."

"Do I have to wait until they're done?"

"The alpha wants to talk to you. Noa..."

When she touched my arm, I couldn't control the flinch.

Hattie took a step back. "Is the wolf energy bothering you?"

I might have told her the truth if I thought it would make any difference. But I didn't think wolves could appreciate what it was like for me, being around them. Probably the same way I couldn't imagine what it was like for them being around me. Already, I felt the pressure beneath my skin. I'd had a brief reprieve, but soon, the pain would crush me. The migraines would start. The nightmares. I couldn't tolerate it much longer.

But Hattie made it clear I wasn't leaving tonight, and all I could do was stay as far away from wolves as possible.

I gritted my teeth and said, "I'm fine. And I can't wait to meet this alpha of yours."

"Oh, Noa." Her smile was sympathetic. "You already have."

CHAPTER 4

Grayson

"Now!"

The command was guttural, but the last time I'd spoken was also the last time I'd worn clothes, and my wolf was unhappy—the obnoxious furry prick.

He preferred his form. Thought the blue scrub pants I wore were too *constraining* for him. I told him he wasn't the one wearing pants, and clothes were polite around females.

He didn't care. He was still reacting to Noa Bishop, to her scent, and the quick, jumbled mix of female with something wild. Levi's blood had covered her, which did nothing to calm his instincts. He'd been ready to make the kill, and any normal human, or wolf, would have panicked at the sight of my wolf as he rose from a crouch.

She hadn't. Even with the wolf in full attack, she'd been thinking. We both heard the thunder of her heart. The rush of blood in her veins. But when she dragged her hands down, tipped her head... she hadn't been submitting. Defiance glittered in her eyes. Resentment.

She fought like someone who didn't understand her strength.

I raked in a harsh breath. The night had come close to disaster. If I hadn't picked up Levi's trail. If I hadn't followed him...

considering the blood loss, it was a miracle Levi made it as far as he did. An even bigger miracle that she'd found him when she did. Then I found her, and I'd been in midair before Levi screamed through the pack bond.

He told me to stop, to gods-damn *stop* while my wolf had been focused on the kill.

Then he told me her name.

Pure fury had been my wolf's reaction. He lived in his emotions, and although he stood down, there'd been no way to explain while he was in that red haze of rage. We were two of the same. The wolf's instinct was mine. My control was his, and he'd watched her through the same eyes that I watched—electric blue for him, the knife-edge of emerald green for me.

I knew who Noa Bishop was because her grandfather talked about her. I didn't know what she was, even though I had the name: *faille*. Her mother had been a *faille*—although she died two years ago—and the only other information came from the old stories, little more than rumor and conjecture.

But seeing her face-to-face, she was just... there.

Fire frozen in ice. Breakable, and yet resilient.

I'd searched for her inner wolf. All I found was an obsidian abyss. An endless sky. Wolf and not wolf. Human and not human.

Strands of hair fell across her face, the silver glinting against the black. Her eyes were a mix of brown and green and gray, reminding me of the deepest areas in the forest. The secret places.

I'd never *felt* anything like her.

Like lightning in a storm.

Something had snapped inside me, stiffening every muscle.

I was the Alpha of Sentinel Falls. I'd battled against creatures of this earth, and those of nightmare. I made the hard decisions, rarely missed an enemy, grew restless when I did.

And I was restless now.

"Do not move," I growled at Levi, rotating my arms to loosen my shoulders. It was a threatening move. To Levi's credit, his wolf quivered, but remained on the wide exam table. I'd been forcing him to shift between human and wolf as much for the punishment as for the healing. Without the constant stretching of his muscles, he'd lose needed agility.

Levi looked younger than he was, with his pathetic wolf-grin turning lopsided despite the pain-filled whine. His goofy pink tongue, with its little black spot, lolled out. One ear flopped. When he yipped, I wondered why he thought irritating his alpha was a good way to explain his behavior.

He put himself in danger, and this time, he wouldn't get a pass from me, no matter how he entertained the pack. He was ridiculous but reckless; adults smiled even as they scolded. Worse, the young pups followed Levi like he was the damn Pied Piper.

I angled my head, and the sound I made carried an anger that had Levi's wolf ducking his head with a whine, wanting to drop to his belly in submission.

I refused permission. Through our pack bond, I issued the order to remain sitting. He obeyed, holding my gaze while his wounded right leg trembled.

"You're too easy on him," Mace rumbled with his usual cheery tone. "He put the entire pack at risk."

"He's young. His wolf is young, and your recruits are just as blind when they're hot on the trail."

"They wouldn't have been alone." Mace tipped his head, popping the joints in his neck. "Levi's the problem. That boy idolizes you, and you let him get away with this shit. When we both know the pack has no place for a rogue wolf."

"My wolf has gone rogue."

"That isn't what I meant, and you know it." His growl sounded like rocks grinding. "Give me a shot at him. I'll run his ass off on patrols, burn him into shape."

Training taught self-control, obedience, and Mace was one of the best trainers I'd ever known. He was first on the front lines, hardened from decades of skirmishes and pack wars. He'd taught me a battle trick or two, and I respected him for it, even when I disagreed with him on policy.

With Levi, I agreed. If the boy didn't grow up, he'd be a bigger risk in a decade's time—if he survived that long.

I stroked Levi's pelt, gray bristle with white on the muzzle. Earlier, Mace had washed the wound, but the overall damp was from the hours Levi spent in the rain. My fingers dug deep, and I gripped the wolf's nape, holding him in position. For years, the pack had poured blood and effort into protective measures around our lands. Wolves died defending the boundaries, and I wanted Levi's wolf to understand what I would—and would not—allow him to do.

He wasn't an eight-year-old child anymore, doing what he wanted. His antics put the entire pack in danger. The females, the pups, the older adults and infirm, and in this moment, I wasn't Gray, his friend.

I was his Alpha. The ultimate authority.

"Now!" I ordered. Levi's wolf bent his head and rolled his shoulders until—with a shudder—a naked Levi emerged. His gangly legs caught on the exam table before he straightened and gripped the padded surface.

"Gray—"

"Alpha to you, pup!" Mace growled. "Know your place."

"Alpha." Levi tipped his chin and angled his head to the side, exposing his throat with a sign of submission, while his brown hair flopped against his cheek the way his wolf ear flopped. "I can explain."

"How old are you, Levi?"

"Sixteen."

"You know the rules about crossing the borderline without permission?"

A flush pinkened Levi's face, but I gave him credit for not looking away. "I know the rules. I can—"

"Now!"

"Shit—" The word ended with a frustrated growl as Levi's wolf reappeared. I ordered him into the shift again before he was settled, and when the teenager emerged, he slumped forward in defeat.

For an instant, I missed his courage.

"You left protected lands alone and without permission—why?"

"I'd been patrolling with Fallon." Levi aimed an uneasy glance toward Mace—who scowled. Fallon was our other alpha, equal to Mace, but the young ones liked her more because she didn't always bark orders.

"She told me to shift and follow the borderline. Check for unusual animal movements, the deer, being where they shouldn't be. That's what I did, but something felt off with the border magic, as if something was testing it. I was coming to tell Mace."

"Why not Fallon?"

"Mace was closer. So was the Bishop house."

Levi's fascination with Leo Bishop's property had been going on for years, and while both Mace and I ordered him to stay away, Levi refused to obey.

"I was careful," he said. "I remembered everything you taught me, but then... the air seemed to change."

"Change how?"

"The same way the borderline did. Vibrating... like something was testing me. To... see if I felt it."

Levi shrugged, and then, with permission, he hopped from the exam table and pulled on the spare scrubs Mace held out.

"I didn't panic."

Mace raised an eyebrow.

Levi crossed his arms with his spine stiff. "I was in control. Then everything got quiet, and my wolf got spooked. He started running, and he didn't see the trap."

I watched Levi shudder. Through the pack bond, I felt the pain, then the terror. The desperate struggle to free himself. Chewing, biting. The decision to rip muscles to the bone if it meant breaking the chain.

I sent a wave of reassurance toward him, and he glanced up with a tight smile and a quick nod.

"Why go to the Bishop house when it's been empty for two years?"

"My leg was bleeding. I thought I'd be close enough to Sentinel Falls for the pack bond."

He was proud. Young. Afraid to admit the exhaustion that drove him to the ground, panting and needing a place to hide.

Levi swallowed as he glanced toward Mace and said, "I thought if a sentry heard me through the pack bond, he'd tell you and you'd come for me. Then she came, and when she started singing, I knew who she was. My wolf was... relieved."

"Why?"

"He thought she... heard him. Not the whine. The... other way. Like maybe she has a pack bond and doesn't know it."

"She can't have a pack bond, Levi," I said. "She has no wolf."

Levi's chin popped up an inch. "She knew enough to submit to you, Alpha. In the mud. I saw her."

The chin pop was the closest Levi could get to a challenge. I was relieved. It meant his resiliency was returning, although I still scowled because Mace was watching.

"Leo Bishop was her grandfather. He took her on rescues, taught her about wolves. She would know what to do from another's knowledge, not because of anything else."

"I heard your command," Levi insisted, his chin moving up another half inch. "You told her to submit. And my wolf said she was... wolf."

"Your wolf is young. He doesn't know what he sensed—but she has no wolf, Levi. I would know."

"That doesn't make her bad."

It struck me that Levi's wolf had bonded to Noa Bishop during those minutes in the grass. Perhaps it was from the stories his sister told him. Or his age, where he saw Noa Bishop with the same hero worship that distorted his view of me, much to Mace's dismay. It meant Levi would protect her, and I needed to remind him why he couldn't.

"Until we know more about Noa Bishop, why she's here, you will stay away from her."

Levi's shoulders stiffened as he turned to the side, and it did not surprise me when he asked, "Alpha, may I talk to you as Gray?"

I nodded toward Mace. He wouldn't stay for a private conversation, and once he'd left the exam room, I looked at Levi.

"How's the arm?"

"Fine."

"Just fine?"

"Yes."

Levi jutted his chin, and my chest constricted at the sign of submission. I was the closest Levi had to a father or a brother. He wanted to speak to me as Gray, and I was still treating him like his Alpha.

I reached out to brush the hair from his forehead. "So, tell me what you couldn't say while Mace was in the room."

Levi readjusted his weight, one leg bobbling, and despite the scrubs hanging on his lanky frame, I could see the man he'd become one day.

"I didn't tell you everything. I left some stuff out."

"Then you'd better add that stuff in now while your alpha's not around."

"When I crossed the border, it was because I felt something off, but not because I thought Mace was closer. I knew he was, but I wanted to find you instead."

"Why?"

Levi's gaze didn't leave my face. "A bunch of us want you to come back. Fallon's worried because the animals are moving around, and she won't tell you because she doesn't want to let you down. She says your wolf isn't ready. But you're the strongest alpha the pack has ever seen. The scariest."

"Sometimes, being strong means staying away," I said.

Levi tugged at his scrubs. "I wasn't strong, Gray. I thought I was, and when I left the pack lands, I was sure my wolf was following your scent. At first, he was sure too, but the farther away we got from the border, the more confusing the scent was, until it wasn't you at all. We were being lured. Hunted. That's when my wolf got scared. He took control and wouldn't listen. He ran and didn't see the trap."

When Levi lowered his head—out of shame in front of me—I didn't move or acknowledge him. If I did, he'd stop talking, and I needed to know what bothered him before I could help.

"I don't want to be a freak, Gray. Unable to stop my wolf."

"I was like you once, battling with my wolf." I let Levi feel the old embarrassment through our bond. "He put me on my ass once or twice before we came to an agreement, and your wolf will do the same to you. That's why we train, to learn how to work as a team."

"I know, but..." Levi squirmed. "Did your wolf notice anything weird about Noa Bishop? Because mine did and it's confusing him."

"In what way?"

"It was when she touched me," Levi said. "It wasn't like the way you heal. Her hands were warm, and it was like... the pain was flowing from me to her. Like, maybe the light was draining from the sky. I know that doesn't make sense."

I stiffened. "Our perceptions can be off when we're in pain. I wouldn't worry about it right now, unless you feel it again."

He dipped his head. "Okay... thank you, Alpha."

"Gray," I corrected him. "So—is there anything else I should know before I turn you over to Mace?"

"One other thing." Levi's throat bobbed when he swallowed. "Whatever scared my wolf—it might have followed me. It will know about her house. About Sentinel Falls and all the wolves living here. Please... I know I screwed up. I'm sorry. Please don't kick me out of the pack."

My anger rose, not toward Levi, but because he'd confirmed my fear. The trap that nearly bled him out hadn't been there for the coyotes, or the smaller animals. No, that gods-damned trap had been meant for *wolves*—and he hadn't randomly stumbled into it. He'd been herded toward it, then toward Leo Bishop's house. An intrusion that could not be overlooked or ignored.

"I'd never kick you out of the pack, Levi, no matter what you did. You and Laura have a home for as long as you want. But you'll tell Mace and Fallon everything you told me."

Levi frowned. "He'll run my ass into the ground for it. She will, too."

"Mace would do that, anyway. He sees your potential. So does Fallon. But only if you get this right from the start. Both you and your wolf."

I gripped his shoulder, and beneath my hand, I felt the knobby bones that would soon have a thick layer of muscle. "A man owns up to the truth and his mistakes."

"I know..."

"Check in with me later," I said. "After you've talked to them."

Levi nodded. As he left the exam room, I saw Noa Bishop through the open doorway. Hattie must have cleaned her up, then dressed her in blue scrubs that didn't fit. A dark bruise covered her arm, one I'd put there. Another marred her face, while strands of damp brunette hair draped around her shoulders.

As Levi approached, Noa's hands trembled. Emotion flared with a heat I could feel before she jerked back. Her face paled, and Hattie murmured something. Noa Bishop wasn't comfortable around wolves, and yet, she'd come close to hugging Levi.

Her fingers fluttered as if she could pet him—his wolf—who was enamored with her and thought there was a connection.

Then her gaze turned to me, and for endless seconds we stared in silent battle. She refused to look away. My jaw clenched. We both remembered those long minutes in the mud.

Hattie frowned, sending a quick thought through the pack bond about Noa and too much wolf energy. She tacked on her signature scold to keep me in line—hadn't I done enough damage for one night?

I stared at the bruise I'd caused, then agreed with Hattie that—*as her Alpha*—I'd wait until tomorrow.

She sassed back, offering a chin dip with the sass. I knew it was gratitude, and I'd never reprimand her. She was more like my grandmother than a pack member, and I ignored my wolf's disapproval, watching while Hattie hustled Noa out of the clinic.

Mace asked if I was done in the mountains—his favorite nag—then asked if I wanted him to follow up with the border or have Fallon do it.

I told him to talk to Levi, then clamped down on further pack communication. No more questions about the borderline, or the odd tracks I'd come across. If my wolf was stable, or how invested did I want to be in Noa Bishop.

What worried me was a *faille* showing up in the Selkirks when new threats loomed in the north.

And if she was the threat.

Or the harbinger.

CHAPTER 5

Noa

THE STORM HIT DURING the night, sending jagged spider lightning across the dark sky. Thunder boomed through the trees, and in Hattie's upstairs guest bedroom, I was surrounded by the chaos.

Hattie's house connected to the general store, although it was private, and when we arrived, she led me up a steep flight of stairs while I clutched the clothes and personal items I'd collected before leaving the vet clinic.

I'd taken nothing else, afraid to dig through a car still smeared with Levi's blood.

"Extra blankets are in the closet, Noa. Try to rest."

Those were Hattie's instructions before leaving me alone. She'd been understanding about the wolf energy, and I thought she warned Grayson Devante because he'd refused to talk to me.

I wasn't relieved.

Grayson Devante was the devil's black wolf. That meant the primary Alpha of Sentinel Falls had wanted to kill me. Or at least, his wolf had, stopping at the last moment and unhappy enough to batter me with a warning growl.

And in the vet clinic, as I'd stared at Grayson Devante... the man's expression had mirrored the wolf, taut with displeasure, as if delaying the interrogation was against his better judgment. But he'd do it, anyway.

We had stared, predator and prey, each waiting for the other to look away. Neither of us did, and I remembered thinking it was two challengers acknowledging each other before the fight.

The image of him, though... alone in the exam room, bare feet, bare chest, wearing blue scrubs that hung low on his hips. His stillness had been alarming, but his isolation haunted, and I'd battled against tipping my chin, or dragging my gaze away from his.

I'd never met a man like him—raw and so silent it felt dangerous. His beauty was monstrous. Hair as black as his wolf, as black as the wolf tattoo on his shoulder that awakened frissons of dark excitement.

As he stared, I knew he expected fear, and when I refused to react, he'd looked... annoyed.

I wondered if cats looked at the mice that way before striking.

If he would look at me like that again.

When Hattie brought soup half an hour later, I'd asked why he hadn't talked to me. She said he had something more pressing to do, but after she left, I couldn't sleep. I thought about my mother, when she explained what being *faille* meant.

No bothersome shifting, she'd said. No dominating alpha in my head, telling me what to do. Without a telepathic pack bond, I'd be free and uncontrolled.

I'd also never know what other wolves were thinking, planning. If I was in danger or not.

That didn't mean I was defenseless. I could sense wolf energy before the wolves could, and I'd know if it was malignant or benign. With practice, I could shield myself from the worst effects of that wolf energy.

But even with shields, being around wolves was toxic. My *faille* body would try to absorb their energy, neutralize it—and fail. I'd have migraines, anxiety attacks. Nightmares where I'd wake with my heart pounding and my skin iced with sweat.

I'd wonder if dreams were real, become trapped in delusion. And when the delusions became unmanageable... I would disappear into an emptiness inside me, filled with a bottomless dark. The place where my wolf should have been. Then she'd warned me that if I ever went there, I'd might never return.

Perhaps my mother had been protecting me, or so deep in her despair she never saw mine. But she told me the truth because she didn't want me to suffer, and I'd used what she told me to blunt the guilt when I chose her over Leo. I used it when I ignored his birthday, failed to send Christmas cards, because I knew contacting him would be hurtful to her.

Even after she died, I'd used it to keep from responding to Leo when he reached out to me. I couldn't do it, allow myself to see him after all those years. The same way I could not allow myself to remember the summers when I ran through the forests, hunting for werewolves.

Lightning sizzled, a jagged slash that left a green afterimage in the night sky. The beating rain grew aggressive, and I tightened the blanket around my shoulders, resisting the cold as I stood in front of the window.

"Noa."

Hattie stood in the bedroom doorway, and I realized I'd hadn't heard her come upstairs.

"I wouldn't bother you, but I heard the pacing."

I tried to apologize, but she was having none of it.

"Oscar's the same way with storms. I brought tea. Chamomile with honey. That always settles him."

She held a tray with two delicate cups on saucers. Faded pink flowers decorated the cup rims, and it was obvious that they'd been lovingly used.

I remained quiet while she arranged a round table with upholstered chairs. Then she said, "I thought we could sit awhile and talk."

And although I was in no mood for interrogating, I appreciated the company she offered. White hair billowed around her face. She wore flannel pajamas, fuzzy slippers, and a thick robe, all different colors, but working together to make this tea ritual cozy. Even... confidential.

"I was sorry to hear about your mom."

"She was tired," I said. "After so many years."

After Stewart's efforts to rehabilitate her.

Without thinking, I murmured, "Toward the end, she was wasting away, like Oscar..."

Then the taste of chamomile turned bitter on my lips, and I said, "I'm sorry, I meant..."

That the slow, defeating loss of a loved one was the same for everyone.

"I understood what you meant," Hattie said with a faint smile. "Losing your mom, then losing your grandfather a few months later—that must have been hard. Leo's passing was peaceful," she added. "I don't know if anyone told you."

No one told me, not until the attorney handling the estate called about Leo's will. I wouldn't have found out otherwise, and never would have known he died alone.

I still woke at night, choking on the shame and guilt.

In the weeks after my mother's funeral, Leo asked me to visit. He'd written a letter, and his scrawled handwriting revealed more than his request. It revealed his age. His vulnerability...

I'd been ashamed to answer him. Ashamed of who I was, what I'd done the last time I'd been in Sentinel Falls. The one man who loved me unconditionally, and I was afraid to face him.

"No one held it against you, Noa. When you didn't come for the service. Leo—of all people—understood."

I didn't deserve her kindness. Even if I'd known, I wouldn't have come for Leo's service.

Not because he hadn't come for my mother's funeral. I knew why. My stepfather wouldn't have allowed him there. And she wouldn't have wanted him to see her degradation.

But for me... I would have insulted Leo by attending his funeral. Offering in death what I'd been unwilling to offer in life: my time, my love. My apologies when the words were too late to matter.

"Today was unexpected, wasn't it?" Hattie asked after a moment. "Not at all what you'd thought it would be."

"I'm glad about Levi."

"You saved his life. The way you saved Laura's."

She meant well. But I refused to turn the saving into a connection I didn't have. Not with these wolves or with this place—although vivid images flashed like terse insults. How adamant I'd been that summer. My hair flying, thin arms crossing, boney legs churning as I'd stormed away from the only place where I'd been happy.

But life shouldn't be the cheap thing that it was for wolves. Where mothers nurtured their children, knowing they would grow up into violence, and I'd rejected everything about wolves with such virulence that my grandfather let me go. Believed it was best for me. Best for the pack. A belief that left Leo alone when he died.

The tea was lukewarm in my throat, and I set the cup aside. "How did…"

"Your grandfather went out on a night like this to rescue a wolf, caught a chill. He died in his sleep a week later."

I stared at the darkened window that reflected the room light now, nothing else. "Is there… a place where I can leave flowers?"

"Not here. The alpha took his body into the high mountains. It's tradition, Noa. It was what Leo wanted."

Looking at her face, I understood the expectation Hattie had, waiting for a request from me. There would be solace in leaving flowers, but I wouldn't ask to go into the high mountains. What I deserved was to feel the regret every day, knowing I'd had the chance to make amends, and hadn't taken it.

"Thank you." I rearranged my cup and saucer on Hattie's tray. "For the tea. And for telling me about Leo. I'm sorry for the inconvenience."

"It's no inconvenience, Noa."

I knew her concern came from her duty to the pack, because the alpha ordered it.

And because of Leo, for whom she still felt affection.

But her concern was not for me. Never for the girl who left. Who made it obvious she would keep leaving, keep wandering. Never home.

I woke to the sweet fragrance of pancakes, a scent so *luxurious* I didn't want to get out of bed. In Seattle, my apartment stank of whatever food the neighbors cooked, but this little guest bedroom smelled like a home, and I didn't want to shower or get dressed because that would mean I was leaving.

I *was* leaving, though, and I straightened the room, put my used towel in the laundry hamper, and went downstairs with my few belongings.

"Sit there," Hattie said when I entered her kitchen, bright with morning sunlight. Plants in jewel-toned pots lined the windowsill. A rose-and-green flowered print covered the cushions tied to ladder-back chairs arranged around an oak table.

"Sit, Noa, before Oscar eats all the pancakes," she added when I hesitated. Oscar grinned above his coffee mug. There was more life in his eyes this morning, and he no longer reminded me of Oscar the Grouch.

"Syrup's good." He smacked his lips. Behind him, Hattie tutted, but I noticed the surprise in her eyes when she placed a heaping plate of perfect, golden-brown pancakes in front of me.

"Thank you," I mumbled around the first bite, and then hummed with pleasure.

"Your mom never made pancakes?"

"She couldn't handle the smell."

I pushed another bite into my mouth, but I hadn't eaten during the drive from Seattle, and the soup Hattie had given me wore off hours ago.

"This is good." I smiled at Oscar so he'd know I agreed with him.

"More syrup." He poured maple goodness over the pancakes stacked in front of me until the syrup pooled on the plate and dripped off the side. I thought about my usual bowl of cereal, how I stood at the kitchen counter eating because the one kitchen chair I had rocked on the uneven floor. The last sit-down breakfast I'd had was years ago, and sitting with Hattie, looking like a grandmother, and Oscar, devouring pancakes, made my hand shake. I set aside the fork and poured a glass of orange juice, forcing myself to sip.

Hattie watched, concern pinching her lips as she said, "I never thought to ask..."

I knew she *had* thought to ask, because she was wolf and thought I'd give more information if the questions came like harmless curiosity.

"Why did you leave Seattle? Leo thought you were happy."

"I was." Until recently. Until instinct kicked in, warning me that the faces I kept seeing were not from random encounters.

After a day spent wandering Seattle, shooting stock crowd photos, I reviewed the images. I was looking for photos that didn't require a model release, and I noticed two men who kept popping up everywhere. I'd noticed them before, standing behind me in the grocery line. Brushing past on a street corner. Lingering outside the mall where I worked. But they were also in the photographs, in three separate images. Three different locations. Looking smug, as if they believed I didn't see them.

Perhaps I hadn't realized how many times I'd seen them, but I must have sensed the threat because—either knowing or unknowingly, I'd photographed them.

My *faille* warning system, I supposed, the same warning that sharpened every sense that night when I heard a noise outside my apartment. A creak in the hall that had me throwing clothes in a carry-on, tossing an empty backpack on the floor beside the carry-on—gods only knew why. I'd dropped the soft items down the fire escape, carried my phone, camera and laptop. My ankle twisted in the alley, but I'd scrambled to my car, drove away.

And if I told Hattie about my midnight dash, or how those men might have followed me, she would tell the alphas, all three of them, who would then add "leading strangers to Sentinel Falls" to their "why Noa can't leave" list.

To distract her, I said, "I'd like to visit Leo's house and post 'no hunting' signs on the property. Maybe find a renter, someone Leo would want living in his house."

Hattie frowned. "He wanted you to live there."

"I can't stay in Sentinel Falls, and I don't want another wounded wolf running to Leo's house and finding the property abandoned."

"I'll look into it, Noa." Which meant she would check with the alphas.

"Whatever you can do, Hattie. I appreciate it."

My sentiment was genuine because I still believed in courtesy, even if the rules annoyed me. And today, I wasn't thinking about alphas, and certainly not about Grayson Devante. My plan was to be gone before he came back from whatever else he was doing.

Oscar brightened when he said, "I cleaned your car. It's parked out front."

I'd been dreading cleaning Levi's blood from my car, and my "thank you" was heartfelt.

"Least I could do for saving that pup." Oscar poured more syrup, then swiped at the drop that fell on his blue flannel shirt. "But if you're goin' out there to Leo's old place, I'm goin' with you. Follow in my old truck. A woman traveling alone isn't wise right now."

"I'm not defenseless." Oscar's beetled brows arched, and I grinned. "I'll show you my bow before we leave. Nothing like an arrow slamming into the ground to make someone think twice."

"Ah..." His head tipped. "You're into archery?"

"State Amateur Champion. Two years running." My teenage accomplishment, but I had a natural ability with archery and used the sport for stress relief. When I held a tightly strung bowstring against my cheek, sighted down the arrow shaft toward the target, a calm would settle over me. I would know I was in control.

"What's your draw weight?"

"At my peak, I was up to 55 pounds." It wasn't a big brag. "I'm old school, use a recurve bow, not compound, and for target shooting. I don't kill."

"Still..." Oscar nodded with appreciation. "I'd say 55's an impressive draw for a girl your size, and a bow with the arrow nocked can make a person stop and think."

I'd thought the same thing last night, when I discovered my bow case in the trunk of my car, pushed to the back where I'd forgotten it. The last time I'd practiced had been more than a year ago, but I wanted to regain the rhythm and strength I'd lost since archery hadn't been on my schedule.

"I've got arrows in stock right now, along with bowstrings. Plenty of zombie targets, if that's your preference. Kids go for those." Oscar finished his second stack of pancakes and smacked his lips again. "Hattie-girl, best you've ever made."

She slapped a gentle hand against his shoulder as she walked past, but her eyebrows arched. "Like you'd remember."

"Aw, now... I remember fine."

Hattie blushed and sent a sideways glance toward me. "I'm not sure what's got into him, but whatever the influence, I hope it doesn't go away."

Knowing that his wolf was silent, I tapped Oscar's hand. "If you shoot, maybe we can have a friendly competition before I leave."

"I'd like that." Oscar's head-dip was more like the one I'd seen him offer Mace. "I haven't held a bow in, oh, a few years now. Like you, it was for sport. No real need."

"The muscle memory will still be there." And if it wasn't, I would fumble, then work through the motions so he could watch.

I sipped the last of my juice. The morning felt so... normal. Deep down, wolves were social animals, needing the pack, and sitting in Hattie's kitchen, the line I'd drawn years ago... the line between the good and bad... it no longer felt as solid as it had once been.

"Breakfast was wonderful." I stood and carried my dishes to the sink—where Hattie shushed me with her hands, telling me I was a guest and she would take care of the mess.

Oscar stood with me. He said he had those 'no hunting' signs I wanted. It would take him a minute, and he'd get a hammer and nails. Help me put them up.

He rummaged through the back shelves in the store while Hattie walked me outside. Her head tipped, and I guessed she was using the pack bond, asking for permission for me to leave Sentinel Falls.

I thought about Leo's house, and if the wolves found the trap. If they were hunting for the poachers, and what they'd do, if they found them.

For once, I didn't feel revolted by the thought of wolf violence. Not after what happened to Levi.

When Oscar didn't join us, I worried that he'd forgotten where we were, or what he was looking for. But a moment later, he walked through the door that whomped, deep in conversation with two men. Both wore tan overalls and heavy plaid coats, and the taller man's voice boomed with indignation.

"I'm tellin' you, Oscar, they said leave before the dang road washed out. Ordered, and it had nothing to damn do with what tore up that storage shed. Like we were all supposed to believe 'em—had to close the mine and get out."

"That mine's been on life support for years," the second man added. "We're a skeleton crew, anyway."

Oscar grunted. His lip poked out, but his grip tightened around the hammer and signs. "Bear, you say?"

"Claw marks on the shed said bear," the first man huffed. "I ain't never seen a bear that size. Strange things in those woods. We're heading for Priest River. Just thought to tell you, in case you were wanting to go that way."

"Hadn't planned on it." Oscar snorted. "But I'll get word out."

As the men left, I sidestepped a stream of dirty water edging the curb. Storm-tossed branches littered the sidewalk. The air was crisp and damp, mixing with the smoky traces of burning wood from fireplaces and woodstoves.

The sun was out, but I shivered, staring at the two women who stood across the street. They were muttering—about me, I guessed, since they sent narrow-eyed glances in my direction.

"Ignore them," Hattie said. "After Levi, then the storm, everyone's edgy. Those two idiots running on about bears isn't helping."

"Tell her to leave, Hattie." The woman in fleece had her arms crossed. "Her kind doesn't belong here."

"Mind your mouth, Jo-Rae Bell." Hattie's lips pinched. "Noa is Leo Bishop's granddaughter, and she belongs wherever he did."

"Doesn't change the fact that she's *'pu*," the shorter woman snarled, shortening one of the uglier slurs for *failles*. *Rompu* meant being broken—like a stick, before it was thrown in the fire. In the past, wolves had attacked *failles*. Broke them into little pieces.

"Should have put her mother down years ago," the same woman continued. "Before we had this problem."

Oscar straightened from storing the signs and hammer on the back seat of my car; he swung around with enough aggression that the woman in fleece stepped back.

But the shorter woman raised her chin. "Your wolf waking up, Oscar? Or maybe you're wearing hearing aids now, turned up enough to hear."

"Karla..."

But Karla stepped forward. "You know how far gone he is, Jo-Rae. Don't see why we need to sugarcoat it."

I placed a hand on Oscar's shoulder and stepped to his side. Bullies were the same, no matter the species. They always picked on the weakest.

Beside me, Hattie had stiffened, and her voice grew angry as she ordered, "Karla. Jo-Rae, both of you go back inside now."

"Not when she's standing there, showing off that silver streak in her hair, bold as day." Karla's lips drew back, and I saw the hint of wolf. "We know what her kind does to a pack."

"I should leave," I murmured.

"You should," Karla said. "And stay gone. Take that old man with you—he's as empty as you are."

I turned to face the two women. I'd done nothing to them, but I wouldn't need to—their vitriol came from a long-standing belligerence toward anyone not wolf. The attitude drove my mother from Sentinel Falls. It was what she'd warned me about, and made me promise not to return.

Leo had also protected me. He'd been a wall, holding back the viciousness of wolves.

But he was gone. So was my mother.

I was still here. No longer a child.

And I didn't care what they thought.

"What I *am*," I said, "is not your concern. I own Leo's house. I'll honor his memory, what he did for the pack, but I owe no explanation to someone who attacks me by hurting others."

Jo-Rae Bell jerked her head, kinky red hair swirling while Karla bristled. Their movements were animalistic; it was easy to imagine their wolf forms. While females didn't shift as often as males, they were as antagonistic, and I needed to remember who to watch for in the dark night.

Hattie placed a hand on my arm. "I'm sorry, Noa. Some wolves in Sentinel Falls—well, they're here because their attitudes aren't welcome elsewhere. They want their bubble, while most of the pack sees things differently."

Hearing such a human phrase as "*wanting their bubble*" from Hattie had me offering her a reassuring smile. "Oscar..."

"He's a little rigid. And that's a good thing, Noa, because it means he's feeling something. Anger, maybe." She crossed her arms as I opened the car door. "Don't worry. I'll ask Mace to remind them of pack manners."

"Not on my account." I slid on to the seat and started the engine. "I'll be gone soon."

And this time... I'd stay gone from the hostility that lurked in Sentinel Falls. As if hostility was not an emotion, but an entity. Sentient. Watching me.

CHAPTER 6

Noa

DRIVING WAS THE CLOSEST I could get to racing through the forest, going on childhood adventures. Dancing over logs and through meadows. The mountains were a blend of blue and green. Snow glistened at the highest peaks. The roadway curved through shadows—but when sunlight hit the puddles—the shimmer was so beautiful that I stared until my eyes hurt.

I left Sentinel Falls behind, along with the bitterness from Jo-Rae Bell and her friend. I knew wolves respected strength, attacked weakness, and they went after Oscar because he was like me. His wolf was silent. Mine didn't exist.

The car window was down; my hair whipped in the breeze. I loved the sense of freedom, wanting to drive and keep on driving. Somewhere... anywhere.

Soon, Noa.

Through the rearview mirror, I saw Oscar following in his faded red truck. His window was down like mine, and he'd propped his arm in the opening. His fingers tapped at the upper door rim, but not with the monotony he'd had while sorting fishing lures.

He drove one-handed while his head bobbed. Perhaps he was listening to the radio. I punched buttons, finding a channel that wasn't all static—country music—but it set the mood, along with the whooshing car tires and the steady passing of pines.

After twenty minutes, Oscar tapped his car horn to get my attention. He pointed to the left. His blinker was on, although I remembered the road and knew the turn to my grandfather's house was coming.

Still, it was nice to have his protection the way I'd had Leo's. I appreciated the kindness. But today would be my last day in Sentinel Falls. I'd wander through the house, say a private goodbye. Then spend the afternoon hiking, looking for traps the wolves hadn't found, and nail my signs on the fence posts.

I'd "leave flowers" for Leo the only way I could, through gestures, since the alpha took his body high into the mountains where I'd never go.

Then I'd continue the life I planned. The alphas could posture all they wanted. They had no authority over me. The future was mine. I'd settle somewhere, cover my tracks. Email the wildlife photographer and ask if he needed an assistant. Maybe I could travel abroad... I'd be hard to find. Gone enough that whoever had been following me would give up.

Just this one last day to get through...

I made the turn, bumped along the road, tires squishing through ruts still muddy from the storm. Oscar followed, his truck rocking. We were both driving slowly because the road seemed more churned up than before. It took longer to reach the curve—where a dozen pickup trucks blocked the road.

I thought, *maybe they're chasing poachers.*

Excitement tightened in my throat.

Then it compressed until I couldn't swallow.

Levi stood beside one truck. The door was open. He was talking to an older man while scuffing his foot in the trampled grass.

Around them, men pushed between the trees, staring down, moving things with booted feet. Others bunched together. Their agitation snapped like sparks in the air, and when I climbed from my car, the taint of bitter iron thickened the air, coating my throat.

Even when I breathed through my scrunched lips, I could taste it.

Ahead, Mace broke from the pack. His spiky blonde hair caught the sunlight, and it should have looked normal. But it didn't. Nor were the scents in the air normal. Or the burning in my eyes.

I wove between the trucks, heading toward the house with its wide deck and the twig wreath on the door, close to running when Mace stepped into my path.

He used his arm to hook my waist. "Stop!"

My momentum knocked him in a half-turn, me with him like we were dancing. His canines punched down. Despite his warning growl, I struggled, pulling at his fingers, surprised when I peeled them back enough to break free. But I didn't stop. He wasn't my alpha. No one was my alpha.

I was not wolf and never would be.

"Noa!" Oscar stumbled in the mud; I didn't like the distress in his voice. "Wait."

Levi rushed with his lanky gait while I pivoted on a crazy backward stride, turning and walking and staring at the men who were circling around. Coming closer.

I was the trespasser, the fraud, the enemy who never should have come here, and I shook my head.

No. Hell no!

Whatever this was—they were the ones who shouldn't be here. This was *Leo's* house. Mine by all that mattered, and I should be walking up those steps to the deck where I played as a child. Going inside rooms that held all I had left of my grandfather. Saying my last goodbye. Letting go of what little remained. Then getting in my car. Driving away.

"Noa." Mace blocked me again.

I pointed a shaking finger toward him. "Move."

The alpha's lips pulled back. Levi braced, ready to defend me. Oscar put a shaking hand on my arm.

But the rumbles from the other men raised the hair at my nape, and seconds passed before Mace raised his hands in false surrender and stepped back.

I heard Grayson Devante's voice.

"Let her come."

A space in the crowd widened. Through it, I saw my grandfather's house, but I couldn't work out what I was seeing. Storm damage? So much?

Worse, the Alpha of Sentinel Falls stood in the doorway. And I didn't want him there. This was Leo Bishop's house—*my house*—the one place I had left to call mine. At least it was mine until I left Sentinel Falls.

Numbly, I walked across the grass. Stopped when my foot kicked the first wooden step. The blue door was open. *Broken* open. Brass hinges clung to splintered wood. The twig wreath was in pieces, and through the dark opening, I could see a hint of wreckage, the disjointed shapes, piled furniture, bent curtain rods. Dark fluff that must be from cushions because it could be from nothing else.

Rubble spilled through the doorway and across the deck. I picked out the shards of broken plates, confused by the damage. But the menace in the alpha's stance turned my mouth dry. I was looking at a warrior. A werewolf in the skin of a man—but still a man who was merciless. Veins ridged in his throat, throbbing with slow, terrifying intensity. Even the way his jeans and long-sleeved shirt fit him was a threat.

I wanted to run.

To hide from this predator.

He was a dreadful unknown. A man more beautiful than I'd ever seen.

A muscle in his cheek feathered—like ice moving. Wicked black claws punched through his knuckles long enough to rip me to shreds. I had no protection against him, and sweat pooled at the base of my spine when I heard his snarl. Pure aggression glittered in his eyes, blue fire mixed with glittering emerald spikes, and I felt a pressure in my head far worse than what I'd felt when I rolled in the mud.

His message was unmistakable. One misstep, one wrong word from me, and I would be down in the mud again. With his canines slashing deep. And no one would stop him.

I took a step back, then stopped. Part of me knew that if Oscar—or Levi—had asked me not to go inside my house, I would have waited outside, allowing the wolves to handle whatever this way.

But a fiercer part of me knew the Alpha of Sentinel Falls said *let her come* because he wanted to see me waver. Prove my weakness.

He represented everything I hated, and I would not give in to his dominance. Lose myself in his energy.

I was the *faille*, the broken one. Flawed. Neither wolf nor human. I had only myself. The person I knew myself to be, and if I gave up that power, then I'd be nothing.

Each step creaked beneath my weight. When I reached the deck, I found Leo's bench in pieces. Great, jagged gouges marked the log siding—from wolf claws. Or something larger, angrier. Streaked blood covered the doorframe; the smears like crimson fingers, clinging, resisting.

And the most vulnerable part of me started to break.

"Noa." Levi gripped my arm.

I looked at him, but he had no words, and I counted my heartbeats. Breathing in, breathing out before I could step inside the darkened house I had not entered for eight years.

It took time for my eyes to adjust to the gloom. When they did, I studied the sunlight slanting through bare windows. Dust motes danced and floated in the spilling light, and I focused on the golden auras that rimmed piles of furniture. The highlight on a sharp corner became an arrow. The curve of an overturned chair resembled a woman's back and hips—and I thought of an Edward Weston black-and-white photograph. How he found an abstract beauty in the mundane, the ugly.

The cruel.

Nothing registered as what it was. For endless seconds, I struggled with a need to identify what I looked at... then the fear... when I identified everything.

"Noa." Levi stood behind me. His voice thickened to a hoarse whisper. "This could have been me."

At my feet, in the middle of what was once my grandfather's favorite room, I counted five—no, six—dead wolves. Ebony globs of clotted blood covered pelted bodies already sunken in around the ribs. Legs stretched—the paws like hands, the extended claws like fingers in a mimicry of running.

Most still had their heads.

One body didn't, and—caught up in the horror—I looked around for it. For the head. Then nausea surged.

Someone had speared the *thing* on a broken floor lamp like a wig dummy on a boudoir stand. Flies buzzed—I hadn't even registered the sound. The jaws gaped; the swollen tongue lolled. A rusted chain draped, arranged around the wolf's ears to dangle like ear rings with gore-covered, saw-toothed traps at the ends.

The pool of blood beneath the stand glimmered like a placid crimson lake, other than the circular ripples that spread out each time a random blood-drop hit.

The head was still draining.

I would not be sick. I would not look at dried-out lips drawn back over extended, broken canines.

I would not think of Levi, lying wounded and bleeding in the grass, yards from where I now stood. Not even when I heard him vomit, then saw him slap a hand over his mouth and stumble through the broken door.

Saliva pooled. I kept swallowing. My skin iced with sweat that I could smell, acrid with fear.

Grayson Devante observed my reaction. His detachment was otherworldly. But I heard his breathing and concentrated on the rhythm while I stared at the bloody writing on my grandfather's pristine white walls.

Bitch. Faille. Leave now.

You're next.

You did this!

I inhaled the sour stench Levi left behind, listening as wolves crowded into the house, thickening the air with a caustic madness. Mace was there. Oscar. Pack members, moving with an agility that was alien. They prowled around, and the enraged murmurs sounded more feral than anything close to human speech. I was witnessing their first reactions—while fighting the wolf energy that swirled and gained strength in this defiled space.

Never had I been so afraid to move. To call attention to myself.

"Ours?" A man I didn't recognize hissed the question, but if he was here, then he was wolf.

"One." Grayson's voice sounded guttural, as if his wolf wanted to shift. "Callum. He bears our pack mark. The others are wild."

Mace crouched down and curled his fingers into the red-gray pelt of the headless wolf. The rough overcoat was dull with the brittle ash of death, but when Mace parted the fur down to the skin, I saw a black crescent moon marking the wolf's shoulder ridge.

Oscar bared his teeth. His hiss was wild and squally. One by one, the other werewolves did the same. Even Levi, looking older. I sensed the solemnity. The reverence I did not expect from wolves. Each man knelt beside the headless wolf, placed a palm on the shoulder mark.

And the weight in that symbolic act filled me with dread.

When they stood and walked into the sunlight, the alpha's strange, angry eyes narrowed. When his gaze centered on my face, I chanted the childhood rhymes in my head as if *liar, liar, pants on fire* would keep me safe.

"They died because of you."

The calm in his voice stirred up my instincts. "I didn't do this."

"You are *here*." And that was enough—my mere presence—for the Alpha of Sentinel Falls to blame me.

"So are you."

He scented the air with a lift of his lip that had me stepping in front of the place where Levi vomited.

"Violence is the hallmark of wolves," I said, my voice cold... so very cold. "You thrive on the terror and blood. Leo showed me enough, and I hated what it did to him—but I never hated *him*. And I did not do this."

The alpha cocked his head, the movement more beast than human.

"You feel no sympathy for wolves who suffer? For those lying dead? Or for Callum, who no longer *has his head*?"

My chin lifted, pulse thundering, but I would not stand down. "I feel sympathy for those who have no choice. But not those who do."

He gestured toward what I couldn't look at. "You assume that, because these wolves were not skinned, it means other werewolves were responsible?"

"Human poachers would not leave six pelts behind. And members of your pack want to do the same to me—cleanse the world of *failles*."

The snarl in my voice surprised me, but the aggression kept me standing when one black claw extended from the alpha's knuckle.

I wondered if he intended to drag it across my throat.

"Who told you that?"

My lip curled, matching his. "Does it matter? It was said. It was meant."

The change in Grayson Devante's stance had me taking a small step back. His canines punched down, slicing his lower lip, drawing blood before he retracted them.

Show no fear, Noa.

"Wolves wanted my mother dead before I was born," I said. "Were you the Alpha then? When she was here? Did you do nothing to protect her?"

"No." His hand sliced through the air. "I wasn't Alpha then, and we're not that uncivilized."

"How do I know?" I gestured, my hand slicing in a mimicry of his. "When I glance around, I see threats on the walls. I hear threats from the men outside."

"They think you lured the enemy here."

"How clever of me, luring an enemy to defile my grandfather's house, a place he *loved*. I loved and maintained for two years."

The alpha loomed over me, despite the space between us. He wore black, but even if he'd worn an Armani suit and had tattoos all over his hands, the intimidation level would have been the same. Some men radiated power no matter what they wore. The kind of power a woman felt in her bones—the kind that told her to run.

His jaw flexed, as if he ground his molars, enforcing a control he'd rather unleash. "We don't like coincidences."

"Because I show up and save Levi from the edge of death?"

Don't prod the wolf, Noa, not when his canines are punching out again.

But then I thought of my mother, how she suffered because of these wolves.

"Why weren't your sentries out here checking for traps before Levi ever ran into one? Why weren't they patrolling the grounds if they're so worried about the enemy?"

"My sentries were in the area."

"Not close enough to help Levi." I stared at what was left of the ruined house. "I can't even say goodbye to Leo."

"Too bad he's not around to hear you."

It was the truth, and I turned my head, restless with no safe place for my gaze to linger. Behind me, the alpha's voice rumbled. "We leave in five minutes."

Not a request, but a dismissive order. He expected obedience. My lips thinned.

"Not *we*," I said into the silence. He'd been halfway to the ruined door, but he swung around. Walked back with a disruptive grace, disapproval scorching my skin, jolting through the defiant wall I hid behind.

Alarm ricocheted like stones in an avalanche.

Dip your chin, Noa. At least pretend that wasn't a challenge.

The alpha's eyes turned predatory. Muscles beneath his golden skin flexed. Heat from his body radiated with a wild scent of mountain streams and snow on pines, and I hated that I liked the way he smelled.

He wanted to frighten me. I refused to look away. He might be massive and sexual, and his dominance had a gritted-teeth kind of edginess that infuriated me. But the danger lay in the way he turned courage into mushiness. If I looked away, I'd signal that he'd won.

Which I'd never let him do.

I defied him with every fiber in my being. My gaze locked with his, and his eyes glittered with what I swore was contempt.

"You carry Leo Bishop's bloodline," he said. "I am obligated to protect you."

"I'm not your obligation." *And already dead... why was I not dead yet?*

"Be grateful for my offer." His tone now vibrated with a menace that flattened my lungs. "I could leave you here to be ripped to shreds."

"By your wolves?" More accusation than question, but I was a *faille*, so he should know what I expected.

His legs were braced. His head tipped back, and he breathed with slow intensity, maybe to keep those canines of his from punching down again. I wondered if he ever tired of the posturing. Then I wondered why I wasn't a babbling mess by now, crushed by his energy.

"By those who did this," he murmured. "I doubt you'd like facing them on your own."

I rubbed hard at my arms.

Grayson Devante turned toward the door and didn't look back. But his voice deepened as he added, "If you want mementos, collect them now."

I sagged when he left, but had no clean wall to lean against, and couldn't believe he'd told me to collect mementos when my grandfather's home was now a hovel. Nothing remained in the ransacked kitchen. The furniture was all but destroyed, and the dark fluff wasn't stuffing from the cushions. It was wolf fur, ripped out in clumps, and while I was grateful the fur wasn't Levi's, I wished I'd believed my mother's warning. I wished I hadn't come back to Sentinel Falls, or tried to save a wounded wolf.

Hadn't put myself within reach of Grayson Devante.

Until this moment, I'd been high on our confrontation, charged with the need to assert my independence while denying the effect he had on me. But with him, I felt like the fool who whistled in the dark while surrounded by monsters. And standing in the middle of Leo's ruined house, staring at... everything... I didn't know where to start. I *couldn't* start. Or make myself wander through the rooms where my grandfather spent his last hours alone. I would see them ruined, bloody from the violence, and never forget. Replay every step I took in my nightmares.

It was hard enough not to sink to the floor and press my face into shaking hands. To grieve losses deeper than I ever expected.

Besides, there were no mementoes left—only a parody of an Edward Weston photograph in blood-red and wolf-black.

Outside, a silence descended, more terrifying than low rumbled voices. The Alpha of Sentinel Falls was issuing orders through the pack bond, and I understood now how massive his power was. How deep pack loyalty went—and it would go against me.

I was the enemy, no matter what Grayson Devante said about protecting me. If I ran, I'd become prey. If I stayed, I had hours or days left before excess wolf energy incapacitated me. I might absorb more energy than my mother could, but over time, I'd reach the same threshold, and the delusions that destroyed her would destroy me.

I flinched when Oscar touched my arm. His eyes were watery, but his lips were firm. "There's a warm coat in the closet. I'll get it while you wait."

I kept my breathing even, my knees locked. Oscar moved broken furniture with more agility than I expected, clearing a path to the hall. His determination meant the Alpha's decision was now law. I was the one refusing to accept it. I had no control. No choice but to be an obligation—and somehow, that involved a warm coat, which made no sense if I was going back to Sentinel Falls.

But when Oscar returned, he held out a quilted woman's jacket—puffy and forest-green, the last item I'd expected to see coming out of Leo Bishop's closet.

"Hattie left it for you." Oscar dipped his head. "She thought if you ever came back, you might not remember how cold it gets in the high mountains."

"I'm not going in the high mountains." But a wave of regret swallowed me up before I turned and walked into the sunlight.

Leo's body was in the high mountains.

CHAPTER 7

Noa

I FOUND LEVI BESIDE my car, stuffing clothes into my backpack.

"Sorry." He made a face. "Alpha wants enough for several days. Put those on too."

He pointed toward my hiking boots while I stood open-mouthed.

"Wear what I can't fit in." Levi stuffed another shirt. "It gets colder the higher you go, but don't get sweaty because the damp won't dry, and the nights will be worse."

I didn't move, but then he reached for a bra, and I slapped his hand. "Stop."

"Can't." His white teeth flashed. "Alpha said so."

Ordered—and it infuriated me.

"He can't order me." And—damn it—I would not let a sixteen-year-old *werewolf* pack a bra for me.

Levi's jaw clenched. "You gotta go with him, Noa. Alpha says you can't stay here. Not after what happened."

The urgency bothered me, and I glanced toward the wolves. Their agitation hadn't lessened, and the wolf energy bled into me while Oscar stood to the side, isolated. His fingers were twist-twist-twisting because Hattie wasn't beside him, patting his arm. Calling him "my Oscar."

I should have watched over him. The way I'd tried to watch over my mother. And should have... with Leo.

"Gray's taking you somewhere secret," Levi continued. "You can't know the way. It'll be through the mountains, hard for someone to follow without him knowing, but you'll be safe there."

Levi crammed a pair of jeans into the backpack while I refused to think about who might follow, or what the hell the secret place was—or if I'd ever leave it.

"I know Gray can be hard. Scary. But he's fair, Noa. It's his job to enforce the rules. Do the nasty work. Sometimes he doesn't like it, but he does it because he knows things we don't always know."

Levi yanked a shirt from the backpack and pushed thick socks into the small space instead. Tossing the shirt toward me, he waved a hand that said "put this on" when I hesitated.

"He's Alpha, Noa. No one goes against him. They don't want to, and it's more than our pack. We respect him, but all those other packs—their alphas can't come close to Gray. Most are scared of him, although they won't show it, and he rescued me when Laura was so scared that she couldn't even shift. He saved her too, like you did, and all that was after you left, so maybe you don't know. But you can trust him, even his wolf—although *he* growls a lot. But don't trust your senses out there, or what you see. You're probably too human, and there's both good and bad magic in this land."

Both good and bad magic—that was new. Leo never mentioned magic. He said werewolves had always existed, along with other immortal creatures, although they were rarely seen.

"What about you, Levi?" I didn't want to abandon him.

"I'm going with Mace." His thin shoulders rolled with a movement I'd watched Grayson Devante make. "We'll take care of things here. Hide your car. Alpha said your stuff would be at... the place... when you get there."

I stared at the shirt in my hands. At my car, being ransacked by Levi. I couldn't look at my grandfather's house. Instead, I tugged the image into my mind of the way the house looked last night. When I pulled to a stop and waited for Leo to come outside, his arm raised in welcome.

Levi's canines flashed, and from the way his eyes glazed, I guessed he struggled with his wolf for control. I put my hand on his arm.

"Did you know Callum?"

"He was funny with a lot of dumb dad jokes. People liked him."

"I'm sorry."

"It's my fault." Levi jerked his chin toward the house. "What happened... inside there. I shouldn't have crossed the borderline alone, and Mace says if I'm man enough to break the rules, then I'm man enough for the consequences."

And what about my consequences? I'd be a fool to ignore the message in dead wolves and threats written in blood. It didn't matter if human poachers or wolves defiled Leo's house. I couldn't fight an enemy who cut off a wolf's head for the shock value. And if the almighty Alpha of Sentinel Falls ordered it, no wolf would let me drive away.

Even if I remained here, my grandfather's house was ruined. And if I stayed in town, the threat would only get worse, between Jo-Rae and her friend. Angry wolves remembering Callum. I couldn't stay with Hattie and Oscar because they'd try to protect me—something *I* wouldn't allow. Not at their age.

The most logical solution was also the most selfish. I needed to hide, and if I disappeared into the mountains with the Alpha of Sentinel Falls, I'd be harder to find. I'd also be away from so much wolf energy. Less likely to react. I could buy time, sneak away when I had the chance. Run where no one would find me.

But it meant trusting the Grayson Devante. Pretending cooperation while I worked on a plan.

Leaving Hattie without saying goodbye would hurt. But hadn't my life always been about leaving without goodbyes?

How could one more matter now?

I pulled on a second tee shirt, ignoring the uncomfortable fit. Oscar stuffed water bottles beside the clothes Levi packed. With stiff hands, I tied the puffy green coat around my waist, then flipped open the hard case that held my recurve bow. Levi fastened the weapon to the side of the backpack. He did the same with the leather quiver that held a dozen arrows—pathetic. What good were arrows against werewolves?

But I was relieved the weapon was there, even if I never used it. I made myself turn and hold my arms out. Levi adjusted the backpack, tightening the buckle at my waist. The weight pressed against my shoulders, digging in, and I gasped at the sharpening impulse to run, get away, hide, close the doors, lock them, pull all the blinds... what I'd felt in Seattle.

Do it quickly, Noa. No second-guessing. Either run or follow him.

Levi said to trust Grayson Devante, but not my senses because they could be wrong.

In my head, I chanted, *liar, liar... pants on fire...* and put one foot in front of the other, following the Alpha of Sentinel Falls. While everything I knew became obscured, lost in the trees. And finally left behind.

For the first two hours, we walked in silence while the irritation chafed. Levi was right—Grayson Devante planned a marathon instead of a hike.

We marched along meandering animal trails, then up sun-drenched inclines and through the blue-shaded pines. I stomped on ferns. Kicked at rotting logs cloaked with moss and sprouting seedlings, and ants, crawling over the woody surfaces, carrying bits of leaf three times their size.

I pushed through spider-webbed branches, swiping at the clingy threads and leaves that snagged in my hair. When we came upon vistas that caught my breath, I wanted to gape, but Grayson Devante set a brutal pace and I refused to fall behind. When the elbow of the path turned, I regretted not having my camera. I could have taken photos. Used the landmarks to find my way back once I escaped.

Instead, I tried to memorize the turns, scuffing with my boot and leaving marks against the rocks. I'd create a trail of bread-crumbs the alpha wouldn't notice as I loitered behind.

His focus was intense. His strength never weakened and our pace never slowed. I glared at his wide shoulders, the flexing muscles in his back. Rubbed at the salty sweat stinging my eyes. But at least the physical exertion lessened the wolf energy rolling from him; I could almost tolerate the agitation now.

My heels dug in as we started up another slope. Oddly, the forest thickened, crowding the path... and when the tang of metal sank into my lungs, I stopped walking.

The alpha was several strides ahead before he noticed and swung back.

I pointed at the ground. "What is that?"

"The borderline."

The line Levi crossed without permission. "Okay, but... *what* is it?"

"Defensive magic."

I frowned. "Like an early warning system?"

"Crossing without permission is a death sentence for those who wish us harm," he said. "So, yes... I warn them first."

The man thought he was amusing. I stopped my backward step, but he still noticed.

"Cross it," he challenged. "Or stay there. I wouldn't stay, though."

I glanced around, wondering what he noticed with his alpha senses that I didn't. "Is something out there?"

"Maybe. If the Green Man is watching, he might take offense. Turn you into a tree."

My eyes widened.

"It's his magic," Grayson explained with dry patience. "That's why you see so many trees. People who offended him."

"You're lying."

"Am I? Look for yourself."

The bastard enjoyed this while I scanned the pines... and... in the twisted bark of an ivy-strangled tree... I saw a man's weathered face.

He winked at me.

A trick of the light, Noa. You can't trust what you see.

The man winked again, while Grayson said, "The Green Man doesn't let everyone pass. I wouldn't take his permission for granted."

I forced myself closer to the invisible line, pressing with my palm against the thickened air, and something uncanny, like liquid metal, oozed between my fingers. I tried to jerk my hand back, but the liquid wrapped around my wrist and yanked me through the barrier, so hard I sprawled on the ground.

My palms burned from the pebbles and grit. My backpack thudded against my head.

The alpha was too far away to have done it. So that meant... the Green Man? The Celtic myth I remembered seeing as carved garden ornaments?

But he wasn't real.

Delusions, Noa?

I glared at the tree where I'd seen the winking man. He was already gone, but in case he could hear, I shouted, "Asking politely would have been nice."

Grayson laughed before he said, "Get up before he throws you back."

The suggestion had merit. If the Green Man threw me back, I could make my escape. But if the damn alpha had been telling the truth... if throwing me back meant turning into a tree...

Gods, Noa. He was lying!

Huffing, I did as he asked, standing and following his lead, scuffing my rocks, noticing the details. The sun seemed brighter on this side of the barrier. Colors were more intense, and the faint scent of blooming flowers teased me while I searched for the source. But when the path turned, a vista opened up, and the view was so wild and magnificent, I just... stopped.

Spreading out around me were the mountains, rising from deep, emerald valleys. A distant river glinted with silver. Overhead, an eagle glided on the wind currents, the white head a vivid contrast to the walnut-brown wing feathers. I walked in awe, stumbling as the alpha crossed another alpine meadow.

When he stopped, I leaned against a human-sized rock, my palms scraping on the heated, gritty stone.

"What's the plan?" I huffed. "How long are we hiking? Do I get a say, or are you a dictator?"

"Dictator."

I dug around in the backpack, still irritated by the earlier turn-you-into-a-tree comment. "What about Levi?"

"He's with Mace."

"What will happen to him?"

"Nothing more than what happens to all the young recruits."

I found the water Oscar packed, unscrewed the cap and gulped the tepid liquid. "Are you punishing him?"

"No."

He was back in alpha mode, all arrogance and clipped answers as he circled the clearing, then walked along our back trail until he found the last scuffing mark. My pulse thumped when he rolled the rock with his booted foot before kicking it into the brush.

He turned toward me, and I held the plastic bottle hard against my lips, wondering how many other rocks he saw me scuff.

Probably all of them.

"You care about Levi?" he asked.

"I care."

I held his strange gaze, unsure if it was the wolf looking at me with those stunning, green-blue eyes, or if it was the man. But I wanted them both to know how I felt.

"Did I make a mistake when I removed that trap? Cause harm?"

"No."

"Good." I gulped more water. Felt the hard swallow.

Grayson's head tipped. Then he leaned in and sniffed, his lip curling as if choking on my human sweat, acrid from the fear and exertion... and two tee shirts... with the puffy coat still tied around my waist.

I was so ripe that I could smell myself. But I didn't feel sorry for the big, bad alpha, annoyed by the scent of an active female body.

He pulled off his shirt.

Sunlight bounced from his bronzed skin and the vicious wolf tattoo that curved over his left shoulder. "Put this on."

I stared at the shirt he held out—not at the ink on his skin. Or the scars on his body that I could now see. "Why?"

"You reek. Anyone following us won't need scuffed rocks. They'll follow the smell."

Unbelievable.

I wrinkled my nose. "Your shirt reeks too."

"It does." He flashed his teeth. "But it reeks of *me* and not you, so you'll put it on."

No way in flaming bright hell!

Being close to him was difficult enough. I wasn't wrapping myself in his shirt, gagging on his male scent with every inhale. His energy would rub all over my skin.

But then I heard the growl. The rumbled sound was deep in his throat, an obvious threat from the wolf, and I snatched the shirt, dropped it in the dirt and poured water over it.

The alpha lunged. I had no warning before his fingers wrapped around my throat, and from the restraint in his grip, I knew it was his choice, if he crushed my larynx first, or snapped my neck.

His canines were out, turning his voice into a guttural snarl. "My wolf thinks you're reckless."

"Your wolf is overreacting," I hissed, feeling his fingers flex.

His gaze locked on mine and we battled through another silent standoff. I should be used to them now.

"Appreciate his reaction. We're entering nymph territory—and nymphs won't bother you if you smell like me."

Nymphs! Immortal creatures not always seen. I hadn't quite believed in them, despite the images in my grandfather's books. But I remembered reading about the light-winged dryads and the bark-skinned hamadryads who lived in trees. Naiads preferred streams and lakes. All of them were fragile beings. Spirits of air, earth, and water.

And none of them would bother me the way the Alpha of Sentinel Falls *bothered me*.

"I thought your border magic kept bad things out," I said.

"Nymphs follow the rules."

Not on my best day did I want to argue that point with him, not when he had his claws around my throat.

But I wasn't sure if the book illustrations were accurate, and I asked, "What do they look like—the nymphs?"

"Not what you expect. But they like their food fresh, and when they're hungry, they'll eat anything."

Anything that didn't smell like him.

I moistened my lips.

Grayson released his hold on my throat, and when he picked up his shirt and held it out, I slid my arms into the wet, disgusting material without another word.

CHAPTER 8

Noa

OUR HIKE WAS NOT going well, at least not for me. Wearing Grayson's muddy shirt was torture. I'd never liked grime, but I hated how his shirt didn't *reek*. Instead, the scent was wild and woodsy, unique to him, and I caught myself rubbing my nose against the sleeve while pretending to swipe the sweat from my face.

Pathetic, Noa.

But needing to smell like him added to my anxiety.

"What else should I be afraid of? I mean, besides being turned into a tree by a garden ornament and nymphs with pointy teeth?"

"You don't know your own history?"

"I couldn't visit unless Leo kept his secrets."

Grayson rolled his shoulders. "If you're curious, we have an archive."

The archive excited me. I loved losing myself in books. Living a life that wasn't mine.

But wolves gave nothing without expecting something in return, and I thought about the somber ritual, with men kneeling next to a headless wolf, placing hands on the crescent pack mark. Mourning Callum.

I'd mourned him too, standing there, afraid to move. And when Grayson offered his protection—I hadn't said the words he deserved to hear.

"I'm sorry about Callum."

I watched his back stiffen before he asked, "Did you kill him?"

"No." I stared at a tiny white flower half buried in the rocks. "But you were right. Callum would be alive if I hadn't come back."

"Why did you come back?"

I gave him the only answer I could.

"Because of fear. The kind that drives you from what you know, toward something you realize is worse, but you can't stop yourself."

"What frightened you like that?"

"Ignorance."

When Grayson turned, he stared at my face, then my throat, over my breasts beneath his smelly, clinging shirt, layered over my smelly, double tees…

His gaze lingered. But there was no way the Alpha of Sentinel Falls saw me as anything of value, and when his lips tightened, I didn't want his pity.

We stared at one another, and I knew the moment when he decided I wasn't worth whatever he was about to say.

The hike continued in silence. I found the downhill grade as hard as uphill, with a steep path that dropped to the flat. And all the while, I stared at Grayson's muscled, naked back… at the edge of the wolf tattoo I could see… until he turned his head to the side.

A muscle riffled across his cheek.

"You're safe on pack land," he said. "The Green Man pulled you through the barrier because he wants you here."

"What is he?"

"The King of the Forest. When you feel his magic, you know you're crossing into his domain. By showing his face in the tree, he honored you. Give him the respect he deserves."

Which means don't call him a garden ornament to his face, Noa.

"What does he want?"

"Gratitude. A reverence for the living trees, and for all the beings who make their homes in the branches, beneath the roots, or in the shelter the trees provide."

The words were reassuring—and the last words I'd expected to come out of his alpha mouth. He hadn't even attached an order to them, or tried to make me feel ignorant for asking. "What about the nymphs?"

"Give them something they want. They'll be bound by magic and custom to repay you."

Now that Grayson was talking freely, I was curious. "What else should I worry about?"

"Witches and vampires. Other wolves."

"Stardust and moonshine?"

"No, but I wouldn't step on the faeries."

I focused on my feet, unsure if I heard teasing or condescension. The shadows told me it was mid-afternoon. In Seattle, my retail shift would be ending. I'd be stepping out into the watery sunshine, grabbing a latte from the kiosk.

I tried to recall the fragrance of brewed coffee. The drone of city traffic, the thrumming from highways.

Instead, silence filled my head, as if those memories had already faded.

Perhaps it was the Green Man's magic, imprisoning me with a beautiful allure. If I forgot what I'd left behind, I'd want what was in front of me and refuse to leave.

But I *would* leave. I didn't belong here, and I picked my way through mounding gray boulders that reflected the sun's heat. Grayson didn't frighten me as much now. Maybe it was the reek of his shirt. Or knowing that reek protected me.

"Why doesn't the Green Man let everyone pass?" I asked.

"You'll have to ask him."

"Will he talk to me?"

"No."

"Just... no?"

"The Green Man talks to the witches," Grayson said. "And the witches talk to everyone else."

"That seems a little convoluted."

"Witches have to earn a living."

"So..." I maneuvered around the large branch blocking the path, a branch Grayson stepped over. "You pay the witches to get to the King of the Forest?"

"Yes."

He put fresh energy into his stride, and I smiled. "Do they share the money with the Green Man?"

"No."

"That doesn't seem fair."

Silence, other than heavy breathing.

Gods, he was easy to irritate.

Why hadn't I noticed that before? And since the length of this hike was his idea, I turned it into a game. Each time I kicked a pebble, the rattle aggravated him more, so I looked for every pebble I could find.

I huffed dramatically.

Hummed a nonsense song.

The longer we hiked, the brighter the sun became until sweat darkened his hair, making it gleam like a black swan. A sheen coated his bare shoulders and the wolf tattoo. His muscles flexed, reminding me of his strength.

My pulse bumped. Then bumped again.

He was too dangerous to look at for long, so I said, "Are we almost there?"

A rumbled sound was my answer. I guessed it was no, or don't ask. Which prompted a satisfying—if reckless—prodding. As if I hadn't already learned my lesson with his muddy shirt.

"I'm asking because we've been hiking most of the day," I said. "And my feeble human legs are getting tired."

Grayson's exhale was exaggerated.

Don't prod the wolf, Noa.

"Do I have to stare at your sweaty back for the rest of the afternoon?"

I breathed through the instant when he halted. Then his hands curled and the claws snicked out. His pivot was enough to send dread through me. I understood why agitated men fell silent in front this man.

He unhooked the backpack at my waist, dragged it from my shoulders. I refused to react. But when he disappeared behind the towering rocks, I frowned. Crossed my arms and tapped an impatient foot.

I counted the minutes. When he didn't return, I grew anxious. Questioned my brilliant decision to harass him.

Argued with myself over whether he'd come back or leave me standing there alone.

I wanted to believe he'd come back, but... would he?

Or would he leave me in nymph territory? Where the hungry nymphs lived... sharpening their teeth... wanting their food fresh?

I was ready to give in. Apologize. Throw myself on the ground and tip my head, expose my throat in damn submission. But then his wolf sauntered out, dangling my backpack from his slobbering jaws.

He dropped it at my feet and chuffed.

I scowled at the jeans sticking out beneath the top flap—Grayson's jeans. And the bulge beneath was shaped like his shoes.

Wolfy bastard!

I wondered how many clothes I had left if he'd made room for his. The wolf pulled his lips back in what I swore was a smile. Then his tail twitched upward—was he giving me the middle finger—wolf style?

Every instinct flamed when he turned and strolled away.

"Okay, fine," I shouted at his backside. "If that's how you want to play it, *wolf*. But this doesn't mean you win."

"And that's how I won my second amateur championship in archery," I said, while the monstrous wolf prowled ahead on palm-sized paws. His tail whipped. Hair bristled along his spine, and he never once glanced around to see if I followed—although he knew, since I'd been carrying on my monologue for more than an hour.

He deserved every minute.

I wasn't the one who shifted into a wolf to avoid a conversation.

"Hitting the target relieves stress, although I don't think you'd understand that, being a werewolf. When you get antsy, you can run wild and howl at the moon."

The wolf chuffed and dug his claws deep, kicking up dirt clods and tossing them backward.

"Petty," I said, dodging out of range. "I was making a human joke."

I felt the breeze from his lashing tail and smiled. Perhaps evilly, but I was feeling a little dark, and finding revenge more fun than I thought.

"You might find this interesting. As a sport, archery is more mental than physical. Sure, you need to be strong to pull the bow weight. But concentration is the key. My mother always cheered me on. You're more like my stepfather. He never saw much worth in a sport that didn't kill something."

The wolf was silent. I concentrated on staying upright while we walked down a steep slope. I'd lost track of the number of hills. Given up on any rock-scraping. I'd started limping ten minutes ago. I didn't think the wolf noticed, but I thought the path he chose became easier. He would bound ahead, leaping from rock to rock on the inclines, growling at me to stay put while he disappeared. I thought he was monitoring our back trail or scouting for a less hazardous route.

Maybe later, I would think about why Grayson's wolf accommodated my human weakness, when the man expected me to carry his jeans and shoes. But I hoped they both regretted their decision to drag me so deep into the wilderness.

"I can't believe I let you scare the shit out of me," I said when the wolf was again leading the way. "That day I saved Levi, you made me roll in the mud, and I'm still annoyed about it. But

I'm thinking now that if I offered to scratch your belly, you'd roll right over on your back and let me."

The wolf snapped at the air as if an insect flew too close to his nose.

"You're very pretty for a wolf. I thought I'd tell you. Maybe handsome—since pretty is reserved for girls, and—"

The wolf paused and swung his head around. The blue-green light in his eyes was more blue than green, and the snarl vibrated low enough for me to get the message.

Okay, then. No talking about being pretty or scratching bellies. Probably no more talking at all, since the wolf seemed as annoyed as the man.

I held up both hands. The wolf chuffed, dug in his claws and circled before leading me toward the silver glint of the river, shimmering in the distance.

I dropped the backpack as soon as we reached the clearing. A crescent of towering gray rocks provided shelter. The rocks still held the sun's warmth. A river was within walking distance, and for a camping spot, I'd seen worse.

Thorny brambles edged soft sand. A stone fire pit surrounded several charcoaled logs. I assumed the wolf knew this place because he paced around the perimeter. Then snatched the backpack with his slobbering jaws and disappeared behind a convenient rock.

When Grayson returned, he'd hooked the backpack over his arm, but he hadn't zipped his jeans, and my pulse pitter-pattered through my veins. I didn't need the glimpse of masculinity. Not after the hours I'd spent looking at his muscled back before he shifted.

"You'll need your bow and arrows," he said as I tugged off his reeking shirt, tossed it in his direction.

"Why?"

He caught the shirt, slid his arms into the sleeves. "I spent an hour listening to you brag about your archery skill. Time to prove it."

I crossed my arms and looked around. "I don't see any targets."

"Yet. You're shooting dinner."

Oh, hell no! I was not shooting dinner.

"I don't hunt. Targets only."

His eyebrow arched, and I'd never met a man who could intimidate with a simple gesture the way he did. "Are you hungry?"

My traitorous stomach growled.

He smirked, bending down to untie my bow, the arrow quiver—both having survived the trek despite being dragged around by an irritated werewolf.

And it was one thing to brag about a human skill because it annoyed the arrogant jerk. I could hit targets all day if I had to.

But I would not reveal my human weakness—the part of me that couldn't kill, not even a random spider seeking refuge in my bathroom.

I'd rather spend ten minutes coaxing the spider outside, instead of squashing it with a tissue. While everything in life was squashable to the Alpha of Sentinel Falls.

"No," I said.

"You're still wolf," he said.

We were not doing the he-said-she-said thing. Not over something like this.

My chin lifted an inch. "I don't kill what I eat. I use grocery stores like a civilized person."

He flashed a tight grin. "Blood in, blood out."

My mouth dropped open. "You'd actually say that to me?"

He stared like I was challenging him.

"First," I hissed, "using the mafia cliché is not only ridiculous but shows a serious lack of imagination. And second, I was never *in* your wolfy club. I'm empty inside, in case you haven't noticed. And there's no way you can change me, bite me, make me want a life with no peace, where I'd be forced to turn into a monster with each full moon. To grow fangs and chase down prey in order to eat. Bury my face in blood."

His canines punched down.

Maybe monster was a little over the top, Noa. The bury your face in blood part, too.

"Do you like to eat?" he asked. "Because I don't see a grocery store nearby, and if you don't use that bow, you don't eat."

Disbelief tightened my lips. "You're making me do this?"

The alpha's jaw flexed with a sleek, animalistic ripple—and wolf energy hit in a heated wave. I pressed a hand to my throat, fighting back the nausea.

Was he trying to *compel* me again? Prove something to himself? Or to his wolf?

But he was the Alpha of Sentinel Falls. He had to know I was broken. That I had no werewolf abilities.

Was he looking for something else, then? For traces of Leo Bishop?

A sign that I had the strength to survive in this brutal world?

Because—in this brutal world—Grayson Devante was the ultimate authority. He decided who disappeared in the mountains. And who returned.

Before he'd let me near his pack, I would have to prove who I was. Prove *what* I was.

If I was a threat or a girl dumb enough to stumble into his territory.

I gritted my teeth. Snatched up the bow, swung the quiver over my shoulder. He could lead the way. Use his wolfy senses to hunt for dinner because I wouldn't help him. And even if we found something, I'd refuse to shoot.

Or shoot wildly and get over the humiliation later.

Grayson turned on his heel. I followed him as we left the rocks and entered a forest where the trees were rough with thready gray bark and patches of north-facing moss.

The shaded ground was uneven, but in a glade, yards ahead, slender blades of spring grass were turning bright green in the late sunlight.

I thought of the Green Man. Honoring those who lived within the trees. "How do you reconcile hunting with the King of the Forest?"

"All living things die," Grayson said. "When they do by our hand, we thank them for the sacrifice—and buy our food the same way you do."

I flinched at the insult. Assumptions were as ridiculous as clichés. And maybe I hadn't changed much from when I'd been sixteen, filled with righteous indignation to disguise ignorance.

"Why am I even here? You could have given me safe passage to Priest River, or Spokane, and let me disappear somewhere else."

"Only a fool sees a kitten when a lion enters the village."

"I'm not the lion." But maybe he was, and I should remember that.

We walked with slow, soft, careful steps. I placed my feet where Grayson placed his. I breathed through my nose. Steadied my pulse and thought about how the scent of wet pine reminded me of secrets and hidden shelters.

I thought about the weight of the bow in my hand and wondered if I could shoot at a living creature if I had to. Embrace everything wolf and *eat* what I killed, because this man asked.

But wouldn't I be betraying myself if I did? Betraying my mother? And Leo, for the way I'd treated him?

I'd hated everything wolf, and the moments I remembered were the moments that hurt the most.

Hearing my mother cry.

Driving away from Leo without looking back.

Standing in the moonlight, hoping that I wasn't *faille*. Then aching with senseless grief when I realized I was.

Grayson had paused. I glanced up. He motioned me to his side, pointing toward the wild hare yards from us.

She was sitting at the edge of the meadow, frozen in place. The leafy bower where she hid did not conceal her. I could see the trembling. The fawn-colored nose twitching. Her pointed twin ears stood straight up and seemed too long and wide for her head.

She held a shredded blade of grass in her mouth, forgotten while she stared for endless seconds.

I wanted to scream and didn't know why. Maybe I wanted to warn her. Maybe I was realizing how insane my life had become, hunting in the woods with a werewolf who wanted me to prove that—while I wasn't a threat—I could kill on command. Shoot an innocent creature. Because there were no damn grocery stores in the middle of nowhere.

This was *his* fault. He was the one who decided my life should be his responsibility because of an archaic rule in his Alpha Law book. A code of honor he had to uphold.

And maybe—in that instant hours ago—I'd been unable to see any other alternative except going with him.

But now? Why was I cooperating, unless something had changed in my thinking. After the Green Man yanked me through his barrier, and I became aware of what I'd never seen before... did I now see the alpha in a different light?

See Leo's life as different from what I'd thought?

I raised the bow with slow precision, a graceful arc that felt natural. I nocked the arrow into place, folded my fingers around the bowstring.

Don't think, Noa. Just do it.

A minute passed, dragged into another minute. I fought the bow's resistance against my extended arm. I'd cocked my elbow out because I had no wrist guard.

The anchored bowstring cut into my cheek. I focused on the wooden shaft. The tip of the black arrow.

I wasn't sure if it was my heart racing. Or if it was the rabbit's heart, thrumming in my ears. Panic fluttered in my throat and I couldn't move.

The rabbit searched beyond me for the threat it couldn't place. Her downy head jerked. The sun was glowing through her too-long ears—turning the flesh translucent, a pinkish-yellow, with tiny ruby-colored veins. I imagined the photograph I would take, how I would frame the pose. The contrast between the light rimming her delicate body and the deep, curving leaves from the bower. The clean green grass.

Her mouth moved with hesitant jerks, start-stop as she nibbled at the food. The grass trembled between her lips. I could sense her hunger at war with instinct. Her inexperience bathed in the late spring sun.

I blinked when my eyes blurred. The arrow tip wavered.

My arm trembled.

Beside me, I felt, more than heard, the alpha's rumbling disapproval. His tension sizzled across my skin, and I knew I was standing beside raw power, a man increasingly impatient and ready to explode at any second. He would never let me forget this failure. Add it to his list of things I couldn't do…

But I couldn't be what he was.

Or accept it. Feel every beat of a dying heart. Inhale the lingering scent of spring grass, where the doe or rabbit or fox last bedded down. The musk of a fawn, or the fear when the predator attacked.

I didn't want to feel the tender resistance of living flesh before the fangs punched down, and rage filled me, that he would try to force this despite my human heart. Despite knowing Leo was a healer. And while I was flawed, my instinct had been the same. To save Levi. Protect life.

Sensory overload made me dizzy. Saliva pooled so fast that I couldn't swallow.

Was this what it felt like—to have Grayson Devante compel a pack wolf?

I opened my mind. Listened. But no voice echoed in the empty space—the space shaped like a wolf. No spark waited in that darkness to be brought to life through some damn alpha's power.

The bond was never mine, and when I released the bow-string, I jerked the bow at the last instant, sending the arrow into the trees above the rabbit's head.

The air exploded. Man became wolf, lunging with rage and unnatural speed.

He disappeared into the leafy bower, and the high, sharp squeal pierced through me.

I turned, falling to my hands and knees, and vomited into the grass.

CHAPTER 9

Noa

WHEN THE WOLF STALKED back into the glen, a body with too-long, pinkish-yellow ears dangled from his bloody muzzle. I retched again. Then pushed from my crouch, gripping the bow, rubbing my thumb against the wood to keep my hand from shaking.

I didn't know the way back and hated having to follow the creature I'd softened toward, believing he cared enough to pick an easier path for me. I'd told him he was beautiful. Wanted to scratch his belly.

Gods, I was so naïve, believing there might be something redeeming in wolves because, for a tender moment, I thought the alpha's wolf cared. But Grayson Devante was no fool. And I wasn't a kitten.

I was strong enough to accept what I was, and know I'd not become like my mother cowering in her bed. Those around me wouldn't offer psychiatric care and call it solace. They would never understand the black hell inside me. The need that was never filled, but ached and echoed like a distant hole in the midnight sky. A missing star in the heavens.

The wolf's growl made me pause, and for the length of two heartbeats, I wondered if he could hear my thoughts. I couldn't hear him, but I'd never thought to ask if the pack bond was a two-way street or not. If the alpha's power was strong enough to eavesdrop, even on the flawed.

In the off-chance that he could hear me, I sent an obscenity his way. The wolf never faltered or flicked his tail. I decided that he either couldn't hear me—or he heard and didn't care.

We trudged through trampled fern that turned to rocky ground and then the sandy crescent framed by towering rocks. The sun had disappeared behind distant mountains, and the forest, the river, and our sliver of sand were now bathed in royal shadows. I crossed to my waiting backpack. Dragged the quiver from my shoulder, set aside the bow.

Each movement took effort. I pounded on the puffy green coat Hattie bought until I'd created a nest. Then I curled on my side and faced the rocky wall.

Behind me, the wolf was growling, digging his claws into the sand. I didn't care what he was doing—preferring my nest, missing my bed, my tiny apartment with the thin walls, where I could hear the neighbors fighting.

But the growling continued until it turned human—and whatever battle the wolf fought, the man had won.

His breathing was harsh when he said, "Don't turn around."

I didn't answer. I couldn't even summon a rhyme to occupy my mind. But I wondered if the Green Man's magic was back when a metallic scent thickened the air. Then the sound of breaking twigs made me flinch. One after another, methodical... and I thought about the slur Karla had used. What wolves did to *failles*.

Acrid smoke drifted. The fire crackled, popped. Not enough to drown out the slippery, skinning sounds—all that remained of the rabbit—and I retched again even though nothing was left in my stomach.

"What happened," he said. "It won't happen again."

I listened to a bird cry in the distance. To the susurration of the river.

To the steady sound of his breathing.

"I've been in these mountains for two months," he said, as if he was speaking to the night and not to me. "My wolf needed the solace. So did I. There are obligations I'm forced to fulfill, and you were right. Our life is brutal, sometimes monstrous. We'd been tracking a rogue wolf. When we found him, he refused to submit. He'd killed and was going to kill again."

Another stick broke. Firelight flared, and I stared at the vivid reflection on the rocks, my back still toward him. My elbows still pulled in tight.

But a small, silent part of me was listening.

"At the last moment, I hesitated."

I tensed at the silent grief he didn't want me to hear.

"My wolf took control, and he hasn't worked through it yet. I was going to let the rabbit go, but he... reacted. So we fight like we did tonight."

I heard him sigh.

"I'm not sure if he's the weak one, or if I am."

I rolled onto my back and glanced across the clearing. Grayson sat on the opposite side of the fire. In the wavering light, I saw the hard, bare curve of his shoulders. His arms, the muscles bunching as he tossed twigs into the flames, then rotated the rabbit impaled on a spit made of wood.

He was naked—which was why he'd told me not to look. Heat rippled across my skin, not from the fire. I stared at his face, the black hair and bronzed skin, smooth over the muscles in his arms and chest. His mouth pulled tight. He held another stick in his hand, prodding at the flames.

And I did not for one instant believe he thought he was weak. Not the dark Alpha of Sentinel Falls. The alpha other packs feared.

Not the man who did the things I'd seen him do, how he commanded the respect that calmed an enraged pack.

I inhaled the scent of roasting meat, but instead of my mouth watering, I rolled back to stare at the rock wall

"I tried to shoot." The whispered confession was an absolution, perhaps for his wolf's sake. "I couldn't do it. The rabbit was innocent."

"Innocence is a liability." Strength was back in his voice, along with a trace of mockery. "And if your mother hadn't fed you fairytales, your aim would have been better."

I shuddered. It was Leo who told me fairytales. My mother's warnings tore me in half, needing to believe her... wanting to believe Leo. Believe in the goodness found in saving wolves. But I saw no point in explaining when it was doubtful that Grayson would understand.

He was moving around again. "The food is here if you want it. I've placed rune stones around the perimeter—they carry magic no creature will cross. You'll be safe tonight."

"You're leaving?"

"Mace will arrive in the morning."

"When?" My voice was unsteady, although hope still burned that he intended no harm.

But perhaps the story about his wolf was a way to gain sympathy. To hide his true intentions.

He claimed wolves were civilized, but he wasn't above lying.

He'd also said life was brutal and monstrous, and innocence was a liability.

I twisted enough to push upright, standing to face him.

"Was this the plan all along? To leave me in the mountains and lie about Mace coming? Then let the nymphs and witches do the nasty work for you?"

Grayson didn't answer. The wolf did, appearing with a violent rippling, and I stared into the green-blue eyes, refusing to look away. Refusing to dip my chin or offer any sign of fear.

Instead, I pointed toward the rabbit on the spit.

"When I see that, wolf—do you know what I think about? I think of Callum, and my grandfather's ruined house. I think of dead wolves and Levi, bleeding out in the grass. And I think of the life you live and thank the gods that I am not like you."

CHAPTER 10

Noa

THE WOLF LEFT, BOUNDING into the dark, and when I slept, fitful dreams plagued me. I thought a monster slept at my feet, but in the morning, I was alone. The sun was watery in a pale sky, and there'd be no warmth from a fire that burned down to an ashy gray. I felt chilled and stiff. The uneaten rabbit was still on the spit and I couldn't look at it, choosing to dig through the backpack for dry clothes. I should have changed last night, but I'd been too resentful. I was still resentful when my clean shirt smelled like Grayson, probably from when he shoved his jeans into my backpack.

I wanted to wash every trace of the man from my hands, from my life, and since I was also thirsty, with nothing but empty water bottles, I stared at the river.

It wasn't far. The wide bank had flattened rocks and water-filled dips carved out by the current. Green reeds poked upward from isolated pools; I guessed the water was shallow. I'd be fine if I stayed out of the center channel, where the river deepened into jewel tones and rushed with a frothy current I could see.

I calculated how long it would take, sprinting across the distance. Five minutes, but not if I was barefoot.

I searched for my boots. When I found them, I gagged.

They *reeked* of wolf piss.

So did the quiver holding my arrows. My bow. Each defiled item sat between where I'd slept and the rune stones, and I wondered if the wolf pissed on my things as a petty way to prove he was in charge. Or if he'd been adding another ring of protection by marking his territory.

But no way in hell was I wearing boots that reeked of wolf pee. My hands already smelled. I notched the bow over my shoulder, along with the quiver, because I wasn't naïve enough to be caught without a weapon. Then I snatched up two empty water bottles, along with my boots, and stormed up to the rune stones.

Magic greeted me, a soft brush against my skin, and I took a moment to study the stones. They were oval, and I couldn't stop admiring the carved designs, the way they seemed to move, a faint undulation beneath the surface.

My legs weakened. The desire to sink to the sand and stare became overwhelming, but then I jerked my gaze away.

Just another lure, Noa. To keep you from leaving.

The sun rose higher. Mace had yet to arrive, and I wasn't even sure if he would. For all I knew, this was another survival test—one I'd pass, if only to spite Grayson Devante. I'd be fine on my own. I would leave without his permission, which I didn't need. And after that little pep talk, getting the water became the goal.

I relaxed my shoulders, arms, hands. Closed off my anxiety, and used my *faille* ability to search for wolf energy.

Nothing disturbed the air, other than a hawk overhead, looping in lazy circles with its head angled down.

The whispered rush of the river grew louder, and I could detect layers of sound, the speed of the water, where the current hurried and where it lingered. Smooth pebbles beneath my bare feet separated and settled with my weight, and it was no more uncomfortable than walking barefoot across uneven pavement.

Stepping onto a flattened rock, I glanced around. Water lapped near my feet, not deep enough to worry about, and so clear, sunlight spangled off the golden gravel beneath the surface.

With my bottles arranged, I moved downstream before dropping my boots into the water. The river splashed playfully. I kicked up little sprays, watching drops decorate the dry rocks. Dragonflies darted. I noticed one with amethyst wings and followed the zigzag flight upstream until I saw something in the current.

Maybe a log, small for a downed tree, but from the bone-smooth look of the wood, I guessed it had been floating a long time. Patches of aquatic grass covered the surface. Stubby branches poked out. And for a reason I couldn't fathom, I needed to capture whatever it was and pull it to shore.

With the first step, I sank into knee-deep water so cold, goose bumps raced the chills up my arms. I stepped back... then stared at the log again.

It was curious, the way it wandered like a compass needle searching for true north, then turned in my direction. I wasn't alarmed.

Perhaps *I* was the true north... and I forgot about the frigid water, the needling pain as I waded. The depth reached my thighs. Rocks beneath my feet felt precarious. But if I could stretch without my toes slipping...

The current grew stronger. I teetered, knowing that if I took another step, I'd fall and the river would swallow me whole.

But I was almost there, with the log drifting closer. My fingers grazed the wet surface, then slid through the slime as the log drifted away. Frustration rushed through me and I grabbed for a broken branch... but as my fingers closed on the branch, the log tugged.

I angled my head, still curious.

Perhaps it was the unexpected weight caught in the current. If I readjusted my grip, took another step...

But then, the hawk screamed, and I remembered what Levi said.

Don't trust your senses out there, or what you see.

My fingers flexed. The log tugged again.

And my pulse beat hard in my throat.

Get out get out get out!

As I scrambled, turbulence bubbled up around the log, spewing foam and all shades of turquoise. A woman surged upward. Ebony hair webbed across her face. Skin paler than pearls gleamed. But her eyes, when I saw them, were inhuman, coal black.

It was impossible to look away.

Her expression was pitiless, her smile dreadful, filled with rows of sharp teeth. She was still lunging, clawing out of the water and toward me, scuttling like a crab.

I looked down, expecting to see her fingers piercing my skin.

But what I saw... black leeches squirming from the splits and cavities in the log. From the aquatic grass and beneath the water, their movements turning frantic as they sensed... *food?*

I backpedaled, sloshing great fans of water, nearly falling when the quiver on my back tangled with the bow.

The leeches were wriggling through the water with a sickening hunching... hunching...

I fought the current and my footing until a leech latched onto my hand. I dug at it with an arrow tip, gouging my flesh.

Slugs kept coming.

I stumbled from the water.

The woman followed, scrabbling on disjointed arms and legs, crab-like, crossing the rocks toward the shifting pebbles. Leeches oozed behind her—a spreading viscous oil.

I gripped my reeking bow, ran and cursed the liability in innocence. Nocked an arrow, aimed, shot and shot again, missing each shot, stumbling backward toward the rune stones.

Although the leeches slowed on the hot pebbles, nothing deterred the woman, and my mouth dried. From my count, I had three arrows left to use if the runes didn't work. I guessed she was a nymph, and I raced toward the semi-circle sheltered by rocks and guarded by magic. I didn't dare look at the creature clicking and hissing behind me. But when I passed the rune stones, I felt the resistance of magic and pushed through with enough momentum that I crashed into the towering rocks that formed a protective wall.

I turned with my bow raised and an arrow aimed.

Not at the crab thing. The nymph had morphed again. She stood outside the stone runes, looking like in image from my grandfather's books. Her gown was diaphanous, flowing with the colors of opals. Black hair fanned around her shoulders. Her feet were bare, and gold anklets jangled as she moved.

But her head cocked as she sniffed the air.

Her lip curled. "Wolf piss."

With my arm stiff, I angled the arrow tip up another inch, so she'd notice I was aiming at her. "What do you want?"

"A meal," she admitted. "But then I smelled him all over you, and I'd rather eat a muck grub than something he's marked."

So, the damn wolf had been protecting me with wolf pee, if this creature was afraid to come any closer.

"If you're hungry," I said, "you can have the rabbit."

"Tempting." Her pointed tongue flicked as she licked her lips. "If I could pass those rune stones to get it. And if I didn't smell that reek."

"That's why I was at the river, to wash it off."

"Maybe you shouldn't wash it off." She pulled a leech from her skin and swallowed it whole. "That reek kept you from being lunch."

"Do you want the rabbit, or not?" I tried not to gag when she searched for another leech.

"For what in return?"

"Not being lunch. Nothing else. Consider it an act of generosity."

"You would give up a bargain with a nymph?" Her laugh clanged, but it wasn't malicious. "You are an innocent."

"Not so much, now. Every minute I'm here, I learn something new."

"Well..." She shrugged. "If the Green Man let you pass... and if that wolf cared enough to leave his scent as a warning... then I'll take the rabbit and thank you."

I inched my bow down as a gesture of trust. The nymph arched her eyebrows. I still wasn't over how rapidly she changed in the river—did everything in this wilderness move that fast?

"Move back. I'll throw the rabbit to you."

She dipped her head, not quite a bow, but with her hands folded in front of her, she took a step back and waited.

"Are the leeches your pets?" I asked as I tugged the spit from the sandy ground, surprised at how deep Grayson had thrust it.

"No. They're quite disgusting and..." She picked at her fingernails. "Not normal for this river."

"Then you're a river nymph." It was obvious that she was, but I wanted her distracted while I moved toward the rune stones. I wouldn't get close; she might grab my arm. But I needed to toss the spitted rabbit across the boundary, and I couldn't pitch it more than a few yards.

"I am." She snatched the spit when it thudded, then used those long fingers to peel off a strip of stringy meat. "There aren't many of us left."

"I know the feeling."

"Are you a wolf?" The eerie head-tip again. "Or something else?"

"Something else."

She popped a piece of rabbit into her mouth like the leech. "What kind of something else?"

"A *faille*."

"Do you belong to him?"

"No."

"Well..." She sucked on her fingertips before plucking at the rabbit again. "Did he tell you that silver streak in your hair was once the mark of queens?"

Spider chills raced down my spine. "No."

"That's probably why he wants you."

"Are we bargaining now? Information for information?"

Her smile turned cunning. "Clever girl."

"Who owes whom?" I asked.

"Such fancy language." She turned the spitted rabbit, searching for another morsel that hadn't turned into dry leather. "We can call it generosity."

I felt something tugging on my arm and glanced down. A leech was gorging on my blood.

"Pull the skin tight and flick it off with your fingernail," she advised. "Cutting them off risks more poison getting into your system."

My heart thudded. How many leeches had I sliced off with the arrow tip? "How... poisonous?"

"I'm not sure. They aren't normal leeches, and wolves are usually immune. But since you aren't wolf..." The nymph sucked on a rabbit bone, then crunched it for the marrow. "Maybe you should ask him to heal you just to be safe."

I looked down at the segmented body. It had swollen to twice its normal size, and I tried to follow her instructions, pulling my skin tight. Sliding a ragged fingernail beneath the pulsing body.

I couldn't get the creature loose.

"Try pinching the narrow end. That's the head. Squeeze until the ooze comes out."

The leech popped between my fingers. Bloody muck coated my skin, and as a proof of how bizarre my life had become... I didn't gag.

"You know the wolf?" I asked as I wiped my hand on the sand.

The nymph shuddered. "Everyone in this forest knows the Alpha of Sentinel Falls. He's quite brutal when he needs to be. His wolf shredded another wolf who challenged him. I'd heard he exiled himself because of it."

"I'd say you heard wrong." *Maybe.*

"And I'd say you're lucky he pissed on you," the nymph said. "Creatures would have feasted during the night, given the chance—fae abominations we haven't seen in centuries."

Centuries?

Since the nymph was sitting on the sand, I sat across from her with the rune stones between us. I left my bow near my hip, within reach, but I was no longer afraid she'd lunge past the magic. She feared the Alpha of Sentinel Falls too much.

"Is this your river?"

"No." Her face sharpened. "My clan—we lived miles from here. But we're scattered now."

"I'd heard rumors of... bears." I offered the information I'd overheard.

She searched for more meat on the carcass that was close to being bone. "Lots of rumors. Not always bears, though."

"Do you have a name?"

"If a nymph gives her name, it's a curse."

"Then how do you know who you've bargained with?"

"She doesn't," Mace said as he stepped from behind the rocks. "And she's lying. There's no curse."

The nymph stiffened and rose to her feet.

"Be careful, Lorriel," he cautioned. "You're a little far from home."

I heard the threat in Mace's tone, rising to my feet like the nymph as I glared at the blonde alpha, remembering my panicked dash across the sand. How long had he been watching?

"You're a little late to the conversation," I said.

"I was waiting to see if she'd eat you." His glance swept back to the nymph. "Where are your sisters?"

"I... don't know." The nymph's gown drifted around her in a breeze I didn't feel.

Mace growled, but then said, "I'm not here to hurt you, Lorriel. I saw the leeches."

"They don't belong." Her anklets clinked when she stepped backward. "They aren't from us. They're an abomination."

"What of your clan?"

"We scattered. Two months ago." The breeze I couldn't feel was now strong enough to lift strands of her hair. Her black eyes blinked—and I noticed the reptilian vertical slit of her pupils. "Predators came down from the north, chasing the game, defiling the rivers. We had to leave."

"These predators—can you describe them?"

Lorriel shook her head. "Shadow forms, moving through the forest. Perhaps dire wolves, if they still exist." She took another step back.

"You'll be safe with us," Mace offered.

"You should strengthen your wards," she countered. "The vampires are moving, too. Talk of war coming."

"There's always talk of war."

The nymph was changing form, becoming as diaphanous as her dress. Her hair whitened into mist, backlit by the sun. "He may not win this time," she said. "Not alone."

"You speak of alliances?"

But the nymph was more fog than solid now, streaming back to the river in gray ribbons that splashed as she disappeared.

Mace snapped, "We should leave."

I bent toward my backpack.

"Leave it." An order, one I should not ignore. "Now. Move."

"I have no hiking boots," I pointed out.

Seconds later, something wet shot out of the river and plopped at my feet. My boots, covered with river-weed, but they no longer reeked.

Mace gestured. "A gift repaid."

I shoved my feet into the wet leather. Then he led me into the pines. His forest-colored clothes blended in with the shadows, and like Grayson Devante, he carried no weapon other than a knife strapped to his thigh.

His confidence was that of an alpha, and something wild, hard and battle-worn. Mace was a warrior. Different from the Alpha of Sentinel Falls, but as deadly. In the human world, he could have gone far on his appearance alone. I imagined his image on glossy magazines or sexy book covers. Even I would have photographed him with the sun illuminating his face. I honestly wondered how many females lusted after him.

But Mace prowled more than hiked, and his vigilance made me wonder what I'd missed in his conversation with Lorriel. They'd both been worried about something, refusing to say what it was.

I was still uneasy when the trees closed in and the river disappeared. I kept pace with Mace despite his disruptive energy. Not as intense as Grayson's energy, although when I thought about his taunt, about waiting to see if the nymph would eat me before he intervened, anger got the best of me, and I snapped, "Be sure to thank your boss for the warning about the river. I might have gone swimming."

"We've never had nymphs in that river." Mace flexed his hands. "You should have been safe."

"He should have checked before he left."

"He added to the security."

"By peeing everywhere?" I shuddered. "Why did I not think of that, instead of doorbell cameras?"

Mace chuffed out what could have been a laugh. "He needed to leave and thought marking your things would be sufficient."

I had to admit Mace was right and released a breath. "Where did the almighty Grayson Devante go?"

"He had other matters that demanded attention."

"Such as?"

"It's complicated."

"More unusual sightings?"

Mace shrugged, staring into the distance. "It's complicated."

Irritation chafed. "I understand complicated."

He grunted as we started up a hill. "I didn't think you could run that fast and shoot at the same time."

"Funny."

"You're lucky you got out of that river. Nymphs use water to enthrall. They're feared for that reason."

"She said the wolf piss stopped her."

Mace chuckled. "I'll bet."

"Were you serious about watching her eat me?"

"Maybe for the first bite," he said with a snap of white wolf teeth.

I wasn't sure if he was teasing.

"You shouldn't have told her what you are," he said a moment later.

"Will she use it against me?"

"Maybe."

I gauged the distance between the two of us and realized it had widened despite my increased effort to keep up with him. "She said the silver streak meant something about queens."

Mace didn't answer.

I took a few more steps, feeling bruised from head to foot. "What do you do for Grayson?"

"I'm head of security. Train the recruits, monitor the patrols. During times of war, I'm the ultimate authority, other than Gray. He can overrule me."

"Does he do that often?"

"He hasn't yet."

I moistened my lips. Tried to swallow—why was my mouth so dry? "How's Levi?"

"Swearing through the pack bond right now. If he keeps it up, I'll be deaf."

I smiled at that image. No rest for the wicked with the pack bond. I imagined them shouting at each other through it, like a radio with no off button.

But I was asking about Levi, wasn't I?

My thoughts were fuzzy.

"What did you make him do?"

"Right now, he's halfway through a fifty-mile hike with a two-hundred-pound pack on his back. But if he doesn't learn, he won't survive."

I heard both the warrior and the father in Mace's voice. Male wolves nurtured the pups differently than the females, but no less lovingly. I wouldn't argue the point.

Instead, I said, "I guess you think I'm broken."

Mace shortened his stride so I could catch up. "In what way?"

"Because of everything, I guess."

Mace was quiet for several strides before he said, "Someone broken wouldn't have escaped the nymph, or had her eating rabbit and talking like an old friend."

"I thought she was nice. Lonely."

Mace snorted. "Did you see the teeth?"

I shuddered. "Where are we going?"

"Somewhere safe."

His voice sounded far away. Like I was back at the river. And he was watching from the towering rocks.

"Where is he?"

"Talking with a vampire."

"Is he talking about the coming war?"

"You're a curious little *faille*."

I took a few lopsided steps, tried not to step on a patch of small flowers... missed and crushed them.

Mace paused long enough to look at me. "Why can't you walk straight?"

His voice echoed like a hollow bell. My lungs crushed inward and I couldn't push them out again.

"I don't know. Maybe it's the creepy leeches." Glancing down, my vision swam as I tugged at my shirt. "Oh, look... I missed one."

I forgot to pinch and pull. Or scrape. I dug in with my fingernails, ripping the black body from my stomach—and with it, I peeled a strip of skin the exact width of the leech.

It was as easy as peeling fruit, while blood ran in rivulets, pooling at the waistband of my jeans.

I looked up at Mace.

"I should go home," I said, and dropped to the ground like a stone.

CHAPTER 11

Grayson

THE MORNING HELD THE lushness of a coastal rainforest, thanks to the Green Man's magic. Cedar, pine, and fir trees covered the foothills and guarded the valley floor. In the meadow, wildflowers thrived. A silvery, ice-fed tributary snaked toward the river far to the south. Toward the north, distant snowy mountains formed an impassable barrier, save for an ancient gap now blocked by a rockslide.

I followed a lost trail, overgrown and abandoned. It led through wild rhododendrons and thimbleberries that spread their hairy leaves on low-arching canes. Already, the plants displayed white flowers and signs of fruit.

The valley hadn't always been peaceful. Ancient—and not so ancient—battles had bloodied this land. Shadows lingered, malevolent spirits looking for the dying. Even the air was uneasy. But the privacy was worth the malevolence, something I appreciated as much as the vampire did.

He waited beneath a tree. "Wolf," he said in greeting. "A wood nymph, the third I've found, either dead or dying."

"In how long?"

"A week. All on your land."

"Where?"

"There." The vampire—Julien Visant—led the way. He acted as an emissary between the vampire sires and the packs, and
his summons was important enough for me to task Mace with
guarding Noa Bishop. We weren't exactly friends, but neither
were we enemies. His hair was dark brown, his eyes were blue,
and his build was that of a slender yet muscular man. Normal.
All vampires looked *normal*. Like the wolves, life was smoother
when the nightmares hid in plain sight.

Julien led the way until I saw the nymph huddled at the
base of a towering cedar tree—*her* tree, the source of her life
force. Vines tangled in her russet-colored hair. Flowers adorned
a translucent gown. But someone had mortally wounded the
tree, ripping the bark away in a full circle around the trunk,
destroying the tree's circulatory system. Sap from the soft wood
bled in thick gold rivulets while the desperate nymph sobbed
and cut bloody strips of her flesh to place over the wounds.

Her fingers were red and ragged—if the tree died, so did
she—but while the tree absorbed her bark-like skin, she could
not save either her tree, or herself.

"She's bleeding out," Julien said. "Can you heal her enough
to stop the flow?"

"She's not wolf." And healing between species was difficult.
Even if I could prevent her from bleeding out, the life force of
the tree was fading. All I sensed was a grief that shuddered in
agony, both for the tree's wounds and those of the nymph.

But I dropped to my knees, stared into her luminous eyes,
green like the new growth of spring. Smoothing my hand
against her forehead, I surged a thread of healing energy.

Her wounds closed, but not enough as she kept shredding
herself.

"Who did this to you?"

"Shadows." Her voice whispered on a sylvan breeze. "We could feel them coming…"

We… the nymph and the tree…

"I'll do what I can for your tree." Perhaps a fool's promise to ease the dying, but I placed my palm against the rough bark, slippery with her blood.

"We… are gone. Save the others."

The nymph turned diaphanous. The cedar's great branches dipped down to wrap around her. Birds grew quiet. The vampire's subtle vibration matched mine.

All predators recognized the moment of death, and both the vampire and I stood silent before Julien asked, "Have you heard from the Cariboo pack?"

"Not in months."

"Neither have we."

"The winter was hard," I said. "Perhaps they moved west."

I offered the possibility without believing it. The Cariboo pack was aggressive, resentful, but the vampires were their trading partners. They wouldn't cut off communication without a reason.

I had my own suspicions about the motives, but I was unwilling to confirm them. During the previous pack war, the vampires sat on the sidelines, picking winners and losers. When the fighting ended, the alphas and sires agreed to co-exist unless the balance of power changed.

A new war would alter the balance, and Julien had already considered that possibility.

At our feet, the nymph was completely gone, and I walked with the vampire back into the sunlight. He was immune—as most vampires of a certain age were immune to the sun.

"The sires are concerned," Julien said. "The evil creeps southward, to the edge of the mountains. Some are moving away."

"Back to Seattle?"

The vampire snorted. "A few are dispersing for safety, but not back to *that* city."

Dispersing meant they could be anywhere. Vampires didn't limit their territory to physical boundaries, but they cultivated a regal image by having a seat of power. A place where the ruling sires held court and granted favors to lesser species like the fae creatures. The nymphs. And those closer in power, like the witches.

The current seat of power was a place they called High Citadel, a remote location on land controlled by the Carmag pack, close to our western border.

"Have you noticed anything unusual?" Julien asked.

"The prey animals are moving around," I admitted. "We thought a disturbance in Canada was the cause, pushing them southward. Our scouts reported anomalies with the wards set in the mountains. Strange energies, tracks we can't identify."

None of this information would weaken our position, and the vampire expected something, a sign of cooperation.

"The sires have heard rumors. Humans, mining beneath the Canadian glaciers. Perhaps there's a disruption in the wards, a weakening that allows old monsters to escape."

"The Cariboo would know." It was their territory, their responsibility. But if the vampires hadn't heard from the Cariboo, and Julien was here, alerting me to wood nymphs destroyed by an evil from the north, then this meeting took on new meaning.

I waited.

Julien crouched down and spread one hand across a clawed, five-toed track in the mud—a track that shadows hadn't made. "Your wolf is quiet."

"He's being polite."

"And he doesn't like me."

I shrugged, while Julien bowed his head with exaggerated courtesy.

"Then, while he's being polite, perhaps you'll confirm another rumor—that you have a new interest in *failles*."

"There's nothing significant in our history books," I lied. "We don't even know if they're real."

"A foolish lack of foresight." The vampire stood, looking at his hand; the mud on his fingers disappeared. "In the old stories, *failles* were mysterious creatures. While their lack of a wolf was their curse, it also hid a dangerous asset."

"A history lesson, Julien?"

"Who knows what is true? Perhaps you should ask her since she's here."

The vampire pushed both hands into his pockets and glanced away. An act of trust, since he'd just admitted to having a spy planted in my midst—someone who'd told him about Noa Bishop. But we both knew I wouldn't kill him. Julien was my best conduit to the sires. I couldn't afford to lose that connection.

"Other packs are noticing the evil," the vampire continued. "Carmag struggles with denial. Even some at the High Citadel believe the rumors are exaggerated. But... if it is true and the girl you harbor is what I think she is, you may have a larger problem than you imagine."

"What do you know, Julien?"

"Three months ago, the sires sent an emissary to the Cariboo pack. He never returned, so they sent another. Then a third. Antoine was powerful, respected. He did not go alone, but again, none returned. And three weeks ago, the sires received his sire ring in a bloody box."

An event alarming enough for retribution. A sire ring was a vampire's mark of status, a connection to his sireline—the bloodline going back to the original vampire sires. It held powerful magic, and for Antoine's ring to be sent in a bloody box meant the vampires at High Citadel faced an unknown but dangerous threat.

"Vampires have enemies," I said. "We all do."

"But you have the history of *failles*. They could contain the evil... and what they can contain, they can also release."

My wolf made his presence known with a low rumble. I quieted him down.

"Vague threats get neither of us anywhere," I reminded Julien.

"We share the history, Wolf. Vampires have records that speak of wolf kings and queens. *Failles*. You say they aren't real, and yet, if more evil seeps into the world, your enemies will not care what you say. They will find out for themselves, and when they do, they won't allow you to keep your advantage. They'll want her for themselves."

I understood what he wasn't saying. "Would the sires attack us?"

"I cannot say."

"What can you say?"

Julien's smile flashed, the first otherworldly sign I'd seen from him during this meeting, which meant he was more than concerned. He was here to warn me.

"For now, the sires hold the truce. But should a few odd creatures turn into a hoard, do not look to the sires for aid. They will not give it."

"Would they want her for themselves?"

"Perhaps. She would be valuable."

"That would be unwise."

Julien nodded. "But there are jewels so rare, others won't care if it is wise or not. They won't hesitate to kill for it, no matter where it's hidden. Not unless the jewel is... protected."

We were both adept at conversations that said little with words, but everything with innuendo, and I didn't like his implication.

"One last bit of information," Julien murmured. "Pack law forced you to kill a wolf. While he was not innocent, there was a provocation behind what he did. A deliberate attempt to discredit you in front of the pack. It was unfortunate that children were present to witness it... but perhaps not accidental."

My canines punched down. "Who?"

Tendrils of black mist swirled around the vampire, turning opaque in the sunlight. "He is gone now. But he was not happy with the result. He hoped to shatter loyalties between you and your wolf, your pack. Be careful, Wolf." The vampire shimmered. "I'll be disappointed if the sires are right and something evil is coming."

He gave me a last look, and said, "And if I were you, I'd be worried about why your *faille* is here."

CHAPTER 12

Noa

I WAS BURNING, GASPING as embers burrowed beneath my skin, searing wormholes through muscles into my bones. Charing my blood. But I was okay. I'd be okay. In a minute, maybe two, I would breathe. Drag in air and the pain would go away.

I gagged as my thoughts cleared. The wolf had me on the ground. He was tearing at my clothes while my hands beat and beat against whatever I could find.

He kept shouting at me not to fight.

How could I *not* fight?

He was wolf.

Get away get away get away.

I tried to crawl from him, my fingernails scrubbing at the hard dirt. Scrubbing and scrubbing. Then he was upon me, and I shuddered. He was wolf, nothing more than a predator, hooking his claws into my clothes to draw me back. A sport to him, while I struggled.

Throughout my childhood, I'd feared this hooking, waiting in the dark while I listened for the *click... click... click* of monsters as they searched for me.

But the monster was here, and I thrashed on the verge of panic. Saliva pooled in my mouth, and a groan slipped from my clenched lips. "*Please...*"

The golden wolf refused to let go. He rolled me to my back while I beat at him, screamed.

He bared his teeth.

"Stop!" The word roared in my head. His hands were ripping... ripping... searching my arms, my stomach where the blood flowed.

He pulled things from my skin. More of the black worms that resisted with a monstrous strength. As if they would take chunks of me with them if they had to let go.

I gasped, too sick to move. The heat grew blistering.

Make it stop make it stop.

The wolf rolled me to expose my back, while his hard, clawed hands scraped across every inch of exposed skin.

My lips pressed into the dirt—it felt so dry. Maybe I was already ash from all the burning, falling apart, drifting through his fingers to float in the air.

"Noa—breathe!"

The golden wolf barked... snarled. But I didn't know that word—*breathe*. He rolled me over and slammed a fist against my chest. I arched up, flopped back down, boneless and unresisting. Was this how it felt to my mother, being close to the wolves? Unable to scream because of the terror?

She'd warned me, and I hadn't stayed away. *Leo*—Leo never hurt me like this. My grandfather was a healer. He was wolf and he should have been here, except that he died and I wouldn't come when he needed me, and now I was dying too.

My eyes were open. I stared at the sky, so clear, vivid, endless. Like the river. I remembered the nymph, and all the shades of turquois, and the white froth. The beauty.

There must be beauty in endless. In floating. Although I wished someone had warned me about worms before I went into the water.

And I wished I remembered what the nymph said—what was it? Worm poison would kill humans while wolves were immune?

Or was it the other way around?

Did it even matter in terms of worm poison, when I was not wolf and not human? Either way, it sucked for me, and I wanted to laugh. I didn't know why. But I wondered if this was what dying was like... because if it was, then maybe it wasn't so bad.

Except for the burning. And the wolf who slammed his fist into me again.

I choked when the air finally flowed into my lungs. The wolf growled and said, "Good girl," so I must have been breathing. Then he said to hang on. But I had nothing to hang on to when I was over his shoulder, my hair falling across my face.

I thought about breathing, sucking the cold in and pushing it out. The fire wasn't burning as hot as before, so maybe the worms were gone and I was okay again. Enough to know the wolf was running—so fast—although he was wolf and they ran fast. Magic fast. Dreadful fast.

Everything was a blur of green and brown, streaking past and making me dizzy. And each time his shoulder hit my stomach, the nausea increased until I pushed up with my hands and vomited down his back.

"*Shit!*"

That word sounded angry, so I said it back to him because I was angry. He threw me over his shoulder like I was potatoes, and he didn't care that he was bouncing me around. Or that his wolf energy made me sick. He'd waited to see if the nymph would eat me, and I wasn't sure if he was teasing or not.

And he hadn't stopped the worms from swarming.

Maybe he didn't see them, Noa.

But you saw them, and didn't get them all off.

I was thinking again, and knew it wasn't a golden wolf but a man who carried me. Still, I saw a wolf shimmering, running beside him when I opened my eyes, and I guessed it was a side effect of nearly dying. Or maybe the worm poison. And then, seeing the gold wolf made me think of the black wolf—the wolf who peed all over my things.

Thinking about *him* made the air choke in my throat. Tears stung and my mouth tasted sour when I heard another voice. Dark, growling.

No no no no!

The black wolf was there—why did he have to come? He left me, and I could be okay if he wasn't here.

Then I was on the ground and his fingers were tugging... hard... gentle. My skin burned again. I twisted, whimpered, beat and beat at his hands. He said words that made no sense. Maybe they were werewolf words, but I didn't question them because the burning dimmed.

Then it retreated.

As if it was sentient enough to be frightened of him.

"I'll be at the watchtower." His voice was a wolf's voice, charged with command. "Let Fallon know, double the patrols, then get back to me."

He gave orders like a king, and I didn't like it. Stood like a beautiful monster, and I was in his arms—and I really didn't like it.

He was taking me to the watchtower, and in my grandfather's books, in the fairytales, the watchtower was never a good place to be. You were either locked up in a dungeon, or trapped at the top of the tower, fighting a siege where you always lost.

I fought. Thrashed, but he told me to "stop" in a way that drained everything from me. Except the anger.

And the fear.

Because he was the enemy.

And I'd never get away.

I was not on a cold floor in a dungeon or trapped in a high tower.

Instead, sweat-drenched sheets tangled around my legs. My hair was stuck to my face with a clammy sweat that stank of me. My skin felt raw, and when I realized the reeking shirt I wore was one of his, I slid from the bed, trying to rip the shirt off.

The material grazed my stomach; pain had me bleating. The Alpha of Sentinel Falls heard the sound. For some reason, he was sitting in a chair, hidden by shadows, watching me.

"Well, this should be interesting," he mocked. "Going somewhere?"

"Water," I rasped, unable to summon enough saliva to ease my dry mouth.

"Is that why you went to the river?"

Nerves invaded my stomach. My thoughts raced off on this new tangent—why was he asking about the river? He shouldn't even care since he left me there.

I took an unsteady step, but my bare feet kept sticking to the floor. I stumbled.

"The river," he prompted. "Where the nymph was. And the leeches."

"I remember the river," I said between clenched teeth.

Grayson leaned forward, his arms resting on his knees. He was shameless in his power, untamed in the shadows, with a predatory stillness that was utterly terrifying. His head slanted to the side as he studied me. "Were you trying to leave?"

"Like you did?"

A muscle ticked in his jaw. "Leaving was necessary."

"Going to the river was necessary." And walking was a farce; I'd only managed three sliding steps, and already, I needed to brace both my hip and my hand against the mattress.

"Always so stubborn." His voice darkened to a velvety pitch that put my teeth on edge. "Why did you go to the river, Noa?"

My legs turned thready. "Why do you care?"

"It's my job."

I turned my head to the side. "Then you're piss poor at it, because you left me with no water in the bottles, and all that water in the river."

"That's why you left? Because you were thirsty? Like you are right now?"

Wasn't it obvious?

I leaned against the bed when the room spun, then slid down until I sat on the floor. With my palm pressed against the smooth wood, I watched my hand flex until my fingertips whitened. He should have known I needed water, if it was his damn job. But he was the Alpha of Sentinel Falls and he thought what he wanted to think, even when it was absurd and wrong.

"Were you thirsty then, Noa?" A dangerous edge had entered his voice. "Or were you calling to the nymph?"

"Don't be a damn ass."

I was tired of the game he was playing. Tired of fighting when everything I'd heard about him was true. He was ruthless to those who were weak, or a threat to his pack—and I was both things in his eyes.

He'd already condemned me, and maybe I was dealing with worm poison because I'd disobeyed his orders. But I refused to sit, helpless, while he watched and asked endless questions.

He offered no help. Only hostility. All I had was myself, in my *faille* world, and nobody knew what that meant.

At least I'd always been resilient, healthy. I'd be okay if I just… moved.

The pressure in my hand eased. I focused enough to look around the room. Through the mess of my hair, I could see a light shining through an open doorway, so bright it made me squint. But if it was a bathroom, I'd find water, and at least I could close the door and he would leave me alone.

It wasn't that far. No rugs on the floor to stop me. I rolled to my hands and knees. Slid my fingers forward, then my knee, catching the hem of the shirt I wore until it tugged. I hated the way I looked, crawling like a child. I wouldn't allow myself to care. Instead, I focused on heaving air into my scorched lungs. Holding it. Pushing each breath out.

"You won't make it," Grayson said. "Although it's entertaining when you try."

"Bastard," I spat, but my cracked lips turned the word into a hiss. My knee slid forward another inch. I focused on my palm next while dark hair fell across my face. The oversized shirt bunched up, revealing my panty-covered ass.

"Aren't you even curious?"

He was patient, asking his questions while the light wavered in the doorway.

"About the worm poison. How bad it's going to get."

"Am I supposed to ask you to heal me?"

"I'd be happier if you begged, since you're already on your knees."

"Asshole." The insult was puny, and it did not surprise me when he laughed.

"Tell me why you're here."

"No." I forced my fingers forward. But every movement surged with fresh pain. I'd moved less than a foot from the bed, but it was a matter of principle now. I wasn't here because I wanted to be, nor did I want to stay. And I'd be damned if I gave Grayson Devante anything while on my knees.

"It's a simple question," he said.

"Nothing is simple with you." My arms trembled and didn't stop until I collapsed on the floor, curled on my side. My cheek pressed against the cool wood. Saliva pooled beneath the corner of my mouth, and my eyes closed as another wave of acid rippled beneath my skin. It worried me.

I'd never been sick enough to think I wouldn't get better. To not know that my body was resilient enough to withstand a head cold or a fever.

But this is worm poison, Noa.

Maybe you should worry.

The creak of the chair meant the alpha had shifted his weight, and he said, "I'm not the one who could turn delusional at any moment. I won't slowly boil on the inside as that poison sets in. Tell me why you're here, and I'll make the pain go away."

I gritted my teeth, even with my cheek pressed against the floor. "I needed a vacation and thought this was the perfect spot."

His canines flashed while his strange eyes narrowed. Fear uncoiled in my throat. But I couldn't tell him all the secrets I kept.

Grayson rose to his feet, stalking toward me, and I thought about the rabbit in the glen. How she froze in place until it was too late to escape.

I had to move, and my fingers flexed against the floor, but dizziness kept me listless. I panted when he crouched down and traced a hard knuckle over the curve of my cheek.

"You shouldn't have gone to the river," he said, pressing his thumb against my lower lip and pulling it down.

I hissed. "You shouldn't have pissed on everything."

He growled, angry, but he'd been the one who dragged me into the mountains, tried to make me kill a rabbit, and then abandoned me because it was necessary. Left me alone with wolf piss all around and no water to wash away the stink. He hadn't warned about the river. He said Mace was coming. But how did I know for sure? There'd been no one else to help me.

For most of my life, I'd had to take care of myself, and I was tired of arguing. Of feeling like prey. I couldn't forget his disdain for the rocks I'd scuffed. He'd kicked them into the weeds. And who cared enough to come and save me? Oscar? Hattie?

They would try, if they knew. But at their age, they'd never survive the hike. And I would never ask or expect Levi to come to my aid when he was so young.

Which left no one other than me.

My eyes turned gritty as I glared at the alpha. He flexed his hands; I tried to roll away, but couldn't make my muscles work. My voice was hoarse when I said, "Don't touch me."

"You'd rather lie here and let the poison fester?"

"I'm... not."

"You're not what?" he mocked.

"Lying here." Except that I was lying there, unable to move while the room spun. The sweat on my body crusted against my skin. I felt genuine fear as Grayson crouched over me.

He pushed aside the reeking shirt I wore and the muscles in my stomach quivered. He was a healer, but my mind turned every action into a threat. I struggled to hide my hand, my arm, when he searched for worm wounds. Then he pressed on my stomach, and the pain unraveled me. I flew to another place in my mind, reliving when I'd ripped the leech free. Tore away my skin with morbid curiosity and no pain, which was rebounding now with blinding agony.

I looked at the alpha's face. His eyes held an odd glitter while his mouth thinned, and I wheezed, "How bad?"

"Not bad."

Then he struck before my heart could beat. Before the breath could leave my lungs.

His claw snicked out, slicing through my swollen flesh.

A scream ripped my throat apart. I gasped, sobbed. Unnatural sounds while spots flashed and I couldn't see.

Grayson cut my hand, methodical, finding every wound on my body and cutting until pain was all I knew. Sickened, I dry-heaved. Sour drool slid from the corner of my mouth. A red haze of panic smothered all thought when he lifted me from the floor.

I thrashed as he carried me toward the light. Kicked as rushing water became a white noise. The shirt disappeared, along with my underwear.

He was still wearing clothes while he held me naked in the shower, but all that registered beyond the pain seemed insignificant. Strong male arms wrapped around me. Steam clouded the air. Heated water ran over my head, into my eyes and mouth, a blinding anguish as it flushed through each slice in my skin, scouring. Burning.

"It's done now," he growled.

I cried. Struggled.

"You can get through this." His low voice reached me. But his strength was brutal and unyielding. His hand closed around my throat, the other around my hips. Water sluiced through my eyelashes while I stared at the black, clotted blood streaming from the wounds he'd ripped open.

Thick rivulets ran across his fingers, down my thighs to my feet. I rocked. Wept with my fingers curled like talons around the corded muscles in his arms, cutting in. He never flinched. This enigma of a man who bargained and abandoned, determined who lived or died—he continued to hold me until the water turned pink. Until my struggles ceased. Then he leaned back against the marbled shower wall and slid down until we were both sitting.

My face was against his shirt, and I hated the beat of his heart. Hated the lift of hard muscles as he breathed. His long legs cradled me, but I hated needing his strength, his warmth, and what he would do if he ever learned the many truths I kept hidden.

Wet hair curtained across my face, and he smoothed the strands back, stroking until the tremors weakened.

The will to fight disappeared like the blood down the drain. I wanted to hide beneath my exhaustion. Let the weight crush me.

"Is this the watchtower?"

"It's near the watchtower," he said. "Which is round and stone-built and cold as hell in the winter. We haven't used it in centuries."

"What about the dungeons?"

He laughed, but it wasn't from humor. He gathered me and rose to his feet. The ability to do that reawakened the fear. His clothes were dripping and cold against my skin before he wrapped me in a towel. As he carried me back to the bed, I glanced around. Artwork hung on the walls. A rock-rimmed fireplace held a wavering, ruddy glow that warmed the air. A table sat beside the wall.

"I'm going to leave," I said. "The first chance I get."

"I know you are."

He moved his hand, and my hair dried. The bed linens looked fresh. What had Levi said about magic? My thoughts became muddled, and when he pulled one of his reeking shirts over my head, my bottom lip trembled.

He was the devil's black alpha, the enemy, but part of me wondered if he wasn't an avenging angel. Someone who could find me in the darkness. See me there.

He put me beneath the blankets and ordered me to "sleep." But I couldn't sleep, and he pulled the chair he'd been sitting in closer to the bed and sang in a deep, vibrant voice. The song made my cry. It was the healing chant Leo always sang... and I thought about what he could never know. About kittens being lions. About dead wolves and Levi bleeding in the grass.

How maybe that was my fault after all.

And the Alpha of Sentinel Falls would condemn me if he ever found out.

CHAPTER 13

Noa

THE FEVER TOOK TWO days to break. Then the chills set in, making my teeth chatter and my bones feel hollow. I crawled across the floor to huddle by the fire, wrapping myself in a nest of blankets. And even though I disliked the alpha's reeking shirts, I pulled on three because they made me feel warmer... safer.

I thought the chill hated his scent the way the fever did.

But despite the shirts, the nest of blankets, I couldn't sleep. Instead, I thought about the secrets I needed to keep.

Wolves thought being *faille* meant having no wolf. They never thought about what we might have in the wolf's place. But I knew, because each night when I dreamed, I slipped into the half-light world deep in my mind... the place my mother said I should never go.

She said if I did... I might never come back.

I thought the real question wasn't about coming back, but *how* I'd come back.

Because when I dreamed, I was not alone in the darkness.

Something hid there, and when I would open my eyes, I'd be standing at the edge of a precipice, looking up at an endless night sky, glittering with stars and holding such a horrible beauty that I couldn't look away. Or rather... I was afraid to look away.

Because if I did, if I looked down at the black, icy sea churning below, I'd see what hid there. And if it ever saw me... claimed me... it would follow me when I woke. And I'd be unleashing something dangerous and terrible into the world.

So I didn't want to sleep. Or dream. And maybe it was the worm poison. Maybe it was something else, but night after night, in the privacy of my bedroom, I walked, circling the room from the bed to the fireplace and back to the bed. I didn't understand why I paced. I supposed it was a ritual. A *soothing* of the restlessness bombarding me, the way my thoughts turned back to the night when I'd saved Levi.

Grayson's black wolf had wanted to kill me. For whatever reason, he'd changed his mind. But when he destroyed the rabbit in the glen, I knew he did it to prove something—how fleeting life could be. No matter the innocence of that life.

And as we'd walked back to the river, each time the last light caught the rabbit's limp ear, my heart had banged in my chest.

Not because the wolf's vindictive act outraged me.

But because—for a heartbeat—I wanted to face him, that wolf.

Find out if I had enough courage to look into his eyes, accept his kind of judgment.

And if that courage would make a difference against the *thing* in my dreams.

Days passed where Grayson said nothing about my recovery, or the midnight pacing. He accepted my resistance to his alpha commands and stopped issuing them. But he refused to tell me when I could leave. Stubbornly, I kept asking.

He never answered.

Some days, I'd hear him talking to other wolves with their voices low, and wondered if they talked about nymphs and a coming war. Or about me and worm poison.

Other days, I slept through the silence, relieved that I didn't have to think about leaving. But when I *did* think about it, I discovered Grayson left the house every night, returning after a few hours. He'd be broody and silent, or tense and aggressive. But I learned his routine, and took advantage of his absence, roaming from room to room, learning the layout of the house—what I'd call a log cabin if it wasn't a serious understatement.

The kitchen looked like a photograph from a glossy magazine, everything pristine and elegant. A well-stocked pantry meant someone had been living here for a long time. I admired the cathedral ceilings and exposed beams. Four bedrooms, four bathrooms. An office I didn't dare enter.

The living room was spacious enough for a crowd, yet intimate. All the rooms had fireplaces, but the largest was there, in that living room, made of natural stone. Perhaps in the depth of winter, the heat dispelled the cold. But I dismissed the lure of firelight at night. Sitting, curled on a couch with a blanket wrapped around, and someone curled beside me.

Beneath my feet, the planked floors felt smooth and warm, but a chill oozed through the tall windows, and I pressed a palm against the glass. A thousand stars sparkled in a midnight sky above moon-lit mountains. Shadows hid the deep valleys. The vista reminded me of an eagle's eyrie, so the *watchtower* was an apt description. I ran through the things wolves would watch for when they were here. Maybe they were like humans, looking for forest fires. Somehow, I doubted it.

Still, I was tense, listening to the silence. Because if Grayson returned and caught me out of bed, he'd guess what I was doing.

He would also be naked.

I'd watched him one night. The alpha would return to the house in his wolf form, shifting before he came inside. Which dredged up memories of the night beside the river, and Grayson, sitting naked, his body reflecting the wavering light.

He'd seemed more approachable that night, stirring up the flames. Talking about his wolf being volatile. I knew that feeling... volatile... I'd lived with it for most of my life.

But as I'd listened to his deep voice, I forgot he was the enemy.

The same way I forgot about passing time now... not until I realized that, while I'd been staring at the night sky and thinking about the wolf, the Alpha of Sentinel Falls had been silently stalking through the house.

My heart thumped. Perhaps he didn't see me, wrapped in my blanket and standing in the shadows. But it was a fool's hope. As he prowled through the living room, he didn't look around because he knew exactly where I stood, and the sickening realization hit me, that he'd always known what I did when he was away.

This time, his intent was to catch me. I slowed my breathing. I wouldn't apologize since that would signal weakness, and I refused to feel guilty for wandering through his house, trying to regain my strength, or for my plans to get away. I'd warned him. He said he knew.

But even if I'd wanted to apologize, it was impossible. Words failed me, and I couldn't summon a single thought that wasn't chaotic... not as I watched him stretch muscles still taut from the wolf.

The fire had burned to embers hours ago, but in the remaining light I could see the rippling strength in ridged muscles, and the blood smear on his shoulder. The impact was bruising. I didn't know who he'd been fighting that night, but if he brought the aggression home with him, then I was in more danger than I thought.

Grayson turned, and as my gaze slid lower, he said, "You're a voyeur now?"

Death waited in his voice, but my focus was on the wolf tattoo. I'd seen it before, parts of it, but now I could see the design. The wolf draped over the man's shoulder, with his head close to Grayson's heart, and I'd never seen artwork so exquisite. So realistic.

For an instant... as I stared... I thought the wolf stared back.

Then the wolf's lip curled, and shock jolted through me.

I told myself it was an effect of worm poison. Or maybe being *faille* with an overload of wolf energy causing delusions.

Tattoos could not be sentient.

But I still said, "Let me talk to your wolf."

The request was impossible. I could no more talk to his wolf than I could talk to the trees because I had no pack bond. But my demand came from an inner knowing I didn't understand, and when Grayson's lip curled with the same disdain as his wolf, I added, "You share the same expressions."

"Perhaps your fever has returned from all the walking you've been doing."

"No." Anger would not frighten me out of this illusion. "He's staring right at me with the same curve to his lip."

I walked forward, but not far. My vision flashed in and out, what it always did in the low light. My eyes would try to focus on either the light or the dark, and the sensation was like a migraine coming on.

But I felt something inside me shift.

And I knew the wolf was as volatile as the man.

"He is angry," I said.

"He has been killing, and he's not done."

"Then let me talk to him."

I wasn't sure if it was imagination or a *faille's* sensitivity, but hostility spiked through the air. I heard the wolf's growl.

A challenge was in that growl... and an expectation.

The same expectation I'd felt at the edge of the meadow with the bow tight in my grip. My fingers on the arrow, unable to let it fly toward the target.

Was I strong enough to do what needed to be done?

Grayson waited with a hunter's patience. Only an infinitesimal tightening of his lips and the steady breathing told me how close I was to crossing a forbidden line.

The most intimate part of a werewolf was his wolf, and asking to speak to the wolf without a pack bond was more than an impossibility.

It was a challenge.

And I wasn't drunk on worm poison now, refusing to tell him why I was here.

I *was* challenging him, allowing the blanket to slip from my shoulders while the alpha's canines punched down hard enough to draw blood from his lower lip.

Violence primed his body, and Grayson's mood slashed from dark to menacing. He licked his lower lip, smearing the blood, and my throat clenched. Sensuality burned in that threat. I heard the snicking of his claws as his hands curled... and I tipped my head the way he did.

Wondered if it was his shirts, layered on my body, that upset him.

Or if he was drowning in my scent the way I was in his, breathing in the rain-soaked pine and wild moonlight.

Seconds passed in silence.

His eyes held the calculating gleam of a predator, focused and unfeeling, measuring each breath I drew in, pushed out.

Something primal and unwelcome went still within me. He was the most unsafe man I had ever met. I did not know his capabilities, but I recognized the sharp edge I was on, how easy it would be to fall.

To slice myself open.

Then the air shifted—an abrupt tipping of that sharp edge—and the wolf shimmered into being beside the man. An insubstantial creature bathed in moonlight.

I understood the wolf was an illusion. He was not in the room, the same way Mace's golden wolf had not been running beside him.

Werewolves were men, or wolves, but not both at the same time.

Seeing this wolf now was another effect of the worm poison, or a trick of the firelight, and perhaps Grayson was right. All my walking brought the fever back, making me delusional again.

But the wolf stared with those strange eyes. The spark of electric blue held none of the cutting emerald facets, and *what* he was—illusion, or sensitivity, or worm poison—should make no difference. If I touched him, I'd find no solidity.

With that decided, I extended my hand, expecting to feel... nothing.

Instead, my palm prickled.

Tiny hairs lifted at my nape.

Beneath my hand, I felt the first faint scratch from a wolf pelt, and the enormity in that sensation settled in. How impossible it was. But my fingers continued to curl, exploring. Seeking proof.

Beneath the fur, I pushed against the muscle of living flesh. I watched the powerful lifting of the wolf's massive chest. Felt the moist, warm flutter of exhaled air and wondered if Grayson was creating the sensations for his amusement. If this was a power of his, and he was using it now to humiliate me into thinking I was *faille* when I was worthless.

Then the wolf and I began talking—a reality more improbable than the wiry pelt against my hand—but I said, "Wolf, I understand about the rabbit. Why you killed it. You wanted me to be strong, but I was weak, and you had to become strong for me."

The wolf lowered his head, his gaze never wavering while his lips drew back and waves of aggression washed from him. He was as unsettled as I was—how was this possible?

But I understood the truth beneath his turmoil.

The wolf struggled with fear. He believed he was feral. He had betrayed Grayson by taking control, killing a wolf in front of children. Hurting a toddler. He'd never felt that wildness before, and his confusion was the source of his volatility.

His grief and his regret. If he lost the battle between control and impulse, the two of them, man and wolf, would cease to be. And it was and would always be his fault.

I wanted to soothe him.

Oddly, frighteningly, I understood I *could* soothe him.

I said, "What you did was right and true. Then, with the rabbit. But also before, with the other wolf you had to kill."

As my fingers clenched in his dark fur, warmth flowed up my arm, drawing the heat from him—and the wolf disappeared while the man erupted with fury.

He moved so fast I couldn't brace, and the crush of his body against mine was savage. We were hip to hip. Thigh to thigh. There was no part of me that did not throb beneath his dominance, the heat of his bare skin.

"What the *hell* were you doing?"

The snarl unraveled me. Harsh breathing scraped me raw, and it didn't matter that I'd violated his privacy by touching his wolf. Nor did it matter that he was a predator.

I'd allowed no man as close as I'd allowed this enemy... this *wolf*. He pushed, prodded, lured me into revealing the *faille* part of me he should never see. The part that knew how to do the impossible. To pull the heat from him.

"I told you he was angry." I spat the words as if they were my excuse, but everything I'd done that night was wrong. Sneaking through his house. Not apologizing when he caught me. I should apologize now, but it was also too late for words I would not mean.

I had touched his wolf, and from the cold emerald green in his eyes, I saw myself the way he did, the captured thief who had trespassed into a sacred place. I should not have gone there, shouldn't have ventured so deep, because I'd left a fragment of myself behind that he now owned.

He lunged forward, and—*oh, gods*—he was so ferocious.

The plunge in my stomach turned into a frenzy when his fingers twisted in my hair. A hiss of heated breath was all I felt before his mouth destroyed mine, bending me beneath the scrape of teeth. The pressure to yield became overwhelming. I'd been kissed before, but never with such wild dominance. As if he was punishing me. Punishing himself.

An avalanche of sexual tension tumbled through me. The surging need was both his and mine, and none of it made sense. I felt the *rightness* in his body taking mine. The hunger beating through my veins with a savage craving.

Alarm flared. My heart turned over, and I wondered when my lips had parted. When his tongue shoved in like he needed to taste every part of me.

I drew back enough to bite his lower lip.

The answering growl in his throat was dark and demanding. Pure possession ran rampant through me, and I felt breakable. Achy and tender when his hand cupped the back of my head. The other curved around my throat, fingers hard yet stroking... and I was no longer fighting. I kissed him back, pushing my tongue into his mouth, ignoring the sharp canines that descended, the thread of blood on my lips.

Something wild unleashed itself, and I didn't care. Didn't care that my heart thundered beneath the heady thrill of his hands.

He angled my head back as if he couldn't get enough of my mouth, couldn't force the kiss deep enough, reach the parts of me he wanted to explore. As if he had every right to explore them.

Once his mouth left mine, I studied his face, unable to get past the furious expression. Firelight rimmed his cheekbones. His gaze skimmed my face as if he looked for something. Then his hands dropped to his sides. He pivoted, stalking out into the night. Leaving me alone in the ember-lit room, pummeled by guilt, and I did not see him again until the following night—when I was caught in a nightmare.

I lay rigid in the dark, my body shivery with cooling sweat while fear cracked through me. My eyes were open, but I couldn't move or crawl away to hide. I couldn't open my mouth, or draw breath enough for a brittle scream.

I was back in a childhood night terror, listening to the *click... click... click...* of the monsters' claws as they approached.

I was that wild rabbit in the glen with the blade of grass on my lips and the light all around while death waited.

The heart beating frantically was my own, while the emptiness inside me opened, the gaping maw expanding into an obsidian night, dazzled by thousands of stars. Churning with a restlessness that wrapped round like a lover's caress.

And I could hear what hid there, in the black lake.

The monster's voice... a woman's voice. Whispering, so close. *Look at me... see me...*

I stifled the sobs with clenched teeth. Stared at nothing until my eyes burned. If I did what the monster asked, if I looked at her, saw her... I would become whatever she was.

But the air against my skin stirred. The sweat on my body dried, and I was no longer in the dark. I was standing on a path blessed by the Green Man. I knew, because everywhere, I saw green—the green of moss, the green of spring grass, and the darker green of ivy twisting around the tree trunks.

I saw nothing odd about the change. Dreams followed their own rules, and after the darkness, the green was a blessing.

When tiny, wispy sprites emerged from the foliage, I laughed at their many colors spangling in the sunlight. They swirled and danced. I wanted to join them. Hold out my arms and see them land on my skin, my open palms. The tickle of their wings was that of the butterflies I used to catch as a child. Such wings were precious. Fragile. Leaving amber smears behind—which I knew meant death to those beautiful beings, losing the powdery coating on their wings.

But I didn't dare touch the sprites, and when they flittered away, I followed, my feet bare, my toes curling in the damp cushion of moss.

The damp came from a waterfall, spilling over rocks and leaving pristine mist in the air.

The waterfall fed a stream, and the stream fed a pool. I tested the water with my toes.

Tiny golden fish nibbled, and I laughed.

A pink-spotted frog leapt from the lily pads to the squishing mud which, when I tested it, was colder than the water.

I hesitated. Part of me knew I was dreaming, but another part was thinking... *is this a warning?*

Then the thought was gone. The mud was coating my feet, and I bent to watch the rivulets wrap around my toes like the ivy wrapping around the trees.

Ivy meant the Green Man, and he was benevolent. While the mud made me recoil with the thought that I should not be here.

That I should not trespass in this place the way I'd trespassed into the alpha's mind.

I should move.

Now, Noa. Step back step back step back.

Too late, though, because the mud twined upward, racing past my ankles, whipping around my calves, and I felt the terrifying tug. Tentacles hid in the mud, constricting, alive, pulling me down, deeper and deeper into a quagmire filled with feeding things, creatures with a thousand mouths that I couldn't see.

I shuddered when I felt them, sucking, greedy mouths worse than the worms.

The pounding of my heart was a drum in my head. Fear crackled like spreading frost through my muscles, freezing them. My lips parted as I gasped out a silent scream. Heaved for breath with lungs that felt broken.

With every wrenching twist of my arms, legs, I did nothing but sink deeper into the mud. I measured each dreadful inch as the muck reached my hips, chest, then my chin, my lips, oozing with thick glee into my mouth.

I gagged as a great, bounding black beast leapt toward me.

It shouted my name.

Shouted again, kneeling on the bed while my head thrashed, my arms flailed.

"Noa!" The beast's hands tightened on my shoulders and his body remained rigid as I bucked against him. "Open your eyes. It's not real."

"I..." It was *too* real, despite what he said, and I couldn't stop fighting the mud that still coated my skin, kicking with my legs, trying to loosen myself from the twisting vines.

"You're safe," he growled.

But my mind thrashed the way my head thrashed, and I wondered if he heard me screaming... *not safe not safe not safe.*

"Noa!" His voice boomed. Arms like bands of iron held me, the biceps flexing, his knees pressing against the outside rim of my hips. We fought and twisted. He continued to speak, telling me I was okay, that I was tangled in sheets and not vines.

He said I was awake enough to focus.

That I should open my eyes.

"Now, Noa!" he repeated, and when I did, I stared into eyes that glowed with electric-blue fire. His body remained braced. He was willing to take the brunt of my anger until I yielded, either from exhaustion or because I could finally listen.

A weakness took hold, allowing my lungs to relax, but I still trembled when he pulled me until I was sitting. Pushed the hair from my face, then slid his fingers through the silver streak, tucking the strands behind my ear. The brush of his knuckles over my cheek was slow, careful, and I knew he did none of this to comfort me.

Because he asked the one question that he'd been asking over and over since the worm poison. When he thought I'd be too ill or too weak to lie to him. The one question I'd stubbornly, desperately refused to answer because it would condemn me for the fraud that I was. The danger I'd brought with me.

"Why are you here?"

I hated that my head felt heavy. My chin dipped, and I hated the jarring upward jerk when I righted myself. Hated the lies I'd told myself, how I could become a photographer and live a happy life.

I hadn't run to Sentinel Falls because I thought I could hide in my grandfather's house before moving on.

When I'd fled from my apartment, it wasn't because a sound had spooked me, or because I thought men were following me.

All of those things were true. But they hadn't been the *reason*.

They'd been so sure I didn't see them in the crowd. Didn't recognize the same leering faces in my photographs.

But I'd learned to see between spaces. Trust the *faille* warnings. The broken part of who I was, and I didn't have to see them to *feel* them.

I'd recognized the threat with every sense I had, and that night, when I drove east instead of any other direction, it was because I knew only one place would be safe.

Where I'd find people strong enough to protect me.

The one place my mother said would be a trap.

"Werewolves followed me in Seattle," I said. "I think they know I'm *faille*... and I think they followed me here."

The alpha breathed in. "Can you describe them?"

"I photographed them."

CHAPTER 14

Noa

I HEARD NOTHING MORE about the wolves in Seattle, or if anyone had checked my camera for the photographs. But two days after my confession to Grayson, I woke to the sound of voices outside my bedroom door.

"Well, that was pretty clueless."

A woman's voice. Then a man's response, indistinct, before the woman laughed.

"I'm sure wearing your shirts softened the attitude."

I sat up in bed, testing my feet against the floor. Moments later, I heard a knock, then the door opened.

"Oh, good. You're awake. I was just telling Gray what an idiot he is."

A young woman pushed into the room while I squirmed on the bed. She was close to my age, with nut-brown hair tied at her nape. Her eyes were the same color as her hair, and filled with a familiar warmth.

"I brought your clothes," she said. "Hattie was sure you didn't have enough, so she added a few things."

I recognized my bright pink bag—the one Levi had been riffling through—and two shopping bags overflowing with jeans, shirts, and a rainbow of softer items. My favorite colors. The sizcs I preferred, although Hattie had access to my clothes for two weeks, so it was easy enough to figure out what to buy.

"She's safer here," Grayson said, and the woman threw him a sideways glance before smiling at me.

"I'm not debating safety. But look at her -- she's swimming in your shirt."

Face flaming, I tugged at the tee shirt, then dragged the sheet across my legs while the woman pointed down the hall, and said, "Gray. Don't you have a meeting to attend? Orders to issue? Enemies to kill?"

"I'm your alpha," he growled. "Show some respect."

"I will when you will."

She patted his chest with an intimacy that bothered me when it shouldn't. Or maybe it was the way Grayson's mouth twitched, as if he enjoyed having her hands on him. Then he said, "You're as reckless as your brother," and a sparkling explosion broke open inside me.

"Laura?" I asked, while she grinned.

"Must be the rebellious streak, huh? I remind you of Levi? Drives Gray crazy, dealing with the two of us. First, we get this bad wolf to leave." She patted his chest again. "Then you get in the shower. Come out when you're ready. We'll talk over coffee."

Coffee sounded heavenly. Laura was busy pushing Grayson with the ease of family, her hands on his back while he pretended to resist. When he gave up, she closed the door with another bubbling laugh.

"Alphas. They're the worst." She looked at me. "I'd hug you right now if I didn't know how overwhelming new people can be. You'll find girly things in that second bag, along with your own stuff. And Gray asked me to bring a few of your grandfather's books, so if you're up to it..."

She hesitated at the door.

"We can look at them."

"I'd like that." I'd never had a friend who knew what a *faille* was, and I smiled as she left. I wanted to feel normal again, and savored the luxury shampoo Laura brought, washing my hair twice because it felt so good. For clothes, I decided on jeans and a light-weight cotton shirt since Laura wore something similar.

I found her sitting in the sun, on the exterior deck I hadn't discovered on my midnight explorations, although I was thankful that I hadn't. For a moment, I took in the view, the fresh, invigorating air, all the while ignoring one disturbing fact.

While the house perched at a precipice, the deck extended out on cantilevered support beams. Not an ordinary deck, either. The deck was thick glass. Beneath my feet, I could see the rocky cliff face. Vertigo hit me. Breathing in, I forced myself to walk toward the waist-high barrier, also glass, there to prevent missteps while creating an infinity edge, the sense of space, dropping into nothing.

But once the dizziness passed, I gripped the top railing, mesmerized by the view. Thousands of trees, with wide valleys and broad swaths of open ground. The isolation was majestic and far grander than I'd ever imagined. The air was crisp and clear enough to see for miles. Silvered finger lakes glittered. The familiar snowy mountains rose from deep green forests, and puffy clouds drifted through the sky on a breeze that was tantalizing and sweet.

This was the world as the Green Man wanted it. And the house was a fitting lair for the dominant Alpha of Sentinel Falls.

A seat of power for the devil's black wolf, high on a mountain top, brushing the sky.

"Come. Sit down." Laura tapped the table, then offered coffee, filling a cup for me. The muscles in my jaw spasmed with anticipation; I hadn't had coffee since leaving Seattle.

"Are you hungry?"

We shared fresh fruit from white bowls. The croissants she brought were flaky on the outside, soft and buttery inside. Perfect. I ate more than expected.

"If my energy is too much, tell me." Laura popped a bite of croissant in her mouth, wiping her fingers on the napkin she left twisted to the side. "Meeting new people is difficult for me, too. But it's so... amazing, finally talking to you."

"I read your note." It was all I could manage when she rubbed at the scar ridging her wrist. After I'd left, I hadn't contacted Leo at all, not even to ask about her—the wolf I'd helped to save—and that shame stayed with me.

She touched the back of my hand. "Leo told me how you adored coming in the summer. He said you played in the woods, completely unafraid."

I wondered how long before she'd been able to return to the woods unafraid. "I would make up stories about you," I said. "How you were happy, maybe had a boyfriend..."

"Don't feel sorry for me, Noa."

I met her steady gaze. "I feel in awe of you. And I apologize if my stories sounded like pity. I needed to pretend because I never asked. I was ashamed of that, and just... hoped." My gaze dropped to where I fiddled with the spoon beside the cup of cooling coffee. "I'm glad it worked out for both you and Levi."

"Gray did it."

Gods, he was the last person I wanted to talk about, and the spoon stuttered from my grasp. I had to dive for it and hope Laura didn't notice.

"When I was... stuck in wolf form," she said. "Gray came every day. He talked to me for hours. Helped my wolf get over her fear so I could shift back. And as soon as I told him about Levi, Gray went out and found him. I've met no one like Grayson Devante. We're all safer because he's Alpha."

What crossed my mind wasn't about being safe.

"You shouldn't be afraid of Gray," Laura murmured.

In the distance, a hawk circled on the wind current, and I stared at it when I said, "I'm not afraid."

"I wouldn't judge you if you were. Gray terrifies his enemies, and Levi told me how angry he was at Leo's house. I'm so sorry about... all of it."

I believed her.

"But," she added with a quick smile. "I'm thankful you were there when Levi needed you. I taught him your song, and that's how he knew it was you."

My lips twisted. "The version Levi heard was more violent than the one I sang to you."

"You kept him alive."

In the sunlight, I thought Laura's eyes glittered wetly, although the breeze quickened, and she turned away before I could be sure.

"Anyway, I'm glad you're back. And it's such a gorgeous day." Laura stood with her arms out. "I can show you around. I'm always uneasy in a new place until I can explore."

"I've peeked through the windows, always at night, so I couldn't see much."

"Then you saw nothing." She looped her arm through mine. "I'll give you the tour."

We trooped through the house, then down steps to a gravel pathway that led through the last thing I expected—a wild garden where flowers spread into the meadow beyond. But we paused on the path so I could turn back to study the house.

The *log cabin* was far more impressive than I'd thought. The steep slate roof accommodated the vaulted, beamed ceilings inside. I secretly admired those ceilings. The same way I admired the craftsmanship in each hand-peeled log. The design of the house was elegant, but with no blind spots where an enemy could approach unobserved.

A perfect fortification. But beyond the security aspect, I was looking at a home with space to breathe. A welcoming place where I'd hang wind chimes if I lived here.

The surrounding meadow beckoned with bare-foot-worthy grass and the earthy, composty scent of renewed growth. The desire to sink my toes deep into the warming soil was irresistible. I wanted to kneel and press the soft dirt between my fingers. Get messy and not care. Plant so many flowers I'd never tire of the scents.

I'd sit in the sun. Listen for the humming of bees flitting around lavender stalks. Photograph the memories.

But I let those wants slide through my fingers. I wasn't willing to attach emotion to a place. I'd made that mistake with Leo's house, and I wouldn't repeat it. Although I paused long enough to stroke the tiny white-and-yellow daisies, savor the velvety petals against my skin.

"The warmth seems early for May," I murmured. "Especially this high in the mountains."

"The Green Man blesses us with the climate. We keep it secret. No one wants a hoard of speculators looking to build the next Jackson Hole."

I held back a laugh. "You'd need better roads."

"And no leeches," she agreed, straight faced.

Her teasing was Levi's—a trait of siblings—which made me curious about her relationship with the Alpha of Sentinel Falls.

He'd spent hours coaxing her through the shift, and I'd listened to her speaking to him without restrictions. Maybe she was more than a friend.

I turned my head to stare into the distance, pestered by a tendril of jealousy I had no right to feel. But I was jealous of her, because the Alpha of Sentinel Falls pulled Laura out of her darkness, while... in my darkness... I was still there.

The path turned, and in the shade, what I saw looked like a purple waterfall tumbling over a moss-covered slope—although it was a living flow, made up of hundreds of delicate mushrooms in all shades of white, pink, lavender. The domed mushroom caps touched at the edges, and I thought of a mob of faeries hiding beneath their umbrellas. All of them scurrying in the same direction. Eager to get to work the way humans rushed in Seattle. Never seeing who was next to them.

The sight was as remarkable as it was breathtaking. I expected winged creatures to flutter from beneath the mushroom umbrellas, moths or butterflies, or miniature sprites with gossamer wings. Completing this fairytale sight.

"I'd love to capture those colors. The shapes." My fingers clenched around the camera I didn't have. "The lighting is perfect, and I'd frame it from all different angles..."

"Gray said you were a photographer."

"My major in college." I looked away. "My mother thought it was frivolous."

"Your work is wonderful, Noa. I searched for you online, and wildlife photography is your niche."

"I mentored with someone." The sigh slipped in my throat. I hadn't meant to reveal personal information, but it was done, so I admitted, "My plan was to email him, see if he needed an assistant. But that's on hold."

"Once Gray's finished with your camera, you'll have it back. And those mushrooms will still be here, waiting for you."

She swung her arm toward the distant mountains. "Those far peaks mark our northern border. It's deep into Canada—but no one goes that way because it's impassable. The Cariboo pack controls the mountains beyond, and they're reclusive. That way..." She turned to the right. "Eastern boundary with the Alpen pack. They're the ones who attacked my pack, so... un-friendly. Carmag pack rules to the west. Their pack is larger than the Alpen pack, but not as large or as strong as we are. Gray considers them an ally."

"Where's Sentinel Falls from here?" I asked, staring at the mountains while I searched for the hidden meaning in what she was telling me—details I would need if I left, as I'd threatened to do.

"The town is there, third valley over. Priest River is another eighty miles to the southeast. Some wolves like isolation more than others, so we have scattered settlements throughout the valleys, even the mountains. Sentinel Falls territory covers hundreds of square miles. But we're all pack."

"Grayson said the real watchtower was near here."

"Beyond those trees."

We wandered through a grove of aspens with dancing leaves and white trunks. Birds chittered, so close they could have been on my shoulder. I touched the bark of a tree and felt the pulse beneath my hand. A life-force moving upward toward the sun.

"Do you feel it?" she asked me while I scrubbed at my palm. "That's the original earth energy, moving the tree sap. In the cities, all the frenzy makes it hard to feel, but we're protected here. And you're probably wolf enough to sense the energy flow."

We left the aspens behind, walked through a grove of clustered fir trees. Brushed past overgrown rhododendrons that were heavy with crimson flowers, then back into the pure sunlight. But the stone tower loomed ahead, perched on the wide crest of a hill, and I felt a sudden, weighty chill that matched the broken edges of the tower stones.

The structure was medieval in style, a drum tower marked by long, narrow arrow slits. The openings were soot-stained, built for archers and air, and impossible slivers of light. Several floors would fit inside the tower, but the centuries had not been kind. The structure was open to the sky. I could see blackened beams, attesting to prior wars, and the edginess I felt might not have bothered me if I thought the ruin belonged to another era.

But the part of me that remembered Leo also knew the wars had not stopped centuries ago. And werewolves were not immortal creatures. They were not undead like vampires, or protected with magic like the witches. And many, many generations of wolves had watched, fought, and died at this tower, protecting the pack.

As I approached the stones, a flock of birds spiraled up from between the charcoaled beams. The wild rustle startled me. I quickened my step, pushing down the thought of men living for endless days inside those oppressive round walls with no end. No corner for shelter, no place to pause. Even the least aggressive wolf would strain against confinement. Especially one that offered little difference between night and day, left or right. Only around.

I would go mad. I'd been going mad during the worm poison, pacing around my bedroom. Had I been sensing the tower from a distance on those nights? Picking up the energy and responding to it?

A breeze touched my cheek, and I shuddered when the sun disappeared behind scuttling clouds. Death had etched itself in those stones, and it uncurled beneath my skin while words pounded through my head like a pulse beat.

Run run run.

"Don't react," Laura murmured. "I didn't come alone. Gray arranged for sentries. You won't see them, but they're watching."

A pebble turned beneath my foot. Somehow, I didn't stumble. "Which means what?"

"Hattie said you're bothered by wolf energy, and the tower holds the energy of many wars. Even wolves feel uneasy when they're near the stones. They're waiting for your reaction... and if it gets to you..."

I kept my eyes hard on the path as we circled the tower's perimeter. "That's why we're strolling? Because I'm on display?"

"Cruel, but yes. Werewolves are two creatures in one, Noa. The wolf is emotional. Suspicious. He reacts. The man thinks, makes moral judgments, balances out the wolf with control. But since the pack has no experience with either you or your mother, they have questions. And they're curious about your reaction, if you react the way they do when they're around this tower, or... some other way."

I took a chance and said, "So... you're saying that I shouldn't do my wiggy dance, hooting and hollering and pumping my hands in the air?"

Laura's laugh sparkled. "Oh my gods, Levi would love that. He'd be hooting right there with you, and I'd say do it for him... but maybe not today. The last pack war was four years ago, and finding Callum was a reminder of the carnage. Then the leeches—we're not sure where they came from, but they're a new species. And here you are, right in the middle of it."

A breath hissed between my teeth. "Is that why I'm here? Because Grayson distrusts me?"

"He isn't punishing you, Noa. We've never encountered worm poison like that, and he was concerned about adverse reactions."

She paused long enough to brush at her face.

"Your resentment is justified. The pack hasn't been kind to you, but they're trying now. Once Gray decides it's safe, he'll take you to Azul—that's our secret. Our sanctuary. It's beautiful, at the edge of a lake, and protected by magic."

"But for now, I have to stay here?"

Laura plucked flowers from the grass and handed them to me. "Until we know more, yes, you do. But I've been searching the archives for information. And your grandfather's books—they should be valuable."

We finished the circuit and wandered through the meadow before heading toward the log-sided house.

"There are always unknowns, Noa. Rivals who want what others have, and the creatures in these lands aren't like those in your grandfather's books—as you've already found out. Being cautious keeps us all alive. We should go inside now."

CHAPTER 15

Noa

FOR THE NEXT THREE days, I was alone. The Alpha of Sentinel Falls never came back to the house, and when I asked, Laura said he was dealing with something in the eastern territory. From her posture, I knew it worried her.

But with his absence, the watchtower house became mine. Every morning, I shared breakfast with Laura on the sun-drenched glass deck. My choice of clothes changed to match hers—my first indulgence after the luxurious shampoo. Jeans and shirts gave way to loose, flowing trousers in pale colors and matching cropped tops. Wolves loved sensuality—and I soon realized it was not in the sexual way my mother implied.

As I listened to Laura, I appreciated how the violence in a wolf's life could be tempered with each sweet enjoyment—the taste of food, the laugh of a child. The touch of a hand in either love or friendship. Wolves, she said, savored life in the moment, knowing horror could strike at any time.

Nor were they hedonistic, the way vampires were. They had sexual relationships, passionate and non-binding. But never in a blood frenzy with writhing bodies and turning humans into werewolves. Because, centuries ago, too many werewolves had turned feral, and now the alphas punished the flagrant behavior.

Some backward packs still held to the old ways—the Alpen pack. The pack that attacked Laura. They stole girls either as forced mates or for the ransom, and I knew Laura was describing her own experience because she rubbed at the scars on her wrist as she talked.

Then we changed the subject and talked about Laura's work as both a healer and an archivist. She managed the research library, which was why she had access to Leo's books. Her healing role was secondary.

"I'm not even close to Gray's ability. I treat the children, kiss their boo-boos, and make sure the vaccinations are up to date. Counsel the young mothers when they feel overwhelmed."

When I asked if she had a mate, she moved on without an answer—which was answer enough. But I continued to wonder about her relationship with the man who'd pulled her out of the darkness. If he could even have a personal life. Or if he was always alone, never settled.

Thinking Grayson Devante could be lonely saddened me. I'd always understood loneliness. I'd had no other *faille* to confide in, other than my mother, and I'd daydreamed about being accepted, loved, despite what I lacked.

But while it was fanciful, thinking I shared loneliness with the primary Alpha of Sentinel Falls, I knew we shared nothing.

On the fourth morning, Laura brought more books, and we sat in the living room, each of us on leather couches. Lamps on the tables cast a golden glow, and the floor-to-ceiling bookshelves turned the room into my favorite place. She opened an Almanac, finding the page dedicated to the Selkirk Mountains. Instantly, I fell in love with the old-world detail on the maps. Illuminated drawings of birds, deer, elk, wildcats, the flora and fauna filled the margins of the book. The workmanship was exquisite. Bees flitted around flower petals. A small ladybug caught my eye, and I smiled when I spotted a hidden whimsey—the tiny faery peeking through the leaves.

Warmth and shelter—that was what flashed into my mind. I was looking at a secret world hidden deep in the Selkirk Mountains.

Laura opened another book and handed it to me. A history book, written in the stuffy language from long ago. But within minutes, I became engrossed in the origin story of werewolves, vampires, and all things unnatural. My breath faltered as I read the opening lines: *In the beginning, there was chaos. Light and dark. Gods and heroes. Those of the blood.*

And as the story continued... as I turned page after page... I lost track of time, falling deep into tales of the wolf kings and queens, their bitter loves and bloody rivalries. They were not alone in the world. Each species claimed an area of sovereignty. The nymphs, the witches. Vampires, the fae creatures. Energy from the Green Man sustained them. His magic ensured that the crops grew, and the rain fell, and the rivers would always be bountiful.

Until the magic weakened and a fissure opened in the earth.

No scholar could explain why it happened.

No moon priest or seer could offer a sacrifice strong enough to appease either the gods or the magic.

Evil was loose in the world. Winged females scoured battlefields, seeking the injured and dying. Shapeshifters lured the unsuspecting into traps. Corrupted forms of known species became walking abominations.

Armies fought, but none could destroy the hoards on their own. Pointless rivalries prevented each species from seeking aid. Then a king rallied the warring factions. A wolf king, arguing for cooperation. If they banded together, the combined force could shore up the magic, trap the evil below the ground until the fissures healed.

A ferocious battle ensued. The kings, with their mighty armies, fought with great strength. But it was the queens who turned the tide. They weakened the evil, siphoning dark energy into their own bodies until the Green Man's magic could prevail. It was at great cost to the queens, and when the battles ended and the war fires burned out, they retreated, while the kings stepped forward to assume the power and rule over the land.

Some kings were benevolent. Others were cruel. But scholars recorded little about the queens. It was said that, during the battles, queens had more power than kings—which made the queens a threat—and as punishment, the kings stripped them of their wolves. Then banished them, with a curse that the punishment would follow their children's children forever, and be known by the silver streak in their hair.

But like all stories, those of the kings and queens faded away. Alphas emerged to lead the wolves—chosen for strength and not heredity. The vampires created sire lines with extensive networks around the world. Witches formed covens tied to their magical gifts. Nymphs and fae creatures evolved into subspecies, taking over the woodlands, oceans, rivers and streams. Even the clouds and the breezes. Some became fierce and dangerous, others delicate and shy, but they all bowed to the Green Man, the King of the Forest, who once again blessed them with the magic... while the terrors of the ancient past became nightmare tales told to children to make them behave.

"What about the missing queens?" I asked.

"Scholars have been arguing for centuries. Some say the queens never existed. Others argued the stories were about political power. Then one scholar found an ancient text. He said it proved queens existed. During the battle, they weakened the enemy by syphoning the life source. But they could do it to anything and anyone, and when they tried to syphon energy from the kings, going into places they shouldn't be... the kings retaliated."

Tiny muscles tightened in my throat.

"The scholar said the text contained a prophesy, that the day would come when the old kings and queens returned to battle with each other. Of course, this was centuries ago." Laura's lips tightened while her face paled. "Superstition controlled the packs, and the scholar was a zealot. He found a girl with a silver streak in her hair and accused her of being *faille*. Tied her to a post and kept whipping until she passed out. He said if she was wolf, she would have shifted, but because she hadn't, it proved everything he was saying. She was a hidden queen, there to destroy a hidden king. And the alpha, being equally ignorant and arrogant, thought he was that hidden king, so he killed her. Many still blame that story for the continued slander against *failles*, even though the ancient text has never been found."

A shiver crept over my skin. "I had no idea."

"Why would you? Leo respected your mother's wishes. It's not a pretty story, and you didn't need to hear it when you were so young."

But I'd needed to hear the story now, because it explained why certain wolves would always be a threat to me. I couldn't blame them, not when parts of the story raised the hair on my arms.

Hadn't I trespassed into a place where I shouldn't have been? I spoke to Grayson's wolf. Touched him. What kind of energy had enabled the impossible? My *faille* energy?

Or delusions from worm poison, Noa?

Maybe Leo kept me ignorant because he loved my mother and she'd asked him not to frighten me. But after she died, he'd reached out. Begged me to come, and I refused. Now I wondered if that wasn't why he left his house to me—so I'd have a reason to return, learn from either Hattie, or Laura, what I needed to know to protect myself.

But I'd stayed in Seattle, wanting to live a human life. Pretending this *other* life couldn't touch me. I hadn't worried about my hair giving me away, or my mother's ravings. The thousands of other missteps I didn't realize I made that exposed my weakness.

My mother had always been afraid of wolves. Not for herself. She'd been afraid *for me*.

Perhaps now I knew why.

CHAPTER 16

Noa

THE NEXT MORNING, THE primary Alpha of Sentinel Falls sat at the table on the cantilevered deck, not Laura. He wore black, the color of his hair, of his wolf, but his posture held the bored relaxation of someone very, very dangerous. I wondered how much of the origin myth he believed, about kings and queens, alphas and *failles*.

Considering how he'd avoided me for days, finding him here meant an ulterior motive on his part. He had the advantage in this situation. I needed his protection, which he wasn't all that inclined to give—even if he had healed me when I'd been so ill with worm poison. I hadn't repaid him with gratitude but with deceit, sneaking through his house. Keeping my secrets. I'd challenged him, touched his wolf somehow, and it had taken a nightmare before I told him about the wolves who were after me.

I would not delude myself into thinking he trusted me. Perhaps he knew I hadn't told him everything—although, after reading the history of *failles*, it wouldn't be safe to tell him, and I sat down, pretending boredom matching his. "Did you chase Laura off once she finished your dirty work?"

"The archive needed her." His shoulders rolled as he reached for coffee—which he sipped with an absent attention.

I unfolded the white napkin beside my plate. If he was slotting our conversation between the more important thoughts in his head, then I'd keep talking. "It was nice, finally meeting her. Thank you for that."

"You're welcome."

"You didn't need to do it. Have Laura educate me about wolf history."

I noticed the infinitesimal tightening of his lips.

"I always wondered, though." My hand steadied as I added cream to my coffee. "My mother never approved of my visits to Leo, so I chose not to upset her by asking for the details. Beyond the children's books, of course, which were hardly accurate."

"Tell me about your mother."

I shrugged. "Not much to tell."

"You were five when she took you away?"

"Yes." I bent my head to the coffee. "You weren't the alpha when I was five, so I'm surprised you're interested."

Again, that infinitesimal flick that drew attention to his mouth, firm, masculine. He set his coffee beside his plate—which was empty, which meant he wasn't here for breakfast.

"Did you enjoy living in Seattle?"

"It was wet and gloomy and smelled like roasting coffee or fish, depending upon how close you were to the Sound. And you?" I stirred my coffee, tapping the cup with my spoon... *tap, tap, tap.* "How do you like living in your kingdom? How many serfs did you pardon today?"

"You're as entertaining as Levi," he drawled, picking up a newspaper and snapping it open, pretending to read.

His attitude made me question our conversation—was it boring? Or was it because my dark hair gleamed from the birch bark shampoo, making the silver streak more dramatic when the waves fell against the side of my face?

I'd worn slender trousers this morning, choosing a soft dove-gray color. The matching V-neck tunic fell past my hips with fluid femininity. The natural blush on my cheeks resulted from sunny mornings on the deck—and before I'd come for breakfast, I'd stolen into the front garden and picked a fistful of soft-petaled daisies, which I set down beside me on the table.

I stroked a finger against the flower stems and asked, "How is Levi?"

"Learning how to be a man."

"Ah." I nodded. "Mace must be teaching him, not you."

The alpha raised his head, lowered the newspaper, and glared. "If you'd rather have Mace as your breakfast companion, I can have him here in five minutes."

His quick, sharp flash of alpha canines made me smile, while the jolting pulse in my throat didn't patter at the thought of Mace joining me.

"You're certainly testy this morning." I snapped my napkin the way he'd snapped the newspaper. "Rough night?"

Grayson refolded the paper, set it aside, and tapped one finger against the surface. "Tell me about your mother. After you moved away, did she have friends?"

"She had acquaintances. Mostly Stewart's business associates."

"He's your stepfather?"

"If we're being polite."

My gaze swung toward the far edge of the infinity deck and lingered there. I couldn't count how many hours my mother spent during those years before she took to her bed. She would rush around, cleaning the house before my stepfather got home.

Afraid of missing some detail Stewart Kline would notice when he walked through the door.

"He liked to discuss my mother's failings," I said. "Until I interrupted him and said I was the one who over-seasoned the roast, or ignored the dust on a windowsill."

And always, my spine would freeze when I faced him. I'd learned how to stare back as if unmoved, while my mother huddled in a corner, her arms wrapped so tightly to her waist that I wondered how she breathed.

The alpha's mouth had thinned. "Did your mother ever correct him? Defend you?"

"I defended myself."

A storm darkened his strange eyes. "Did she ever meet with other wolves?"

"Gods—no." I barked out a laugh. "She detested wolves. That's why we left Sentinel Falls, because she couldn't handle the wolf energy. Or the attitude. In her last years, she hid in her bedroom and rarely came out."

The alpha's finger flicked against his coffee mug, once... twice... "What about your stepfather? Did he meet with wolves?"

I pushed the croissant away. "He told my mother werewolves didn't exist, and it was her delusion. We couldn't even say *wolf* in the house. We had to call Leo *him,* as if he had no name. They were always fighting because my mother refused to get better... those were Stewart's words... as if she could change what she was. And when he got tired... *tired* of her."

My teeth snapped.

"He sent her to a private hospital that treated depression. She spent six months there, and when she came home, she was so changed I didn't recognize her."

My mother—Andrea Bishop Kline—the woman who once laughed and danced with me when I'd been five. The woman who said we were going on a glorious adventure of our own and moved us to Seattle with such hope in her eyes. That woman lost a third of her weight. Most of her hair had fallen out, so they shaved her head. Taking away her ebony hair with the silver streak. Her identity. Her memories.

They took everything that mattered, and while I grieved that loss, what stayed in my heart was the day I looked into her eyes and realized she was no longer there. That she was lost in the black, wolf-shaped hell inside her, where I could never reach her.

The muscle in Grayson's jaw flexed. Perhaps he was giving me time to relax and not feel like this was another interrogation.

Time wouldn't help. It wouldn't relax me. I was tired of trying to be one thing or the other. To fit into worlds that weren't mine. I was not wolf. I was not human. I was *faille*—whatever the hell that meant—and what I wanted was a place that belonged solely to me. A twilight place, where only those who could understand were allowed inside.

"You may never know what it feels like to have leeches feed on you, Grayson," I said with my throat still tight. "Perhaps you've felt things far worse. But what my mother felt when the doctors strapped her to a chair twenty different times, rammed a rubber ball into her mouth. Gave her electric shock therapy to cure her wolf delusion—that is something I can't describe. Other than telling you it was a thousand times worse than any wolf energy. She couldn't function after that, let alone meet with random werewolves."

"What about you? Did you ever meet with any random werewolves?"

I bared my teeth at him. "I knew better."

"The men who were following you." His canines flashed at me the way I'd flashed at him. "We identified them from your camera. One was from the Alpen pack. The other was Callum."

CHAPTER 17

Noa

THE PRIMARY ALPHA OF Sentinel Falls dropped that information—as if he wanted my reaction—and I gave it to him.

Our truce was over, if it ever existed. He was once again the unforgiving man who stood in the middle of Leo's house, surrounded by wolves who died because of me.

A tiny, bitter smile twisted my lips. I shoved hard against the chair as I stood. When I heard the clatter against the deck, I hoped the chair broke into little pieces—which was better than me, breaking into those pieces.

Leaving the sunny deck, I walked through the shadowed house as if the clench in my stomach wasn't real.

As if that clench hadn't come from realizing *who* ended up with his head speared on a lamp pole—the man who'd stalked me in Seattle.

I should have expected a wolf from Sentinel Falls to betray me. Wolves had long memories. They hated my mother. And I'd been foolish enough to run here, believing they would help.

What I hadn't expected was Grayson Devante's nasty little test to see how I would react. If I was guilty or shocked.

Because I was a *faille*, wasn't I?

I'd trespassed where I didn't belong, and did things I shouldn't have done. I might be that ancient, *ignorant* threat the scholar ranted about. The girl marked by a curse because she couldn't shift. The girl who could endanger Grayson's precious pack.

But why stop with superstitions? Why not be modern? Perhaps I wanted revenge for what the pack did to my mother. The men shunned her. The women called her trashy. And hadn't Hattie questioned my reasons for saving Levi? She thought I'd been trying to curry favor for selfish reasons. Ingratiating myself with a pack I wanted to destroy.

But I was okay. I'd be fine—hadn't I dealt with Stewart? Watched my mother fade into nothing without falling apart?

So what if I was *faille*? It meant being sensitive, not only to wolves. I was *empathetic*—a high school counselor told me that, which meant I was a sponge. I soaked up emotions that weren't even mine because living in someone else's life was safer than living in my life. Then she asked me about Stewart, and my mom, and how were things at home these days. And I smiled and smiled and said things were fine until she gave me advice, which I never followed.

But I was good at it, faking my way through life. I was a functioning adult. I knew how to get a job, live on my own. Pay my bills. Buy food. Take photographs and sell them on the internet. I was capable, and maybe I got migraines from wolves. But crowds could trigger migraines. The smell of car exhaust. Driving over a high bridge at night with all the oncoming head-lights blinding my eyes—it didn't mean I couldn't function.

And I didn't have to stay here.

I could leave. I *would* leave. There was nothing here for me. Nothing of Leo. Not even the hope of being safe, since a wolf from Sentinel Falls had hunted me and the alpha thought I was involved. Did it matter?

He didn't trust me.

I didn't trust him.

Or need him. I'd hike back to town, use the money in Leo's trust fund to survive—since I didn't need it for a destroyed house. I'd buy a new camera. Another car. Drive, wild and free, and not stop until I was somewhere else, far away from wolves and their energy.

I would leave as soon as I could find the road.

There had to be a road nearby, right? Because how else could you build this house, here on this mountain, without a way to transport the materials?

How else could Laura get here with all the items she brought, the stack of books, clothes—the food? None of it could have magically appeared.

So don't think about nymphs, Noa. Or worms. Or the Green Man, throwing you on the ground.

Or that there was no road in sight.

But I'd get through this. Already, I was calm.

So very calm.

I was standing in the front garden, ripping wildflowers from the ground, when Grayson found me. I pulled another stem through my fingers and said, "Levi told me he knew Callum. That everyone liked him—and there Callum was with his poor head cut off and speared on a lamp."

I forced the words out while Grayson stood in silence. The day was brimming with spring, glorious. Overhead, birds sang, and the sun was so bright it made all the shadows crisp and dark. I reached for another wildflower—then stared at the trousers that flowed and brushed against my legs. Stared at the tunic that slid so luxuriously against my skin. I wished I could tear the clothes from my body, along with everything they represented. The sensuality of wolves. Living for the moment.

But wishing was pointless, and I ripped another wild plant from the earth, spewing dirt clods from the roots the way I spewed words.

"Did you know why Levi threw up his guts that day? He was *ashamed.* All he could think about was how it could have been him—his head on that pole instead of Callum's. While his almighty *alpha* curled his lip at the weakness and said nothing."

My fingers curled around another flower stem. The petals trembled.

"Then every wolf in that defiled room bent a knee and mourned Callum. You mourned him. Even I did. I stood there and *mourned* the man who terrorized me in Seattle without knowing who he was—and that makes me sick to my stomach."

I pulled against the sharp-edged stems until they scraped across my palm. Until my skin was stained green.

"I felt guilty. *Responsible.* I thought Callum was dead because of me. Because I ran and some damn enemy followed me—and *he'd* killed Callum to frighten me. So that made it my fault."

The breath in my throat felt like crushed glass.

"But now, I understand why your wolf was so angry the night I talked to him. The world is black and white to you, Grayson—but all the colors of emotion for your wolf—and it's no wonder he hates you."

The low growl served as a warning. I'd crossed a line with that hate accusation—which wasn't even true. But I wanted Grayson to hurt the way I hurt.

I made a dangerous mistake in coming here. Asking for help. Trusting him.

Allowing him to control my life.

He still said nothing, and I stared at the wildflowers wilting in my hand. They had no stamina. No Green Man's magic to keep them alive. No more than I did.

"I don't know why the Green Man won't let them last," I said. "They're dying from the moment I pull them from the ground."

Because they're fragile, Noa. The way you are fragile. Unprotected in this world.

And I couldn't survive here, any more than the ruined flowers in my hand could survive without roots. No place to call home.

My eyes burned, and I told myself it was because of the sunlight.

Not because the Alpha of Sentinel Falls moved toward me with dark grace and strength. He took my hand and loosened my grip. The flowers fell to the ground. But the stain remained on my fingers.

My entire body felt stained.

"The mountain ranges both west and east," he said. "They linger in winter. The deer and elk struggle with the snow, exhausted and picked off by predators. The Green Man blesses us with milder weather. Here, everything thrives. Living things find sanctuary. And these wildflowers, once separated from his energy, wilt to remind us we are all connected."

He folded my palm open, tracing his forefinger over a green stain that disappeared beneath his touch.

"I'm sorry I forced you into our world the way I did. Sorry I left you by the river, and I'm sorry about Mace's delay. What you did with the nymph was impressive. And with Levi—he said his wolf thought you had enough wolf to have a pack bond. You soothed him, and you did the same for Laura, even when the violence of our lifestyle upset you."

He stroked my palm, and another streak of green stain disappeared.

"But when you talked to my wolf, touched him... that was something different."

A tremor raced down my spine.

"I've told you before that my first obligation is to protect the pack. My second obligation is to protect you."

"I am nothing."

"I disagree. In the old stories, a *faille* could incapacitate all things made of energy—wolves, supernatural creatures, magic. She was a weapon, or a savior."

"Which one am I to you, Grayson?"

"Both."

He stroked my hand again, erasing the stain, and I disliked the sensuality in each stroke. I wanted to ignore the way my pulse thundered, and how the callouses on his skin were rough and grounding. But still... a kernel of calm rooted itself beneath the skin.

A stillness that came from him.

"If you choose to leave, I will give you safe passage." He continued stroking, even though all the stains were gone. Rhythmic, hypnotic. "If you wish to return to any city but Seattle, I'll make sure you're settled."

"But if I live somewhere else..." I stared at my hand in his. "There is no place where I'll be safe, is there?"

Grayson folded my fingers inward until I formed a fist.

"I wasn't at the river with you because I was meeting with a vampire. He found a dying nymph beside her tree. The tree was ruined, and so was the nymph, but she spoke of shadows, coming from the north. The vampires are on edge. They're aware of the menace—and they are aware of you. So is the Alpen pack. The Carmag will also know of *failles*. We all have libraries filled with ancient texts. And if war is coming... I want the advantage."

"You want a myth," I whispered. "One of the blood queens."

Shadows drifted from him, tendrils that curled into the air. Magic or power that I never expected him to have. But what did I know of this world? For the last eight years, I'd been pretending to be human, working hard to fit in where I would never belong.

"You are a *faille*," he said. "Rare and coveted. Feared and hated."

"Callum..."

"Had a cousin who married into the Alpen pack. Mace found the man, and I had a discussion with him."

I looked away. That was where he'd been, doing what worried Laura. But I saw no damage to him, no visible wounds. I imagined the cousin hadn't fared as well.

Grayson's tone was devoid of emotion. "The Alpen have been hunting Levi for months. We thought they hunted you for the same reason—a trade for Laura. We were wrong. They want you because you're a *faille*. Callum remembered your mother, and when he told the Alpen, they ordered him to find you. Frighten you so you'd leave Seattle, then snatch you when no one was looking. When he failed, they used his head to defile Leo's house and make you run again."

Blunt, Noa. But Gray isn't Leo. And real isn't pretty.

"For now, you're safe," he said with the menace I'd heard in that ruined mess at Leo's house.

For now...

I faced him. Frost splintered down my spine, but it strengthened me. This man was a fortress against the world. Revered. Feared. But he granted no redemption, no respite.

"There's always a cost with you," I said. Not because I was angry, but because I knew he was about to offer a devil's bargain. A choice that was no choice at all. "I'm not that kitten after all, am I, Grayson?"

"No more than I'm a fool." His canines flashed. "And a weapon that does not recognize itself is harmless. There are wolves who would rather disarm you before you discovered what you are. Even more would kill you."

"They believe in myth and fairytales. Scholars who argue over semantics."

"What they believe is that you possess a power that could be used against a growing enemy—or twisted for their own benefit."

He was ruthless with that dark, velvety voice.

"And if evil is escaping from the north, be it myth or fairytale, no one will be safe. Not the wolves or humans living in Sentinel Falls. Or those living in the mountains. None of the warring packs will be left unscathed. Not the nymphs or the witches, the vampires. The animals that shelter here. Until finally, when every living thing has been consumed, corrupted, the evil will bleed into the human world."

Affecting those I knew. The photographer who took me under his wing. My stepfather who never understood, or believed what was behind my mother's illness—although he deserved destruction.

But I had friends from school, and people I'd worked with every day, who didn't deserve what would happen. All of them had hopes, dreams for the lives they wanted to live.

And this dark alpha saw me as a weapon—although I was a broken weapon. One he put back together after the worm poison, who had nightmares, and would never be strong enough to fight evil.

"If you choose to stay, I will protect you," Grayson said. "I will train you, and I will use you."

The touch of malice and shadow and power in those words quaked through me. Despite that, I said, "Then there is no difference between you and the others."

"I will never imprison you. Never use those you love to force your compliance. There is no hiding from this, Noa. Talking to—touching the wolf—while the man stands there is beyond our abilities, and yet you did it. Either you find out what that means, use what you are, or you give up. And the enemy wins."

A frigid shadow kissed my skin. Grayson said he wouldn't use force, but he'd been forcing me all along with decisions made before I could breathe or argue. He tried to compel me. Dragged me through the mountains so I wouldn't know the way home. Then left me alone by the river. Perhaps out of necessity, as he claimed. But perhaps it was more. To not only see *if*—but *how* I survived.

Didn't that mean I should run?

"Your mind is racing," he taunted. "You're wondering how far you could get on your own. Wolves will always hunt you. The witches run both the east and west coasts, and they don't like wolves. So I doubt they will help you. The nymphs might bargain with you, but they have their own rivalries. Vampires are in every city, so even if you changed your name, they would identify your scent and track you down for the bounty—or for their own advantage. Who wouldn't want someone rumored to be a remnant of the ancient blood queens? A prize like that is beyond rules or civility. And as for what the humans would do to you, well..."

His amusement closed around my throat like claws. "I don't suppose electric shock therapy would save you."

"Bastard," I spat at him.

Grayson shrugged, a beautiful, lethal blow without lifting a hand. As if I wasn't worthy of his anger. "Perhaps it's time to learn what your mother should have taught you."

I wanted to hate him for that statement, but he was right. I could run, hide, and never be safer than where I was. Where every day was a battle of will and power.

The Alpha of Sentinel Falls was no friend. And he frightened me because he understood my weakness, my fear. He couldn't compel me through the pack bond. But with the worm poison, he'd learned how I fight. How I needed to defy him, drag his shirts from my body. Sneak through the house at night and feel like I had control.

He had always known I would challenge him, rather than submit, which was why he pushed so hard. Pushed until I realized the choice he offered was between more than risk or security, life or death.

There was one fear I had above all others, even dying. The fear he exploited by reminding me of the human world. What they would do to me.

I was terrified that I'd end up like my mother, strapped to a chair, screaming into the darkness. Feeling parts of myself dissolve until all that remained disappeared into the black lake inside me. Where a monster lurked—but the Alpha of Sentinel Falls found me there.

Somehow, he'd known how trapped I was in that delusion, and he'd pulled me out, his hands on my arms, his voice cutting through the panic while I beat and beat at him.

He could have let go. Left me there in the nightmare. But he hadn't, and I'd been wrong with my envy when Laura said he'd pulled her from the darkness.

Because he'd done the same for me.

And while logic told me this was the only choice I had—to stay with him—there was a history of *failles* that talked of kings and queens, rivals and power.

Where only the kings survived.

Grayson knew why I hesitated. He knew what we could become—if we did this.

If the old tales were true.

And even if they weren't, I knew he would destroy me.

Would it matter?

He nodded and took a step back.

A bird overhead screamed the way the rabbit screamed.

"You'll..." The breath I pulled in was jagged. "You'll have to help me. Because I..."

His body tensed.

"Don't know where to start."

The alpha's white teeth flashed. "You wanted to leave flowers for Leo. We'll start there."

CHAPTER 18

Noa

GRAYSON'S IDEA OF STARTING involved a hike. His first order was to change clothes, and as I pulled on jeans and a cotton shirt, shoved my feet into hiking boots, I felt a knotting fear.

I would learn what I was—either a weapon or a freak—but I'd learn it from the man who would use me.

Do it quickly, Noa. Run. Or follow him.

Once before, I'd thought those words, then followed Grayson into the high mountains. I'd made the choice for Levi, Hattie and Oscar. To protect them.

But I'd been thinking of myself too. Buying time. Wanting to go on with my life.

The choice now was selfish for another reason. I could not protect those I loved if I remained ignorant. I would always be vulnerable unless I faced what I was... even if that meant nothing more than not wolf, not human.

For a moment, I breathed.

And I knew what Leo would say.

Follow him.

When I returned to the garden, Grayson was holding the wildflowers I'd ripped from the ground. The petals were fresh, as if they still grew in the soil, and I didn't question it when he handed them to me. They were flowers for Leo. The goodbye I believed I'd never have.

We used the path through the trees that Laura used. My boots sank into the soft, meadowed ground. The sweetness of spring floated like butterflies. I thought of the other mountain ranges still struggling with the thaw. The nymph, the swarm of leeches. I thought of Levi's smile when he finally met me—not as a wolf pup bleeding out, but as a teenager on the cusp of manhood.

I thought of the Alpha of Sentinel Falls holding me in the shower while I cried. And when he walked from shadow into sunlight, I had the absurd desire to photograph him. To capture that wild edge. The tilt of his head, the muscular power in his body. Such an image would turn a few heads if I uploaded the photo online. Not that I would. The image was one I wanted to keep private, locked in my memory.

And he'd sink his canines into me if I revealed who he was. Or that werewolves existed.

"Will the house be safe?" I asked, turning once to glance over my shoulder.

"It's warded. Visitors need permission to enter."

"Is there a road nearby?"

"Yes. It's warded too, and hits a dead end a mile away. The Green Man rearranges the landscape each time someone uses the road, so the uninvited can wander these mountains for hours and never find the house."

"Must be hard on the delivery guy," I said, standing in awe when Grayson tipped his head back and laughed.

I'd never heard him laugh. Or even thought he could.

"You aren't afraid of me, are you?"

"I've seen you naked." I shrugged. "Hardly intimidating."

A smile flirted with one corner of his mouth. "I liked you in my shirts."

"You liked your own reek."

But it felt comfortable, this new space between us. Where we were in the same orbit. Opposite each other and yet... not in combat.

Ahead, I recognized the grove of trees where the mushrooms fell in a lavender torrent. When Grayson walked by, every mushroom in the cascade turned in his direction, drawn by magic or out of respect—I didn't know. But the mushrooms moved back into place when I approached, a fluid, lavender ripple that settled into normal.

No matter. I was not the dark Alpha of Sentinel Falls.

But I would absolutely hate it if those mushrooms were destroyed.

"What kind of evil are we talking about?" I asked.

"Save it for another day. This one's too nice."

I glanced around and agreed. "Do you spend much time here?"

"This is my home, but no. I'm not usually here."

"Where are you, if not here?"

"For the past two months, I've been out there." He stared toward the rugged mountains and valleys. "My wolf needed the respite."

I remembered... "And now?"

A minute passed before he answered. "Now he is your ally."

Through a gap in the trees, I could see distant valleys and hills, the mountain ranges. Those to the north looked like serrated arrowheads, and what lived beyond had worried Grayson enough to use my mother's experience against me.

She had suffered. I'd been unable to stop it. And to protect myself from that future, I'd accepted his devil's bargain. I would be the *faille* against his alpha—and hope the ancient stories about kings and queens were inaccurate.

That he and I—we were not destined to destroy each other.

But we were starting, and the quiet rage I'd felt over being coerced disappeared with the offer to leave flowers for Leo. "Where are we going?"

"The old watchtower."

I frowned. "Leo's near there?"

"Yes. But the tower is a favorite of mine. As a kid, I would sneak up there and play."

"How old were you?"

He shrugged. "Maybe eight. I'd gone looking because everyone said the tower was dangerous and ready to collapse."

"Red flag, meet bull." I pushed harder to keep up. "I see why you're fond of Levi. He's another version of you, isn't he?"

"Like recognizes like."

Gray held a heavy branch until I passed, then let the branch whip back into place. Drops of dew pattered like raindrops against the ground. The forest canopy was thicker here, but the shadows interspersed with spangles of sunlight, making everything look alive.

When I studied Grayson, the way he walked... silent, vigilant... imagining him as a boy became difficult. But it was easy to see him playing in the forbidden areas, the riskier the better.

"Where were your parents, if you could run wild in the forest?"

"They were dead," he said. "I was a ward of the pack. The mothers loved me. I could talk them into anything."

"You had no permanent home?"

"Not until I built one for myself."

The flowers dipped in my hand. I stroked one petal, then the stems, thinking about the wild garden outside the log house, and how he removed the green stains from my palm. Erased them as if I'd never been angry enough to rip flowers from the magic that sustained them.

"I never knew my father, not even his name." My gaze remained on the flowers as I spoke. "I don't think my mother even knew it. The pack called her names I didn't understand until I was older. Until I saw her with Stewart. I know people thought she was self-destructive, but she was trying to… prove something to herself."

The alpha changed directions, moving back into the sunlight while I continued to confide. "I think she wanted to prove it to me too, because she didn't want me disappointed the way she was."

"Disappointed in what?"

"Not being wolf enough."

"Did Stewart ever beat her?" The quiet question still held a sharp edge.

"Not with his hands." I stepped around a tiny mushroom growing in the middle of the path. "He attacked her emotionally."

We stopped near the crest of the hill. The expansive view swept in all directions. Watchtowers were built around the views, since their purpose was to watch for an approaching enemy and sound the alarm.

The weightiness of the stones had the same chill, but this time, an underlying shimmer softened the sensation. The way it pressed against my skin… I tried to put a name to it and failed.

"What games would you play here?" I asked.

His smile sliced. "War—what else? I'd fight off the invaders."

"I did the same when I was young, sneaking into the forest around Leo's house, despite the predator warnings. Run around like a wild thing, chasing shadows and hoping one day I'd see a werewolf who wasn't Leo."

"And when you did?"

"I ran screaming."

Grayson started up the last slope toward the blackened tower doorway. The temperature dropped despite the sun burning in the sky.

Uneasy, I swept a strand of hair from my eyes. "Did you ask the sentries to watch the day Laura brought me here?"

"Yes, and they knew the instant you faltered."

"Laura said I shouldn't do my wiggy dance."

"That might have set them off," he agreed. "But they're used to Levi, and they needed to see your sensitivity to the Green Man's magic. Know you're not a liability."

"I'll always be a liability without a wolf."

"You don't need a wolf to react to the magic." His stride never altered, as if our conversation was normal. "In battle, you need to feel the wards and know where to go. It's less work for the wolves who protect you."

I watched my feet, not wanting to trip. "Why would they protect me?"

More alarming, why would I be in battle? Although, I wouldn't pretend I didn't already know that answer.

"They'll protect you because of Leo," he said. "You spent summers here, and whatever you have—real or imagined—you've always tried to help. With Laura. Levi. The wolves won't forget it."

He waited until I reached his side.

"Besides, you proved you were pack."

I crossed my arms and glanced away. "Say worm poison survival and I'll kick you."

"No." His voice was an alpha's voice, commanding yet gentle. "Wolves threatened you, but you didn't go to the human authorities. You came home and asked for help."

I came home.

The idea unsettled me after years of believing I had no home. I looked up, and Grayson's strange green-blue gaze never wavered.

"The pack will protect you," he said, then set his shoulder against the warped tower door. The grinding scrape of wood on stone ended with silence. I heard a soft exhalation, a long-held breath releasing. Glancing down at the wildflowers gripped in my hand, I realized they were still fresh.

My hand trembled. "Leo's... in there?"

Grayson stood with his body halfway through the doorway, one foot already lost in the gloom. His hand braced on the stone surround as he looked at me. "I can take those flowers if you're not up to it."

But layers of meaning hid in that remark.

There was a question. A challenge. And, once again, an expectation.

The breeze quickened, teasing strands of my hair until they fanned across my cheek, sticking to my lips. When I reached to brush them away, my fingers caught in the silver streak. The flowers gripped in my opposite hand glowed, translucent, while I remembered the mushrooms, turning in graceful unison to watch the Alpha of Sentinel Falls walk past.

And when Grayson disappeared through the doorway, I followed him into the ancient watchtower.

CHAPTER 19

Noa

THE TOWER ROOF WAS gone, and only bare skeletons remained of the upper floors, planks over supporting beams. But as my vision adjusted to the gloom, I saw the wooden steps anchored to the stone, spiraling around and upward. Thin blades of sunlight slotted through the windows. Birds took flight from the charcoaled beams overhead, a flurry of black wings, stirring the air, sending whorls of turbulence in the floating dust motes.

Grayson picked his way around the piles of wreckage, the pieces of rotted floor boards and steps, dust-coated and scented by the animals who sheltered here—rodents, the birds who fed on them.

The flowers trembled in my hand when I thought of Leo, buried in the dark.

He loved the light. Needed the wind in his face. Sunlight on his skin.

I looked at Grayson and choked out, "I can't imagine you playing here."

He frowned, and I moistened my lips before saying what I'd meant to say.

"I can't believe you left Leo here."

"I didn't." He ran a hand over the rough stones, letting his fingers trace the old joints and gritty mortar. "Leo's somewhere else. But before we go there, Noa, I need to know how hard you're willing to fight. How far you'll go to find the truth. There's no half in, half out beyond this point."

An alpha's ultimatum, a line that, once crossed, would forever strand me on the other side.

"I'll always be half in, half out of your world," I said. "I can't change what I am. But I shot at a nymph when I couldn't force myself to shoot a rabbit. Is that far enough for you?"

Dark energy misted around him. I wondered if he knew, or if I was the only one who could see it.

"Did you want to kill that nymph?"

"I would have killed if I had to, and thrown up my guts afterward."

"You wouldn't be the first. It never gets easy."

"I don't expect easy."

"What do you expect?"

My fingers cramped from the grip on the flowers. "I expect what you expect. I need to know how far you'll go. If you'll teach me how to fight and survive... because I'm tired of feeling terrified."

For a long minute, our gazes remained locked, and then he said, "There's an anomaly with the Green Man's magic. We call them pockets. They're hidden spaces between spaces. Some are small crevices. Others form passageways, shortening the distance between one area and another. But like the borderline, magic isn't always seen. It's felt, so a pack wolf needs to feel the vibration before he—or she—can find the entrance."

The stone floor was cold beneath my feet. "Can any wolf feel the vibrations?"

"Our energy is keyed to the passages. It's the same for the other packs. They can't find our passages. We can't find theirs."

The Alpha rubbed his palm up the wall, studying each soot-darkened stone. I wondered how many wolves, over how many centuries, did the same thing. Searching for something solid to believe in. Hold on to during the lull between the battles.

"You're sensitive enough to feel the magic, but doorways move, Noa. Like the road."

The alpha watched when I swallowed. "Why do they keep moving?"

"For security. Some pockets are shortcuts or storage closets, but others lead to protected spaces, where the women and pups hide if an enemy attacks the pack."

He shifted his stance to face me.

"And the fewer people who know about them, the safer we all are."

I was on the other side of that line now, with no turning back. I held his strange gaze.

"Why are you telling me this?"

"There's a doorway in this tower. I discovered it as a child. Show me where it is, Noa. And I'll show you where Leo is."

Shock kept me from reacting. "Everything's a test with you, isn't it?"

Grayson shrugged and said, "It has to be."

Glancing around the cluttered space, at the tower that vibrated with wolf energy, I felt the squirming sensations beneath my skin and knew I'd never discern one energy from another.

My voice sounded raw. "What if I fail?"

"Don't."

I breathed in and glanced around again, taking my time. Dirt and rubble cluttered the floor. Dust coated everything. Cobwebs draped across the narrow arrow slits and from the broken stairs. A rickety twig table lay on its side; I wondered if children built it when they played here.

And what would a child do to entertain himself?

No—that was wrong.

The right question was what would Grayson do when he came here, if he played the way other children played.

I righted the table and left the flowers there—still as fresh as before. As if the flowers were an unturned hourglass. Waiting.

The alpha crossed his arms and lounged against the wall. My jaw clenched. He enjoyed challenges, and if I wanted to win, I had to be like him.

Think like him.

I studied the floor. The flat, fitted stones were smooth from centuries of wear. I saw no cleft that might suggest a place to lever up a stone. Besides, what secret doorway would hide in a stone floor? In a panic, in the middle of invaders crashing through the door, there wouldn't be time to move blockages, then move the stones... and then I laughed.

I was thinking like a human, someone who didn't know about magic. Thinking *solid*—when I should think of air like molten silver. How I had to push through the resistance. What floor would be like that, without every Sentinel Falls warrior falling through? Not a secret, then.

And doorways move, Noa.

I worked my gaze along the curved wall, looking for anomalies. The rocks had the look of granite, while the floor resembled gray slate. Pits and scars marred the stones, and crude, ash-gray mortar filled the joints. The wear of age was everywhere. The marks of battle. Then I altered my thinking again, no longer searching for the obvious clues. I needed to be that boy who discovered the door on his own.

He came here to play—what would he do?

He'd go to war... fighting off enemies. Taking risks.

Then I thought about the Green Man, winking at me. Yanking me through the barrier.

If this was his magic, wouldn't it have his sense of humor?

And if so... then I had to play.

Not stand here imagining it.

I sorted through the stacked rubble, the broken railings from the spiral stairs, and found a piece of wood. It was close to three feet long, and the rounded surface would fit my hand without leaving splinters.

I tested the weight.

"Interesting," Grayson drawled.

With a wave of my pretend sword, I grinned in his direction, then leapt onto the stacked woodpile that wobbled as I balanced.

The alpha flashed a feral grin.

I flashed a rude hand gesture and hated that I loved his laugh, rich and deep in his chest.

The bottom two steps of the stairway were gone, but the framework survived. Looking up, I tried to judge the worthiness of the remaining steps and how secure they were, anchored in the wall.

"I wouldn't try them," Grayson warned.

"Why not?" I shot him a glance. "When I'm sure you tried them every time you came here."

"It's your risk."

His amused smirk made me feel like I was plunging down a steep precipice. I didn't care. The flowers for Leo kept me going, and I refused to admit defeat so early in the game.

But would he do something drastic if I couldn't find his damn doorway?

I shuddered.

"This is training, right?"

"Wrong," he said, as if he hadn't heard the tremor in my voice. And I had a clearer picture of what "all in" meant to him.

The cobwebs clinging to the wooden framework soon clung to me, and I wiped my hand against my jeans. The stack of wood tipped as I shifted my weight, but I didn't need to stretch far to reach the first solid step.

"Why is it," I asked, searching for a handhold on the wall, "that I could get through the wards at the river, but the nymph couldn't?"

"The magic protected you and not her."

"Are doorways like that?"

"They keep things in, and other things out."

The crevice I found fit my fingers. I gripped my fake sword and held on as I balanced, then climbed the remaining steps, reaching the makeshift landing that dipped but held.

"So, if I find the doorway…" My palm scraped against rough granite. "Will it let me in?"

"That's the test. Finding it means you pass, and the magic lets you in."

"But if I don't find it… the magic doesn't get mad or any-thing?"

"No."

I thought he sounded more interested now. I glanced back the way I'd come, but didn't see him against the shadowed wall.

Overhead, beams creaked. I wiped at the grit drifting down and glared up at the alpha's grinning face. He was already on the upper floor.

"Too much for you?" he mocked.

"Cheating, now?"

"The test is for you. I already know where the door is."

I scrambled up the next six steps to where he stood. "How did you get up here?"

"Jumped."

"Will I be finding a pocket or a passageway? When I find this doorway of yours?"

"It's not my doorway. It belongs to the Green Man."

"His glorious *hidden* doorway," I corrected.

"Better," he drawled. "But it's not hidden. He left it in plain sight. Let's see if you're as clever as he is."

I scowled. "You keep changing the rules."

"Life changes rules all the time. If you want to survive, you need to adapt."

What remained of the floor was a semi-circle of wood planks with inch-wide gaps. Looking down, I stared at the stone below and wouldn't survive falling that distance. Wandering toward the nearest arrow slit, I traced the rough stone, imagining archers with longbows, moving from side to side, facing the enemy from multiple directions.

But as I stood at the slice in the wall, I realized dark energy remained in the view. I felt it like a shadow cast by a faint sun, and then... I could see them... wolves caught in ancient battle. Hear them... the madness and pain and fury.

I turned from the window, losing my balance before the alpha gripped my arm. He was sunlit pine today, a heady male spice, and I breathed in while turning my pretend wooden sword, watching the way light fell across the broken end.

"The mushrooms turned in unison," I said. "They watched you as you walked past. I'll never be like that. Have what you have. I'm not like the old stories."

He remained quiet. I swallowed once, turned my hand again, testing the resolve I needed to feel... and I wondered. If this wood had been a real sword and I'd been in that battle, would I have used it? Wielded it against an enemy?

Or was I only strong enough for a child's game, dancing through sunlight and shadow, racing along the fallen logs?

I looked around. Another set of stairs circled upward, hugging the curving wall, but that floor was more precarious than where I stood. "When you played invader, did you do it from here?"

"I'd throw spears through those windows," he admitted. "Scare the birds with my war cry and dance around in a little circle."

"I have trouble imagining that."

He slid strands of my hair behind my ear. "What did you see through the window?"

"Shadows. A battle. Blood. Bodies piled, and the birds circling. I saw creatures swarming the hill. Felt the energy. My mother warned me what to expect... and maybe that's what the scholars meant when they said *failles* syphoned the energy because I can't turn it off."

"We don't have to do this today," he said.

"No. We do it today."

Sunlight flickered through the narrow window, and he nodded, understanding the rest of that statement—*or we don't do it at all.*

We started down the stairs. The alpha went first, and I grew confident when the steps held his weight. From the higher perspective, I could see the table with Leo's flowers. Angled sunlight fell through the open doorway, spilling across the floor, highlighting the dust motes. They looked golden in the light, but swirled as if caught in a vortex too far away from the door to be the breeze.

I paused.

Grayson halted three steps below. He looked back at me, and I tipped my head, watching as the dust motes floated toward the wall and disappeared. When I angled my head to the side, I caught a shimmer from the corner of my vision that also flashed out when I turned back to look.

I heard Grayson's steady breathing.

"The doorway," I said. "Do you feel it? Or see it?"

"Both. If you're lucky."

He walked down the remaining steps, jumped to the floor, and held out a hand to me. I took it, and when I was steady, I picked up Leo's flowers.

And followed the dust motes through the wall.

The magic felt as it did before, the ooze of liquid metal as I pushed through the stone that became insubstantial beneath my hand. Then I was in a dark space, illuminated by bioluminescent plants. Vines snaked up the hewn walls and spread across a ceiling made of glossy black obsidian. As I gazed upward, I saw the familiar inky night, black, yet filled with stars—the horrible beauty that lived inside me.

When Grayson joined me in the tunnel, I asked about the stone. He said obsidian was sacred to wolves.

Distantly, dripping water plinked. The air was fresh and moist. A whispering breeze stroked my face and felt curious… sentient. Then the vines moved. Tiny butterflies emerged, their wings a delicate blue-tinged white. They circled the alpha, grazing his hair, his shoulders before floating toward me. I held my hand flat and felt the tickle as the creatures settled, touched, then floated away and disappeared back into the vines.

"What are they?"

"They're like the mushrooms."

"Are all pockets like this?"

"Not all."

I noticed the flowers in my hand. They'd taken on the same glow. Each petal shimmered, the tiny veins pulsing. Feeding off the bioluminescence—such an odd thought, *feeding*. Perhaps they were like me. Unable to stop absorbing the life force surrounding them.

"Is Leo in here?" He would have loved these lights, the glowing, living things. Found peace here.

"No."

The Alpha placed his hand against my back, as if he understood my need to feel settled.

"He's in Azul. This is a passageway to get there. Azul sits beside a lake, hidden in a secluded valley. It's inaccessible to the outside world except through these shortcuts. I found it by accident."

I imagined him easily now, that boy playing in the tower, finding the doorway and searching for invaders here.

The idea made me smile.

"Did you tell anyone you found it?"

He grinned. "Not when I was eight. It was my private place. But after the last pack war, I owed it to the pack."

He'd realized the strategic advantage.

"We developed the area, small sections at a time. Wolves live there full time. Others cycle in and out. The archive is there, as well as a clinic. If war comes again, the women will take the children and shelter in Azul while the men fight. Everyone understands that security depends upon secrecy."

"I thought Sentinel Falls was everything."

"Intentionally." Grayson's fingers pressed against my back when my steps faltered. "For safety. Pack members have to earn the right to know. Only in a dire emergency will the others be told."

I wondered who he meant. Perhaps those in Sentinel Falls who preferred their own bubble?

"Leo knew," he continued. "I asked him to develop a facility for wounded wolves, and those too old to defend themselves. He created a safe place where they could live out their lives in dignity."

I breathed in against the ache and... released a small sorrow. If Leo's body was in Azul, then he was also safe. Protected.

"When Hattie told me you'd taken Leo's body high in the mountains, I imagined him out in the open, lost somewhere," I murmured. "I hated you for it."

He remained quiet.

I moistened my lips. "But now... I need to thank you. For giving Leo peace."

Grayson dropped his palm from my back. I shivered at the loss. He pushed ahead, his dark hair gleaming in the bioluminescent light. Small creatures scurried through the shadows. I heard their scuttling legs and thought of the nymph.

"Is it safe here?"

"Two months ago, I would have said yes."

"The evil we'll talk about on another day?"

He glanced over his shoulder. I shrugged and said, "It's amazing how you've kept this secret in a world filled with technology. Cell phones track everything. The lack of privacy is appalling."

"Perhaps in the human world." Grayson guided me around a curve in the rock passage, dipping his head beneath the lowering ceiling. "But for some reason, the satellites don't register the lights from Azul. We're self-sufficient, and people go about their lives like they would in any rural town. Unmolested by outside forces."

I knew *some reason* meant *someone*.

The Green Man. King of the Forest. I pressed the flowers to my chest, and dipped my head until I could inhale the delicate scents, sending a silent apology for calling him a garden ornament.

I thought the flowers twitched. Then we reached an abrupt left turn around the sharp rock, and at the end of the new corridor I saw shimmering light and what looked like a cave opening. And the man waiting there... was Leo.

CHAPTER 20

Noa

"BREATHE," GRAYSON COMMANDED.

I gripped his hand, curled my fingernails hard into his skin. If this was another test...

Leo spread his arms, and I thought about the day I arrived, how hard I'd wished for him to come outside.

"Noa, girl. I'm right here."

I stumbled forward and buried my cheek against Leo's shirt. Between us, we crushed the flowers, but I didn't care if Leo was crushing them. He was alive. And I didn't question it, not then.

We lingered. The alpha took a position on one side while I clung to Leo's other arm.

And it registered, the awkward way my grandfather walked.

It registered, how the alpha supported him.

But I left the questions for another time. It was enough knowing I was with Leo again.

We pushed through the magic into bright sunlight. The pristine valley, the sapphire lake... houses. I couldn't take it all in and I turned to the young man waiting—brown hair, lanky build. Wolf. I guessed he'd been Leo's escort. He stepped forward, asked if I needed help. I smiled, mouthed a quick "thank you."

But I wasn't letting Leo go. The man nodded in return. Took Grayson's place at Leo's side. We walked along a paved street lined with shops, crowded with people. I saw windows displaying books, a café with tables in the sun. Flowers were everywhere. And wind chimes. The older women waved as we passed. A few men dipped their heads to the Alpha of Sentinel Falls, but the children were not as impressed by power. They raced, giggling and shoving to see who could tackle Grayson first, hang on his arms while dragging their feet.

I had to laugh.

Grayson laughed, too, taking time to touch their heads and then shoo them back toward their mothers.

"I'm worried for you," I said. "Facing a mob like that."

"They keep trying to take me down."

"Never."

His gaze locked on mine for an instant before he looked back at the street. Rustic log buildings stood beside modern structures of wood and glass, but everything belonged in the landscape, sheltered by pines and graceful, draping fir trees. At the center of town, a two-story building dominated with stone and tall windows—the archive, Leo said, as we passed. And not to worry about the sunlight through those windows, since the books were deeper inside. On two floors filled with shelves, plus two levels below ground for the rare books, centuries old.

Leo kept pace, although the pace was slow, and when the brown-haired man released Leo's arm, I realized my grandfather felt embarrassed. He didn't like the feebleness, so I held his hand like the child I'd been, letting him lead me toward a pretty cottage set back in the trees. The flagstone path led to a deck with wide steps, a railing with slats, and a log bench beside the door. Leo stomped up each step, one step at a time, grunting as if he hated showing weakness. While I wondered if he hated revealing pain.

Hattie greeted us with a tea tray in her hands, which she set aside. A smile creased her face. Her eyes dampened as she first patted my arm, then helped Leo into a padded chair.

"Don't overdo it, old man," she teased.

"Bah." Leo swatted the air. "I wasn't missing that look on Noa's face."

The prick of stems against my palm had me staring at the flowers. They were still fresh, no worse for wear after all the crushing.

"I can take these for you, Noa," Hattie said. "We'll put them in water. Why don't you sit down?"

I thanked her and sat on the couch, staring at Leo. A blanket covered his legs. A cup of tea sat on the table within reach. His hair was grayer than I remembered. More lines etched his face.

When Hattie returned, she sat in a straight-backed chair, concentrating on the tea she wasn't drinking. Grayson remained standing while the man who walked with us introduced himself as Leo's assistant. His name was Blaine O'Donnell. He'd helped Leo build the clinic in Azul, and he was proud of their accomplishments.

Small talk, it seemed, designed to put me at ease—since everything felt surreal. Leo wasn't dead. Azul was the result of a pack war four years ago, due to an event that happened four years previous: Laura's escape. She'd been the *girl* who'd gotten away from the Alpen's alpha. He'd lost influence and still blamed her, along with everyone who helped her. He decided to stir up the wolves. Go hunting.

That meant attacking Sentinel Falls.

The Alpen had always been marauders, opportunists. The attacks were indiscriminate. No one in Sentinel Falls territory was safe. But the Alpen were also cowards. They preferred the weaker, remote settlements. They raided. Destroyed buildings. Stole livestock. Killed women, children, old men.

Grayson and Mace led the retaliation, and the fighting lasted two years, escalating as the Alpen became more demented. Too many wolves died. But prisoners were taken, and after what Grayson described as persuasion—while Hattie glanced away—they discovered the motive.

Laura was the excuse. The purpose was anything Alpen could gain. The Carmag pack refused to get involved. They saw it as a fight over a stolen wolf, and anything that hurt Sentinel Falls was a gain for them. The vampires also abstained, although they meddled behind the scenes. The war ended when Grayson met the Alpen's alpha in battle, and Alpen's new alpha signed a truce.

I glanced at Hattie. Her expression remained grim. She rose to her feet, took the tea and retreated to the kitchen. When she returned, the pot on the tray was steaming, and the fragrance of spice filled the air.

"Gray didn't trust Alpen to hold with the truce." Leo's voice was hoarse. "I didn't think they'd forget about Laura, or those who helped her. I decided to go to Seattle and... warn your mother."

His throat bobbed as he sipped the tea. I looked at Grayson's set expression, saw the condemnation in his green-blue eyes.

I'd been in college during the two years he'd been fighting. Busy with my dreams. Sneaking off for superficial moments in motel rooms. Spending six months with the photographer. I hadn't gone home because Stewart said every time my mother saw me, the old delusion resurfaced, and the thought of my stepfather's reaction to Leo was chilling.

Perhaps that explained why my mother ended up with an incurable depression.

"What did my mother say?"

"I never saw her." Leo plucked at the blanket covering his knees. "There was an accident."

"He was ambushed." Hattie's lips were white. "Leo was driving the med-van on a back road. Three pickup trucks cut him off and forced the van over an embankment. They left him for dead, trapped in the wreckage, miles from the nearest town."

Not an accident, then. But meant to look like one.

My gaze darted around the room, from the vase of flowers, to the table close to Leo's hand. Then through the window. I could see the sky, bright blue, a few puffy clouds drifting.

"We didn't know Leo was missing," Hattie said. "We thought he was in Seattle, and eighteen hours passed before we learned what had happened. Someone found him, but they'd called the rescue services who took him to a human trauma center. By the time Gray got there, it was too late."

Too late for a proper wolf healing. I listened while Hattie talked about surgeons, multiple fractures in Leo's legs, and how grateful they were that he could walk.

When she said Leo couldn't shift with steel rods embedded in his femurs, my throat spasmed.

And when she added that Leo's wolf had gone silent, like Oscar's wolf, I turned my head toward Grayson.

The Alpha of Sentinel Falls met my stare with his own. The silent menace stilled me. He'd been unable to help Leo—and then I felt a stirring, deep in my mind, like ice breaking on the surface of a black lake.

The *thing* that hid there was rising, listening.

"Are they dead?" I asked. "The ones who did it?"

The alpha gave the smallest of nods.

"Good." The word tasted like venom in my mouth. Like I'd snarled, feral. Cunning. It startled me... because the sound wasn't mine.

"There's more, Noa," Hattie murmured.

I looked at Leo.

"It was my decision not to warn you," he said. "After the accident, I knew they were watching me, but maybe they didn't know about you being on that rescue. You left right after, and hadn't come back. I thought you'd be safe if I didn't call attention to you." His voice shook as he stared at nothing. "Then Andrea died. I took a chance and asked you to come. We were going to tell you about the Alpen. Ask you to stay. But when..."

He gripped his bony knees, covered by the blanket, and I knew what he'd been about to say... *when you stayed away*.

"Leo agreed with me," Grayson said. "If the Alpen thought Leo died, they'd stop looking for revenge. We wouldn't go to you, but if you cared enough about him, you'd come to the funeral. If not... maybe the house would lure you back, and we'd tell you then."

I stared at my hands, clenching the tea cup. Even before I knew of him, the Alpha of Sentinel Falls had been offering a devil's choice—the illusion of safety when there was none. I'd thought Leo's house was a place to hide when it had been a seductive trap.

A trap you didn't see, Noa.

I stared at him. "If you wanted me here, why all the tests?"

He flashed sharp canines.

"To see how deep your hatred went. And how desperate you were, since you hadn't bothered to come when your beloved grandfather died."

Hattie's face paled. She stared at Grayson. He was unrepentant, even if his strange eyes flashed with more blue than green.

I wanted to give him credit; at the time, he hadn't known the Alpen wanted a *faille*. He believed what Leo believed, that the Alpen were after anyone who'd helped Laura. Why draw attention to me if the Alpen didn't know?

But he'd also believed I didn't deserve to be told. I hadn't cared enough. Then I was here, telling him werewolves were after me. He saw Callum and an Alpen wolf in those photographs I'd taken. Went to the eastern territory to question a man. Returned to question me, putting the pieces together. And maybe he hadn't appreciated my value as a weapon the first day we met. Or even when he dragged me into the mountains. But he'd known when he made his bargain with me.

And the bitterness in those thoughts erased any credit I'd give to him now.

We were stalemated in the credit department.

Leo, though... when I looked at him, I thought of all the nights I'd grieved and wished for one more day. One more chance to make amends.

I'd earned the guilt and regret, but not two years of believing a lie when someone—*anyone*—could have come to Seattle. They could have told me he was alive and warned about the Alpen, instead of letting me figure it out on my own.

"When you died," I said to Leo. "I didn't think I deserved to come back, not after choosing my mother over you. All the years of pretending I didn't love you because it made it easier for her."

"Noa..." Hattie whispered.

The tea spilled when I set aside the cup.

"I've been frightened all of my life, not knowing who I was, what I was. If my mother was sane or totally delusional..."

Hattie tried to pat my arm; I shoved to my feet. The circumstances of life had always trapped me. I was too wolf to be human—but human enough to trust too much. I never realized how easily I could be manipulated, coerced into every step I took.

There were nights when I cried, days when I lived recklessly—anything to blunt the pain. I could never trust myself, never knowing if I was as broken as my mother. I'd turned to Grayson, took a chance. Trusted him. Revealed my fears. And he hooked his claws in deep. Offering to heal those wounds with his bargains and promises and choices.

He is alpha.

You are faille.

He will destroy you.

"Noa."

Leo rose to his feet, but when his blanket tumbled to the floor, the way it looked... carelessly discarded... my mind blanked and I was in his ruined house, surrounded by broken furnishings, breathing in the hot, vile scents thickening the air. Staring at blood and dead wolves and vicious, pointless carnage.

Fear rose. The thing inside me writhed.

Saliva flooded into my mouth. I couldn't force air into my lungs.

"Breathe." Grayson was beside me, his voice cold.

My fisted hands shook—how the hell did he know what was happening?

"Loosen your fingers," he ordered.

"I can't."

"You can. This is nothing. Remember the rabbit? How she froze in the sunlight?"

A sob choked in my throat.

"She was beautiful, wasn't she, Noa? Innocent, young, with golden light all around, and all you wanted was to photograph her, preserve that moment of life."

"Stop." My jaw ached. My eyes burned. "You killed her. Your damn wolf *killed* her."

"Remember that," he snarled. "What happens to the weak. What happens to those who can't move through the fear. There's always time to grieve later. To be angry. To hate me—but not if you are weak."

"I despise you." I spat the useless words, but I'd called him every other name and nothing stabbed through that shell he kept around himself.

Grayson nodded, as if he accepted my disrespect. Maybe it was the truth. But my fingers slowly uncurled. The writhing inside me calmed, and a moment later, he stiffened.

"What is it?" Hattie demanded.

Leo took an unsteady step, ready to stand between me and the alpha's wrath—because Grayson was staring as if I was that traitor again.

"The sheriff from Priest River is waiting at the vet clinic. He isn't alone. Stewart Kline is with him."

I sucked in a breath. Why had Stewart come? I was nothing to him. But that never stopped him from denigrating Leo and Sentinel Falls, and now he was waiting at Leo's vet clinic?

"I'll talk to the sheriff." I wasn't sure about what, but I needed to put Stewart off. He'd probably come up with some story about me, why I left Seattle.

"You will remain in Azul," Grayson ordered.

Silence ruled for a heartbeat.

Then my spine iced the way it always iced when facing Stewart. I stared at the Alpha of Sentinel Falls, unmoved, unwilling to back down. Taking the brunt of his anger as if it never touched me. Never hurt.

"I will go."

"You will not," he snapped. He meant it, too, if the blue fire blazing in his eyes told me anything. Seconds later, emerald sliced through the blue.

I associated the two colors with the twin parts of him—the man and the wolf.

The wolf was the electric blue, full of power and emotion.

The man was... the strength in gemstone, the depth of mystery, the sensuality with a sharp edge that could and would destroy me.

"Stewart Kline is looking for me." But I wasn't that girl Stewart could control through threats to my mother. She was gone, and maybe this was me, reacting, feeling, breathing. Maybe it was wolf energy, or worm poison, or fear, but I was tired of trying to fit into the world.

The damn world could fit me for once in my life.

I refused to waver when Grayson's gaze sharpened. Tension vibrated between us, two powerful forces clashing... then resettling.

Grayson relented first. "If you go," he growled, "you'll do as I say."

I thought Hattie snorted, but when I glanced over, her face was impassive.

And I pushed my answer to Grayson aside.

There was no *if* in this part of the story. I would make my own choices.

Grayson Devante could make his.

CHAPTER 21

Noa

A PASSAGE FROM AZUL opened within half a mile from Leo's old vet clinic, and I tramped behind Grayson, keeping up with his aggressive stride. We'd be having words once this confrontation was over. But I knew Stewart, and Grayson didn't. My stepfather was here for one reason—to prove he wasn't wrong.

Stewart was a bully. What made him dangerous was the way he manipulated reasonable, intelligent people. Strangers believed him despite the truth staring them in the face. And Sentinel Falls represented my mother's delusion. If I was here, that meant it was my delusion too, and he could throw me into the same institution he'd used to cure my mother.

I glanced around the forest and knew how far we were from the clinic. Sunlight filtered through the canopy of trees, the branches swaying, whispering...

Grayson was several strides ahead. He would handle Stewart his way, and I would handle him my way, not stand at the edges waiting for permission.

I stopped and braced one palm against a tree. The faint vibration welcomed me.

"If you're real," I said to the Green Man. "I need your help."

Overhead, the leaves rustled. Beneath my palm, the bark warmed, softened, as if my fingers were sinking into moss.

THE WOLF IN THE WATCHTOWER

Sparks tingled against my fingertips, and despite the logic that said I was imagining everything, I asked for what I needed.

The air shimmered beneath a nearby tree, and the item I'd requested glinted in the sunlight, half-hidden by tall grass. It could have been there all along, but when I picked up the heavy weight, it felt cold. I heard the dull clink. My fingers recognized the rusted texture, and—not daring to doubt—I sent a quick "thank you" to the King of the Forest, and followed the Alpha of Sentinel Falls as he stalked into the vet clinic.

We used a back entrance. The door opened onto an exam room, awash with the antiseptic scents that wrinkled my nose.

"Wait here." Grayson gave the order without a backward glance, and I doubted he knew what I held in my hand. The way he slammed the door was enough to convince me to cooperate, at least for the moment. Wait and listen, then find the advantage and make my entrance.

I listened to the voices through the door.

"Ned, what can I do for you?"

Grayson was aggressive with that tone, and Ned—probably the sheriff's name—mumbled something back.

The words sounded apologetic, and hearing Grayson use the man's name instead of Sheriff meant they knew each other, putting Stewart in a weakened position.

I had to admire the subtle tactic.

"This is—"

"I know who he is." A pointed pause. "What can I do for you, Mr. Kline?"

My stepfather cleared his throat before he said, "I'm looking for my stepdaughter."

I cringed at the title. Stewart had no legal claim to me. I was the baggage that came with my mother. The skinny girl who stood up to him while his wife cowered in the corner.

"Noa Bishop. She quit her job through text and left Seattle in the middle of the night. Her mother was unstable, and Noa—she could be in the middle of an emotional crisis. None of her friends have heard from her, but she inherited an old house and might be here, trying to hide."

"We've been out to the house, Gray," the sheriff said. "Looked like recent damage. I wouldn't have gone inside, but with the broken door... you understand my obligations. Had to make a wellness check."

Even through the clinic door, the drawn-out silence felt threatening. I chose my moment to enter, allowing the door to slam behind me.

Looking around the cramped space, I saw Grayson, relaxed enough to make me wary. Mace stood to the side and behind Stewart—while a tall woman stood across from him. Her blonde hair hung in a single braid down her back. She wore leather pants, a long-sleeved shirt, boots. Fallon—the other alpha, I guessed, when she nodded toward me. Then I scanned the other two men in the room.

The sheriff's hat was off and tucked beneath his arm. Stewart's expression held the same smarmy confidence I'd seen him use with the doctors treating my mother, and so, so slick, in his tailored clothes and short brown hair.

"There *was* recent damage." I threw the three illegal saw-tooth traps toward the sheriff's feet. The chain rattled as the mess slid across the gray linoleum floor, and I caught Mace's smirk, then his quick side-glance toward Fallon. She stepped away from the couch and closer to me.

The sheriff looked up from the traps—still bloody, thanks to the Green Man—and I glared at him.

"Poachers were on my land, trapping wolves for the bounties from those ranchers down on the flat. Your area, Sheriff, so you may know which ranchers I'm talking about. When I destroyed their traplines, they returned the courtesy by trashing my house."

"You weren't there... Ms. Bishop?" He guessed my name since I hadn't introduced myself. It didn't fit with my planned outrage. My attack on Stewart he wouldn't see coming.

I wasn't the Noa he'd shouted at all those years ago.

"I'd been in town with Hattie. The storm tore up the road, or I would have been there. In the morning, I found six dead wolves in the house, all the furnishings trashed, so if you saw blood, it was because the wolves had been *skinned* and I haven't gotten it cleaned up yet."

I watched the subtle flexing in the sheriff's jaw. He was processing the picture I painted—using the false detail of skinned wolves for shock value and to explain the blood. I could guess Stewart's version, that I'd trashed the house myself, proving my fragile mental state.

"Grayson said I'd waste my time pressing charges. The poachers were unknown. And that you..." I let my anger settle in. "Or others like you didn't consider poaching an important crime."

The sheriff pushed at the chains with his boot before glancing up at Grayson. "I'll look into it, if you'd like."

Grayson shifted his stance. "We know who did it."

The sheriff's nod came with a chin tip—*wolf*, I realized. Probably pack, by the deference. All the better, if dead wolves were involved. I guessed Grayson was explaining through the pack bond while I played this game with Stewart.

My glance slammed back toward my stepfather. "Why are you here?"

Stewart rocked on his heels, hands in his pockets to hide the fists I knew he'd formed. "I was worried about you, Noa. You know how your mother could get—"

"I know you drove her to it."

"I never—"

I arrowed my glance toward the sheriff to see how he was reacting. "When I came home one summer, she was digging up the backyard. He'd stolen a book from her and buried it—taunted her with the knowledge. She was trying to find it."

Stewart smirked and glanced at the sheriff as if to say, "see, I told you."

I sent another silent request to the Green Man, walked behind the reception counter to the small refrigerator I knew was there and opened the door. A bottle of beer waited. When I stood and glanced through the window, I swore I saw the King of the Forest's face in the trees.

He winked.

The bottle cap disappeared. I swallowed a gulp, walked back to Grayson and offered the beer like we were more than friends. His fingers closed over mine, and the bastard made me help him lift the bottle, tip the beer to his lips.

Emerald amusement glimmered in his alpha eyes. My jaw clenched. But this pretense was something I started, and the sheriff was wolf. He'd know what our interaction meant. It was Stewart who needed the message.

To make it clear, I said, "As you can see, I am fine. I don't need to explain where I go or who I live with."

Grayson took that cue to heart. He draped a possessive arm around my back. But when his hand moved beneath my breast, I wrapped my arm around his waist, tried to pinch his side, finding little in that damn wolf's muscle to grip.

At Grayson's low laugh, Mace smirked, and I didn't dare look at Fallon—oh, yes, we were definitely having words after this meeting.

Stewart kept arguing. "You didn't answer your cell. I was concerned."

"You never were before."

My stepfather wasn't getting the message. Or else he didn't realize a graceful loss was his only choice. He turned to the sheriff. "Her mother suffered from acute depression and anxiety. She had uncontrolled delusions relating to Sentinel Falls—"

"And Stewart's solution was to lock her up in a mental institution where they—"

"Ned." Grayson stopped me in mid-rant. "Would you mind waiting outside?"

Even I shivered at that Alpha tone. Ned nodded and turned on his heel, resettling his hat as he walked toward the clinic door.

Cool air wafted in, laced with sunlight, and when the door clicked shut, Stewart glanced around. The corners of his mouth tightened.

Mace now stood behind my stepfather.

When Grayson pulled his arm from around my waist, Fallon moved close enough to take the beer, set it aside. Then she nodded toward the exam room door.

I shook my head.

She shrugged and stepped in front of me.

I took one step to the side. The ticking of the wall clock counted off the seconds while the tension in the room ticked with it.

"What book did you hide in the backyard?" Grayson asked, surprising me with that question—with noticing what I'd said.

Stewart jerked. "Some foreign book. Andrea couldn't even read the language, but she kept... obsessing over it, and I wanted to get rid of it."

"Did hiding help?"

"No. She went into one of her rages. Destroying the back yard. When she found the book, she went psychotic, pacing around, clutching it. *Drooling* all over it." His mouth twisted with disgust, a hint of what my mother had endured. "I told her I'd call her psychiatrist if I ever saw it again."

My breath halted when Grayson took a lazy step forward.

"You liked to threaten Andrea, didn't you?"

Stewart paled. He stumbled backward, reversing directions when he realized Mace was there. His lower lip moistened. "I never threatened."

"Noa tells a different story."

"She..." Stewart swallowed, then amended what he'd been about to say, turning it into something innocuous. "I wasn't always perfect. Neither was Andrea. But Noa wasn't there toward the end. She doesn't know how ill her mother was."

"You thought her mother had delusions?"

"Andrea's psychiatrists said she was unstable, perhaps a... a traumatic event here in Sentinel Falls. She hated this place."

Stewart's first mistake was his disdain. The way his lip curled as he glanced around at the walls of the vet clinic, the photos and notes, then to the gray confetti floor. The worn-down spots that revealed the subflooring.

His second mistake was ignoring the way the alpha breathed, slowly, steadily.

"When I realized Noa's apartment had been ransacked, and none of her friends had heard from her, of course I was concerned. You don't know Noa the way I know her. She's believable. Lucid. People see her as a victim because they don't understand her sickness. How she's caught in the same delusion that killed her mother."

Fallon's balance shifted into a ready stance. Across the room, Mace's face became unreadable. Grayson took another indolent step that raised the hair on my arms.

"Noa's mother talked of werewolves, didn't she? In her... *delusions*?"

Stewart forced a tight laugh. "She believed she was a werewolf, but she couldn't turn into a wolf." He flashed white teeth. "Made it hard for her to prove."

"You don't believe in werewolves?"

"I'm not that irrational."

Grayson attacked before I could blink. His claws were out and wrapped around Stewart's throat. His canines had punched down. Even the bulk of his shoulders had a monstrous curve to them, as if he'd halted his wolf in mid-shift.

The Alpha of Sentinel Falls tipped his head, an infinitesimal, uncanny movement—a movement his enemies feared. "Do you believe in werewolves now?"

I watched the slow tightening of Grayson's claws, the drawn-out moment as the tips punched through the skin on Stewart's throat.

Beads of blood sparkled.

My stepfather's face turned bone-white.

"Andrea Bishop was mine," the alpha said. "You tortured her. Killed her."

Saliva dribbled from Stewart's mouth. His lips moved as if he could deny the accusation while his throat bobbed.

Grayson tightened his hold.

"Noa Bishop is also mine."

Mine... the vicious word ground through me, leaving an odd mix of terror and comfort. Then the air trembled with a vibration that iced my skin. Over the past few days, Grayson had revealed fragments of his power, but he was dropping the shield.

His claws bit deeper. Light caught on his canines.

Fallon heard my indrawn breath. She reached back to grip my hand. Either to steady me, or keep me from running when Grayson spoke again.

"And whatever you believe, the lies you tell yourself, know this—*Stewart.*" It was the wolf's lip curl I saw. "If you breathe a word of what happened today. If you ever say her name again. Talk about her, drop little hints, write it out on paper... I will know." His voice deepened into a silky threat. "And I will rip your fucking head off."

The stench of urine filled the clinic.

Mace choked and said, "I'm not cleaning that up."

Stewart's knees gave out. Only the alpha's hold on his throat kept him upright.

I wrenched my wrist from Fallon's hold and pushed past her. "Grayson..."

His claws did not lessen the depth they'd already dug into my stepfather's skin. Blood ran in thick threads, staining Stewart's pristine shirt.

Terror had turned my stepfather's eyes into a vacant glossiness... and I touched Grayson's arm.

"Alpha…"

When his head turned toward me, what I saw in his eyes had me tipping my head to the side, exposing my throat with an offer of submission. "Please."

His gaze narrowed, and the striking electric blue in his pupils flashed as he tracked the tears running down my cheeks.

"Please," I whispered again. "No more… rabbits."

I was speaking to Grayson's wolf, reaching out to him, waiting until shards of emerald formed around the blue—and in that instant, I felt a tug in the center of my chest, as if the part of me the alpha owned made a claim.

"Fallon." Grayson jerked his head in a "come here" movement. She moved to my side, her hand gentle on my arm.

"Noa," she said. "Come with me. It will be fine."

My legs were wooden as she pulled me back through the exam room, then out into the sunlight.

The air cooled my face. Havoc made it hard to think. I struggled with the emotions—not from the confrontation with Stewart, but from that tug in my chest. The way I'd tipped my chin to him.

Fallon stroked her hand down my back. I felt the steel in her touch, though. A warning, when she said, "Gray knew you were there. Even if he wanted your stepfather dead, he wouldn't have killed Stewart in front of you. He would have ordered Ned to do it, far from here."

"How do I know that isn't…"

But I knew—because I knew what kind of alpha Grayson Devante was. He made a choice and followed through. And perhaps his choice had been for me to see him, hear him defending my mother and me—threatening the man who had abused us.

Fallon was right. He wouldn't have killed Stewart with me standing there. Instead, he was giving me a gift, showing me what he'd told me weeks ago: *blood in, blood out.*

No matter what I was, or what my mother was, we were Sentinel Falls pack by birthright. The pack would defend us.

And I was home.

CHAPTER 22

Noa

WE GATHERED FOR DINNER that night at a table overflowing with food. Everyone was there—Leo, Hattie, Oscar. Fallon and Mace. I sat across from Grayson. This was my house, he'd told me earlier, where I would live whenever I was in Azul. It was similar in style to the watchtower house, but two stories, and set in the pines, not on a precipice. A wide yard kissed the edge of the lake. A wooden boat dock extended out over the water, with two Adirondack chairs waiting at the far end. In the evening light, the water shimmered with all the shades of blue—then the crimson from the setting sun. The view was breathtaking.

Inside, the furnishings were enough to make my jaw drop—fine woven carpets, designer leather seating both comfortable and elegant. The vaulted ceilings had cross beams and hanging chandeliers. A floor-to-ceiling rock fireplace added ambiance and warmth. The view through the cathedral windows framed the lake, with darkening hills on the far shore. For a long moment, I stared at the glimmer of distant lights—other houses, close enough for comfort and far enough away for privacy.

But what had me standing, silent, were the photographs hanging on the wall. My photographs, downloaded from my website—the wildlife images Laura said were my niche. The enlarged images were beautifully framed, gracing every wall that wasn't covered with bookshelves.

On a library table, my camera waited. My bow—unstrung—and a quiver of arrows hung on a wall rack designed for them. The flowers I'd brought for Leo were at his house, according to Hattie. But she'd picked more from his garden and those were the flowers now gracing another table in the living room.

I hadn't known what to say. I still didn't know as I watched the group around me laugh, relaxed and playful after the day's stress. Wolves, I remembered, lived in the moment.

Hattie's meal overflowed with comfort foods: a succulent roast, garlic mashed potatoes, fresh green beans. Rolls still yeasty and warm inside. She enjoyed cooking, she'd said, when I offered to help. Now, I toyed with my fork, enjoying the silent pleasure in watching Leo, his eyes bright and his laugh joyful. Oscar sat beside Leo, but he kept glancing at me throughout the meal, and I wasn't sure why.

Mace said something that made Fallon toss a grape at him, which he caught and popped into his mouth, snapping his teeth loudly.

"These three have known each other since childhood," Hattie said, wagging her fork at the alphas. "Don't let them gang up on you."

I was curious now. Since Grayson remained silent, I looked at Fallon. "How did you meet?"

"I met Gray first," she said around a sip of wine. "I tagged along because he knew all the cool places to play. Now Mace—he was something else."

Mace crossed his arms and pretended to glare. "I was not."

"Were, too." She grinned at him, then looked at me. "He was twelve when he had his first bar fight."

I gasped. "How could you even get into a bar at that age?"

"I was tall for my age, looked older than I was. And a fine female thought she wanted company, so..."

Mace flashed his canines, proud of his achievement.

Fallon pitched another grape at his handsome face.

"Don't believe *that* for an instant," she crowed. "He'd broken in and was trying to steal beer when the owner caught him—a pack wolf—who dragged him up to Sentinel Falls to see the old alpha. Turned out, Mace had been on his own for a while, fighting, surviving, offering his services to any pack willing to pay a twelve-year-old to do grunt work. But the alpha wasn't about to let Mace off the hook."

"What did he do?"

"Adopted Mace into the pack," Hattie said, gesturing toward my plate and raising her eyebrows as if I hadn't eaten enough. "By that time, he had two delinquents on his hands with Gray and Fallon, so one more wasn't a stretch."

"Why were you on your own?" I asked Mace.

He shrugged and went back to eating. "I was never one for authority. My parents joined a pack that didn't feel right to me, so I left."

"When you were twelve?" I couldn't believe it.

"When I was ten." Another proud canine flash, although I thought it looked strained. I wondered what else had gone into that decision. "I liked making my own rules. And no way was I belonging anywhere." He motioned with his fork. "These two knew it. Wouldn't leave me alone."

"The alpha made us train together." Fallon sent a quick glance around the table. "He said we'd make a good team because no one else wanted a bunch of rebels. But while Gray and Mace were the same age, I was three years younger. One day, Mace was so furious. He wanted me to prove I was good enough to be with them. There's a sacred pool beneath the real Sentinel Falls. He knew there were nymphs in that pool. But he didn't know they were friendly to female wolves while males were forbidden, so... when he said if I swam across and back, then he would, too, I saw no reason to tell him."

Her laugh was evil in a way that made me smile.

"When I didn't get ripped to shreds, he jumped right in. Got about twenty feet out before the nymphs found him. Gray had to trade our weapons to get him back, and I still don't think he was worth it."

"Oh, no." I laughed, shaking my head at Mace. "Surely, you're worth it now, being the alpha's second."

The alpha's second grinned. "Gray tried to warn me about disrespecting wolves I thought were weaker than I was. He said one day I might need a skinny female on the battlefield, but I was thirteen and wouldn't listen. So he let me learn about rivalry and pride the hard way."

I looked around the table, then back at Leo. "I never knew there was an actual Sentinel Falls."

"There's a waterfall," Grayson said as he leaned forward for his water glass. "One valley over. The old stories talk about a female wolf who stood guard at the top of the falls, protecting the sacred pool against an invading force. She fell defending the nymphs."

"That's why the nymphs like females?"

"A gift repaid."

I grew quiet. Oscar smiled when he handed Hattie his empty plate, and she refilled it for him, surprise wrinkling the skin around her eyes. Even Leo was leaning back in the straight-backed chair he needed for support.

"I never knew much about pack wars," I said. "About females on the front lines."

The idea made me shudder.

"That was centuries ago." Fallon tipped her head to the side. "You should train with me."

Mace barked out a laugh. "With you and the twelve-year-old pups?"

She glared at him, but Grayson was chuckling, and I guessed this was a common dynamic between the two seconds—each of them proud alphas, constant rivals.

"It's not a bad idea." He sliced another piece of roast. "You need to regain your stamina," he said to me. "Learn basic defensive moves."

He'd already assumed I would agree, the way he assumed I would remain in Azul. Our bargain, how he'd teach me, and I'd find out what kind of weapon I'd become. I gripped the wineglass. "I'll think about the training."

Grayson turned toward Fallon. "She'll start in the morning."

I sputtered, but my protest fell on deaf ears. Maybe I should agree, since I'd told Grayson I was tired of feeling terrified. It was having him *decide* for me that was bothersome.

I was chewing on my lower lip when he looked at me. "Did your mother ever tell you what book your stepfather hid?"

"Not the title. I knew she was desperate. She said no one should find it, and I thought she meant Stewart. He liked to gaslight her by moving her things and denying that he did it."

"About that." Fallon hesitated, then held Grayson's gaze. "The nymph story."

She adjusted the fork beside her plate.

"Three years ago, when you and Mace were fighting in the eastern territory. I came across Andrea Bishop in the forest, near the pool. At first, I thought the nymphs hurt her. She was dripping wet, and there were cuts on her arms. She told me she'd given something to the nymphs for protection, and she was leaving, so I shouldn't worry."

A quick glance toward Leo before she went on.

"Leo had his hands full with the wounded, and I needed to finish my patrol, so I told her to go back to Sentinel Falls because it wasn't safe in the forest. Then I left. I never saw her again, and never asked Leo because I remembered the hurt when Noa left, and thought I should leave it alone."

Mace looked at Leo. "Did you know Andrea was here?"

"No," my grandfather said. "And it's hard to imagine her in that pool. Andrea couldn't swim, and she wouldn't leave something with the nymphs because she didn't trust them."

"Maybe that's why she was there," Grayson said. "Because it was the last place people would look if she needed to hide a book." He rubbed a hand across his face. "Looks like we'll be visiting the nymphs. Find out what they'll want in trade."

Fallon frowned. "Noa has to do the negotiating."

I stiffened. "Why me?"

I had no desire to visit with nymphs again.

Fallon held my gaze and smiled with what looked like sympathy. "Because your mother said something else. She called it insurance. No one could find the book unless they were like her."

Without a wolf.

"Well..." Grayson leaned back and stared at me. "Train hard, Noa. You're going to need it."

The training began when Fallon pounded on my front door at six in the morning. I'd dragged myself from bed and still struggled with my shirt when I met her at the door.

"Tie up that hair, sunshine." She grinned. "Then get your ass moving."

I frowned. "Are you always this perky in the morning?"

"Yes, so toughen up, no-wolf."

I snatched a hair tie from the counter and followed her out the front door. "Grayson said the pups liked you more than Mace because you didn't bark orders."

Her laugh rippled. "He lied. They like me for my perky personality."

We joined a group of boys and girls, all between ages nine and twelve, and as a group, they smirked when I jogged in place, trying to loosen up.

"So, where are we going?" I asked, looking around.

"The lake circuit," the pups shouted, glancing at Fallon, who had a smirk of her own that matched theirs.

If I'd been smart, I would have complained of cramps and begged off training.

Instead, I refused to let a bunch of pre-teens think I couldn't handle whatever "the lake circuit" was. Although, staring at the reality a moment later, I figured it out on my own.

"You have got to be kidding me."

"Nope." Fallon flashed alpha teeth. "Fall in, everyone."

The lake circuit followed the shoreline, through the trees and scrub, up hills and down. Every mile, there was a break in the running—long enough to maneuver through an obstacle course made of logs. Then more jogging. More throwing myself over barriers, crawling through mud, barking my knuckles and knees.

Fallon would fall back and tell me to pick up the pace. She threw in the new "no-wolf" nickname because it pissed me off. She called it motivation, while I called it something else.

Then we reached the rushing stream that fed the lake. A torrent of white water tumbled over sharp rocks before falling twenty feet, a wavering bridal veil at my feet. White foam and azure blue glittered through the water's churn, seductive enough to remind me of river nymphs. And sentient water, pulling at my legs with iced fingers.

I forced myself to cross the wood-planked bridge. Boards bounced beneath my pounding feet. But the misty air cooled my heated skin, and despite being tired and terrified, my feet didn't slip on the wet wood.

Trees whispered all around, and I wondered if the Green Man watched.

If he was amused.

By the fourth mile, my thighs burned and my legs had turned rubbery. I lagged at the back of our little pack, staring at *children* who could run faster than I could and with more stamina. I had to admire their seriousness, though, and tried to emulate the focus, push myself.

One girl slowed until I reached her side. We jogged in unison, her arms pumping, her auburn hair woven into two braids that bounced against her back.

"I heard about you," she said.

"Yeah?" I puffed out a breath. "What did you hear?"

"That you saved Levi. And I wanted to thank you, in case no one else thought you needed to hear it."

I stopped, air heaving in my lungs while I braced my palms against my knees. Saliva dripped from my open mouth.

"How do you *do* this?" I panted.

"Come on, no-wolf. This is *easy*. Wait until it gets hard. Then you can drool."

"What's your name?" I asked as she jogged off.

"Catrina."

"Thank you, Catrina. I needed to hear it."

She waved, and I pushed my legs into motion. Followed her along the dirt path until we reached the next set of obstacles—a series of wooden walls. I straddled the first three-foot wall, but the second wall was four feet. I braced my palms, tried to heave my body high enough to sling a leg over the top the way I'd watched the girls do it.

It took me three tries before I hooked a heel, rolling my body enough to fall over the rim, landing like a landed fish in the dirt.

But at least I'd made it.

No such luck with the last wall. Six feet high, ten feet wide, with thick ropes hanging from the top. I imagined my graceful self—feet against the boards, palms shredding. Butt hanging out as I tried to go up and over the way the boys did...they were half my size and damn laughed as they raced upward like the wolves they would soon be, strong, agile. The last three girls matched the boys for speed.

Then it was my turn.

Thankfully, there were no witnesses.

Gripping a rope, I tested the knot at the top, hoping it would fail and fall in a coil to the ground. I'd claim defective equipment and keep going.

But the damn rope held, rough and twisted in my hands.

I backed as far as I could, then made the short, three-step run toward the wall. Slammed one foot against the boards. Then the other and... slipped, twisted, slapped against the wood.

I hung there with my eyes closed, listening to my heart thud. Feeling the sting of exhaustion and failure and sweat in my eyes. My body ached. But I gave it another go.

Backed up. Ran again.

I admitted defeat after the third try. My hands were raw. There was no strength in my legs. I gave up, sliding down the wall until I sat with my legs splayed, eyes closed to shut out the sunlight, the dirt.

Fallon walked back. I heard her soft footsteps as she rounded the wall and sat cross-legged beside me.

"I'll have to buy the beer now," she said.

Turning my head, I peered at her. "Buy what beer?"

"Gray and Mace said you'd last until the walls. I said you'd stop with the second mile and the mud pits—which means I buy them the first round of beer tonight." She slapped my thigh, then rose to her feet. "You should join us."

"I have a date with a bathtub and hot water," I said. "If I can move before the sun goes down. Otherwise, you'll find me frozen here in the morning."

"Doesn't get that cold." She twisted to stretch the muscles in her back. "I can have Catrina show you the way back."

I shook my head. The trail was well-marked, and I didn't want a child offering escort duty to a no-wolf.

I pushed to my feet and trudged toward the path.

"Hey," Fallon called after me; I glanced over my shoulder. "You did good. I'll use your name tomorrow, Noa. Be ready at six."

CHAPTER 23

Noa

THE FIRST WEEK FOLLOWED the same pattern. I dragged my-self out of bed, ready by six. Then a few hours with my grand-father. Blaine O'Donnell and I would walk with Leo, visit the older wolves, the injured, those who would never shift again. We talked, shared coffee or tea or the occasional beer. One man sat in a wheelchair with a blanket covering his missing lower legs. His name was Halwyn, and after asking permission, I touched his gnarled hands, feeling guided to soothe him. The warmth that flowed from him to me was familiar now, and when we left, Blaine murmured, "You have your grandfather's gift, Noa. Whatever you did, it comforted him. I heard his wolf whine for the first time in over a year."

And whether the comfort was Leo's gift to me, or part of being a *faille*, what mattered was helping wolves like Halwyn. Slowing down the process—if that's what I was doing.

There were days when, after visiting Leo, I would visit Lau-ra. She took me to the second basement level—the ancient book archive—with wide mahogany tables, reading lamps, and a comforting leather scent. I wanted to curl up in a secret corner and read.

Stacks of books would sit between us—recorded histories of ancient werewolf packs. Vampires, along with witches, nymphs and other creatures. The Green Man. Legends from around the world. Cultures paying homage, using different names, but the meaning was the same.

By the second week, I could complete the lake circuit, other than the six-foot wall. Fallon jogged at the lead, followed by the boys, but I had a posse now—one by one, the girls had joined me, jogging at my side and urging me on. We wore our hair in single braids like Fallon's, and when the pink stripes started showing up in the girls' hair, matching the silver streak in my hair, I stumbled. My eyes kept blurring, the sting coming on so suddenly, I always blamed the sun.

It was Laura who told me why Grayson wasn't around. He was in Sentinel Falls, meeting with pack elders, representatives from the outer settlements, and although I didn't ask, she told me the real reason why the Alpha of Sentinel Falls spent the last two months in isolation.

The night Grayson told me the story, after his wolf had killed the rabbit, he'd sanitized it by saying the wolf was a rogue. But the wolf had turned feral and was killing his way toward Sentinel Falls. The alphas tried to divert him but couldn't. It was a busy weekend, people shopping, visiting. The pack knew the man, knew his family. When he was cornered, they argued for mercy.

"Was mercy the norm?"

Laura shook her head. "The law doesn't give the alpha a choice. Once a wolf turns feral—once he kills as a feral—the sentence is death, no matter how desperately the family hopes for a miracle. Once the darkness takes them, they're lost."

A chill grazed my skin.

She told me Grayson tried to force the feral to submit. Give the man one last chance to prove he could reclaim control. But a ball bounced into the road. A toddler ran after it, and when the mother saw the danger, she dropped her groceries and ran after the child. With all the movement—the feral noticed. He lunged. The Alpha met him in midair. Took him to the ground. But the Alpha's wolf slipped the tether in that instant—long enough for the kill. It wasn't clean. Or quick, and when he realized the toddler was bleeding, and other children had been watching...

"Grayson regained control immediately," she said. "But his wolf was volatile, and he exiled himself far from the pack."

Mace and Fallon talked to him. Several elders in the pack sought him out. No one faulted Grayson. They understood, and said each of their wolves would have done the same thing, given the circumstances.

Grayson had asked for time, and it was granted. But the pack missed him, his guidance, protection, and they were all relieved he was back.

That night, I couldn't sleep. I kept thinking of the line I'd crossed with my hand deep in a black wolf's pelt, telling him I understood why he felt the need to be strong. That his actions had been right and true.

I did not know—nor could I explain—how I'd known weeks ago that the wolf's fear was about becoming feral, like the wolf he'd killed. Or that he'd killed in front of children. Hurt a toddler.

And the answer—I also knew but could not explain—lay somewhere in the star-filled darkness within me.

Where the nightmares lived.

Week three began with a change in the training. Fallon met me at the door, told me to grab my bow and arrows, and meet her in the meadow.

The pups were there, gathered in a group; at the end of the field, I saw a range of archery targets.

"In battle," Fallon began, "you must use every tactic. What if you can't let your wolf out, but still need to fight? How would you defend yourself?"

She glanced around at the hands that shot up, then called on a cocky boy with red hair who preened when she acknowledged him.

"We have brute strength." He rocked on his heels. "Even with the vamps, we could take them down without being wolves."

"If you got close enough." Fallon braced her feet. "Vampires can disappear in an instant. Snatch you and be gone before your friends can help."

"I'd still beat on them," the boy boasted.

"What if they dropped you? Say, from a thousand feet up... what then?"

The girls laughed.

The boy's face turned red.

"The first solution is the impulsive one," Fallon said. "I want you to have a hundred choices for every situation. With the discipline to stop, think, then act. Battle is as much mental as it is physical."

She looked at me.

"Noa, why don't you show these pups something they've never seen?"

A boy laughed and said, "What—how to shoot at nymphs and miss?"

Catrina whipped toward him and growled, "I'd like to see you face a nymph without peeing your pants, Davie Johnson."

He tried to flash canines he didn't have, and Fallon interrupted with a growl of her own.

I hadn't realized my exploits were so well-known—although wolves were social creatures. It shouldn't surprise me that Mace let the information slip.

"I'd never seen a nymph before," I said as I walked toward the targets. "I didn't even believe in them, but I saw her teeth and knew she wanted to eat me... maybe I was scared enough to miss."

I tested the bowstring, ran my fingers along an arrow shaft, checking the fletch.

"What I love about archery is how it levels the playing field."

Glancing toward Fallon, I waited for her nod, then slotted an arrow and took a position in front of the target row, starting at the right and moving to the left. Large, growing smaller. Near, then farther.

Muscle memory was a wonderful thing. I raised the bow, sighted on the closest target.

"The first time I used a bow, I missed everything I aimed at."

I let the arrow sing from the bowstring; the shaft thudded deep into the center bullseye.

"I didn't improve overnight. It took months of practice. But then, I'm not entirely wolf. I can't even get over that six-foot wall, so maybe you'll learn faster than I did."

I slotted a second arrow, turned and fired a clean shot. Then again, moving through the targets in rapid succession, each target smaller, more distant, some wavering on flexible posts. My skin heated. My breathing settled, and I lost awareness of those watching.

The bowstring sang and the arrows thudded, one after another. When I hit the last target, I started over again. Quivers appeared at my feet. I guessed they held the arrows Fallon intended to use in training. My shoulder twinged from the non-stop movement—pull, sight, release—but I repeated the circuit, large target to small, each arrow hitting beside shafts already buried deep.

I could have split the shafts if I'd wanted to waste the arrows. I didn't though, and I kept shooting until hay bales slumped from the impact. Bits of golden hay floated on the wind. Two of the flexible posts broke—and I looked at Fallon.

"Do you have anything you can throw in the air?"

A crowd had gathered around us, beyond the pups, and a young man ran toward the town, reappearing minutes later with a stack of paper plates.

Fallon took one and pitched it into the air.

The arrow pierced the center. More plates flew, and I hit them one by one, letting a few flutter away rather than shoot above the watching audience. Maybe I was showing off, needing to prove I wasn't weak. Did it matter? Archery gave me a peace that I craved, and control was a drug I'd missed for too long.

Fallon threw another plate. I let it flutter to the ground.

At the end of the field—farther than any target—the Alpha of Sentinel Falls stood with a plate held in one hand. His challenge was obvious.

I listened to the soft collective gasp as I sighted down the shaft and let the arrow find its target.

"And that's how it's done, boys and girls," Catrina said beneath her breath. "How a no-wolf fights."

That afternoon, Leo spent time with Oscar, leaving me with Laura. The archive was quiet, other than Laura's hum each time she found something. Books littered the table, and her scrawled handwriting on yellow legal pads marked our progress.

"I've found something new." She peered at the crinkled parchment. The journal had the mustiness of age, but it wasn't offensive.

"*A Brief History of Kings and Queens.* Written by someone named Ovid and translated later by other scholars. The style of writing is archaic. I'll paraphrase for you."

She marked the inked passage with a paper beneath her fingers. "He talks about the ancient queens raising the silent ones—I'm not sure what that means—but queens were healers. They could calm the agitated. Bind the wounded." She looked up. "That sounds normal when men went to war and women tended the casualties. Then he contradicts himself, calls the queens wicked creatures who amassed armies and unleashed vile abominations." She studied the flowing script, squinting where the ink feathered into the parchment. "I think this says the kings and queens were fated enemies, doomed to battle, and only one will win."

Her expression grew troubled. I wondered if she thought of the other ancient scholar's text, the one that talked about hidden kings and queens. The one used to kill an innocent girl.

"Research is always inconsistent," she said. "With different interpretations of the same events. Remember the time—scholars used magic or the gods or evil to explain what we understand as normal."

"Maybe." A soft moan escaped when I moved my arm.

Laura frowned. "What hurts?"

"My ego." I rubbed at my right shoulder. "I overdid it today and I'm paying for it now."

She huffed. "Fallon's been working you too hard."

"Not Fallon." I dug deeper into my shoulder muscles. "She wanted an archery demonstration. I embarrassed myself by showing off in front of kids who outrun me every day. They jump higher, move faster, when I can't even get past that rope obstacle."

Laura closed the book in front of her. "Why is training so important?"

"I made a bargain with Grayson. He said I was in danger if I didn't learn what being *faille* meant, and he could help me."

I stared at the darkened ceiling where exposed beams hid in the shadow. "He offered his precious protection. All I had to do was let him find out how to use me, if I have some voodoo talent. In case there's a war or something—and it's hilarious, you know?" I sucked in a half-breath. "Thinking I can terrorize anyone when I can't even get over a six-foot wall."

"Who do *you* think you are?"

"I'm no-wolf right now."

Laura tipped her head. "No-wolf?"

"That's what my posse calls me." What I preferred over Noa. *No-wolf* held no expectations. "It started as an insult. Fallon called it motivation."

Laura snorted.

I smiled and said, "The girls jog beside me now, instead of racing ahead. They put pink stripes in their hair as a sign of solidarity, which I'm sure their parents don't appreciate." I linked my fingers together. "But I can't be a mentor to them. No one should be like me when we don't even know what that means."

"They're frightened. You hold out a light. The hope that even the weak can fight back." Laura's fingers pressed hard against the polished table. "Years ago, when the Alpen came... my pack wasn't prepared. Our alpha was old, peaceful. The men were off working, and it happened so fast. The Alpen just... killed. Women, children, the old ones. It didn't matter. They ripped us apart, herded the girls into a pen like animals. Their alpha saw me, and I'll never forget that smile. The hated satisfaction. His... proud victory."

She breathed in.

"He knew I was a healer. For the fun of it, he beat me, then said I was free to heal myself. They tied ropes around my wrists. Dragged me when I couldn't walk. They didn't stop unless it was to finish off someone who hadn't already died. Even the girls they left behind. The dogs who followed. It took them a week before they felt safe. I wasn't the only girl. There were two others. I didn't know them. They dosed us with wolfbane powder—not enough to kill—but to keep us from resisting."

Her grief radiated, and I shifted my position, stretching until I could touch her fingers. She inhaled again, her hand jolting.

"The Alpen spent a month raiding. They'd collected one other girl, but she died before they got me. I heard about her from the other girls. We stopped. I guess so they could get drunk and celebrate. I remember the tent. No light. The bucket in the corner. Blankets that stunk of urine. How, when it got dark enough, they came for the older girl. They dragged her outside, passed her around until she stopped screaming." Laura breathed in. "The other girl curled beneath a blanket. But I knew... I knew I had to get away, right then, while the Alpen were distracted."

I pressed against her hand, waiting. Letting her know I was there.

Laura's mouth trembled before she whispered, "I told the girl beneath the blanket to come. I begged. She wouldn't move and I... left her behind. Hating myself for the cowardice, because I couldn't face what those girls faced."

Her hand juddered. I curled my fingers around hers—all I could reach without moving—because I was afraid if I moved, she would not put the rest of her nightmare into words.

"Gray reassured me. He said what happened to those girls wasn't my fault. I wasn't the monster for leaving, and I hadn't chosen who lived or died. I'd been choosing Levi. Choosing life. Because he'd die if I couldn't find him, and leaving was the one best thing I could do to save us both. He said what made my choice honorable was the pain I felt for those other girls. Because they'd been too afraid—or unable to choose life for themselves."

Her hand turned until her palm was facing up toward mine. Brown hair fell in waves. She bent her head, pressed her cheek to the curve of her arm. I stared at the scar on her wrist and now knew it was the rope burn. And as I measured how deep it had gone... my grief felt shallow against hers.

"Gray told me to hold on to that pain, Noa. I'll feel it for the rest of my life. But it proves my humanity. How I value life. He said I should treasure that proof, because, for werewolves, it's so easily lost. I know that. I've tried so hard to believe him. But at night, in the dark, I still hear those girls pleading."

Her head lifted, her brown eyes sparkling in the lamplight that fell across the table, the ancient books and her notepads.

"Gray also told me there is light and dark in everyone. I'm strong and weak, and it's the same for you, Noa. What you offer those girls is the hope they can be like you. Spit at the world and say... try me, asshole!"

I swallowed the hollowness, and said, "Grayson said a *faille* was both a weapon and a savior, and maybe that means I'm his light and dark. But instead of a wolf, I have a nightmare place inside me. Something lives there, Laura. Something terrifying. I think it's the weapon he wants, and if I ever let it out, I'll be like that feral wolf. I'll go into the darkness and never come back."

Laura stood and came around the table to pull me into a hug. I'd never had someone who would hug me with true understanding. Silent support in our grief.

She leaned back with her hands still on my shoulders.

"Listen to me, Noa. Grayson has to worry about the pack. That makes him hard, even brutal. But you don't have to be like him. You are strong, honest, with such an amazingly brave spirit. And if this is something you can't do... don't let him force you."

CHAPTER 24

Noa

WHEN I RETURNED HOME, exhaustion and pain kept me from climbing the stairs. I collapsed on the lower steps, thinking I would sit for a while. I woke to Grayson lifting me, carrying me upstairs to the bathroom where water in the contoured tub steamed and fogged the air.

He stood me on my feet and asked if I needed help.

I groaned when I lifted my arms. He pulled off my clothes, lowered me into the warm water. I kept my eyes closed. Wolves were casual about nudity, but I wasn't. It still bothered me, the care he'd taken when I was ill. The many times he'd seen my naked body.

The few times I'd seen him.

But once I was alone, I floated in water that was soothing and scented with flowers. The petals drifted, brushing against my thighs, my knees, toes. Little eddies swirled as I moved my hands, let the petals wash across my stomach—pinks, reds, white, purple, bright yellow—the colors of spring. Rebirth. I breathed in the sweet fragrance, enhanced by the steam, and wondered if the flowers were whimsy. Or medicinal—because the spasms in my shoulders eased.

I lost track of time, and when the alpha returned, he pulled me from the water, wrapped a towel around my nakedness.

Then I was flat on my stomach on a bed with fresh linen. His hands were on my shoulders. The scents of eucalyptus and spearmint filled the air—from an ointment he massaged into my skin.

With my lips pressed into the pillow, I murmured, "Why are you here?"

"I'm a healer. Laura said you had need of me."

"Laura talks too much."

"I asked. She answered."

Of course. He was her alpha, so she would tell him what he wanted.

His thumbs pressed hard against the tender areas. I didn't want to move. My exhale was slow as I sank into the soft mattress. "Why did you come to the meadow?"

"I heard the no-wolf was shooting targets." His fingers stroked down my spine. "I thought she'd like to shoot at me."

"Another one of your tests?"

His laugh was low; the sound uncurled in my belly.

"I thought you'd miss."

"You knew I wouldn't miss... so why?"

Why did he stand at that distance with a target held too close to his chest?

His hands smoothed over the curve of my hips while his calloused thumbs eased the pain in the small of my back.

"I wanted *them* to know you wouldn't miss. That you wouldn't hesitate, no matter who stood there."

"Why?" I floated in a lethargic haze; Grayson didn't seem to notice.

"I want them to trust you in a crisis. Feel as safe with you as they do with Mace or Fallon."

I scrubbed my cheek against the pillow and whispered, "No one's safe with me. I have no wolf."

"I know."

"Then why?"

"We have a bargain." One that included visiting the nymphs, and he'd waited long enough. That was why he was back in Azul, holding up targets.

But as Grayson's skilled hands continued to press and stroke, I breathed through the loneliness in lying on a bed with this man's hands on my body. Knowing it meant nothing more than a healer mending his broken weapon.

When I woke, I found Grayson's note on the kitchen table. *Be in the meadow at seven. Bring your weapon.*

I slid the leather quiver against my back, strung the bow as a precaution. I'd already braided my hair, dressed in clothes with enough stretch to twist, shoot, run—Fallon's favorite mantra. She'd said the wrong clothes would cost me the one second of time I might need to save my life.

A less than comforting thought.

I found the Alpha of Sentinel Falls standing in the grass where the dew sparkled in the morning light, and when I reached him, he turned and walked away.

The lack of communication annoyed me. A simple "hello" shouldn't have been too hard, not after he'd had his hands on my naked back last night. *Healing* me so I'd be useful to him this morning.

But fine, if he wouldn't share, I wouldn't ask. We were going to see the nymphs. Ask them for my mother's book. It was almost like a childhood rhyme, stomp-worthy, but rather than chanting, I focused on the landscape and not on what seeing the nymphs meant.

As the sun warmed and rose above the trees, Grayson turned toward the conifers and the shimmer marking the passage. He disappeared through a hazy veil. But as I approached, the magic pressed me back.

I halted.

Then Grayson was there with his fingers gripping my chin, not hard, but with enough dominance to tilt my face. "It's your choice, Noa. I'll ask. But I won't force. Tell me you've reached your limit, and I'll send you home."

The alpha jerk expected me to say yes, send me home. Prove how weak I was.

I yanked my chin from his grasp, gave him a smile that didn't meet my eyes. "What else did Laura tell you?"

It was amazing, how quickly he pretended innocence. "She told me not to bulldoze you."

"Afraid I'm half in, half out?"

His tension flashed too fast to decipher. "No rabbit in the glen?"

"None." I stepped into the passage, ignoring the thrumming against my skin, waiting for my eyes to adjust. I'd wrapped my arms tightly at the first chill. Now I kept my elbows tucked in to keep from touching anything.

The walls were obsidian, but instead of vines, bioluminescent spider webs dangled from the ceiling in messy, knotted masses, looking like blue neon flickering on a rainy night. Thumb-sized spiders lurked in the crevices, shiny, black, with needle-thin legs touching the anchoring web filaments, waiting for the faint tug of snared prey.

Mud squished beneath my feet, and the scent of something rotting made me shudder. I couldn't shake the nightmare memories with the scent, the dark. I wasn't sure how long I'd tolerate being underground.

I glanced at Grayson, my eyes half-shuttered. "How long will this take?"

"Not long," he said, stepping around to lead the way. I scowled at his back. Not long could mean anything. Laura said ten minutes in a passage was like an hour above ground, but I'd forgotten to ask how far the sacred pool was from Azul.

I watched where I put my feet. Ducked beneath the veils of webs. The passage was too narrow, too dank. I kept waiting for something to change and it didn't. Not until I felt feathery legs race across my throat. I squeaked, slapping at the sensation, and he said, "The spiders aren't poisonous."

"The way leeches weren't poisonous?"

"Turn back if you're afraid."

"You make it tempting." He was several strides ahead of me, but I still wanted to push at him since he seemed so willing to push at me. Pick a fight. "But if I turn back, you'll win, and I won't let that happen."

"I'll win either way," he said, so arrogant I sputtered with an insult... until a walnut-sized black spider dropped from the ceiling to his back. I wanted it to bite him.

An instant later, the spider fell, sizzling into nothing. Whatever alpha power he'd used, it wasn't a normal wolf trait. Magic must have come with the job.

"Show-off."

I heard his laugh, but couldn't fault him after I'd shown off with the archery targets.

My steps dragged through the mud until the webs and spiders ended and the bioluminescent light came from lichen on the rocks. The passage floor was stone worn down from use, but the air turned frigid and my teeth chattered. Nothing helped, not cupping my hands or blowing on my fingers. The chill stabbed to the bone until heat drifted across my skin. I'd felt that warmth before... from him.

"Can you stand ten more minutes?"

"Yes." But it was a lie.

My teeth still chattered when I followed Grayson out of the passage and into the muted sunlight, dimmed by an old growth forest. Around us, sparsely flowered shrubs fought for light beneath the canopied trees. The stillness left me breathless. No sense of where we were though, or how close to the sacred pool. No deep-throated rumbling from a waterfall, which meant more walking. The braid thumped against my back. At least the air was warm. And I was above ground, although the forest shadows were uneasy.

When a bird squawked, I glanced at Grayson. His stride never faltered. His gaze swept from left to right, what I expected from an alpha, but he seemed more relaxed. Perhaps he preferred the fresh air, too. Seeing the sky. I blew out a breath. I was tired of the silence, the feeling of walking on damn egg shells with him. I'd thought we'd both given up small parts of ourselves that day at the watchtower. Eased up on the conflict. Trusted enough to confide.

"The reason I went into the river that day," I said. "I thought I had to stop the log without knowing why." I waited for his shoulders to stiffen, some form of judgment. "I couldn't fight the thrall. I didn't even realize what it was. That's why I've been avoiding... nymphs, if that's what you think."

Why he'd questioned if I was half in, half out, ready to go home. After he'd shared the secret of Azul. Put the pack at risk by trusting me.

Grayson aimed for a break in the trees. "I didn't think you were avoiding anything. When I asked Laura, all she told me was that your muscles hurt. Then she reminded me of the importance in respecting who you are and not my selfish needs."

"I don't think it's selfish to want a weapon, Grayson. Not when you have a pack to protect."

"You'd just rather it wasn't you."

I paused, about to rasp out a lie, but he deserved more. "My mother warned me before she died. Two of those warnings have come true. What terrifies me is the third warning."

And all he said was, "If I know anything about you, Noa, it's that you're not the kitten."

I couldn't think of anything worth saying after that, no snappy comeback. The forest was silent, the air slowly warming even in the shade. But my skin chaffed. Something skimmed across my hand. I swiped at it, still worried about spiders.

But not spiders. What I felt was...

I searched my memory for words to describe it: a drifting feather on a breeze. No, more like the hot-cold snap from a Fourth of July sparkler I'd once held too close to my hand.

I rubbed at my wrist. Glanced at Grayson's back as he hiked ahead of me.

Then I felt it again. Sparks...popping off my skin with the sting of nettles.

I stopped, locked my feet in place. Tiny hairs lifted on my skin. Grayson looked back, and I mouthed the words, "Do you feel that?"

His body braced, the muscles rippling into readiness. But he shook his head, and doubt crowded into my throat. It could be wolf overload. I could be sensing what wasn't there.

I counted through my inhale, waiting for the calm. Followed with the exhale.

Overhead, the sun wavered. The breeze quickened, then stilled with the weight of a dropping stone.

I stared at the trees. At the spaces between them until my eyes ached. Then I scanned the meadow, too bright with spangled sunlight... was that what I sensed? Innocuous sunlight? Spooking me because my vision hadn't adjusted yet?

But... no.

I eased the bow from my shoulder, shrugged until the quiver slipped. An arrow fell within reach; I nocked it against the bowstring.

Grayson looked at me. I looked at him, then watched as he scanned the tree line. His continued silence made me lurch to the side. I didn't know why.

But the sting on my skin turned snappish, and it wasn't natural.

The taste of ash was in my mouth—and that wasn't natural, either.

When he looked at me again, my gaze slid to the left, a subtle, flitting movement toward the meadow. The trees were sparce, and the air there had expanded with spangles, coalescing into a vertical slit.

I thought of the nymph's reptilian eye, and a shudder rocked through me. "What is that?"

Grayson studied the meadow where the sun had turned blinding.

I asked, "You don't see it?"

All he did was narrow his eyes, turn slightly and shake his head... *no.*

The slit was growing wider, beyond a hand's width, and the need for him to see it became urgent. I leaned toward him as if body language could convey more than words. "Twenty feet back, between those two trees. A dark seam, forming in mid-air. Three feet above the ground. Getting... longer."

"I don't see it." His canines punched down. "But I trust what you see."

Relief flared in the instant before the air exploded.

The flash was brilliant enough to be sheet lightning. But not sheet lightning. Whatever it was, I didn't hear it.

I *felt* it. An expanding wall of storming energy, sinking beneath my skin... deep into my bones... down into the hollowness inside me.

Stirring up the dark with chaos. Cracking the ice floating in that black inner sea.

The *thing* inside me began to rise.

"Grayson."

"Follow my lead," he said, firm, calm, issuing instructions I could follow without thinking. "Run where my wolf runs. Keep him between you and whatever comes through. Shoot and do not hesitate. No matter what you see. If I fall, there's a pocket—a mile from here. Stay to the north and you'll feel it. Go inside. You'll be safe."

I nodded, but he pinned me with a hard gaze. "Shoot to kill, Noa."

The command held the burn of a flash-freeze. Beneath my feet, the ground trembled. I thought a herd of *something* stampeded toward me... when *nothing* moved in the meadow.

Grayson was already shifting. His shoulders were ridged, arms and legs elongating. Clothes were replaced with a black pelt, and the wolf was leaping when the thing behind the reptilian eye screamed.

My blood turned cold. The seam cleaved open, and a beast tore through the gap, cloven hoofs gouging the dirt. The head was grotesque, with a soot-colored boar's snout and curving yellowed tusks. Saliva dripped from its jowls. A ridge of wiry onyx hair spiked along its spine.

My bowstring *twanged*. The arrow flew true. The sickening wet thud when the boar hit the ground seemed as unreal as the heaving sides, the flailing hooves, digging ragged trenches in the bloody ground. I wondered if the creature thought it was still running. But I couldn't decide as a second beast burst through, trampling the first.

I reached for another arrow. The screams were otherworldly. Blood splattered. Then the black wolf was there, claws ripping, canines sinking in deep as more creatures poured through the gap.

I couldn't look away until some *faille* instinct jolted my attention from the wolf and toward the ground. Yards from where I stood, a gash was opening and a swarm of six-legged creatures scuttled up and out in a teeming flood, their mouths gaping, eyes beaded with crazed intensity. Translucent bodies revealed the pumping hearts and veins and brains, and I shot and shot. But when a they drew close enough to see their eyes, I hesitated.

The blues, greens, browns registered as... human.

I gagged, spit at the bile in my throat. Grayson talked of witches. Of nymphs that were never what I expected. In a world guarded by an ancient Forest King, I could be looking at anything.

Shooting at... what could be no different from what I was. A failure of creation. Broken. Used by those with more power.

Then I heard the Alpha's order in my head: *shoot to kill, Noa. No matter what you see.*

To my side, the wolf fought. I did the same. Arrows pinned the bodies to the ground. Others massed in to consume what was still moving, and an atavistic fear strangled me. I couldn't process the sounds beyond rattling, crunching... *chewing*.

I bit my lip, tasted blood. Stared through blurry eyes. Sweat dampened my palms until my grip slipped on the bow. The arrow wouldn't nock. I struggled, losing track of how many arrows I'd already used.

But I was okay. I'd be okay. What I told myself was nonsense, but it kept my mind numb. I breathed through my mouth. Pushed the sounds behind the wall in my mind, then deep into the darkness where the other fears lived.

I chanted *liar, liar, pants on fire* while arrow after arrow flew from the bow.

Bodies flopped from severed legs or blinded eyes, and still... I breathed.

When I thought the quiver should be empty, more arrows appeared.

I didn't question the arrows, or the way rocks moved from my path as I ran, then reformed behind me.

The wolf was snarling, his massive claws tearing through muscle and bone and blood-drenched earth. I ran behind him, choking on the stench of rotting meat. A blood-red sun shimmered, but it wasn't the sun that was red—a bloody mist beaded my eyelashes. I smeared it across my cheek.

When I forgot to tip my elbow out, the bowstring ripped through my shirt, abraded the flesh on my arm. Arrows flew toward anything that moved, other than the wolf. I didn't stop to think. To sort out what I was seeing, although I knew... this was what I'd sensed when I peered through the arrow slits at the watchtower. An unrelenting enemy. A sea of crimson and inhuman screams, of gasping breath and terror-tightened muscles.

We worked as a team, the wolf and I. He charged the hoard flowing through the slitted eye. I aimed at what came from the ground. The too-sweet scent of decay was not a Sentinel Falls scent. The moist, putrid oil of viscera that coated my skin was nothing like what I'd experienced at my grandfather's vet clinic, even with the severely wounded. My arms ached. The abraded area throbbed. But the black wolf destroyed without pausing.

Blood flecked his coat. Claws and canines dripped red saliva as he shredded bodies, leaving ruined flesh scattered across the trampled grass. He was stunning in his lethality, and watching him, I couldn't catch my breath. My lungs clamped down with both awe and fear. Bodies and blood pooled around him, and still the boars came, tusks reddened when they ripped into the black pelt.

I'd never watched a wolf kill the way the Alpha of Sentinel Falls killed. Efficient, precise. We left a path of carnage. Fought, ran, breathed until all I knew was run, turn, shoot. Each yard gained toward safety stretched like a mile.

The sounds wore on me. I tried to shut them out and failed.

Each time I shot, I tried to keep my hands steady.

And failed.

The world narrowed down to arrows and a bow. I stumbled and went down on one knee. Struggled upright again.

I did what Grayson asked. I followed his lead. Ran where the wolf ran. Keeping to the north.

And then the enemy withdrew.

I stood in that silent lull, frozen and numb until the wolf crashed into me, growling for my attention.

He raced along a cliff base, cluttered with thorny bushes and sharpened rocks, treacherous to the unwary or the exhausted. I let what air there was into my lungs, unable to control my breathing. Muscles tore as I kept pace with him.

I might have cried with relief when I felt the magic, stumbled through an opening in what looked like solid rock. Outside, the wolf postured and raced, but inside the cave, it was quiet and as dark as a gray night. I dropped until I was sitting on the sand, staring at nothing. The bow, the leather quiver—both lay near my feet. Blood turned to rust on my hands. When the wolf leapt through the veil, landing close enough for me to smell the reek of battle on his pelt, I drew my knees to my chest, wrapping my shaking arms.

The wolf raged, his eyes blazing and his growls bouncing off the obsidian walls. He sank into the cave shadows, disappearing until I was alone.

While outside... the trees were moving.

CHAPTER 25

Grayson

My shift back to dominance was violent. I stood naked, scanning the cave. I wasn't done killing. Neither was my wolf. His aggression became mine, and we both still hunted the enemy—*fuck!*

I'd been blind to the passage opening up. If Noa hadn't felt it. Warned me in time. She sat on the sand, her breathing forced. She wouldn't be moving until the trembling stopped. Besides, the magic wouldn't let her leave until I told it to—a small blessing in this fucked-up day. I stalked deeper into the cave, through an angled passage to a cavern lit by iridescent mushrooms, thousands of them covering the walls and pulsing a silvery light.

No one had entered since the day I left months ago. The air was cold and undisturbed, other than the gray fog from my breathing. Sand covered the cave floor, and in a circle of stones, the stack of wood burst into flames as I passed. The thready smoke would disappear through a crevice in the ceiling and reappear miles away. Alerting no one to the cave's location.

Likewise, the landscape outside had already changed; the King of the Forest liked to shift trees and shrubbery around.

Play his little games.

Fury overwhelmed me. I stood rigid with a bone-deep resistance. Fought the impotence that once had me screaming at the sky. Only I'd been on my knees then. So gods-damned angry. My wolf had torn up the ground. Lost a bit of his sanity. We'd disappeared for a month without explanation. Still hadn't given that explanation. One look at my expression when people asked was enough for them to turn away, change the subject.

I could smell Noa's fear, the way I'd heard her desperate inner chanting: *liar... liar... pants on fire...*

The way I'd felt her terrified remorse each time she let an arrow fly.

Heard her when she'd been in a nightmare.

I'd stood there that gods-damned night when she touched my wolf, and fucking let her—when the only reason she could do that was the one reason I could not control.

My palms felt gritty; I still dragged them across my face. Every part of me resisted, and I swore again, startling the mushrooms until the light wavered and dimmed.

But anger changed nothing. I shut down the emotion and stalked to a carved niche holding the extra clothes I kept on hand. I shoved my legs into stiff jeans. My face felt like stone when I looked at Noa. Her arms were strained as she gripped her knees. The braid draped over her shoulder, damp and blood-specked. Wisps of hair had come loose. She looked lost, but coddling a woman like Noa Bishop would do nothing. I'd allow no tenderness between us. She was in shock, and I needed to push and prod at her until the anger broke through.

My hands fisted. "Get up."

She didn't move.

I dropped into a braced crouch in front of her. "This is what we do, Noa. We fight. We bleed. And then we get up."

She tipped her head, lips pressing into a thin line. "I'm not you."

"You'll still do as I say."

"No."

I surged to my feet. "It's no wonder you can't get over a six-foot wall. You're weak. Now stand... the fuck... up."

"And you... are a damned... ass," she hissed.

"So you keep telling me. Make the anger useful. Put your weight on the balls of your feet. Center yourself and push upward with your thigh muscles."

"I know how to stand."

"Then do it, unless you want my hands on you when I drag you to your feet."

Her anger was a storm that matched mine, and I regretted never having met her mother. Never having seen Noa as a child. I'd been the Alpha the last time she'd been in Sentinel Falls, but off on my path that hadn't intersected with hers.

She was still in full rebellion when she demanded, "Why do I have to get up?"

"We have a bargain. You're already in pain. If you stay in that crouched position much longer, you'll be no use to me."

Her glare glittered with the secrets of the forest. "Do you know all the names I'm calling you right now?"

I flashed some alpha canine in return. "Fallon said you were tough. I think she lied to make me feel better."

Fury brought color into her face, but she broke from the catatonic state she'd been in for the past ten minutes and rocked forward on her hands and knees. When she finally stood, her body shuddered as if she couldn't stand straight.

"Go sit by the fire."

"Why?"

"You're hobbling like an old woman when I want you ready to run."

"You're demented if you think I'm running anywhere." But she plodded through the sand that didn't soften beneath her feet. "Besides, I see no difference between sitting where I was and where you want me."

"You'll be warmer by the fire."

"I'm already warm."

She was fighting me again. I wanted it… needed it. When Noa reached the stones around the fire, I heard her stifled groan as she sat down. Water had been heating, and I dropped a cloth into the small pot, then pushed it toward her. She focused on scrubbing her hands, wrists, avoiding the angry red area on her arm. I could heal it for her, but I wouldn't offer. It wasn't wise for me to have my hands on her right now, not unless she asked.

"We'll stay here for the rest of the day," I said.

"I can't stand being with you for another day."

"Time passes differently in the pockets. Tomorrow will be here before you know it."

Noa shushed her irritation, rinsing the rag, twisting as if she twisted something else. Some part of my anatomy, perhaps.

I tried and failed to ignore the part of my anatomy I wanted her hands on. When she'd wrung what life there was in rags, I tossed it with the dirty water, then settled a clean pot near the flames, taking my time, giving her space to adjust while I prepared a tea. Something to counter the adrenalin in her system—if she'd relent enough to drink it.

"I've warded the cave," I said. "We're safe here. No energy trace in or out—either mine or yours."

I watched her reaction. She gave none, other than a brief twitch in her hand before she accepted the cup of tea.

"It's hot," I warned.

Her lip curled in acknowledgement.

"Sweet," I prodded.

"Drugged?"

The sarcasm she summoned choked the laugh in my throat. I reached for her tea, drank deeply, then handed it back. "Proof enough for you?"

"Yes." Her lips pressed the cup where mine had been. I wondered if she knew and did it deliberately, with defiance, or if it had been instinct.

"Tell me what that was, Grayson. Pouring from the ground, through the air."

"I'm not sure." I took a moment to settle in the sand, on the opposite side of the fire, allowing us both the distance. "They smelled of corrupted power."

"The ancient wars with kings and queens—they fought creatures like that?"

"Probably similar," I admitted. *Probably worse.*

"What were those... splits that opened up?" She cradled the cup, but her fingers trembled and her elbows pressed in. "Were they passages?"

"I've never seen one open like flesh being cleaved by a knife."

She shuddered. "Why did I sense it and you didn't?"

"There's only one way—someone keyed the passage to your energy and not mine."

"That isn't possible."

"You are a *faille*. None of us knows what's impossible."

Her inhale dragged like she was drowning. She set aside the tea, then dug stiff fingers into the sand. Fear leaked from her like gray tendrils, and even while I refused to name what it was, I reached through a mental connection we shouldn't have and brushed across obsidian... blacker than night yet filled with stars.

For wolves, obsidian was a sacred stone. Born in fire, the swirling liquid turned into solid waves—opposites in the same element, echoing the twin souls of man and wolf.

Except that Noa had no wolf, and what I felt instead of a wolf, what I could not explain, was what Levi had described. The pull of light as it fell into the void.

I sipped tea that was no longer hot, while Noa clawed her fingers through the sand.

"The ancient queens could draw the evil to them," she said, making swirls that reminded me of runes. "Manipulate the magic."

"Perhaps that's what happened today. Somehow, you manipulated the magic."

"You're saying I invited monsters into the world?"

The sand drifting from her splayed fingers formed little mounds, hour glasses measuring her thoughts. I leaned forward to adjust the pot of bubbling tea.

"I'm saying that today could have been a test. From someone else, not me. Someone using magic to see how—or if—you reacted to that passage opening."

"Why?"

"To see how early a *faille* could detect the danger. And if she'd warn the wolf or stay silent."

"Who would do that?"

"I don't know. But from the first day, Noa, when the King of the Forest yanked you through the barrier, he's been protecting you. He's never done that before, which is why we're visiting the nymphs tomorrow, despite what happened today."

Her fingers clenched. "So you did lie about my mother and the sacred pool."

"It wasn't a lie." I stopped my canines from punching down. "Call it withholding judgment."

She arched an eyebrow. "Until *after* the nymphs ripped me apart?"

I guessed she was thinking about Mace, waiting to see what the river nymph did before he intervened. "I wouldn't let them rip you apart, Noa. You're too valuable."

"But you knew the nymphs hadn't protected my mother because she was both wet *and* bloody when Fallon found her."

I was proud of her for figuring it out when Fallon hadn't. "What did that mean to you?"

"That my mother wasn't wolf enough to be protected by the nymphs. And the warning she gave Fallon, that only someone like her could retrieve the book, guaranteed it would never be found. Because any *faille* would be ripped apart, and no female wolf would try."

"Why did she do that, Noa?"

Her hand trembled in the sand. "You tell me."

"After your stepfather buried the book, your mother recognized the danger. She couldn't keep it with her, and hiding was her only option because she couldn't destroy it."

Bitterness sharpened the forest colors in Noa's eyes. She rose to her feet, arms tight, and wrapped around her waist. "Why couldn't she destroy it?"

"Because blood magic protects ancient books, Noa." I let my canines punch down. "Books that hold secrets. The kind of secrets your mother tried so desperately to hide from you. Especially from you."

CHAPTER 26

Noa

NAUSEA KNOTTED IN MY stomach. My mother had been many things, but I'd never thought she'd hide a book with nymphs who would attack me if I tried to retrieve it. I couldn't stop pacing. Stop the urge to flee—but the horrors outside kept me from leaving. Grayson remained where he was, sprawled on the sand, silent and frowning. He'd known all along what my mother meant, and I wasn't sure how I felt about him keeping that secret. He was always testing me... no, not testing. Asking me to work through each challenge on my own.

He wore jeans, nothing else, and if he kept clothes here, this cave belonged to him. A place where he felt comfortable.

The muted glow from the mushroomed wall chased the shadows. Firelight illuminated his skin, highlighting the scars on his chest and abdomen. I saw what remained of a gouging slash along his ribcage. From the look of it, he'd had the scar a long time, and I couldn't—wouldn't fathom what kind of creature had done that to him.

During the fighting, I'd been more terrified for the wolf than for myself. Years ago, I'd hated the pointless carnage, seeing it from one side—my side—but Grayson fought for dominance, not for glory. He took the fight to the enemy from a desire to end the bloodletting, not prolong the death and destruction.

Now I searched for the wound his wolf received during the fighting. One of the tusked creatures had sliced through the wolf's pelt. When I saw it happen, a scream had strangled my throat. I'd been afraid to let it out, distract him. Maybe because it sounded like a sob.

The jagged red line on Grayson's forearm looked raw enough to be new, and I asked, "Is that from today?"

"Yes."

"How quickly do you heal?"

He stretched his shoulders as if the muscles were tight. "Quickly."

I sat down, dug deep into the sand, and watched the fine grains sift through my fingers. "They would be fools."

His mouth tightened. "Who?"

"The ones who challenged you. When I watched what you did..." I met his strange blue-green gaze. "I understood what power meant."

A mocking smile slipped across his lips. "That wasn't power, Noa."

But the mushrooms on the wall pulsed as if they agreed with me.

"Whatever it was, can you teach me? I want to learn the composure you have, so I don't panic the next time."

Grayson's eyebrow arched. "You were focused today."

"Out of fear," I admitted. Even after training with Fallon, my focus had been mindless. I'd forgotten about breathing and balance, flailing away... while the wolf never faltered, never wasted a second's worth of energy on doubt.

Instead, he'd moved in a deadly dance. I'd been the opposite, stumbling, shaking, loosing arrows without even sighting the targets... driven by a terrified hope that enough arrows flying could somehow keep those creatures at bay.

I stared at the flames between us. Dread pulled at me, thinking I'd somehow called those monsters into being. "I must seem ignorant to you."

"No one taught you as a child, and when you left, you didn't want to know."

"I think we're past what I didn't want to know."

Grayson reached for the glazed pot and added more steaming tea to his cup.

"When the Green Man created passages, he made thousands of them. I doubt even he knows how many. The only way we know about them is because the magic responds to specific energies, and if it's not our energy, we're blind to what might be there."

He leaned toward the cup I'd left in the sand, pouring more spicy tea.

"We've never had a passage open up like the one did today. As if someone figured out how to weaponize the magic, use it with passages. And I need to understand how that happened."

"You think is has something to do with me."

"I won't let harm come to the pack, Noa."

One black claw had punched through his knuckle.

I stared at it and said, "I'll leave before that happens."

"You can't leave."

"I *killed* things today. Listened to their dying gasps and realized I was becoming like..."

Like him. This alpha sitting across from me.

Hadn't I'd screamed at his wolf after he'd killed the rabbit? How I thanked the gods I wasn't like him?

Grayson was unmoved. "The Green Man made his choice."

I wiped two fingers over my eyes. "I didn't ask him for anything."

"Neither did I."

I wondered what he meant. The depths this man kept secret worried me because I hadn't noticed the different levels before, how he would drift into his thoughts, focused on what I'd never see.

I understood solitude. The intense version was isolation, without what I considered a human touch. Perhaps I'd forgotten how close to human werewolves were, emotionally.

"When the old alpha died," I murmured. "Did you want to become alpha?"

Grayson refreshed his tea, his attention on the steam swirling upward. "The magic chooses the wolf. The man has nothing to say about it."

Then no, not his choice, but I could see Grayson accepting the responsibility. He gave no excuses, accepted none from those under his command. He killed without mercy. Healed with skill. He had no one in his life, other than the two friends he'd had since childhood. Perhaps Laura and Levi were on that list. Hattie and Oscar. Leo.

I held the tea so steam concealed my expression. Grayson Devante would never walk away from his commitment or his honor. He would protect his people until he was dead.

He was the wolf in the watchtower.

And what was I?

Protected by the King of the Forest, but flawed enough for friends and enemies alike to test me.

Was I drawn toward something horrible? Or was it drawn to my energy? Perhaps that terror already lived inside of me. Perhaps it was the magnet...

I leaned forward, breathing through my mouth. My heart thundered until I was dizzy, nauseous, thinking of the wildlife photos covering the Azul house walls. How naïve I'd been when I'd taken them.

I'd believed I was in control, at peace, unaware of the spiderwebs waiting to ensnare me... but I was caught now. The stickiness crept across my skin, and I felt the tugging from a stealthy spider I couldn't even see.

Hot tea splashed on my fingers. I gritted my teeth and asked, "Why do you have the wolf tattooed on your skin?"

Grayson's voice was neutral. "It's the Alpha designation. The tattoo appeared when both the wolf and I accepted the obligation, and it will remain until that changes."

He was telling me what I already knew. Alphas had one way out, death through challenge or battle. Beyond that thread of knowledge, I was the outsider with no understanding of werewolf traditions—*my* traditions—and maybe I was tired of being an observer, defending myself out of desperation.

Maybe I no longer accepted living in a world I refused to understand. A world that swallowed me whole.

More than once, I relived that night when I trespassed like an ignorant thief, daring to touch his wolf because it should have been an illusion. Maybe I resented the part of me I'd left behind, the connection that Grayson now used, because I would never get that part back.

I'd known, when I felt the tug on my chest weeks ago, that he'd set the hook deep. But if that hook tethered me to him, then it also tethered him to me, and he didn't like it. The night he found me in the nightmare and pulled me from that darkness, I thought his anger came from the questions I refused to answer. Over and over, each time he asked, *why are you here?*

I wondered now if he'd been asking for his own sake.

If we were the same.

Both of us, caught in the web spun by the Green Man's magic.

The mushrooms pulsed, picking up on my frustrations. "The tattoo on your shoulder," I said. "The pack mark... runes on trees and the stones... they all hold magic, don't they?"

"Most tattoos hold magic," he agreed. "The runes always do."

"How does the magic get there?"

"The King of the Forest puts it there."

I shifted my position in the sand, staring upward. Shadows huddled near the ceiling, in the corners, creeping closer, as if they sought the warmth from the fire... or wanted to listen.

My clothes felt tight. Specks of blood and what I didn't want to identify were still on my shirt.

I looked at Grayson. "You said he was protecting me."

"Yes, but he doesn't do it for free. With all magic, there's a bargain involved."

"Like with the nymph—when she tossed back my boots."

Grayson nodded. We each stared at the flames, but were likely lost in the same thoughts.

I drew a pattern in the sand, moistened my lips. "What bargain could I have with the King of the Forest? I didn't even know he existed before he pulled me through the barrier."

A muscle feathered in Grayson's jaw. "Perhaps it's an expectation for something in the future."

"Because I'm a *faille*?"

"You'd have to ask him."

I leaned toward the fire. "If I asked you to paint runes on my skin—would they have enough magic to protect me from the nymphs in the sacred pool?"

An alpha stillness settled as Grayson tipped his head. I wondered if he'd ever considered painting runes on human skin. Then his eyes narrowed, and he said, "I can design protective runes, but the magic isn't in paint."

I held his strange green-blue gaze. "What would you use?"

"Ink."

Permanent. A tattoo embedding the magic into my skin.

I thought of the book my mother didn't want me to find.

Then the chill I'd felt in the meadow, watching the air rip apart.

The old stories of kings and queens, alphas and *failles*, destroying each other.

Fated to be enemies.

When the fire popped and tiny sparks flew, it was hard not to flinch.

"What kind of ink?" I asked.

"Ink from the mushrooms in this cave. Iridescent, visible in the dark and deep shadow. The pattern would start on your back, along your spine. Over your shoulder. Down your arm. The curve of your left breast."

My chin lifted. "Can you do it now?"

Shadows swirled around Grayson. "Tell me why."

I dug my fingers deeper into the sand. "Because I have to face the nymphs, and I want those runes on my skin."

"Why?" he asked again, and the thoughts flowed through my mind, words I would never say. *Because I want the runes as my* Faille *mark—like your Alpha mark. Because the dark inside me might rise and I'm frightened. Because I need a way back to you.*

Grayson said, "I'll do it now."

I breathed in and felt an inner stirring, as if the dark inside me heard those thoughts. And his answer.

My pulse quickened. "Will it take long?"

"It won't take long, but the magic requires a ritual."

The hair on my arms lifted.

"What kind of ritual?"

"A promise. An acceptance. Magic isn't free. There's always a cost to using it, and once it's done, Noa. It can't be undone."

I looked into Grayson's eyes and thought I was staring into lightning, while the dark inside me shuddered and grew quiet.

"I trust you," I said.

He rose to his feet and strode to another niche in the wall. I unlaced my hiking boots, curled bare toes into the gritty sand, savoring the rough texture against my feet. When I slid the soiled shirt from my body, the magic whipped it away. The same magic left my hair clean and my skin dampened as if I'd stepped from a shower. When a fresh shirt appeared on the sand, I reached for it.

"Leave your shirt off," Grayson said with his back still turned. "And the bra. Wrap yourself in the blanket. It will be easier for you."

Beside me, folded neatly on the sand, a white blanket fluttered into being. This was Grayson's magic, or cave magic... or even the Green Man's magic... and I didn't want to ask. But I appreciated the gesture.

I folded a cashmere softness around my shoulders and buried my nose in the scent—his scent, permeating every nook and cranny in this cave.

"You come here often, don't you?" I asked, watching the muscles flex across his back, noting the inked wolf's tail, which I half expected to flick in approval.

The black tattoo didn't move.

Disappointment skimmed across my skin.

"Not often," he said. "It's one of my private places. No one else knows about it."

Now I knew, and I regretted taking that solitude from him. "I'm sorry."

"For what?" He sounded genuinely confused.

"For stealing sanctuary."

"You stole nothing. I wanted you here."

Grayson's approach was quiet, but in the firelight, half dressed as he was, his masculinity left an imprint. More than visual. I had to prepare for his hands on my skin. For the power that left me feeling tender and raw. Night-dark hair fell across his forehead. Once again, his scent reminded me of all things primitive and dangerous.

I bent my head, turned away to hide my expression. One look, and Grayson would know how he affected me. The alpha who slaughtered those creatures in the woods as if he did it every day.

"I'll need to sit behind you," he said, his bare feet halting close to my thighs. "Turn away from the fire."

I scooted around.

He settled with his legs pressing against my hips. The blanket loosened from my shoulders and draped, exposing my back to him. I didn't do it. I didn't feel him do it—perhaps the blanket was like the cave, responding to him.

"I'll numb your skin."

"No, I'd rather feel it."

"Let me know if it becomes too much," he murmured. "You'll feel pain when the magic bonds."

My fingers folded into the blanket's edge. "Will I glow in the dark?"

"Like a thousand stars before the dawn."

Grayson's breathing was steady. He shifted my braid to the side. I stilled, waiting while he arranged the bowl; ink shimmered with swirling opals. The metallic scent filled my lungs. I felt his hand against my nape—and the light from the mushrooms pulsed as if they followed a drum beat I couldn't hear.

Perhaps it was an invitation to war. Or a ritual older than time. But when Grayson traced two fingers down the length of my spine, my body went loose at the sheer eroticism in that stroke.

When his fingers slid upward, my lungs expanded, then emptied until a drift of air remained.

With the next downward stroke, my eyes closed while every sensation felt the way sunlight felt on the Green Man's side of the magic... heightened. Pure.

Image after image drifted through my mind... the sparkle of light on dew-covered grass. An arrow, arching through the air. The spaces between trees... the branches... until I saw the faint threads of leaf veins.

On Grayson's third downward stroke, the images shifted, and I saw him as the storm beyond the horizon, approaching with terror and exhilaration, while I waited on the shore with arms wide.

Our connection seemed vital. As if he would remake me.

But this was *magic*.

Ritual.

The luminescent mushrooms pulsed, gaining strength and speed; each concussion pounded through my veins. Grayson traced the curve of my shoulder, down my arm, pushing aside the blanket until it fell to my waist.

In the cool air, my breasts tightened. My nipples pebbled. I heard his indrawn breath. We were both half-naked, and that similarity crackled with tension when he touched my forefinger. Then he dragged a stroke over my wrist, inside my elbow, never pausing, never altering the pressure as he traced over my shoulder, then down across the slope of my breast before ending where my heart hammered.

My eyelids fluttered. My shoulders pressed back, and the sensations changed until I felt like melting sin, like someone I didn't know, supple, strong, beautiful.

As if I was his lover. His consort.

I wondered if this was the magic, sinking into me.

Or the ritual. The promise and acceptance.

But the sensuality of wolves overwhelmed me, and by the time his hand returned to my back, I was bent over, fighting the arousal. The space between my thighs was slick. An aching throb pulsed, then pulsed again.

My scent rose in the air. Dismay was a small whimper in my throat.

"It's natural," Grayson murmured. "Beautiful. Never be ashamed of your scent, Noa."

I felt drunk on his words. He pulled the bowl closer, tapped a slender bone needle against the bottom as he dipped into the pearlized ink, then shifted his body to the side.

"I'll begin here." He touched the rounded tip of my shoulder. "Where your pack mark belongs. You'll feel a sting."

I shivered, not from cold or fear, but from acceptance, formalized.

The first prick felt feather-light. Then I felt a tugging, the way his tether had tugged. I gasped.

His thumb pressed against my skin. "Don't be afraid of it."

"I'm not afraid of the pain."

"I meant the magic," he said. "How it claims you."

I turned enough to look at him, while the sand beneath me seemed to shift. "Do I have to call you Alpha now?"

"You may call me an ass if you prefer." His smile sharpened. He inked the next rune, and it felt like silk being drawn over my skin.

"Have you numbed me?"

The sting returned, but it was his roughened touch, drifting with a lover's caress, that had my scent rising again, mixing with his, becoming more potent than I ever imagined. My fingers curled.

The breath hissed from between his lips. "Happy, now?"

His voice had lowered to a rough growl, and I understood when his canines brushed against my shoulder, the curve of my neck. An aroused werewolf wanted the feel of teeth against skin, and his deep inhale shuddered through me before he pulled away.

"The numbing isn't only for you."

I peeked at him. "You tattoo females often?"

"No." His fingers moved to my left breast, and the touch was so intimate it permeated every part of my body.

It took immense effort to change the conversation.

"Have you ever encountered creatures like the ones we killed?"

"Similar. Not like what we fought today, but... unexplained." He dipped the bone needle into the ink, then refocused on my breast. "Creatures like that killed my parents."

I gripped the blanket. "You were young?"

"Too young to help my mother."

He finished with the small rune, moving to my collarbone.

"She pushed me into the house, told me to hide. But I grabbed a stick and watched through the window. She was screaming."

The bone needle tapped against the bowl, a brutal sound. "She'd locked the door to protect me. My father ran toward her and shadows ripped him apart. When the alpha came, I told him I'd seen shadow dogs."

His voice hardened at a memory I didn't think he liked sharing.

"Years later, when the Alpen attacked, survivors talked about shadows, and we thought the Alpen manipulated the magic. Mace sent spies into their settlements, but we could never find proof."

I glanced at him over my shoulder. "Manipulating magic seems too sophisticated for a backward pack like Alpen."

"Not if they've recruited a witch." His attention was on my back as he inked more runes. "The tree nymph talked about monsters without substance. But we found five-toed tracks in the mud. And what you saw today—it's possible the witch found a way to manipulate the passage magic. Force spelled creatures through to attack you."

Remembering the human-like eyes staring at me, I wondered if I could ever forget, or atone for killing beings no different from what I was, unwilling pawns caught up in magic. But perhaps I'd used all the grace I deserved when I made amends with my grandfather, and guilt was all I should expect.

"Mace has a team with him," Grayson said. "Scouring the area for remains. Maybe Leo can identify what we're up against."

"I didn't think much was left." Not after the cannibalism.

"I'd rather no evidence was left behind," he said.

For others to discover. To wonder about, Noa.

I turned my head, watching Grayson ink the final runes on my arm, and as the pattern emerged, I sensed something ancient and immortal creep into the cave. The air changed, snapping with static electricity. Light from the mushrooms became jerky. The fire flared on a fretful breeze.

Unease fell like a single, frigid raindrop on my shoulder.

Grayson seemed oblivious to the changes, and a fleeting alarm made me dizzy.

Was this like the meadow, when I sensed what he could not?

Monsters coming through?

I didn't think so... because dark descended, not spangled light, and I knew where I was, deep in the wolf-shaped void in my mind, standing beneath a sky shimmering with a thousand stars, above a black abyss where the *thing* lived...

I knew because I felt it... sentient, clawing upward.

Heard it.

See me see me see me!

My lips stung with a spreading frost. Dread stiffened my muscles, and when Grayson dipped the bone needle into the ink, pierced my skin for the last rune, what I *felt* forced my back to bend until I was arched like the warrior's bow, ready to break beneath Grayson's strength.

I heard my bones crack.

A woman screamed.

Nausea hit, while beneath my feet, an edge crumbled, and while I knew I was not physically falling into the abyss, I also knew it was the alpha's grip that kept me tethered.

If he let go... if he did not finish this... I would be lost, and my fingernails cut into his skin.

"Hurry," I begged.

Grayson's face was stone. The last mark was incomplete, and I knew why he hesitated.

The runes on my body held the promise.

Finishing the last mark was the acceptance.

But... what if it was more?

No time no time no time.

Seconds remained—a fleeting heartbeat—before the magic would be sanctified, or withdrawn, and I would fall.

The dark inside me pulsed, and I knew I could not stop. Could not give in to the rising fear. To the woman's scream.

With my lips barely moving, I ordered him... *ordered* the Alpha of Sentinel Falls.

"Do it."

His eyes glittered.

"Do what, Noa?"

"Finish the last rune. Now."

CHAPTER 27

Noa

I SLEPT, BUT IT wasn't peaceful. Maybe it was the wolf energy that kept me on edge. Maybe it was the magic.

Or maybe it was the enormity of what I'd done.

I pushed upright. Tangled hair swept across my face and I left it that way, afraid to see Grayson's expression. Afraid of the last rune he'd inked on my skin.

The designs flowing along my back, shoulder, and down my arm felt cool. Even the small mark on my breast.

But the rune on my wrist burned with a heat that reduced me to ashes.

Grayson sat beside the fire, still wearing jeans and skin and nothing else. I felt like the interloper. Everything in this cave belonged to him, responded to him, and when his eyes narrowed, I knew he was looking for weakness.

The tee shirt I wore was one the cave provided. I'd pulled it on after he finished the last rune, my fingers trembling so hard I'd barely gotten it over my head. Then I'd curled down on the blanket, exhausted and avoiding the questions that thrummed like my heart.

The silence between us had grown awkward, and even the *faille* void inside me was quiet. My gaze skittered around. The blue glow from the mushrooms reminded me of a child's nightlight to keep the monsters away.

But what if monsters don't care about nightlights, Noa?

"Why is it so dark in here?"

"Magic requires the dark to settle," he said. "You needed the rest."

"How long was I asleep?"

"Two hours. We have time before we leave." Grayson rocked forward to pour steaming tea into a cup that he held out. "Drink this."

"I don't want your tea."

He waited a long beat, then set the tea aside. "What do you want, Noa?"

His tone made me nervous; I dug my fingers into the sand. "Tell me what you did with the last rune."

"What you asked me to do."

So calm, that answer. I sucked in a difficult breath, glaring at the wolf tattoo he'd inked on my wrist. It wasn't white or iridescent, but fierce and black, and I rubbed hard at the wicked little twitch that felt... wrong. "It doesn't look like the Green Man's runes."

"Because it isn't his rune. It's mine."

"You couldn't do his runes without adding yours?"

"Apparently not." His canines flashed—a brief warning, before he said, "Poor little Noa, thinking it would be easy. When easy isn't what you got. I warned you magic wasn't free. There's always a cost. You should have asked what it was before you ordered me to finish it."

My skin dewed. "I'm asking now."

"Our bargain, embedded in your skin."

Permanent. His promise of protection, in exchange for my cooperation with no question about half in, half out, when his mark was inked for all to see. I couldn't even blame him because he'd hesitated.

I'd been the one who begged.

He asked what I wanted him to do, and I let fear drive me. Ignorance. When everything I felt—the changing air, the snap against my skin. The thing rising in the darkness. The woman's scream. What if I'd been experiencing a *faille's* natural resistance to wolf magic? Nothing more?

I would have known the answer if I'd asked instead of trusting him, when what I should have remembered was how the Alpha of Sentinel Falls did not allow excuses. Not for himself and not from others. He saw his world in black and white, in decisions and actions and doing what was necessary.

I hated that word. *Necessary*.

Hated the black rune on my wrist that ensured I'd be his weapon, available at his command. I rubbed hard, as if I could erase the mark, forget the carnal ache I felt when he put it there.

"Break our bargain," I hissed. "I know there has to be a way."

"There's a way," he agreed. "But why would I want it broken? You were so wet, Noa. Panting so sweetly each time the ink penetrated your skin." He leaned forward to readjust the pot of steaming tea. "You asked me to finish it. *Ordered* me."

I lifted my head, my lips tight. "I don't want this."

"Your scent makes you a liar."

The smugness was more than I could take. "Is this because you think I'll leave? Some... leash to keep me here?"

"I told you I'd use you. Don't look so surprised."

I held out my wrist where the black rune was raw and stark compared to the other runes. "You also told me you wouldn't force me."

"I didn't. You asked."

"Take it back."

"Too late."

Firelight honed his face. His mouth thinned, and each breath I took jerked inward. Hadn't I wondered how far he'd go to get what he wanted? Now I knew. He'd go as far as he had to, and my tone turned bitter. "Does this mean I have a damn pack bond in my head?"

"Pack communication connects through the wolf you don't have."

"At least I won't hear you yelling."

His smile turned sarcastic. "How unfortunate, when I hear *you*."

My heart froze. "You can hear...?"

"For weeks now," he snarled. "I've had to listen to you rage because you never learned how to shield your thoughts."

I bared my teeth at him—a woeful attempt to intimidate, but having him listen in on my private thoughts was abhorrent.

He knows what you fear, Noa... what you desire...

My hands curled into fists while heat spread from the wolf rune up the length of my arm. "Tell me how to slam that door shut, and I'll do it now."

"I'll have Fallon teach you." Grayson poured more tea for himself before he said, "She's perfected the art of shutting me out when she's angry."

"I see her point. You're a bastard who can't let go even when you're wrong."

"While you're terrified of the dark inside you," he cut back with the same sharp edge. "You wanted my mark. Begged for it. Needing me to come into that dark abyss and save you."

I shuddered. The fact he even *knew* that was terrifying, and I reached for the most vicious thing I could say. "You let your wolf run for two months because you thought he was feral. Maybe you both are."

An icy breeze swept through the cave. Grayson's face was bleak when he said, "I did you a favor by marking your skin."

"You'll forgive me if I'm not grateful."

The fire guttered. I glared at the cup of tea he'd left within reach, then poured it on the fire, hoping to snuff out the flames. They continued to incinerate the charcoaled wood until Grayson tossed his tea. The flames died and my heart hammered in my throat.

"You have five minutes before we leave." He rose to his feet. "Fix your hair."

I'd never heard him sound so adamant and cold. I wouldn't bend, or offer an apology—not that he'd care since his attention had already moved on.

Far from me.

I would do the same.

Fighting with Grayson was pointless when he could hear my thoughts, so I marched behind him and thought about the word *bastard*.

It had a nice cadence, and I thought it more than once.

Grayson prowled ahead as if he wasn't listening. Maybe he could turn it off, and lied about it—the listening.

It wouldn't be the first lie. He was stubborn. Conniving. Telling me things with innuendo that I could interpret any way I wanted... wasn't that the same as lying? I wanted to believe it was lying because then I wouldn't feel bad about my secrets. Then I hummed to myself to keep from leaking those secrets by thinking about them.

We marched in single file along a path that wove through tall pines. Sunlight slashed, and although I flinched, it was only sunlight. Insects droned; the air warmed. The monotony of staring at the alpha's back made my eyes blur. He wore black because the cave apparently loved him, while it didn't feel the same about me, since I still wore the wrinkled tee shirt I'd slept in. At least my jeans were clean, and my boots... and thinking about boots led to putting one foot in front of the other, which led to all the relationships I'd ever had.

One relationship, sad compared to the other girls I knew in college. I'd kept it casual. A boy in my photography class who was shy, awkward... safe. We kept our heated moments to motel rooms because he had plans for his future. I pretended I did too, and we went in knowing it was sex and nothing more.

Last year, a new girlfriend took my place, and when he told me about her, I wasn't angry. I wanted him happy and working on his plan, while mine... I could be halfway there if I overlooked all the strikes against me.

"Did you enjoy having that boy inside you?" Grayson waited by a downed log. He'd crossed his arms, and I halted in the middle of the path.

"Listening in again?" I asked, bitter because I'd forgotten about the listening thing.

"Tell me if I have to kill him."

My heart beat once, twice, before I wondered about my motives. If they'd been less than pure, thinking about motel rooms and sex for revenge. If he could turn off listening, but hadn't.

He was the Alpha of Sentinel Falls. He ought to have that power when thousands of pack members could be screaming at him.

But what did I know about wolves?

Nothing, Noa.

I couldn't even tell if he was serious when he talked about killing. Then I wondered if the heat I felt in the wolf rune matched the heat I saw in his eyes. After a moment, he said, "If you don't like my darker side, then don't flaunt your men in my face."

The tightness in his arms worried me, and the thought flashed… the cost of magic. He'd hesitated at the last moment. Was that because I wasn't the only one paying the price? Was he paying a price, too?

I pinched the rock-hard muscle at his waist as I walked past. "Poor little alpha, thinking it would be easy."

"Such threats, coming from a voyeur."

"In your dreams." I stalked ahead of him, stomping on the memory of his naked body in the firelight. A body that—in no way—resembled the thin, fumbling *boy* in the motel room.

Branches crunched beneath my feet. I didn't know where we were going, only that Grayson kept pace, dragging his finger down my spine to get my attention.

"This way." He tipped his head close. "And keep thinking about bastards if you don't want me thinking about sex."

"Bastard." The word blurted out.

"Better." Something dark and sensual shot through his gaze before he tamped it down, adding, "I don't share my sexual partners, so consider yourself warned."

With that, I gave up on the war of words. I would never win with an alpha who thrived on challenges, even if his willingness to flirt slammed into me. I didn't expect it from him, any more than I'd expected our mutual arousal when he'd inked runes on my skin. But *sex* wasn't a place I dared go with him.

I focused on the path because I could hear the thunder of the waterfall, and that meant we were closer to the nymphs. Moments later, I stood with my hand pressed to my throat. The flow poured over the rim of a towering promontory, falling into a terraced upper pool before plunging over a second rim with a force strong enough to create its own breeze.

Around me, needled tree branches swayed. A rainbow glittered in the rising mist. At the base of the falls, I saw a moss-covered log with a single white flower sprouting upward, hopeful, growing inches from the water that churned with fizzy, flamboyant foam.

The foam turned into a wide stream, feeding the sacred pool, tree-lined and ordinary, but with a width that made Mace's challenge to Fallon impressive.

And there—below normal hearing—the vibrating hum of magic. My fingers curled around nothing because I had no bow, no arrows. Grayson said the weapons would anger the nymphs, and he'd flashed his arrogant canines when he'd said it.

I'd thought he was more afraid of an arrow in his back.

"So, now what?" Surrounding the sacred pool was pure wilderness. Pristine, extending for miles. Gorgeous enough to linger. Not that I trusted beauty these days, or silence.

"Now we wait," Grayson said.

"How long?"

"As long as it takes."

"Maybe we should throw a rock or something to get their attention."

He stared at the water. "They know we're here."

"How do you know they know?" I pretended my back ached, twisting to one side. Then the other. "Do they own the sacred pool, or do they need your permission, since this is pack land?"

"They own the pool, but without my permission, the water might not flow."

"No one has that kind of power."

Grayson shrugged, as if it wasn't worth the argument. I wondered if it was, but then he motioned me forward, and I wasn't sure if I was ready for the nymphs.

"Sit down," he said. "This could take time."

"I have nothing but time now."

He sighed... still so easy to annoy.

"Noa."

I held his stare, feeling a little wicked. Like his rune when it twitched. But the rocks looked comfortable enough with the layer of thick moss. I picked one, perched on the edge and studied the waterfall. Then the sacred pool. No matter how I tried, I couldn't picture my mother having the strength to hike here, let alone go in the water. No secret could be so precious, unless she'd been driven by desperation, or by delusion.

A distant memory clouded my eyes. My mom, digging up the backyard, wearing a nightgown with her hair flying. She'd always seemed... helpless. What if that was pretense, and she knew more about *failles* than the horror stories she told me?

Grayson pulled something from his waistband. He cradled it in his hand, but it wasn't a rock he pitched high over the water.

The item was long, narrow, and metallic enough to glint in the sunlight. Then it sank beneath the azure water without a ripple.

We waited. I picked at my fingernails. Stared at the moss, at the pine needles matted beneath the trees, and the tiny butterflies that flitted in the warming air.

When a jay screeched at us for trespassing, I searched the tree branches to see where he hid.

A dragonfly flitted by and I stared at the translucent wings.

I sighed. Shifted my weight, then thought about my favorite rhyme—in case Grayson was listening.

Maybe *liar... liar...*

He growled. "Patience is a virtue."

"This is me, being patient." I kicked at the pine needles. "I'm sure things thrown into bottomless pools take a long time falling."

His shoulders rose as if I amused him. "Believe me, they found it before it went far."

"Maybe *they* aren't interested, since no one has responded."

"They're interested."

I heard the smirk in his tone and knew nymphs expected bargains. He'd made an offer, and we were waiting for the acceptance.

I was also bored and gave in to curiosity. "What did you throw?"

"The scabbard for a ceremonial blade. Something their High Priestess wants. She'll need time to get here."

"Doesn't she live in the pool?"

"She's the Lady of the Lake. The spiritual queen for all water-based nymphs—even the mist and cloud sprites worship her. She holds a hereditary title that traces back to the ancient ocean gods. Her palaces are scattered around the world, so she'll be using the passageways."

"I thought the Lady of the Lake was an Arthurian tale. Part of Camelot."

Grayson snorted. "Metis is quite real, and she won't appreciate the comparison to the Welsh lake faeries. She's an oceanid."

A chill crept across my skin, furtive and halting before it disappeared, and I said, "Maybe we don't need the book."

"Too late."

His favorite words.

I stared at the center of the pool, where a ripple moved outward. Then more ripples, bubbles frothing to the surface. The agitated water turned every shade between green and blue, and—rising out of the chaos—the tip of a spear. Followed by a second, as two females rose from the depths.

Each wore a gold helmet with winged cheek-plates, the metal etched with strange sea creatures. White chitons hit mid-thigh. Laced sandals protected their feet and legs. Across the chest, crisscrossed bandoliers carried an array of wicked knives, and all of it, the chitons, the weapons, the helmets—and the females—were dry.

They stood on a platform that rose until it floated on the water. The women resembled living statues, stunning and flawless, gripping the spears with webbed hands. But I could see their black, inhuman eyes, and worried over the pressure swelling in my ears.

"Her sentinels," Grayson murmured. "Be cautious with your movements."

An understatement. I wouldn't be moving anywhere near those women, and I thought hard about holding him to his promise of protection—in case he was eavesdropping in my mind again.

His head tipped as if his neck was stiff, and I supposed it was the derogatory little jab I'd tagged on at the end that annoyed him. And because I could, because it eased something in my chest, I jabbed at him again: *better than thinking about sex.*

He glared over his shoulder.

I bit my lip to avoid laughing and turned back to the sentinels. A mist coalesced behind them before disintegrating to reveal another female striding forward.

She was graceful, unhurried. A queen approaching her throne, looking neither left nor right as her arms brushed against her amethyst gown. A filigreed silver girdle hung low on her hips. Matching crystals studded the gown's hem; they dazzled like an ocean's spray, while the hem floated with the lightness of spume on the waves.

Her regal posture matched the silvery blonde of her hair, fashioned in an intricate knot crowning her head. There, a spiked coronet nestled. Faceted amethysts spat shards of light from each spike, but the encrusted diamonds radiated the icy glitter of star-shine, formed galaxies away. Traveling through the eons to grace a High Priestess who was as cold and more deadly than the stars.

The Lady of the Lake walked along a narrow causeway that proceeded her, halting several feet from where the water lapped against the verge of mud and grass. I wondered if she used magic. If she had a wall of protection in place.

I let my gaze drift over the features fit for a queen. The symmetry was perfect, and yet, her beauty hissed with pure heartlessness.

Silver bracelets clinked as she flicked her wrist, and in her hand, she held the ceremonial scabbard Grayson had thrown into the pool.

"Lady." Grayson held her black gaze.

"Wolf," she said with a slight nod, so the title was not an insult, but an honor. She held up the empty scabbard, crafted in bronze with gold runes etched into the surface. "You have my attention. I hope you aren't wasting my time."

"I am interested in a bargain between us," he said.

"A... *bargain*? You present me with an empty scabbard, then expect me to barter for the Blade of Nereus like it's *some bauble* at the fair?"

The dark of an ocean's depth was in her voice, but there was no unease in Grayson's tone when he said, "That is what I expect."

"Your arrogance is astounding, Wolf."

"As is yours, Lady."

The High Priestess drew her lips back. "What are your terms for this bargain?"

Grayson slid his hands into his pockets. "You have something I want. I have something you want. The High Feast of Galatea is within a month. Your lineage traces back to the sea god, Nereus. If you retrieved his blade in time for the ritual, you would become legendary."

The Lady of the Lake closed her fingers around the scabbard and I counted my breaths, waiting for the ancient metal to disintegrate beneath her grip. The Feast of Galatea would be a sacred rite for all water nymphs. Galatea turned her slain human lover into a river spirit. If Metis was descended from Nereus... I felt hollowed out, realizing the importance Grayson placed on my mother's book, if he'd trade the Blade of Nereus for it.

Metis asked, "What is it you wish in return?"

"A book was entrusted to this pool three years ago. We would like to retrieve it now."

"Why?" The question tolled like a death bell, and the wolf rune beneath my skin moved, stealthy and alert.

"It holds sentimental value."

The Lady of the Lake turned the scabbard until reflected light shot out in all directions. "You expect me to believe a sentimental *book* is worth our sacred artifact?"

Her tone was reptilian.

I took a tiny step back.

Grayson shrugged. "It belonged to Noa's deceased mother. She would like it returned."

"This... *faille*?" Metis narrowed her gaze as she looked at me. "We have heard of you."

"And I have heard of you," I said, thinking about the stories of King Arthur, which she didn't need to know.

Grayson choked.

Gods, Noa, stop thinking! She could hear your thoughts like he does.

But perhaps not. The Lady of the Lake dismissed me as if I was a crustacean beneath her shoe before looking back toward Grayson.

"The queens were destructive," she said. "That is why they became *failles*."

"They also aided the kings." The warning in Grayson's voice made me wonder if he was more of a threat than she was.

But—no! Wait a minute.

When did this become about queens and kings, and not about my mother's book? My pulse pattered with what I didn't know.

Grayson ignored my frantic thoughts and said, "She has the Green Man's favor."

"He's a doddering old fool," the High Priestess sneered. "A king without a throne or a kingdom."

"His power still reigns here, Metis. Enough to stop the water flowing into your sacred pool."

Grayson waved his hand. The river spilling over the cliff splashed and sputtered and then *diminished*, before resuming the flow.

My heart thundered.

Grayson said, "We are not enemies, Metis."

"Neither are we allies." She held up the scabbard. "Where did you get this?"

"The King of the Forest found both the blade and scabbard in a crevice in Greece—someone was careless."

Her nostrils flared. "How long has he had the artifacts?"

"Centuries. He had no reason to return them until now."

"Because of that... *girl*?"

"He seems fond of her. She wants the book, and—" Grayson sent a lazy glance toward the two sentinels who stood behind their High Priestess. "In exchange for that privilege, I'll return to you what he entrusted to me."

The pounding of the falls faded to an unearthly thrum. When I looked up, the flow of water had turned into a weakened stream.

I wasn't sure whose power was responsible. If Metis was descended from an ocean god, she could probably control water. But so could Grayson, if that wave of his hand meant anything, although I suspected he had the Green Man's help.

The way the Green Man helped me confront Stewart with illegal traps. And a bottle of beer, which I shared with Grayson, my arm around his hard waist while his draped around my shoulders.

But the talk of kings and queens had me frowning.

Grayson waited. The temperature dropped. Sharp frost pricked at my skin when the High Priestess turned her fathom-less gaze back to me.

"Do you know the story of Lycaon, girl?" she asked. "He held a feast in Zeus's honor, then tried to trick the god into eating human flesh. As punishment, Zeus turned Lycaon into a werewolf and cursed his descendants. I would tell you this because of what you are—beware the enemy who says he is your friend, then holds a blood feast in your honor."

"Your tales are entertaining, Metis," Grayson murmured. "But I would not test the wolf."

The simple, brutal warning meant the Alpha of Sentinel Falls was present and dangerous. Each sentinel placed a hand on their bandoliers and angled the spears forward.

Every sound scraped across my skin—the lapping of water against the shore. The distant cry of a bird. A worried breeze eddied around the amethyst gown, but Metis did not turn her gaze away from me.

I realized how nauseous I'd become.

Grayson stared at the Lady of the Lake before tipping his head to one side. "Water is vital to you, Metis. At least ask the Guardian of this pool what she knows."

After an instant, the surface of the pool quavered with inch-high waves, overlapping with increasing frequency until a female rose to the surface, her dark hair streaming against her pale skin. She reached the causeway, dripping water on the dry surface. Her gown was translucent blue, clinging to her thin body, her long-fingered hands reminding me of the river nymph.

The female halted a foot behind the sentinels. She waited, trembling until the High Priestess ordered her forward.

Her steps were hesitant. With hands clasped, she dropped to her knees.

"Lady." She bowed her head. "How may I be of service?"

"You are the Guardian of this pool?"

"Yes, Lady," the nymph whispered.

"You have heard the request. Was a book left here in your care?"

"A woman came three years ago. When I found her, she was near the upper falls, wet and bloodied. She claimed to have hidden a book, but we would have known if she'd entered the water. We thought she'd thrown it in, so to be safe, we searched both the sacred pool and the one above. Even the cave behind the upper falls. We found no book, Lady. She had no wolf—like this one." The nymph nodded toward me. "We thought she was half-mad, imagining things."

Dizziness hit. I wasn't breathing. If there was no book... but there had to be. My mother wouldn't have gone to such lengths, coming here behind Stewart's back, keeping Leo in the dark. Then telling Fallon—knowing Fallon would tell the alpha.

The surface of the pool was still churning, small wavelets dissolving as more nymphs appeared. They did not look friendly. The sentinels widened their stances, one foot in front of the other.

The Lady of the Lake stood like a statue while water bumped against the shore, but her oceanic gaze leveled on me while she spoke to Grayson.

"You claim a bargain. Taunt me with stolen property in a trade I cannot make. Why should I not put a blade to your *faille's* throat? Cut her until you give me what is mine?"

"Because you are neither foolish nor reckless," he said, still smiling with the cold confidence that had the trembling Guardian inching closer to the water.

The wind rose, thrashing through the fir branches closest to where we stood. Grayson breathed in, raised a lazy hand, and the rocks edging the waterfall rolled together, slowing the water's flow to thin ribbons.

A mourning wail rose from the nymphs.

My gaze swept toward the upper pool. I tried to imagine my mother there, on those slick rocks, clinging to the roots of trees for balance. A cave opening loomed. Stones moved, black and glinting in the sunlight, and my heart... stilled. The wild thoughts calmed.

I thought the words as hard as I could, hoping Grayson would hear what churned in my mind.

What if the book isn't in the pool but in a pocket in that cave? And my mom told Fallon only a faille *could find it as a message to me?*

There was no other *faille* except me, and a heartbeat passed before the wolf rune on my wrist warmed.

"A favor, Metis," Grayson drawled. "Allow us to search for the book."

The sentinels glanced at each other, then back at the High Priestess. Their fingers tightened on the knives in the bandoliers. My hands shook, but I glared at the oceanids. Their overblown aggression wasn't any different from the women in Sentinel Falls who bullied Oscar.

Or Stewart, when he bullied my mother.

Ice stiffened my spine, and my lips were tight when I said to Metis, "It isn't such a difficult request."

Her gaze centered on mine... and the ice in my spine became something endless, the glacial cold of a distant star, cracking through my bones.

Then the black rune on my wrist pulsed with a heat that spread from my hand up my arm and down my back.

The ice retreated, and the Lady of the Lake blinked her reptilian eyes.

"The request is indeed difficult," she said. "Males cannot enter the sacred pool, a lesson the wolf learned long ago."

"We're not going into the pool." Not my best decision to challenge her, because the High Priestess raked her gaze down my arm until she reached the black rune.

Her mouth tightened.

"You are more reckless than the Dread Lords," she sneered at Grayson. "If you have tied yourself to her with ink."

He waved his hand toward the waterfall—which kept up the trickle of water without interruption. "Allow us to search the cave, Metis. Regardless of what we find, I will return the Blade of Nereus to you."

"She will go into the cave alone."

"Agreed."

"Alone?" I gaped at him, my pulse beating.

The Lady of the Lake turned toward me, her lip curling. "It isn't such a difficult request. We'll await your findings."

And with a thunderous roar, the rocks exploded, allowing the waterfall to resume at full force, crashing down in a wave of churning, foaming water.

CHAPTER 28

Noa

GRAYSON LED THE WAY. He'd been too quick to agree with Metis, stalking off and expecting me to follow while the Lady of the Lake smirked. I didn't want to bitch at him about it. Not in front of her. But he treated me like his pet *faille* when the almighty Alpha of Sentinel Falls was powerless. His *alpha-ness* meant nothing to the nymphs. He wouldn't be allowed near their sacred pool. All he could do was haul me to the top of the cliff, and I'd have to find the way down by myself.

I stared at his back, silently calling him every name I knew.

His stride never altered.

But he absolutely knew what I was thinking because his rune twitched.

My palms grew sweaty. I needed to stop chewing on my lip; the raw spot was swelling. Loose pine needles made footing slippery, while I hopped from worry to worry. I didn't know what to expect with caves. If they were dark and wet. Maybe I shouldn't trust the nymphs. My mother didn't trust them. Did I even know there'd be a pocket in that cave? Couldn't that be my damn imagination again? Wolf energy mixing with nymphs?

I had no idea how to reach the cave, and even if I did, I was terrified. Grayson had to haul me through a steep gap in the rocks where the mist pooled, and I pressed back against the wet stone. "I don't like heights."

"Then don't look down."

My jaw locked hard enough to ache. "Forgive me for being too human, but sheer drops get my attention."

Grayson looked at me and scowled. "You've been fine on the deck." The one made of glass.

"There was a railing on the deck."

He offered no sympathy. "Trust Fallon's training. Doubt makes your body stiff. One misstep, and you're over the edge before you can react."

As if to prove his point, my foot slipped in a crevice. Grayson snatched my hand, his fingers tight. "Hold on until I tell you to let go."

"Is that an alpha order?" I didn't believe he offered the security for any other reason than expediency, but I held on to him—even after we were away from the edge and back between the rocks and trees, climbing upward. The sound of the water was still alarming. Not the kind of alarm that warns you to step back, but the kind that says you're already caught in the undertow and going over the edge. Crushed beneath tons of water thundering down on the rocks below.

"I'm sure Metis is enjoying this." Then the nerves stung at my nape, and I worried again. "Can she hear my thoughts?"

"No." Grayson blew out an exasperated breath. "But stop shouting them at me."

"Stop listening if you don't like what you hear."

I yanked my hand from his. He swung back, pressing his finger to his lips with a *shushing* gesture, and that amusement set me off. I pictured a vulgar gesture in my mind. His bi-colored eyes glittered in the sunlight. We were at a standoff.

Then a flash of movement caught my attention, and I spun to scan the trees. Nothing was there, and when I turned back, Grayson was twenty feet away—damn him. He couldn't even wait in case I'd sensed something he hadn't.

Metis said he was as bad as a Dread Lord, and while I wasn't sure what that meant, it was easy enough to guess by the name. I wouldn't complain, though. Metis was far more bloodthirsty than the children's books portrayed her. I was convinced that Grayson's black rune kept her from crushing me. Which made me feel ignorant again. What I didn't know about oceanids and nymphs and sacred pools could be dangerous.

Or caves. Shouldn't I know the layout of the cave if I was supposed to go there? How deep was it? Would I be able to see once I was inside?

When the water slowed to a trickle, I'd noticed the low, arched opening, and I worried about moving water, how close I'd be. Was there an overhanging rim? A space behind the water where I could shelter?

I sorted the questions the way Oscar sorted fishing lures—tap-tap-tapping through each one. If my mother made it to the cave, then I would, too. I'd push aside the doubt.

Remember Fallon's training. Think, she'd said. Breathe. Move.

I breathed. I moved. Catching up with Grayson's long stride left me panting, and the thought of asking him for answers made my skin itch. Going into the cave blind would be worse. I'd be vulnerable, so I asked, "What are the rules for this cave?"

"Caves don't have rules."

"Then the runes." I rubbed at the chills on my arm. "The runes must have rules."

He shrugged. "Do you feel anything?"

"They're cold."

"Maybe they think you're not grateful."

My throat compressed. How many times had I thought the word *bastard* while we were hiking? I'd rubbed at the wolf rune as if I could erase it, never imagining magic would debate my worthiness. Another thought raced. What if the cold was normal, and *the bastard* was using ignorance against me again? He said doubt made me stiff. But wasn't he creating doubt by telling me I wasn't grateful enough for the runes?

He did you a favor with that ink on your skin.

Grayson glanced back with a ghost of a smile.

I clamped my lips tight and began chanting, *liar... liar... pants on fire.* He could listen to *that*, if he was so nosey.

Grayson led the way until we were above the falls. The river flowed from the north, snaking through old growth pines before plunging over the promontory's rocky edge, and the view captivated. Looking past the waterfall and into the distance... toward the mountains and sheltering forests... my throat tightened.

I wanted to be part of this place.

I yearned for a sense of belonging. Except that belonging *here* meant giving up everything I believed in.

It could even cost me my life.

Below, the sacred pool glittered in the sunlight. I could see the Lady of the Lake, watching. Her sentinels were beside her, while hundreds of agitated nymphs stirred up the water. All of them, waiting for the bloody spectacle if I slipped.

A shudder passed through me. I'd never been at someone's mercy before. Leo had always protected me from the pack. My mother protected me from life until I needed to protect her from Stewart. Now, I was at the mercy of a book my mother hid.

A book Grayson and the King of the Forest wanted enough to summon the Lady of the Lake. Offer her a priceless artifact.

Either do it, Noa. Or run.

The only time I ran from fear was when I left Seattle. I'd come to Sentinel Falls for protection, and Grayson offered his. He saved me from worm poison. Reunited me with Leo. Inked magic runes on my skin when I asked.

I felt like I owed him for doing that—even when it irritated me. I owed him for fighting those creatures and leading me to safety, and I would do what my mother had done. Go into this cave alone and not bitch at him about it.

With my back stiff, I studied the waterfall's rim, searching for the way down to the pool—there, steps carved into the rock face, descending to a lower ledge. Random puddles of water shimmered in crevices and dips. A gap in the ledge reminded me of the rapids along the lake circuit, where water flowed and I'd had to cross a bridge with no railing.

There was no bridge across this gap, though. A single board spanned the distance, so rotted, it dipped in the middle.

"You could have warned me," I croaked, gripping my elbows. "I might be dead after this."

"I gave you my rune, Noa." Grayson lifted my braid and settled it behind my shoulder. "And your mother made it to the cave with nothing to protect her."

"About the cave... I could have been wrong about a pocket."

"I don't think you were wrong."

I chewed on my lip again. "Maybe you shouldn't trust me."

"It's not only me, Noa." His fingers brushed my shoulders, then slid down my arms to curl above my elbows. "Metis also thinks you're right. That's why she's allowing you to look through the cave. She knows what you are, but not what it means, and she doesn't like unknowns."

"So... I'm the experiment?"

He loosened my hands, laced his fingers through mine. "You're the *faille* who stood up to the Lady of the Lake."

I turned away from Grayson, from what he said, but I couldn't forget the trembling nymph dropping to her knees. The wailing in the sacred pool when the waterfall weakened.

I stared at the blue water that flowed like silk toward the cliff's edge.

Then it dropped into nothing—an infinity edge with a deadly appeal.

Desire gripped me, a need to creep forward. Inch my feet toward the slanting curve of rock, despite the vertigo. I saw it as a test of courage, to see if I was brave enough to peer over the precipice and slip into the dark.

Mist sparkled. Birds darted into the spume in a devil's dance above the raging tumult. I watched the rush of water, felt it pulling me along, and my heart thundered against the quick, chilling impulse to jump and join the birds.

"Who stopped the water?" I asked.

"I did."

The admission broke whatever thrall I'd been under. "Your effort didn't last long."

"Metis is an enemy we don't want. I left her pride intact."

The runes flitted beneath my skin. A fragile connection formed between us—the magic and I—and I understood what they meant.

"She tried to restart the waterfall, didn't she? But her power is limited to the pool. You control the water." I remembered how he'd said that, and I'd wanted to argue.

"I gave her the win," Grayson murmured.

"No." I knew him well enough. "You wanted her to underestimate you." The same way he wanted me to assume his motives were pure. "I hope she skewers you when I don't retrieve that book."

Grayson's chuckle was a darkly sensual sound. "You will, and she won't. Pretend you're training with Fallon. With your posse. You know everything you need to know."

I dragged my gaze from the precipice and checked my clothes. My shirt was damp, but tucked into the waistband of my jeans. I refastened the tie at the tip of my braid so the hair wouldn't fly loose. Grayson knelt and loosened my boots to tuck the hem of my jeans in tight around my ankles.

"The runes will guide you," he said as he re-tied each bootlace. "Trust what they tell you."

"Even the wolf?"

"Especially the wolf." He bit each word with a cutting humor as he stood. "Although I'd rather you trusted me."

"It won't work this time," I said. "I'm on to your strategy. You tell me one thing to get me to do the opposite."

He grinned.

I pressed hard on the black rune, pricked by the wicked twitching beneath my skin. Only it didn't feel so wicked this time. It felt like Grayson, circumventing Metis. He'd found a way to be with me in the cave, through his rune, but it rubbed me the wrong way, because it felt like he didn't think I could do it. Go in alone.

I said, "You don't have to worry."

"It's my job to worry."

What he always said.

And because he always said it, my anger felt wrong. Then the memory flashed and I was no longer standing at the top of a waterfall. I was in the watchtower house, beneath the shower, and he was holding me, his arms tight while the worm poison leached from my body. His lips pressed against my wet hair and he told me over and over how the pain would end soon. That he was sorry.

But I'd be fine. I'd be okay.

The memory was so vivid that I took a stumbling step back. I didn't care if Metis saw me and thought I was weak.

I didn't want *Grayson* to think I was weak.

The first move was easy. The stone steps were wide, but I took my time, testing the footing. There'd been a rock formation near Leo's house, surrounding a leaf-filled bowl in the earth where water gathered after the rain. When I'd been a child, I would climb over the rocks, pretending to be a princess heading down to a secret grotto where a prince waited on a white unicorn.

I had been fearless then, and these stones were no different now. I balanced with each careful step. Dragged my fingertips along the ridges of stone. Heat moved up my arm. My breathing eased. The steps followed the curve of the cliff, with straight runs before a new set of steps. I thought of the iron fire escape hanging outside my apartment building in Seattle. The vertical downward ladder, then the flat landing.

I was below the rim now. I didn't look up, trusting Grayson to be standing there, watching. He was silent, but when I thought of him, the wolf rune stirred.

"Jealous?"

A sharp little twitch.

"Poor baby."

A veil of water bounced off the rocks and splattered against my face. Cool beads weighted my eyelashes. I blinked and watched my feet each time I took a step, avoiding the deeper puddles. When I breathed in, the scent of the moss was peaty, hinting at a bog. In the crevices between each horizontal bar of rock, I saw bits of abandoned bird nests, tiny broken egg shells, sodden feathers, and twigs too far back to wash away.

My thoughts fell into a cadence, while another part of me drifted. Out of all the people I knew, I'd loved no one other than Leo and my mother, and I'd made so many mistakes with them. Maybe I wasn't good at loving someone. Love felt like a commitment ending less-than instead of more. I hadn't even tried with that boy I'd spent weekends with because I'd known, going in, that he wasn't what I wanted.

But I also knew that if finding my mother's book helped Grayson, protected him somehow, then I'd do it even if it was a mistake.

A pebble skidded beneath my foot. My hand shot out for balance, slapping nothing but air, and I threw my weight sideways. My head slammed against the rocks. Light spangled as I landed on my butt, and when I could see again, I realized how close to the edge I was, sitting in a puddle with one foot hanging above a sheer drop.

Gods, Noa! You're giving Metis her bloody spectacle after all.

I leaned back against the stone, waiting for my heart to stop pummeling my throat. The sun warmed my face enough to close my eyes, and the pink behind my eyelids became the pink of the rabbit's ear. Then it was the pink my posse wore in their hair. So brave, those girls, and their act of defiance. Solidarity with the no-wolf.

The pummeling in my throat was gone when I pushed up-right, brushing my palms against my hips. Ahead was the gap with rushing water and the broken board. A small stack of extra boards lay nearby. I dropped one across the gap, refused to doubt myself. Then I was on the other side and behind a small cascade of water.

The overhead ledge sheltered me from the bluish rush of water, no worse than being in a shower. The next ten feet would put me behind the deluge, and I forced myself to cross the distance the way I'd crossed all the obstacles on the lake circuit, without a pause.

My body followed each command until I was standing inside the cave, trapped by the vibration of moving water. It was like a freight train rushing past, so visually disorienting, I wasn't sure if the water was moving, or if I was.

Then I needed to widen my stance, or I'd be on my knees. In awe, realizing Grayson Devante had controlled that flow, moving the rocks. The same with the cave when trees rearranged themselves. He credited the King of the Forest, but he also said magic chose the wolf.

A wolf strong enough to wield it.

I wondered why he hadn't slowed the water for me, and then knew it would anger the Lady of the Lake. He'd chosen not to make her an enemy. Did that mean he had faith in me?

I had to think of it that way.

The cave resembled a cornucopia, wide at the mouth, arching well above my head, then curving behind black rock. Stagnant pools of water glimmered. The air smelled of fish and something vague, swirling with the air currents. Through my boots, I felt a seeping damp, and my wet jeans kept my muscles tense. I wasn't sure where to start, or how to start, and I was biting on my lip again, tasting blood.

Passages needed to be sensed, or seen, and if I was right, then I'd do what I did at the old watchtower. Edging along the perimeter, I probed the curves and angles in the dripping rock, watching from the edge of my vision and waiting for the light to bend.

On the floor of the cave, scattered shale lay in haphazard stacks. I knelt to graze the surface before snatching my hand back. Something awful had touched those rocks. And the vague smell... I recognized it now. The smell was the same as the meadow, the carnage, and I jerked upward.

But... the scent was old. The burn on my fingertips was real, but dulled. Something had been here...

Not now, Noa. Not recently.

Were the runes talking to me?

Or the *faille* part inside? The part I hadn't heard from since the moment Grayson inked his wolf rune on my skin.

The warning had me moving, sliding my fingers through a green slime—algae that hung in moist sheets and threads, glowing each time I touched it. My fingerprints were eerie and pink. They also faded within seconds, and I'd not find the way back by relying on the slime.

I forced myself to concentrate, always stepping to the left, with my right arm toward the front of the cave, and if I hit a dead end, I would switch to the other side and reverse the process.

Clammy air felt too thick to breathe. The light was dim but not diminished. Water dripping from the ceiling ran in wintry trickles through my hair. With an angle to the left, the cave closed in, and I moved faster, dragging my hands over the wet and ooze, the crevices and jutting edges.

I found nothing. And with nothing, doubt crept in, that my mom had gotten this far. That she'd been lucid enough to find a pocket and hide a book. I remembered the half-frenzied look in her eyes, that day in the backyard, and if delusion drove her, then all I did now was chase her phantoms.

I should admit it. Tell Grayson how damaged she'd been toward the end and that we'd find no answers here.

My throat ached with it, the failure. More for Grayson than for me. He'd already paid a high price. Trusted me. Traded a priceless artifact, risked angering an enemy, and I couldn't even achieve this one goal. But I'd run out of anger, and I was sick of the guilt in being broken... it shouldn't hurt so much this time. I'd known for eight years what I was. Eight years, when I could push the disappointment or whatever it was down where I wouldn't feel it. Pretending was the only thing that kept me functioning. Pretending to be human. That I was normal and had a plan. How I'd be a photographer one day and sail with the wind.

Pretense was what got me through each day, and I'd been pretending with Grayson... pretending I was strong, when... I pressed both palms against the slime-covered rocks, resting my forehead against my wrists. I needed the cold ooze against my skin to quell the heat each memory brought. To ease the pressure in my throat.

I leaned in, needing to push my fingers deeper into the muck, needing the pressure against my forehead to keep my eyes from stinging.

Something odd pricked my skin.

I pulled back. Burrowed through the slime with my fingers.

A spark caught my attention: a speck of gold.

I couldn't tell what it was, but once I worked it free, my legs gave out. I slid down and sat on the dank stone, my knees pulled up. My arms wrapped while I stared at my hand.

In my palm... a guardian angel, hanging on a tarnished chain, the kind of tarnish that came from a cheap necklace a child might buy for her mother.

I wanted to cry. I *should* cry... but I couldn't. It took weeks of saving my allowance before I asked Leo to take me to Hattie's store, where I remembered seeing the angel necklaces on pretty, decorated cards. I wanted one for my mother. Leo helped me wrap it in red paper, and when I'd given it to her, she said it was perfect. But she never wore it, and I never knew if it was because the cheap metal irritated her skin, or because the angel came from Sentinel Falls. She kept it in a jewelry box, small and round with frayed white velvet, and every time I would see a jewelry box like that, my eyes would sting.

They stung now.

Not from the memories.

But from all the ferocity bubbling up. So much anger over what I didn't know about my mother. She told horror stories about why I should abandon Leo... never return to Sentinel Falls. When she kept secrets of her own. Secrets the angel in my hand proved.

Was the necklace a sign from her? Because she wanted me to find the book?

Or had my mother's delusions been worse than I ever imagined? Maybe she came to this cave to cram the angel into a muck-covered crevice because she hated Sentinel Falls. Wanted no ties... not even a cheap trinket on a tarnished chain.

I thought of the days when I listened while she ranted. When I asked what was wrong, she would tell me to be happy and not ask questions she couldn't answer. She acted like I should be the mother because I was stronger than she could ever be. And I tried to be strong. Even when I stood up to Stewart.

But I'd resented having to do it, and the summer when I left for college, I let the space between us widen. I didn't go home when I could have because Stewart told me not to come. He said I upset her. And I agreed because then I could pretend that I wasn't selfish. I did it for her. The same way I convinced myself not to see Leo. And while I'd mended the rift with my grandfather, the last time I saw my mother, she hadn't known who I was.

I did cry then, for a moment, because the runes twisted beneath my skin, telling me to move. I pushed upright, tucked the angel in my jeans and slid stiff fingers through the muck, testing both sides of the crevice. Looking for some sign that proved my mother hadn't abandoned the necklace here. That it meant something.

And there—a softening in the rock.

Gritting my teeth, I pressed harder. My hand sank into what felt like thick mud, cloying and cold. Then the mud ended, and the space began, no different from a child's game, reaching into a closed paper bag on trust.

Still, my heart hammered.

No spiders. Please, no spiders.

No creatures from the other side.

The muck on the rocks smelled of decay. I shook as I leaned in, my fingers brushing through the space. Nothing toward the front, other than a hard, smooth surface with a vertical wall. I imagined a stone box, and slid my fingertips across until I felt the other vertical wall—a square space, then. I pushed and flicked until one fingernail scraped across an edge.

The object slid backward.

I flicked again. Whatever it was, it moved, then stopped an inch beyond my reach.

I paused.

Was this a game? A trap? Was the pocket luring me deeper?

Or was this like reaching for that box on the top kitchen shelf? The one that always popped away from my grasp?

My right hand was inside the pocket up to my wrist, but the runes were on my left arm. I glanced down. They pulsed, muted even in the shadowed light. I felt no warning twitch from Grayson's rune. The pocket couldn't be more than an arm's reach for something to be hidden there.

I breathed in, pushing until I was elbow-deep, finger-walking across the stone, feeling for whatever was there.

Then I found it, solid, wedged at an angle against the wall. Leather binding, textured and dry. If I leaned in...

Hold still hold still hold still.

The thought was frantic enough for me to notice the temperature in the cave. It plunged close to frigid, and a malevolent fog formed. Seconds passed before I realized the fog was the violent puffing of my breath.

But instinct stopped me from moving.

The mud surrounding my arm was freezing. I fought the urge to drag myself free. The pocket might not reopen. I'd lose the book. It seemed... elusive. Teasing me, and I wondered if it didn't want to be found. Perhaps it was the book and not the temperature that thickened the mud, pinching my skin.

Was the pocket closing?

Was this a trap, after all?

My thoughts turned feverish. I didn't want to think of my mother manipulating magic, but she was also a *faille*, and

Grayson said no one knew what *failles* could do. Other than what the ancient stories described...

I clawed with my fingers, desperate to find the book. When I touched it again, the crushing mud around my arm turned my fingers numb.

Think, Noa!

Energy was keyed to pockets, and this one had opened for my mother's energy. It had opened for mine.

Two energies, Noa...

Wouldn't my mother need her energy to put the book there, but mine for me to retrieve it? Was that why she left the necklace wedged in the stone—because it was the key? We'd both touched the necklace, left traces of energy behind. It made enough sense that I dug the guardian angel from my pocket. Around me, the algae throbbed with a crimson light; the beats mimicked a living heart, and in the faint glow I saw tiny, spidery creatures crawling from the crevices in the walls and the ceiling.

Terror stabbed in my throat and I slammed the tarnished charm against the hardening stone.

The mud softened.

I thought the book was within reach, and my fingernails split as I scraped, tried to claw a fingerhold, sagging with relief when I grasped it.

Too soon too soon!

The instant I touched the leather cover, a flash-burn heat raced up my arm while beneath my feet, the cave shuddered. The air expanded like a balloon close to breaking. I felt, then heard, stampeding hooves echoing in the dark.

My vision flashed like fireworks. The moisture on my face became ice. In my mouth, the taste of bitter ash dried my tongue while the din of the waterfall turned tumultuous.

A woman screamed. The absolute fury burrowed beneath my skin, deep into my bones... along with the horror. I'd heard that scream before, when Grayson inked his rune on my skin.

I yanked the book free. Tried to run across a cave floor that spun in slow, loopy ovals. The ceiling tilted. My feet slipped.

Through the dinning noise, I heard my name.

"*Noa!*"

Fallon. Shouting, running toward me—she grabbed my arm. From the shape of her mouth, I knew she was ordering me to move. When I tripped, she yanked me upright. The waterfall raged. Slashes of water hit my face until I gagged, hugging the book while Fallon dragged, and then pushed me along the ledge, across the creaking board. I didn't glance back, even when the board flipped into the water from the weight of our feet. The sky was too bright. Fallon's hands were firm against my back as we climbed the stone steps. At the first flat ledge, I paused, tipping my head, gasping as I stared upward.

Overhead, Northern Lights danced—how odd to see them in daylight and this far south. They were deep purple, blood red.

"Who broke the sky?" I asked.

"Metis thinks you did." Fallon forced me up the second group of steps, up and up, until Grayson was there, his hands outstretched. He shackled my upper arms, hauled me to the top.

"Get her back to Azul." I'd never heard him sound so dangerous. So... angry. "I'll take care of Metis."

"Creatures have been in that cave," Fallon snapped. "I recognized the scent."

"Lock everyone down."

That did not sound reassuring, I decided. Not reassuring at all.

But what worried me more was the book.

I couldn't let go.

CHAPTER 29

Noa

When Mace marched me into the forest, I hugged my mother's book and pretended it wasn't glued to my hand. A contingent of men joined us. Wolf aggression pulsed as they fanned out, moving through the forest with stealth while I stumbled and made so much noise, I probably defeated their efforts.

I felt rigid and chilled. The sky continued to writhe, and I hoped I wasn't responsible. When I glanced at Mace, he was stoic—the way he'd looked when he led me from the river and I'd been so ill with worm poison.

I never thanked him for saving me that day.

"I'm sorry," I said, trying to keep up with him. "You're always cleaning up my messes."

He didn't answer, and I puffed out a breath as his stride lengthened.

"I wanted to thank you," I added. "For saving me again."

"Gray sent out the order," he growled, as if it wasn't his idea. "You didn't come out of the cave, and he wanted everyone here. Then the runes went crazy. We all felt them before they went silent."

My lips wouldn't work. I remembered how the runes had numbed.

"Gray thought it was Metis, but Fallon was the only one who could go in and get you out."

Because she was both female and wolf. She'd risked her life for me, and I focused on the book, heavy in my hand but still dry despite the mist and wet of the waterfall. "I was fine."

"Debatable."

We hiked between tall pines and through a meadow before I grew brave enough to ask, "You don't like me, do you?"

"I worry, because your posse thinks you're a fighter. Someone who doesn't give up."

"I gave up at the six-foot wall."

"And that—right there," he growled. "The arrogance in failing. That's why I can't decide about you. If your influence is good or bad."

My lips twisted. "There's no arrogance in falling on my butt in the dirt."

"There is when failure is your excuse."

A branch cracked beneath my foot, spiking up, stabbing at me the way Mace stabbed with words. I could see myself as he saw me, sitting in the dirt at the base of a six-foot wall, proud... relieved.

I stabbed back and said, "No wonder the young wolves like Fallon more than they like you."

"Fallon teaches them how to run." His canines flashed. "I teach them how to survive. And it doesn't take a wolf to get over that wall, Noa. What it takes is commitment, and if you can't commit, then I can't trust you."

We returned to Azul, a hike that took less time than I'd spent in the cave. My mother's book was now with Laura at the archive; I'd been able to unglue my fingers and let it go. Then I'd gone home, showered, dressed, and picked up my camera. Walked out again, posturing like a photographer, hiking along the lake, kneeling for a closeup on a curling fiddlehead fern because framing my world through a camera lens made life easy.

I could see it now. The arrogance in failing.

In my human world, I'd lived with people I didn't really know. Hid in the crowd and never noticed how lonely life was. I was a coward, and I refused to get over that six-foot wall because then I never had to face what came next. Mace realized it, and he said he taught wolves how to survive instead of run—because he knew I did one better than the other.

That made three times now that he'd cleaned up my messes while I kept making them. I wandered to the end of the boat dock behind my borrowed house. In the evenings, the dock was the perfect place to watch the sun disappear behind the far mountains. Two Adirondack chairs angled toward the water, but I preferred to perch on the dock edge, where I could see the rippling reflections.

The water was crystal clear. Tiny fish darted after the gnats that landed on the surface. Submerged blades of grass moved in the gentle, lapping currents.

Laura promised there were no nymphs in the lake, although she didn't blame me for the caution, poking me in the ribs and admitting she'd rather not be nymph lunch if she had a choice. And I'd said, well, certainly not without ketchup, and she'd laughed and laughed—and, listening to her, I'd wanted to laugh like that, too. Have a moment where nothing mattered except joy.

Leo found me when the sun was turning the sky crimson. I heard the tap of his cane, the soft groan as he settled in the Adirondack chair. I fretted about him getting up again, but I could help.

"Noa, girl," he said. "You like watching the ducks?"

"Yes." I turned my head as a green-necked mallard lifted off the lake, trailing drops of water from orange webbed feet. "I should bring bread next time. Feed them."

"Bring them lettuce," he said. "More like their natural food."

Small talk I appreciated. Setting the camera aside, I smoothed a finger along the grain in the wooden dock. "I found the book."

"I know."

"It was strange, realizing she was stronger than she let on, and for all those years... I believed her."

"People hurt others out of love, and maybe that doesn't seem right," Leo said. "But maybe that's the way it needs to be."

I thought of Grayson telling me the worm poison wasn't bad, right before he sliced me open. Then I thought about this strange world where I was drowning because I couldn't swim.

"I can't do this."

"Gray said the same thing when the old alpha died. He had three challengers in as many days, men older than he was, men he knew, respected."

"He killed them?"

"The challenge was theirs. The choice to walk away or die was also theirs, while the wolf chosen as Alpha has no path except to stand and fight. That's our tradition, Noa, girl. The magic chose him. The way I think magic has chosen you."

I wiped two fingers across my damp eyelashes. "I don't want it."

"Neither did he when it came, but power is a gift. Gray's healing ability has saved many wolves. I think your healing ability can do the same thing with silent wolves. Oscar is better. I feel lighter when you're around. My wolf whines now, and I'm grateful for that."

I pushed to my feet, hands shaking when I bent down to retrieve my camera.

"There are two sides to every blade," Leo said as I helped him stand. "Both can be sharp for different reasons."

We walked toward the house that glowed with golden light. Hattie was busy inside, preparing a meal. Oscar hummed as he set the table. We shared braised pork chops and thumb-sized potatoes, roasted apple slices and turnips in a spiced sauce. Vegetables from Laura's garden.

Hattie bragged about the veggies being organic as she arranged bowl after bowl on the table. Fresh fruit glimmered in the light. Warm rolls were soft in the middle. We ate and talked. I paid attention to Oscar, smiling when we made eye contact. He was more animated. Hattie beamed, and if I was responsible, I sent a thread of gratitude out to whatever power had given me the gift.

We didn't talk about magic, or being *faille*, or my mother's book. No one mentioned creatures in the forest or a strange sky. The conversation moved toward the Night of the Beacons.

As excitement filled Hattie's voice, I felt it. She described the Night of the Beacons—her favorite holiday after Christmas. It came when the late-spring warmed, but before summer's heat. She claimed it rivaled the Fourth of July for nighttime displays.

Through all the summers that I'd visited, I'd never been in Sentinel Falls early enough for the celebrations. I'd heard about them, of course.

Centuries old, the Night of the Beacons was a hallowed event, celebrating a dark time in ancient pack history. The enemy lurked in the north, building massive armies, while the packs struggled toward cooperation. The settlements were sparce, scattered throughout the valleys. Beacon fires became the communication system. Sentinels manned the wooden pyres, watching for the first flame. Then, beacon after beacon lit the mountains, the crags and sharp ridges, even the valleys, warning the wolves.

Modern celebrations included family groups lighting bonfires in their yards, or building them on the high ridges. Competition between settlements was fierce over who could build the largest beacon fire, and the night filled with the magic of yellow and ruby flames. On the following day, the annual Gathering took place. All the species attended to reaffirm the truces. Peace continued for another year.

"Think of the mafia," Hattie said. "People smiling through their teeth. Enemies at the same banquet, toasting one another."

She shuddered. "We're hosting this year. There's a rotation—although Cariboo hasn't taken part in decades. The vampires hosted last year. Thank the gods we don't have many witches in the area. They rarely come, while the nymphs do, but then they pretend they're above rivalries."

I thought of the Lady of the Lake, her amethyst gown swishing, the diamonds glittering in her hair, and the warning not to mention the Welsh lake faeries because she'd be offended.

Then I thought of the Alpen and stood to collect the empty dishes. I carried them to the kitchen, where Hattie joined me.

We gossiped about meaningless things until she decided I was tired and everyone needed to leave. The quiet afterward drove me upstairs to my bedroom, but I couldn't sleep. I thrashed beneath the sheet for two hours before giving up.

Wrapping a thick blanket around my sleeping attire, I shoved on floppy slippers and wandered back outside, drawn to the dock where I'd spent the afternoon. Frogs croaked. The moon was high in the night sky, and the reflections on the water wavered with ribbons of light. But I felt a stirring in my blood and knew Grayson was behind me before he said, "Noa... may I join you?"

I nodded, adding, "I couldn't sleep."

"Neither could I."

He was a mystery in the dark, with the pull of a new moon. I couldn't look at him, even while I breathed in his scent. My pulse hitched when he lowered himself to the decking. Warmth radiated from his hardened body. I plucked at my slippers. I'd set them aside so I could dangle my legs over the dock edge, swing my feet without worry they'd fall off.

Grayson's long legs swung next to mine, and it was like we were two kids, waiting for the fish to leap. Listening for the splash. I wondered if peace felt like this, or hope, waiting for some sign like it was Christmas morning.

"Did you look at the book yet?" I asked.

"I looked at it, but I couldn't read it."

"Why not?"

"It's written in a language I've never encountered. Laura's more of an expert than I am. She thought it might be a language you could read."

"If it isn't English," I said, "we're out of luck."

Grayson tipped his head, and I joined him in staring at the endless sky, a black void, yet filled with more constellations than I'd ever seen. Even the Milky Way, two bands of ice-white stars with a black space in the mid—my mind flashed to a gray seam opening in spangled sunlight, and the gasping sound I made was humiliating.

Rocking forward, I lowered my head toward my knees.

"Breathe," Grayson murmured.

"I can't."

His hand settled on my back, his fingers rubbing in small, soothing circles. "Was today too much?"

"No." My hair swung loose and my nose felt clogged and runny. Gods, I was a mess, and I hated being a mess in front of this man. It seemed… important not to disappoint him. "I'm having a moment, that's all."

"A weeks-long moment," he said. "I'm sorry."

"This isn't your fault. I seem to be the wild cannon in this scenario."

He chuckled. "Metis thought so."

"How can you laugh?" I rubbed my nose as I straightened. "She was horrid, and that awful story she told about being invited to a secret blood feast? I knew she meant you."

"I'd never invite you to a secret blood feast, Noa," he said with a tug to his lips. "I'd order you to go."

"Such an alpha." I skimmed my toes inches above the lake water. "Did I really break the sky?"

"No, solar activity, or an earthquake beneath the northern glaciers caused an electrical storm."

The glaciers guarded by the Cariboo, the ones everyone worried about.

My fingers gripped the dock edge. "Leo said I've been healing people like Oscar. He said the magic chose me, and I think you already guessed it, but wanted me to find out on my own."

"You sound thrilled," he drawled.

I brushed at my hair, sliding silver strands behind my ear while I glanced back at my swinging toes. "It's not that I'm ungrateful, but I'd rather have magic that let me turn someone into a frog or something."

"Only you, Noa. Thinking of frogs right now."

I loved the soft way he laughed. Easy enough to dissolve the tension. We were talking like two friends who meant it—the friendship. Perhaps that's where the courage came from, to tell him what I hadn't told him before. I talked about the cave, what happened with the shale and the scent. The muck that glowed, and the dripping, icy water.

I told him how I'd found the guardian angel, what it meant, and how it saved me from the mud.

I described the freezing air; the creatures scuttling from the crevices and the ballooning sensation of a passageway opening.

Then I admitted to the fear I felt each time I heard the woman's scream. I thought it was a warning, that she screamed the word, "*No!*"

Then I told him what I had instead of a wolf, the sentient *thing* that seemed drawn to him, rising closer to the surface each time he was around. I thought it was the weapon he wanted, an evil seeking the light. How that terrified me.

And throughout the confession, his hand was steady on my back, moving in soothing circles, while I stared at my swinging feet above the moonlit water as if none of this was real.

"So... how much trouble am I in?" I asked when he remained quiet.

"Mace covered up what happened in the meadow, but I can't guarantee no one else knows about those creatures coming through."

He tucked the blanket around my shoulders, and it was his turn to talk. He told me if not for the lights in the sky, Metis would have believed I was harmless, and the book was a meaningless journal my mother left behind.

But the Lady of the Lake's agitation alarmed the nymphs, and because nymphs were horrible gossips, by tomorrow, every species in the Selkirks would know I found something in that cave.

Then the packs would remember the ancient history of kings and queens, and the assumptions about *failles* and how they disrupted a pack.

They'd worry about the book. About me and my reasons for being here.

I'd be the weapon, the advantage the Alpha of Sentinel Falls held over them.

Or I'd be the curse like the queens of old.

I'd be hunted. Hated.

Grayson had said those things before, but this time I knew it was a thousand times worse because I was no longer his secret.

"We need to quell the alarm," Grayson said. "Present you as harmless. Let the packs think I caused those northern lights—or Metis did."

Since they'd already battled with the waterfall, Grayson's solution had possibilities. He was the Alpha of Sentinel Falls. Magic chose him. Empowered him.

I wanted to believe what he said. I would have believed him, except that while he talked, I'd been shivering, and not from the cold.

The wolf rune on my wrist was burning, and I knew immense power hid beneath the simple design. I'd felt the twitch, more sentient than the other runes, and as I dragged the blanket toward my chin... I knew Grayson had lied to me.

"What does your mark mean?" I asked, watching a black-feathered bird, a night hunter, dive toward the lake. "The truth, this time."

He breathed in, then turned his head away. "It means I've claimed you, and will fight to protect my claim."

My pulse thudded. "You mean it's a mating mark."

"Not always. That mark represents a bargain between two people, Noa. I didn't offer it casually."

I rubbed above my aching eyes. "Tell me the rest."

"Everything I told you was true. A bargain begins, and it ends, and what it means is up to the two people involved. The wolves will see that mark and believe we've agreed to an exclusive relationship. Sexual. That's what Metis thought, and I let her believe it because it explained my interest in getting the book for you. But after what happened today, you can't hide, or it will look suspicious. The pack will accept our relationship out of respect. My enemies will be skeptical. They'll also be hesitant. They won't touch you if it means challenging me."

"Then you meant it as protection."

"Yes. But for that to work, I need your cooperation. During the Night of the Beacons, the pack elders will want to meet you. They're not all friends. At the Gathering, my enemies will be there, and I'll ask you to do things you might not want to do. You'll still have to do them."

I kicked at the water. "Will the Alpen be there?"

"I can't stop them. Laura will hide in Azul. So will Leo. I have a traitor in the pack." He scrubbed a broad hand over his face.

"Someone planned the incident with my wolf and the feral. He tried to cast doubt upon my ability to lead, and until I know who that traitor is—or was—I can't trust anyone."

Anxiety rippled across my skin. I'd put so many people in danger by coming here. I'd thought of my own fears when it couldn't be about me, or even Grayson. It had to be about convincing both friends and enemies alike that we were harmless lovers, and not potential conspirators.

"If I can't do this, how will it end?"

As soon as I said the words, I regretted them. But his jaw tightened. And perhaps honesty was what we both needed, what we'd come to this lake to find.

"We can end it now. I'll break the bargain. Numb your hand, cut through the rune. Blood nulls the magic and you'll be free to live as you wish."

The words were a punch to my heart, and I was glad for the rising breeze that covered my tightening grip on the blanket. As he had with the ritual, he offered to blunt the pain.

I'd never feel the wicked little twitch again. Our bargain would end with a thread of blood to make it real. Such a simple solution. I could close my eyes, refuse to watch when it happened.

Then I'd be free. So would he. No more risk for him, while I'd go on with my life. Take my camera, travel the world. See what I wanted to see and never know what I was.

And if... if there was evil coming from the north, it wouldn't be my problem to solve.

I wouldn't have to face what came next.

But endings shouldn't be so easy, and I said, "What if I stay?"

He shifted his weight, bracing on his arms, his palms on the wooden dock, his fingers close to mine. "We continue our bargain. Pretend we have a sexual relationship, at least until the Gathering is over."

What he wasn't saying became obvious. I'd need to be convincing. Because—despite his reputation—his enemies would challenge him if they thought I was worth the risk. Other wolves would come to his defense. Mace, Fallon, Levi... they'd be hurt. Killed. A pack war would follow, destroying innocents like those who sheltered in Azul. Leo and the other silent wolves. The girls with pink stripes in their hair. Laura. Wolves I'd never met.

How much blood was I willing to spill for my mistakes?

Grayson had inked runes on my skin when I asked, and what he wanted in return was such a small thing. A pretense—what I'd been doing most of my life. When we'd both seen each other naked. I could touch him and make it look genuine. Turn my face toward his, lean into his side. Allow him to stroke my back, my arm. My throat.

He'd kissed me in anger, but I'd lost myself for a moment. During the ritual, my body had responded to him.

He hadn't been immune. The attraction was there for both of us. Perhaps that was the real danger.

My heart raced, and I would not... I *would not* think of the damn rabbit.

And yet... there she was, bathed in yellow light, her eyes trusting me while the real danger loomed at my side.

He wasn't the danger, though.

The danger had always been in my hesitation. In the rabbit's hesitation. The inability to decide. To be committed before someone else reacted.

"How much time do I have?"

"Two nights before Night of the Beacons. The Gathering is the following day, and when it's over, you can stay in Azul, or somewhere else, if that's what you want. I'll protect you. The wolves will believe you went back to Seattle, and if someone searches, the leads will take them nowhere."

I chewed on my lip. "What do you want me to do?"

He turned his head, his blue-green gaze spearing me. "I want you to have the choice, Noa. But if you stay, I'll need you to trust me."

He'd told me once before that life changed the rules, and I had to adapt if I wanted to survive. I wasn't good at adapting, but if I needed to trust someone, Grayson was the better of the two of us.

A calm settled. "Then I guess I trust you."

Grayson rose to his feet and held out his hand. But when his fingers closed around mine, I could not help but worry. Not for me. I'd be fine. I'd be okay.

But I worried about what the next few days could mean to him if I failed.

CHAPTER 30

Noa

TWO DAYS LATER, I was on the glass deck at the watchtower house. I'd asked Grayson why the deck was glass, and he'd said that, if an enemy attacked from below, he wanted to see them coming. The idea left me unsettled. While the cliff face was sheer, the pale creatures who swarmed the meadow would have no trouble climbing over those vertical rocks.

When Laura arrived, I went inside to greet her. She'd brought three friends, women from Azul. Leticia was a brunette in her late twenties. Cossa was also a brunette, thinner than Leticia, while the petite blonde—Vasha—reminded me of Mace with her spiked hair. Except that she'd tinted her blonde spikes purple.

They carried cases filled with lotions, makeup, hair supplies because it was the Night of the Beacons and I needed to look gorgeous.

"Not that you don't always look beautiful," Leticia said as she pushed me toward my old bedroom. She chatted on about how tonight would be special... while I struggled with different thoughts.

Looking toward the bedroom corner, I remembered how Grayson sat in a chair, silent and watching. I stared at the bed where he saw me at my worst, sweaty, my naked body marred by worm wounds and tangled in the sheets.

The polished floor was where I'd crawled from him. And there—he'd crouched down and delivered a swift and brutal pain.

In the bathroom, I sat in the deep tub filled with scented water and stared at the glassed-in shower, remembering the beat of his heart when he'd held me.

Then I thought of the cave. The firelight and the pulsing mushrooms with their soft glow.

His hands on my body.

I recalled the pinprick-pain from the bone needle as he'd inked the rune on my breast. The brush of his knuckles. His canines against my shoulder, and the dark sound in his voice when he'd asked, "Happy, now?"

And when Leticia knocked on the door and walked in, I lied and said it was the luxury of scented oil that kept me in the soaking tub for so long. Not those memories.

Once out of the bath, the women took charge. Vasha wrapped me in a fluffy robe. I sat in a chair so she could work with my hair, while Cossa sat on a stool and stared at my abused fingernails, arguing with Leticia over white or pale pink polish. When they asked what color dress I was wearing, I looked at Laura with a deer-in-the-headlights expression.

"She's wearing red."

"Ooh…" Cossa's shoulders shimmied. She dipped her little brush into a clear gloss and painted. "I'll add red as the accent." She tapped at my cuticles. "Rub lotion on these fingers daily." Then she frowned when she noticed the callouses from the years of archery.

"Her mark of honor." Vasha worked on an elaborate knot at the back of my head. "We'll have those soon."

The conversation drifted, and before I knew it, they'd dressed me in a floor length red gown that skimmed my body. The off-the-shoulder design had a sweetheart neckline and showcased the runes on my skin. I suspected that was why Laura chose it.

Earlier, I'd peeked into the walk-in closet, overwhelmed by the evening gowns and cocktail dresses. Heels from Jimmy Choo sat in cubbyholes. On shelves, I counted more casual jeans and sweaters than I could wear in a year. Below were tennis shoes and sandals. The drawers overflowed with sexy silk panties and bras, and while I wasn't a prude, I wondered who had been in charge of the shopping.

If this was Grayson's idea of what his lover should have on hand.

My skin tingled as the reality sank deep. I'd have to pretend tonight. Be convincing, when not all pack members were friends. Laura said some elders backed the rivals who'd challenged Grayson. Those rivals died, and while the elders swore loyalty afterward, the Alpha of Sentinel Falls would always have adversaries within the pack.

I tugged on the neckline of my dress, willing it to cover more. Then I realized the neckline was on purpose, along with all the primping. Somehow—these beautiful women understood what was at stake, although none gave the knowledge away. And I added three more names to my list of those I wanted to protect: Leticia, Cossa, and Vasha. Friends who worked so hard to make this pretense convincing.

Vasha pinned a band of flowers in my hair, framing the knot she'd designed. She called them the alpha's flowers because his mark was on my wrist, and flowers were a traditional warning to other males that a female was off limits. Leticia applied my makeup. Cossa fussed with the gown, and when I looked in the mirror... I didn't see myself. I saw a goddess... a lover... a consort to the Alpha of Sentinel Falls.

Of course it wasn't about anything but pure illusion. Convincing the pack I was a delicious tidbit for a lustful male. Entertainment, but underneath, completely harmless.

Would it be enough? If Grayson's enemies already feared me as a *faille*, would how I looked, or what I did, ever be enough?

Nerves made me want to throw up. Sitting on a boat dock at midnight made it easy to imagine myself doing this, pretending to be his lover. But wolves were sensual creatures, and they'd see through me in a heartbeat.

I gasped for breath.

Laura held my hand. Her finger traced around Grayson's mark.

"It's not what you think," I choked.

She had to know, but her finger circled again with a subtle, comforting pressure. "But what it is, Noa... cherish it."

Laura and her friends would celebrate in Azul. I understood why, but I also missed their comfort. I'd be on my own. Faking my smiles, flirting with the right laugh over drinks. A casual hand on Grayson's arm. A murmured secret over dinner. The days were getting longer, which meant the evening would seem endless, waiting for the dark and the beacon fires. But I'd smile and smile, and be fine.

I'd be like Metis, a queen walking to her throne, striding toward the crowded living room. As I made my entrance, the dress swished. My hands swung at my sides—no damp fists to give me away.

The house had been transformed. In the living room, light from the chandeliers reflected off crystal vases overflowing with flowers. A chef worked in the kitchen; the aromas made my mouth water. Black-suited men matched the women in designer gowns. I guessed twenty couples—a manageable size. Conversations added a white noise, punctuated by laughter. Wolf energy was tolerable.

I kept measuring my surroundings. These were *wolves*, after all. My audience... and I needed to read the room. Use my *faille* senses to recognize the threats.

No familiar faces, other than Fallon. She wore a flowing black mermaid gown, sleeveless with a plunging neckline. Her hair remained in the signature braid, and she said, "don't judge," when I raised my eyebrows.

"Not in the least," I teased. "You look stunning." Then I glanced at the flaring, floor-length hem and asked, "Are you wearing boots beneath that?"

When Fallon frowned, I came close to laughing. Did she *need* to think about what shoes she wore? Perhaps she'd never considered hiding boots beneath the sexy dress. With Fallon, she preferred her fighting clothes, although I heard the click of high heels when she walked, and when a server offered champagne, she grabbed a glass and drained it before the man could move away.

"You look as tense as I feel," I murmured as I glanced around. Still measuring.

"It's tradition." Her head tipped with an alpha's grace. "We dress in the glamourous clothes, drink the most expensive alcohol, and show how civilized we can be. Security is a nightmare—try shifting in a thousand-dollar dress. But the alpha orders and I obey." She swapped her empty glass for one with water and winked. "He's looking for you, by the way."

Her voice carried to the women close enough to hear. I knew my dress revealed the runes and the crescent pack mark on my shoulder. The pearlized tattoos could have been temporary, a pretty painted design on anyone else but the—I wasn't sure what the females were calling me.

Was I the alpha's dalliance? His... distraction?

The insults thrown at my mother had been harsher—I'd been too young to understand when I first heard them. Not the tone, though. The disapproval, and I wished I'd accepted that glass of champagne because the same disapproval followed as I crossed the room.

Grayson waited on the cantilevered deck. He possessed the honed menace of a man who knew what he was and who he owned, and no one, not even me, could consider him as anything other than extraordinary.

He was magnificently, profanely male in a black tailored suit, white shirt, and narrow black tie—and I trusted him. Despite our history. The way he'd trusted me the day we confronted Stewart. As I approached, his chest lifted on a breath, making me wonder if I'd interrupted something. Because he wasn't alone.

"I'm sorry. Fallon said..."

"Noa." Grayson wrapped his fingers around mine. "I'd like you to meet Mosbach, one of our pack elders. He came down from his mountain to join us tonight."

The white-haired elder was stiff-postured yet gregarious, reminding me of Stewart when he spoke to my mother's doctors. His beady eyes tracked me. Devoured me—and when he peered down his nose with that arrogant expectation, I wondered if I should shake his hand or curtsy.

I did neither because Grayson's fingers flexed around mine, and I took that as a warning to do nothing.

"Mr. Mosbach," I said, while his fake smile most likely matched mine. "I hope you don't mind my interruption."

"Not at all, my dear, when I see the rumors are true."

"Rumors?" I blinked.

"The pack mark. On your shoulder. If you weren't born with one, the next best thing is to have the alpha put it there."

"Oh—*that!*" I amped up my smile, pretending I didn't hear the condescension the way Mosbach pretended he hadn't meant it. "It was really sweet of him. But I wish he'd told me it wouldn't wash off before he did it."

Grayson squeezed my hand. I squeezed back, ignoring him, and stared at Mosbach, at the elder's pasty face. He was *so* like Stewart. "You'll be at the Gathering tomorrow?"

"I wouldn't miss it."

"Oh, good. Someone else I'll know." I turned toward Grayson, trying not to react when he stared at me... like he couldn't decide between irritation or amusement. I decided a little push would help him. "See, darling?" I patted his arm. "I'll be fine."

Grayson smiled, but a predatory glitter entered his bi-colored eyes. Maybe that last part was overdone—like the bury your face in blood remark I'd made once before. And when he pulled my hand to his lips, when he kissed my knuckles, I felt the prick of canines before he said, "You'll excuse us, Mos. I have something for her. I've waited long enough."

Grayson wasn't asking for permission. Wolf culture had protocols even the elders followed. Grayson Devante was the ultimate authority, and with a stiff nod, Mosbach stepped aside.

But as we walked back inside, I was afraid my little push had been toward irritation, because Grayson refused to let go of my hand. He wove through the crowd, dragging me along, acknowledging the greetings without slowing until we were down the hall and inside his office.

"Breathe," he murmured when he closed the door.

I hovered near the massive desk, leaning against it after Mosbach. I still felt the oily creep of his gaze along the neckline of my dress before centering on the pack mark.

This was Grayson's private domain, though, and I glanced around, curious. I'd never explored this room during my midnight explorations—the door had always been locked. It didn't surprise me to see bookshelves lining one wall. Bookshelves were everywhere in the house. A modern computer sat on the desk with several monitors. The view through the windows was equal to that on the cantilevered deck—breathtaking.

As he unlocked a desk drawer, I watched his hands, the way his fingers moved. White shirt cuffs peeked out beneath the tailored jacket. Black obsidian cuff links glittered, cold and hard. I was seeing a different side of him, someone as cultured as he was deadly, and although I knew that for tonight, we were pretending, the sexual vibes he gave off were bruising.

I traced the desk's edge. "Who is Mosbach?"

"Someone we'll discuss later."

He turned with a flat jeweler's box in his hands. Light glittered off the necklace nestled on black velvet, a choker with five rows of matched diamonds. I couldn't calculate the worth. "The necklace is on loan," he added. "You'll wear it tonight. Turn around."

For once I obeyed, too stunned to argue. I couldn't process why the Alpha of Sentinel Falls would order designer dresses and get exorbitant jewelry on loan, when all he had to do was say we were lovers. His mark on my wrist was proof enough. I didn't think lavish displays worth tens-of-thousands would convince the skeptics.

But his hands lingered at my nape, fastening the clasp that took longer than I expected, and his scent crept up on me, spice and woodsy pine. I thought of dark nights, cool breezes... and when his canines brushed against my shoulder, and I couldn't stop the flinch.

"Relax," he murmured. "I'm leaving my scent on you." Then he straightened. "Turn around."

I obeyed a second time, still amazed by diamonds that warmed to match the heat of my skin. But as I touched the faceted edges, a part of me still said, *he just hooked a diamond collar around his pet* faille's *throat.*

The idea lingered as we rejoined the guests. I paid no attention to the raised eyebrows when the wolves noticed the small fortune now added to the designer gown—adornments I could never have afforded on my own. Grayson continued to hold my hand. I stood at his side, marveling at his ease with the elders. Friends and rivals. His political skills were a joy to watch. Wolves agreed or challenged, but always with light-hearted banter.

We pretended. Smiled, nudged shoulders as if sharing a private joke. Grayson's breathing remained steady, save for the few deep inhales when I touched him. He kept his hand on me, either at my back or around my waist. It felt natural. Until I was curled against his side, his heat flaring through my elegant dress—and I realized how tall he was. How much cleavage the plunging neckline exposed.

His head was bent. A smirk twitched at his lips, and I squirmed, aware of the elders' wives, their pinched expressions. The tight hands, gripping champagne glasses. Censure was the ice no one wanted to thaw, and when Grayson leaned in, I blocked him with my shoulder.

He misinterpreted, turning more fully into me. "Every elder here is drooling."

I glared at him.

"That was a compliment, Noa. The way you look…"

"I get it." I pushed away, straightening the gown where he'd wrinkled it. "They get it, what you want and why I'm here. You didn't have to dress me like my mother."

He frowned. "I didn't."

I wondered if he didn't understand. If he hadn't heard the whispered comments I'd heard, how some things never changed, and I was like my mother in more than one way.

She'd thrown away self-respect for a night of passion. Flaunted herself without shame, without even knowing her lover's name. Despite the vaunted sensuality of wolves, their open-minded attitudes toward consensual sex seemed to be reserved for wolves.

Not *failles*.

"Has someone said something?" The flash of alpha anger was there—what I'd seen the first time I faced him in Leo's defiled house.

"Not to my face."

Comprehension darkened his eyes. "I'm sorry."

I didn't care. This was the plan, wasn't it? Let the pack believe the performance we gave. We both agreed to it, even if the hurt was unexpected and sharp.

"I'm sorry, Noa."

I brushed off the repeated apology with a tight smile, and although he said nothing more, I thought his body remained tense. We sat together through a wonderful meal I struggled to eat, not because the food wasn't delicious, but because my mouth was so dry. As the evening wore on, we drifted apart. But I would feel his gaze on me, look up, and find him staring with his eyes narrowed.

I wondered if he was listening while the women chatted. They told me about the festivities, what to expect. They marveled at the alpha, so, so generous with those diamonds at my throat... and did I think I'd be leaving soon?

My face hurt from smiling, from pretending. A headache throbbed with so many people and their insensitive questions, and while wolf energy hadn't bothered me for weeks, the irritation was back, scraping beneath my skin.

I waited until Grayson wasn't looking and stepped outside, drawing in deep gulps of cool air. The sky was still light. We'd have another hour before the beacons lit. I wasn't sure I could get through it.

"Too much for you?" Mace sat on the glass deck, looking as uncomfortable as Fallon in the formal attire—a wolf irritated by his sheep's clothing. I'd learned by now that once an alpha, always an alpha, and none of them could turn off the vigilance.

"I didn't mean to intrude."

"You didn't." He waved the glass he held. "Join me? Whiskey. The bottle's on the table."

Glasses, too, I noticed. A bucket of ice with tongs. I added ice and poured enough whiskey to cover the bottom of the glass because, while I had no desire to aggravate my headache, after the last hour, I needed the alcohol. Fool that I was, I'd thought Grayson's mark on my wrist would at least earn me a whisper of respect.

"Some wives are hard to take," Mace said when I settled in the chair beside him.

"It's me. I don't get over six-foot walls and I'm not good with crowds."

He snorted. "And you're tired of all that passive-aggressive shit the wives call conversation."

It was never about what Mace said, but how he said it that stung. We'd had conversations before where he'd been critical. Mace didn't accept failure any more than Grayson did, but he acted as if something about my failure tonight was important, and it pissed him off.

"I know what's at stake."

"But you'd rather hate Gray for putting you in that dress with diamonds at your throat."

"No."

"Lie."

"Fine." I rattled the ice in the glass and felt as bitter as the taste of whiskey on my lips. "Think what you want, Mace. I won't change someone who's too stubborn to listen."

"You aren't stubborn?"

"I'm wearing the dress, aren't I? I have his damn diamonds around my throat like it's his hand."

Mace flashed his canines. "You've got the elders drooling and their females fuming. Too bad it's not enough for them to respect you."

"For the damn gods, Mace, I get it." My glass was empty, and I lunged up to get more. "I'll never be good enough, wolf enough, loyal enough, or committed enough for you. Get in line behind the wolves inside who laugh like I can't figure out it's at me."

"You're tougher than that. Where's the Noa who beat me to death when I was trying to help?"

My lips twitched. "She was drunk on worm poison and angry because you wanted to watch the nymph turn her into lunch."

"And you'll never forgive me for it, will you?"

"Probably not. At least not for another decade or more."

Mace sipped his whiskey while both of us stared at the purpling hills. "Gray would intervene before then. He doesn't like discord in the ranks."

"I'm not in the ranks."

"Yes, you are, Noa. Like it or not. Once Gray pulls you into his orbit, he doesn't let you out—and those women in there? They won't respect you until you believe you deserve it."

The need to argue died on my lips; I sipped the whiskey instead. This conversation was the longest I'd ever had with Mace, but maybe it was easier to talk without either of us noticing what we were doing.

"When Gray was six," Mace said. "Creatures slaughtered his parents, and he sat there for two days with a stick in his hand, guarding their bodies until the alpha came. Because that's who he is. He protects those too weak to protect themselves."

I licked the taste of whiskey from my lips. "He's a knight in shining armor?"

"Some wolves see him that way." Ice rattled in Mace's glass when he refreshed both our drinks.

"But not you?"

"He doesn't want the shining armor. Years ago, he kept after me. Wouldn't let go. Made me shit-faced angry about it, but I ended up with something I'd never had. He gave me dignity. Self-respect. A place to belong. When he wanted to build Azul, I told him it wouldn't work. We'd never keep it secure. But he did it anyway because he knew the pack needed safety and I'd work out the security. With Gray, it's more than duty, or obligation, or because the magic chose him."

I shifted in the chair, stared at my glass while Mace continued, "He fights. He doesn't accept defeat, and in all the years I've known him, he has never offered his mark to anyone. Not to me. Not to Fallon. But he offered it to you, Noa, and whatever bargain you made with him…"

When Mace turned to face me, his eyes were hard in the light. He was the alpha I'd met on the first day. The predator who stalked through the general store hunting me.

"You will uphold your end, or I will slice through that wolf on your wrist. Do what he should have done, if he had any sense."

"I'll uphold my end." I clenched my lips. "But maybe you should slice it anyway if he shouldn't take the risk."

"I won't, because he wants you."

The glass clipped against my teeth as I sipped. "Why?"

"He faces threats you can't even imagine. He does it because he believes he'll make a difference." Mace thumped his glass down on the table beside the bottle. "He believes in hope, Noa. What about you? What do you believe in?"

I was still asking that question twenty minutes later. The whiskey burned in my stomach, making me nauseous. I'd lost my sanctuary when the elders and their wives moved outside. The glass deck was crowded and noisy, and I retreated to a far corner, safe in the shadows. Turning toward the distant mountains, I tipped my face toward the cooling breeze.

"The beacons will light soon," Grayson said from behind me. "Come stand with me."

I jolted out of the reverie I'd fallen into and blinked. "I can't watch from here?"

"You can't see the fires from here." He leaned in, brushed his nose close to my ear. "You are not your mother. Now... come stand with me."

The command was deep-throated and dominant. *Wolf.* As were the wolves gathered around us. I needed to see them beneath the human side, understand them. Wolves were emotional, erotic creatures. They were also ruthless. The woman who gossiped the most during dinner had stepped closer, and when Grayson spoke again, he pitched his voice loud enough for her to hear.

"Please, Noa." His lips warmed my throat where the pulse beat. "Stop being angry with me."

Was I? Angry with him? Or with myself?

Because maybe, when I saw this dress... when I saw *him*... I'd believed for an instant it was real.

Wanted it to be real.

His knuckles grazed down my arm, then up again. It was the way he'd touched me during the ritual, and my body softened.

"You are... breathtaking."

Wildfire whipped through me. "I think you're talking about the view."

"There's only one I'm interested in."

The wolf rune on my wrist twitched. My heart beat as Grayson clasped my hand and pressed it against his thigh.

"Now, come," he murmured. "Stand with me."

The demand was ruthless. I knew this was pretend. But when his thumb traced small circles against my skin… when I felt the flex of the hard muscles in his thigh… saw the faint feathering of the muscle in his cheek…

I breathed.

Relented.

"Fine," I said. "But I'm still angry."

"I know." His fingers tightened. "It's the same for me."

CHAPTER 31

Noa

THE FIRST BEACON FLARED when the first star blinked on in the night sky. Then a second flashed from an opposing hill. Within seconds, crimson pyres illuminated the dark... a third, a fourth... while I gripped the glass railing, silently counting. Ruby flames danced on the hills. Beads of light glimmered in the deep indigo valleys. Distant mountain pinpricks reminded me of stars that had fallen from the sky.

Gratitude ached in my throat for the gift Grayson had given me. We stood where the view was the best; I leaned forward, trusting the hold he kept on me so close to the barrier. The glass was nearly invisible in the dark, enough to trigger my fear of heights. But his arms were steady around my waist, while around us, the elders argued over which beacon was the most spectacular. The betting was furious until flames leapt from a snowy ridge in the distance. An explosion sent sparks pouring over the edge in a glorious crimson waterfall, and Mosbach shouted in triumph.

"He wins every year," Grayson said. "That's his mountain. His seconds usually come for the glory, but the Gathering is in Sentinel Falls this year and he had no excuse."

"You sound like he isn't welcome."

"He was unexpected." Grayson frowned as the crowd moved toward the French doors, returning inside where more food and drink waited. Then he left with the excuse of discussions that couldn't wait until morning. Mace and Fallon circulated—I could see them from where I stood. When Mace disappeared, I guessed he was checking the sentries. Fallon was monitoring those inside.

All the elders knew about Azul. They'd be staying in guest houses before attending the Gathering. Although the evening was slowing down, I wasn't ready to leave, not yet. I needed the solitude and wanted to watch the last beacon fire burn out.

"Did you enjoy the spectacle, Ms. Bishop?"

Mosbach lurked in the shadows, the way a spider lurks, waiting for the hapless moth. I didn't doubt he despised me. Despised the pack mark on my arm even more than Grayson's rune on my wrist. What I didn't know was why he'd come back outside, and why he was talking to me.

But I knew Mosbach hadn't come tonight because he wanted an award. Awards meant nothing to wolves like him. He valued power.

I turned to face him. "My grandfather told me about the beacons," I said. "I never thought I'd see them."

"I hope the experience was worth the cost."

We were alone, other than two hulking bodyguards blocking the French doors, and something crowding had entered Mosbach's posture, as if he was backing me into a corner.

"Have you ever skinned a rabbit, Ms. Bishop?" he asked. "Not after it's dead. While it's still alive. They scream—oh, not with the first cut. Seconds later, when the ripping starts."

Every muscle in my body froze while the elder waved a hand toward the space beside him. "Sit down."

He'd claimed one of the two chairs remaining on the deck, and my gaze skittered from the empty chair to the empty deck, then to the blocked door.

The last thing I wanted was to sit near him, but the body-guards stood ready. They would force me if I didn't obey.

My hands fisted in my lap when I sat. Around my feet, the dress pooled like blood, and when I looked at the deep shadows beneath the glass deck, I was back in my nightmare, perched above the abyss.

Only the monster wasn't hiding in the dark.

He was sitting next to me.

"I'm afraid I don't know your last name."

"Mosbach is sufficient. The name comes from an extinct wolf believed to be the ancestor to gray wolves, which makes my history as curious as yours."

An elder named after an extinct wolf... speaking to the *faille* with her own extinction history. Perhaps mortal enemies, if one wanted to believe the old superstitions.

I studied his suit, tailor-made, signaling money and influence. When he smiled, his fleshy lips were repulsive, his eyes black, and I was no longer thinking about the spider.

I thought about a seam opening in a sunlit meadow and creatures pouring out. About slamming my mother's guardian angel against thickening mud and pulling a book free, a book no one could read.

About breaking the sky.

Despite the cold, my skin was damp. A server approached with a tray, two glasses, and a bottle. Mosbach gestured toward the table as if he expected the delivery, and the action was proof enough this meeting was not accidental.

When the server offered a glass, I kept my hands in my lap, and Mosbach chided, "Take it, my dear. It's only cognac. Far too expensive to be poisoned."

I did as he asked, and he nodded.

"That wasn't so hard, was it? Dropping the charade?"

Maybe this was Mosbach making polite conversation with someone he despised. Maybe I imagined the menace because I was guilty, but I'd endured everything that evening to protect Grayson, protect *wolves* I cared about, and I wouldn't betray them. "I don't know what you mean."

"Of course you do." The elder *tsked*, although it sounded like a hiss. "It's been painful watching you pretend. You try so hard, wanting to belong—but you don't belong, do you? And you're realizing you never will. Because you're different. But you keep trying, hurting yourself, hurting others, and then something bad happens, and you go along with it. When no one appreciates it. No one stands ready to help or even tries to understand how you feel. Then, despite your best efforts, you end up here, trapped in something you can't escape."

If snakes could smile, they'd look the way Mosbach looked—abhorrent.

"Tell me about your bargain with Grayson, why it needed to be inked on your skin."

"A bargain is between two people," I said. "What it means is between them."

"Not when it affects the pack." Mosbach swirled the drink in his hand, bent his head and sniffed. "I hear you handled yourself well in that meadow."

Through the French doors, laughter filtered, giddy and frivolous, while fear was a long, bony finger sliding down my spine. This *wolf* knew about the creatures in the meadow. Did he know I might have brought them through? Sensed them before the Alpha of Sentinel Falls could sense them?

"Mace did a thorough job cleaning up the mess," Mosbach said. "I'd expect nothing less from him. But he hasn't decided about you, has he? Does he look at you with suspicion? Despite his undying loyalty to his alpha?"

I refused to answer, since bullies like Mosbach liked to poke and prod for an emotional reaction. They fed on it.

"You don't have to answer if it's easier for you," he said. "Information is a commodity, my dear, and the forest has nymphs. Horrid gossips—so imagine my surprise, not only hearing about you, but realizing how dark a secret our Grayson was trying to keep."

I went still. "There are no secrets."

"Everyone has secrets. It's foolish to deny them. Although your secret came from an inept Alpen spy. He told me all about you. I wasn't sure I believed him. Pain makes a man unreliable, so I came here tonight to see if what he said was true."

I couldn't count the threats laced through those words. Mosbach seemed capable of torturing a spy, or ordering it done while he watched. Perhaps waiting for the scream.

And for the first time since Grayson inked the magic on my skin, I believed I needed the protection against *wolves*, and not nymphs.

The elder's gaze sharpened.

I breathed. "You should talk to Grayson."

"I shall, but perhaps I wasn't clear. I know about the meadow. The unnatural creatures you killed. I see the runes on your skin, and I can guess why he put them there. To protect you. But from what? Not from the nymphs. Not when the Lady of the Lake was more afraid of you than you were of her. And that is the first of many, many questions I have for you, my dear. Other elders, too, are wondering, pretending to be so pleasant inside while I'm out here having this delightful conversation."

I thought of Mace checking the sentries, and Fallon mingling. Even Grayson's urgent meeting—were his enemies within the pack so bold they would betray him beneath his own roof? While accepting his hospitality?

Or were his friends protecting him while Mosbach held his little interrogation? To discover if a threat existed. Then eliminate it—suspicious, judgmental, *vindictive wolves!*

Either way, if Grayson found out... or if Mace or Fallon did... I didn't doubt blood would spill. Once again because of me.

I glanced at the last beacon light, flickering from a distant hill, and chanted, *liar... liar... pants on fire* to calm my mind. To keep Grayson from listening to my thoughts. He hated that chant. "I can leave tonight if that's what you want."

"I'm afraid it's too late for you to leave. The damage has been done. The packs expect to see you at the Gathering tomorrow, and if you aren't there... well, someone will have to go after you. Bring you back."

"Then why are we even having this conversation?"

"Because of what you are, my dear." Mosbach's eyes glittered. "The superstitions surrounding *failles* can be tenacious. We've spent generations trying to weed them out, and I can't let you undo all that hard work. I couldn't let your mother do it either, but she was smart. Do you know what made her smart?"

I shook my head.

"She knew when to cut her losses. She didn't stir things up, become a catalyst. Because she knew a catalyst was dangerous. A spark that ignites a fire, and if the alpha isn't willing to put that fire out, it might encourage others to do it for him. The vampires, for instance. They might sweep in, snatch the spark away, and the others might let them do it. See it as solving a problem."

Ice crystalized in my spine. "The others might have a greater problem, giving the spark to the arsonists who sat out the last pack war."

"So... you have claws." He sat back, smug, entitled. "I wondered, since our alpha rarely bothers with women beyond a casual dalliance. But you are right, my dear. No one wants the vampires involved, or rivals going after Grayson's whore."

I kept my expression blank, ignoring the hostility designed to bleed me. "I'm not his whore."

"Of course you're not. That was harsh, and I should have used a kinder word. But the last pack war was over a stolen wolf, and we don't need another. Although you are exquisite. I see why Grayson put his mark on you."

The elder made a moue with his lips, igniting an alarm that seeped into my veins. I had to push it down, deep down, where the monster stirred.

Mosbach gestured to a man I hadn't known was there. He held a blanket.

My hands clawed around the cognac glass. Liquid sloshed.

"She's chilled." The elder spoke to the man while he looked at me. "No point in suffering if you don't have to."

It took a moment before reality sank in. The man arranged the blanket around my shoulders, tucking it tight. But not tight enough for Mosbach, since he leaned forward to adjust the folds. Then his hand dropped to my knee, his fingers squeezing. I jerked away.

Mosbach leaned back and savored his cognac. I could hear voices inside the house, laughter. The breeze fluttered the dress hem, cooled my skin. The blanket was a straitjacket that I shrugged off. And Mosbach went on as if there'd been no interruption. That we were two friends sharing drinks on the deck, and we'd have plenty of conversations such as this in the future.

"The Gathering is tomorrow, with so much at stake," he said. "We must all play our part. Grayson is the Alpha, but he can't rule without the support of the pack elders. And this is where you come in, my dear. Our little catalyst, our... spark... blazing innocently away. Oblivious to the risks. How many elders will trust him tomorrow, after their wives realize how you lied to them tonight?"

I went rigid. "I didn't lie."

"Oh, I'm sure they won't see it that way." Mosbach smiled and swirled the cognac in his glass. "Ah... I've upset you."

"No."

"Of course I did. You've gone pale. The cognac will help."

He leaned forward, pushing his glass against my lips. Revulsion whipped through me, but the bodyguards shifted, and I separated my tight lips enough to sip while hoping I wouldn't retch.

"I didn't support Grayson as Alpha." The elder settled back, satisfied—over what, I wasn't certain, forcing his cognac on me, or not supporting Grayson.

"I supported my nephew in his challenge. But he died, my nephew. It was a gruesome spectacle. Challenge battles are always hard to stomach. You don't want to see one."

I asked tightly, "Why would I see one?"

"Because he put his mark on you. Broadcasting to the world that he'll kill to protect you. When we both know it's a lie. And tomorrow, the Gathering will be far more perilous for him than for you, my dear. If his enemies discover the truth, he'll look weak. Wolves kill the weak. Oh, we'll call it a contest with as many opponents as it takes. Do you want to watch him battle, bleed, fall from exhaustion, and know all that violence was because of you?"

"He's not weak."

"I didn't say he was, but you endanger him. Along with everyone you love."

"They've done nothing."

"Which makes the injustice more unbearable—the suffering of innocents. It's like listening to the rabbit's scream over and over."

Mosbach crossed one knee over the other while I shook from head to toe.

"Challenges never end with the alpha's death," he continued. "No alpha assumes power without having to kill at least one wolf. Then the old alpha's allies, their families. Friends unable to swear loyalty. All dead. The bloodshed goes on, so much damage spreading like wildfire. All from one harmless, tiny, oblivious spark."

"I am harmless."

"You are far from that, my dear. I think you're the advantage he hides behind his back."

Perhaps Mosbach was trying to warn me, but I felt panic swell, and beneath the red dress, my knee jerked with the urge to run. "What do you want from me?"

"Cooperation." He ripped the glass from my grasp, then gripped my wrist, jerking my hand upright, his fleshy fingers digging into the wolf rune. "No one will believe this unless you have his scent not only on your skin, but in you. And your scent on him. In him."

I yanked my hand free, rubbing at the reddened flesh.

"Convince me by tomorrow, and I'll support him at the Gathering," Mosbach said. "The other elders will, too. If not, know that scent on your shoulder and a few diamonds won't fool his enemies. He'll need to fuck you to do that."

"Noa?" Fallon's voice sharpened as she shoved past the bodyguards Mace held in place. Then Grayson was striding out on the deck... so very far beyond anger as he scooped me up from the chair. What I felt in his arms chilled me. I couldn't speak as he tightened his hold, and while I didn't know what order Grayson issued through the pack bond, I knew Mosbach didn't like it by the way his snarl rumbled.

Mace's sentries surrounded the elder, closing in. Then Mosbach's men arrived, and I couldn't stop the shivering that wracked through me.

CHAPTER 32

Noa

WOLVES THRIVED ON VIOLENCE, but what Mosbach provoked was violence on an emotional level I wasn't sure I could handle. Hours ago, Grayson handed me off to Fallon. He'd been so enraged that I went with her without protest, letting her push me into the bedroom and close the door. She wanted me away from the arguing wolves, and once I was alone... after I stopped shaking... I took off the glamorous dress. Pulled the flowers from my hair, unwinding the intricate knot Vasha fashioned with such hope.

I couldn't remove the diamond choker because I couldn't figure out the clasp, and I'd have to face Grayson eventually, if only to ask him to do it.

But I wasn't looking forward to that meeting, so after I undressed, I tugged on one of his reeking shirts because it felt right, having something of his wrapped around me.

And maybe that made me foolish enough to scream at the moon, at the gods who thought this situation was hilarious. I could pace with my arms wrapped tight, chew on my lip and pretend nothing had changed. Lying to myself about traveling the world, taking photographs. Creating my safe reality.

Or I could accept that the silver in my hair was the mark of queens. And a queen did not cower or let life happen to her because she could not make a choice.

It was past two in the morning. Grayson was still up; I heard him moving around and knew he couldn't relax. After finding the fluffy robe, I pulled it on over his shirt, belting it at the waist as I walked through the house the way I'd walked weeks ago.

I found Grayson in the living room. A low fire guttered in the fireplace, casting a golden light. He sat on the couch with one arm stretched along the back cushions. The other was bent as he stared at the half-empty glass in his hand, and I wasn't sure how to reach him if he wanted solitude.

"Second thoughts aren't worth it," I murmured. "All they do is keep you awake."

"You should be sleeping," he said around a sip of whatever he was drinking.

"So should you." He'd left out the cognac bottle, and after pouring a glass, I turned to look at him. He still wore the black suit, but the jacket was off and the shirt tightened against his shoulders as he drank. His bare feet were propped on a low coffee table, and I stepped between his legs, sat down on the table's edge. While he moved his feet to the floor, I took it as a positive sign when he didn't stand or move away. Lazily, curiously, he simply watched as I arranged the robe, shifted my position so my knees were between his.

We both sipped the expensive alcohol while I wondered if he was still angry. Not with Mosbach, but with me. I'd known his ferocity, when he stormed out onto the deck, was because I'd used that childish inner chant until it was almost too late. But still... he was there, and I'd clung to him, hiding the disappointment when he handed me off to Fallon.

We were alone now, with no Fallon between us. My gaze drifted over the tiny scar near his left eye. A muscle feathered in his cheek the way it always did when I annoyed him, or when he fought his moods. I grew aware of the latent power in his body, leashed, yet crackling with tension. He was the Alpha of Sentinel Falls. But I could not stop what I'd started, and asked, "Did you kill him?"

"Kill who?"

"Mosbach. Because I know you were angry enough. He's one of your elders, accepting your hospitality while stabbing you in the back. But I hope you didn't, because I think he was trying to help."

Grayson scowled. "He'll be happy to know you're pleading his case."

"Where is he?" I asked, licking the alcohol from my lips. "Do you have a dungeon where you hide your enemies?"

The look Grayson threw me was irritated. "What the hell did your mother tell you?"

"Fairytales and nonsense. But every hero has a dungeon somewhere. Sometimes he even ends up in it himself, and then the princess has to rescue him."

I reached out, daring to push back the dark hair that fell against his forehead. "I think you're in that dungeon right now, but it's in your head, and worry keeps you there. Tonight didn't go as well as we'd planned, and—honestly—it was nobody's fault."

"It was my fault Mos cornered you on the deck," Grayson said, bringing the glass to his lips.

"It was my fault for coming here weeks ago," I countered, daring him to continue with the guilt game.

"I should have guessed why he was here."

"Yes, you are the all-powerful Alpha, and Mosbach is a rude, pudgy little snake." I watched him over my glass rim. "He told me you killed his nephew."

Grayson's scowl deepened, but he couldn't be too annoyed because he hadn't pulled his arm from the back of the couch.

I drew in a breath. "He also warned me about what could happen tomorrow if no one believes our ruse."

"I'll deal with tomorrow."

"I know you will. Brilliantly. But there's nothing wrong with asking for help. I've asked you for help plenty of times and you've never said no."

I set aside my glass, then took Grayson's glass and set it beside mine. "What's at stake tomorrow is important to you, but also to me, because I have people I love. People I want to protect. And your enemies will circle around, looking for ways to hurt you. Hurt the pack."

"I won't let that happen," he said.

"Neither will I."

Grayson's strange eyes narrowed. He was broody, lounging like a predator. My stomach dipped as I leaned forward to loosen his tie and tug it from the shirt collar.

"We both know Mosbach is right. No one will believe we're lovers when they can tell we're not."

I unbuttoned the top two buttons on his shirt as I spoke, smoothing my hands toward his shoulders, aware of the strength there. The danger in petting the wolf.

"My mother told me something else about wolves. The importance of scent communication."

He gripped my hands to hold them still. "I'm not sleeping with you because of some damn thing that old man said."

I moistened my lips. "No. We... are sleeping with each other... because we have a bargain. I won't be the reason your enemies challenge you. Not after the many times you've protected me. Let me give this gift to you."

"No."

When he lunged to his feet, I remembered how tall he was, but it was worse with him towering over me while I sat on a low table with my knees pressed together and my fingers curled. "Why?"

"Because your hands are clenched."

I stared at my fingers, at the whitened tension he saw there, but then I stood. The lack of space between us meant we were pressed close enough to feel the hard arousal he couldn't control. "You aren't immune."

"I've never been immune." His canines flashed. "That doesn't mean you owe me anything."

His voice was low, his scent a mix of cognac, pine, midnight spice... drowning me. "That's not why I'm offering."

He breathed in... and my hands were at the buttons on his shirt, one by one, until I could slide my palms around his waist.

"I know you want to keep me safe. I want the same for you, and I thought if I wore your reeking shirt, it would help. But I don't think it's enough, and you know it's not enough. You'll still be stubborn about it, because that's you, Grayson. All alpha—and it has to be your idea, or it isn't right. But tomorrow, the world could change, and I don't want regrets in the morning. Knowing I didn't do everything I could tonight to help you."

I loosened the robe until it fell from my shoulders to the floor.

His chest lifted with a slow breath, and I breathed in the way he did. I was hardly a seductress in his reeking shirt, with the hem brushing at mid-thigh, the neckline sliding off one shoulder. Beneath, I wore no bra, only black silk panties, and the diamonds that glittered at my throat.

I touched them. "I left the necklace on because I couldn't figure out the clasp."

"Turn around." His voice was dangerous as he added, "I'll do it."

Dutifully, I obeyed, trembling when his thumb traced a small circle over my shoulder. He swept my hair aside, then attended to the clasp, taking his time. As he slid the necklace free, he used both hands, caging me, holding the diamonds in his palm.

"I liked seeing you in these." But then he moved away, set the diamonds on a nearby table and kept his back to me. "Go to bed, Noa."

My pulse thundered. Gods—why had I thought I could seduce a man so far beyond my experience? Grayson was the damn *Wolf* of Sentinel Falls. So far from the boy in my photography class who'd been afraid to touch me. I'd had to walk that boy through his first fumbled attempt at arousal, showing him with my hand... I'd be pathetic, trying to do that with a man like Grayson.

But then, the images Mosbach planted in my head flashed, the blood and endless challenges, death and a rabbit's gods-damned scream. The muscles in my back spasmed as I asked, "I can't be half in, half out, but it's okay for you?"

His posture stiffened. "I said I wouldn't sleep with you—"

"Because you think I'm obligated?" My temper flared. "In what fantasy world do you live in, Grayson? I wouldn't have offered if it wasn't my choice."

"A choice Mosbach manipulated," he snarled, swinging around, his strange eyes glittering. "And you're too gullible not to realize sex with me makes it worse for you."

Cold, hard words. I couldn't clamp my lips tight enough, fast enough. "You're right. Sleeping with an *asshole* could be worse. I'm sure I'd hate myself in the morning."

His eyes looked a bit glazed, flashing between cobalt blue and emerald. But he was all male, all dominance, and I couldn't stop the backward steps I took when he pushed away from the table and walked toward me.

This was the wolf I should fear, not seduce, and my back knocked against the cold window before Grayson pressed his palm against the glass, leaned in.

With his free hand, he gripped my chin. "Convince me you want this."

"I offered you a gift. You threw it back in my face."

"Convince me."

His thumb pressed against my lower lip and I jerked free. The scents now rolling from him were heady… male arousal, cognac, anger… yes, anger had a scent, like crushed roses at midnight, cold spice, woodsy secrets. He was bulldozing me. Pushing the way he'd pushed after tattooing his wolf rune on my wrist, daring me to fight with him.

I wouldn't do it.

"Convince yourself," I said as my mouth dried.

A muscle ticked in his jaw. An inner war darkened his eyes, but I recognized the battle in a way I couldn't explain. As if a part of him said, "*We are the same.*"

And a part of me said, "*No… we are moth and flame.*"

He moved closer. I breathed. His knuckles brushed against my thigh, drifting beneath the shirt hem. His fingers spread, pressed against my skin. The calloused stroke of his thumb inched higher, tracing little circles until I pressed my teeth into my lower lip. Sucked in another breath.

His gaze never left my face. I knew he tracked each tiny shudder. Each time my lashes fluttered. When I looked away, and when I looked back again.

How I stifled a soft moan.

"Tell me you like this," he ordered.

"Tell me you like doing it," I hissed while his lips twisted.

"Always so stubborn."

"Always such an ass."

My gaze locked on his. We battled as I'd always known we would, two equals clashing. The green in his eyes sharpened. His hand became relentless, as if he needed to wring every last shiver and trembling confession from my lips. Force me to say what my scent already gave away.

My lips parted as he played with my silk panties, at the wet that pooled.

"Interesting," he mocked. "How your body can't lie."

I shuddered at that truth. "Convincing enough?"

"Not yet." His growl was a soft seduction. He slid the silk aside and found my swollen clit, teasing with the same erotic circles he'd used on my thigh. My body jerked at the friction. I gripped his shoulders and couldn't stop my nails from digging into the hard muscles that flexed and bunched beneath his open shirt.

He rubbed again, a soft laugh rising in his throat. "Say it."

But this was his war and I wouldn't surrender. I'd already given him my terms, and he'd rejected them. I wasn't begging now.

He growled, his thumb still doing wicked things while he pushed one finger inside.

Tremors rocked through me. I bit hard on my lip. His hand flexed while I willed my body into stillness... but a second finger joined the first, stretching me, curling upward. He pulled out and then pushed in again.

A whimper caught in my throat.

"Better. But I want the words."

He circled my clit while his fingers pushed with a pressure so perfect, I was sure my eyes had rolled back in my head. I couldn't get enough. Couldn't get him deep enough, hard enough. Couldn't reach him intimately enough to know if he felt the same way.

"That's it, sweetheart. Give me that orgasm you're trying so hard to stop."

"Bastard," I gritted.

"You say that with such anger when this was your choice." His head bent until I felt the scrape of his canines against my throat. "And call me darling when you roll over the edge."

Wave after wave of full-body pleasure pulsed through me, my breath hissing in my throat as he increased the pace, his fingers finding the sensitive spot that had my hips lifting. His palm rubbed against my clit until a small, helpless sound parted my lips.

"*Asshole!*"

He laughed.

"*Bastard!*"

"I love the arguments you make when you're dripping all over my hand."

His tongue stroked my throat and the quick, sharp brush of canines was utterly catastrophic. My hips jerked. The sounds I made were throaty as I ground against his hand, my grip hard on his shoulders. As my head tipped back, his mouth took mine, and I'd never had a man kiss me like that before. He devoured, took even the breath in my throat, his pumping hand destroying me with the first pulsing release. His thumb pressed, rubbed, and he brought me up again, pushed me over in a second shuddering orgasm... but as the tremors weakened, he withdrew and pulled me against his chest.

We were both breathing hard, but while my hands were at his waist, my cheek against his chest, I knew our storm was not building. It had already passed, and when he cupped my face, kissed my forehead... I didn't want to let go.

But nothing could stop him from pulling away.

"Now, go to bed, Noa," he said. "Please, just... go to bed."

CHAPTER 33

Noa

"TIME'S WASTING, SUNSHINE," FALLON said the following morning. "I brought clothes."

She tossed an outfit over the couch, and from the leather, I guessed it was a long-sleeved black shirt with a tight-fitting vest and pants—what she always wore. With a flip of her braid, she added, "I'll do your hair if you want."

Bleary-eyed, I gulped my coffee. "I don't look good in leather."

"Leather means you belong in Gray's inner circle."

"I'm not good at inner circling."

"I'll warn you about the major players." She helped herself to coffee, then said over her shoulder, "You'll be with me or Mace. You can't be alone, so if not us, you'll be with Gray."

I felt less than charitable about that order. "I won't know what to say."

"Follow your instincts when you meet people you don't know."

If I'd followed my instincts, I would have ignored her knuckles hammering on the door. But instead, I'd squinted into the sunlight, scowling at the birds chirping and the green hills wiped clean.

No hint of the beacon fires that had burned so vividly the night before.

No hint of what happened on the cantilevered deck or in the living room, where I'd humiliated myself.

I wondered if she knew about my failed seduction. Or that I'd been alone in the watchtower house when I woke up. If she knew the abandonment still hurt.

Maybe someone like Fallon would have handled Mosbach differently. But if this ruse with Grayson failed, I'd do more than damage his reputation. I could destroy the peace Grayson fought so hard to maintain—with his elders. His wolves. Even if I could forget the sick gratification in Mosbach's voice when he described the rabbit's scream, I could not forget those who would suffer unnecessarily. I'd watched Grayson fight. I knew no one would survive a challenge, and few would take the risk. But there would be damage. Blood. And I'd be responsible for that.

The coffee was bitter on my tongue, and I dumped it out. "I'll get dressed."

An hour later, we'd completed the trek from the watchtower house to Azul, then from Azul to Leo's old vet clinic, where pickup trucks waited for the short drive to Sentinel Falls. The weather was mild, and the town festive. Crowds mingled along streets swept clean and lined with flowering planters. Streamers fluttered from roof overhangs. Everywhere, the swirl of color and movement drew the eye. The café's doors were open in a show of hospitality. Outside Hattie's general store, a man I didn't recognize monitored an open grill stacked with sizzling meat.

Side streets hosted chairs beneath open-sided white tents. Flags snapped in the breeze like colorful war banners, identifying tables loaded with food and drink. Fallon explained each flag. The nymphs had stripes of blue, brown, and green for water, tree, and woodland nymphs, the three major clans in the territory. Flowers covered their table. Dishes held fresh fruit, nuts, prepared fish. Rainbow-colored juices sparkled in glass urns, contrasting with the vampire's table, which, like their flag, was draped in black. I didn't look closely at the refreshments, but it was hard not to ogle the beautiful men who gathered around. "Do all vampires look like that?"

Fallon laughed. "Enough of them."

"Maybe it's a prerequisite," I murmured, staring at a man with long salt-and-pepper hair, mesmerizing gray eyes, and a sex appeal that stroked against my skin.

"Maybe it's their diet." Fallon nudged me with her elbow. "Don't stare too long. Vamps have no boundaries."

I glanced at the other flags that whipped and fluttered. "Who else is here?"

"No witches, at least not enough to have a flagged delegation. The packs are here." She pointed to the left. "The red flag with the two wolves in battle—Carmag. Sentinel Falls has a blue field with a white diagonal stripe."

She frowned as two men pulled the fabric cover from a yellow flag that, once unfurled, revealed a black claw-slash through the middle ground. Three other men set up a table draped in yellow bunting. Five more carried boxes and chairs.

I monitored every movement. "Alpen?"

"We were told a limited delegation," Fallon said. "Not over three."

I counted ten and altered my stance. I'd known Alpen would be here, but seeing them unnerved me.

Fallon tipped her head, and I guessed she was communicating through the pack bond. Moments later, I recognized five Sentinel Falls pack members as they ambled along the crowded street, talking casually, yet closing in and alert.

"You'll stay away from that end of the street," Fallon warned, as she moved me in a different direction.

I copied her swagger and hoped I didn't look ridiculous. "Doesn't the Gathering forbid hostilities?"

"Any attendee caught violating the rules is exiled for five years."

The urge to roll my eyes had me blinking. "How often do you have violations?"

"Rarely. Not even during the pack wars. But Noa..." Fallon closed her hand around my elbow, stopping me. "Everyone here has their own agenda. And no matter how you feel about Gray this morning, trust him."

I held her steady gaze. "I'd like to get through the day without problems."

"We all want that."

Ahead, the blue flag for Sentinel Falls caught my attention. Blue represented the entire Selkirk territory, while the white diagonal stripe proclaimed the Sentinel Falls authority by sheer power and numbers. Women surrounded the table, arranging platters and bowls. Children played soccer in the street, laughing, shouting insults back and forth. I thought of the children in Azul, hanging on Grayson's arms, trying to drag him down. The memory smothered me before I pushed it away.

I saw Hattie, sunlight tangling in her white hair as she directed the women. Oscar was nearby, standing with a group of older men who laughed at some joke. A band played in the distance—lively Celtic music.

"Carmag," Fallon said. "They love their music. Anson Salas is their alpha—early thirties, muscular and handsome." Her eyes sparkled. "I might let you meet him."

She laughed when I elbowed her, then sobered. "Alpen's alpha is Lec Rus. Julien Visant is the vampire emissary. An ally. Anyone else, and I'll give you a name. We'll be in the receiving line before the Gathering starts, but everyone keeps a distance, so... no touching to worry about. Smile and nod, but don't chant the liar... liar."

I shot a look at her, and she grinned. "Oops. Gray let it slip."

"He said you could teach me how to keep him out of my head."

"Chants work. I can teach you more. But he's the only one who can hear you, so maybe leave that channel open today."

She was talking about the near disaster last night, when I'd shut Grayson out. I tugged at the leather vest that felt constraining. Levi loped past, waving at me and nodding in deference toward Fallon. Grayson stood in the distance, his hair raven-black in the sunlight, his muscular frame towering over the surrounding men. They were animated, holding glasses in their hands. I took a moment to settle myself, testing the wolf energy at this end of the street—so different from Alpen's energy.

Instead of heavy and dark, I thought of summer grass freshly mowed, filled with warmth and the lazy drone of insects. A nymph stepped into our path. She wore a gossamer blue gown with flowers scattered on the skirt and twined in her long auburn hair.

"Lady." She bowed her head toward me, then toward Fallon. "Alpha. I offer greetings."

"Nia." Fallon returned the nymph's greeting, although she didn't bow. "Good to see you."

"We are pleased to be here." Nia held out her hand, palm up, then gestured toward the laden table. "Please. We offer our hospitality." She looked at me again. "Lady, we would be honored."

"I'm not a lady," I murmured, thinking of Metis, but I focused on the food at her table. The iced drinks sparkled. The strawberries and succulent raspberries drew my attention. And because the sun had grown warm while leather was uncomfortable, I envied Nia's gown. The fragile blue material played with the breeze. Flower petals fluttered, and I asked, "Are you a water nymph?"

"I am woodland." She picked up a plate, adding choices while my stomach rumbled. "Alpha?"

Nia offered Fallon the same courtesy, although she accepted less than I did. But enough that I didn't feel odd, standing there and sliding food into my mouth. As we ate, Nia chatted about the other nymphs present, then took our empty plates and offered the chilled drinks.

I sipped and sighed. "I've never tasted anything this wonderful—like I'm biting into a fresh peach and an orange at the same time."

"It is from our orchards." Nia's smile widened, revealing pointy, perfect teeth. Her over-long fingers flexed as she folded her hands in front of her. "We are pleased you like it. And I offer our apologies. Word of your kindness to Lorriel has reached us. The Lady of the Lake also extends her... apologies. For any dispersions upon you which were unintended."

Fallon shifted her weight. Nia bowed again. "I have kept you."

"It's alright, Nia," Fallon said. "I will give the Alpha your message."

"Thank you."

As we walked away, I murmured, "What was that about?"

"Diplomacy," Fallon said. "And repercussions, perhaps. The nymphs are worried, beyond what happened at the cave."

I chewed on my lip, deciding to remain silent.

"We hold the Gathering at city hall," Fallon continued. "Each species sends a representative, plus a guard or assistant of their choice. The doors will close. They'll discuss minor conflicts, new areas of concern. Envoys settle major issues months in advance. Agreement is a formality."

A gaggle of children rushed past in a raucous game of tag, bumping into Fallon before she stepped aside. When a small boy tripped, a girl stopped to help him up. Both Fallon and I smiled at the consideration.

"We'll still have discussions, not long. Then everyone signs the treaty," she said. "They stand, make formal toasts no one believes, and fake the friendships until it's time to leave."

Hattie waved from her table, and I waved back. "Where will I be?"

"Inside with the rest of us. As the host, Grayson may have his full court around him. He could have twenty armed wolves if he wanted, but the optics would be aggressive, so he'll settle for the three of us. That doesn't mean we aren't all on guard."

"Mosbach said—"

"Noa." Fallon's tone was sharp, and her hand closed around my arm. "The elders support Gray, and no wolf will challenge the Alpha of Sentinel Falls today. Not in his home territory, and not when he's hosting the Gathering. Annihilation is the penalty."

I shuddered at the menace in her voice. But I also recalled Grayson telling me Mosbach manipulated me, and I was too gullible to realize it. Perhaps there was more to pack rivalry than I imagined.

My braided hair felt heavy against my nape. The leathers were stiff, and I asked testily, "Why did I have to dress this way?"

"Because it's tradition," Fallon said. "And the shirt hides the runes on your skin."

"Will they still protect me?"

"Yes." She rubbed her hand against my back. "But the wolf on your wrist surpasses them all, and that's the mark Gray wants everyone to see."

Hattie hugged when we reached her, then pushed me back at arm's length, studying my face, my clothes. "Oscar... she's here."

Oscar beamed as he walked toward me, standing straighter than I remembered. A woman hovered beside him, and I recognized her: an elder's wife. Miranda Kirk, early sixties, but the wrinkles on her face came from worry and not age.

"Noa," she said. "I owe you an apology for last night. All the wives do, although I'm not sure all will admit it. I'm sorry I behaved as if you weren't welcome. You were more welcome than I was, and it was my awkwardness at fault."

Hattie added, "Like those in Sentinel Falls, established cliques can be... insensitive. They remembered Andrea, and perhaps some behaved rudely out of embarrassment."

I understood Hattie's explanation because I'd felt a similar resentment toward the wolves for eight years. Emotions were never perfect. But Miranda Kirk was trying, and I touched her clenched hands.

"I was rude and immature eight years ago," I admitted. "I owed everyone there an apology for the way I stormed away. But I've never attended a beacon night, and I was grateful for the opportunity."

Miranda's tension eased. "Bless you. Hattie was telling me about what you did for Oscar, and I know... it's not appropriate for me to ask, not today..."

I guessed where she was going and asked, "Do you know someone like Oscar?"

"My brother." She twisted her hands, looked away. "I thought, if you could visit him someday, maybe hold his hand for a moment."

"Is he here today?"

"He's sitting in the shade. I can't leave him. He forgets where he is and wanders off and then it upsets him."

I touched Fallon's arm. Told her where I was going and why, how she could see me the entire time.

After she approved, I matched Miranda's careful pace across the tufted ground. "What's your brother's name?"

"Albert." Her step faltered. "He was always so strong."

We didn't go far. I could still hear the voices around Hattie's table. Albert sat in a chair, shoulders hunched, knee bouncing with the same repetition Oscar had the first day, when he'd been sorting fishing lures. I wondered if constant movement was a way to soothe the silent wolf inside.

In the shade, the air was cooler, and being out of the sun and away from curious eyes was a relief. I didn't mind the subdued energy around Albert. I found it relaxing. Birds rustled and chirped messages as they hopped through the trees. From somewhere distant, a dog barked. The Celtic music turned into something haunting. Bagpipes, mourning a loss.

I breathed in, breathed out.

There was goodness here. When I looked at the people filling the street, mingling, dancing... it was hard to see them as wolves. Or vampires, witches, nymphs. As enemies.

"Albert," I said, taking care not to startle him. "I'm Noa. Your sister told me about you."

His knee bobbed. His fingers were knobby with arthritis and his skin had the dryness of leather.

"May I sit beside you?" I wondered how Miranda handled him. Did she reassure him through her voice? Or through touch?

Albert remained mute, but I asked permission before I touched him, skimming my fingers across his veined skin. Then I settled my palm and felt the trickle of warmth flow from him to me. I didn't understand the magic. If I had to describe it, the easiest would be to say I was draining the pressure, easing him within his own skin.

We sat that way for twenty minutes. Albert's knee bobbed. And then... it stopped, and he looked up, dazed. "Mira?"

"I'm here." His sister placed her hands on his shoulders. "Thank you," she mouthed to me.

"I can see him again," I offered. "Maybe your husband can make arrangements."

In Azul, I thought. Albert would be safe there, with the other silent wolves—if Leo could convince Miranda to allow her brother to remain. No one, it seemed, had suggested it, or if they had, perhaps either Miranda or her husband hadn't wanted to agree.

But she'd asked for my help, and apologized for the Night of the Beacons. Perhaps I'd misread the emotions last night.

Then the runes rippled beneath my skin, and I couldn't discount the unease that caused, when the magic had been quiet before. I'd forgotten, during the moments with Albert, how healing a silent wolf might bother those in attendance today.

Remind them of the old stories, stir up the alarm my ruse with Grayson was supposed to quell.

Shadows clustered beneath the trees, but as I stared, I decided it was the shrubbery that hadn't been pruned back. Albert's knee bobbed again, jerky. The breeze cooled. The runes shivered, and I looked at Miranda. "Take your brother and go back to your husband. Stay close to him. Tell him to be alert."

She whispered, "Is something wrong with Albert?"

"No, nothing. But... sometimes, I get these funny feelings around wolves."

"I'm like that, too, only it's around witches." Miranda smiled, but I wanted to jump out of my skin, get up, and race back to Fallon.

Miranda didn't notice the impatience as she urged Albert to his feet, patting his shirt, holding his hand.

I stood and took a small step.

"We'll leave now," she said. "I'll make up an excuse to go home."

I nodded, then hurried back to where I'd left Fallon; Mace was waiting in her place. I walked up to him, herding him toward the middle of the street. "Pretend we're sharing a joke," I said.

He dipped his chin and looked at me.

"Mace," I hissed. "Act normal. I think there's something wrong."

He flashed alpha teeth and rumbled a laugh that sounded genuine. But he scanned our surroundings in a way that reminded me why he was the Alpha's second.

"Describe what you're feeling."

"Something's here," I said.

"Like in the meadow?"

"Not quite. But the runes are acting up." I shaded my eyes, watching the children kicking a ball around. "Can you get them away? Without being obvious?"

Mace laughed again, swiping a piece of fruit from the nymph's table and popping it in his mouth. But his eyes narrowed, and a moment later, Levi loped across the street to snag the bouncing soccer ball. He held it above his head and laughed like it was a game. The kids mobbed him, and they were off in a merry game of chase while Mace glanced at me.

"We call him the Pied Piper. He'll get as many as he can to Azul."

I looked toward the blue flag. "What about the older women?"

"Hattie's making suggestions now."

I could see her directing ladies like a group of clucking hens; they disappeared down a side street. Sweat pooled at the base of my spine. The need to pinpoint the edginess kept me tense, but I felt nothing like the meadow, before the passage opened. No snapping against my skin, or the taste of ash in my mouth. Even the runes had grown cool.

I stared at the wolf rune. "I could be wrong. The Alpen have me on edge. And I was with Albert, which always throws me off, and—"

"Then you're wrong and we're all happy," Mace said, his hand warm against my back. "The formalities are about to start."

With the streets emptying, it was easier to see the delegations moving toward the pillared building I knew was city hall. Flags flew above the entrance, declaring cooperation and friendship, while the bright yellow sun cast knife-edged shadows. Music still played in the distance, then came to a halt amid a round of applause. Perhaps the musicians were taking a break.

Mace closed his hand around my arm. "Gray knows the status. He wants us there, pronto."

"Pronto?" I teased to ease the tension. "That's a word I never thought you'd say."

"Noa's got balls are three words I sure as shit never thought I'd say, but I just said them to Gray. He said I'd better hope they weren't mine—arrogant bastard."

"That's my name for him." But I was grateful Mace understood. He made this easier while putting precautions into place. And maybe tomorrow we'd all sit around and laugh about it.

Someone had cleared the nymph's table. Flowers were all that remained, battered slightly by the rising breeze. I wondered about the fragile-looking women, where they'd gone, and which two would attend the Gathering. If Nia would be one of them.

The vampires were also nowhere to be seen—I'd not considered it before, but vampires and wolves were mortal enemies. I doubted they'd be comfortable lingering.

Grayson stood with Fallon on the white marble steps of the city hall. He noticed us while speaking to tall man. Mace urged me forward.

Grayson gripped my hand, pulled me to his side. "Noa, I'd like you to meet Julien Visant."

A vampire, according to Fallon's briefing, and I tensed as his gaze drifted over my braided hair and the clothes that matched hers. Did I look like an equal? Or a harmless girl wearing leather to conceal her human vulnerabilities?

"My Lady." Julien bent his head. "An honor to meet you."

I heard only the deference in his voice and nodded in return. "And you, Mr. Visant—although I don't get all this 'my lady' stuff."

He wasn't the first to call me that today.

Grayson murmured, "Noa's not familiar with our customs."

"But charming." The vampire had a diplomat's ease. Brown hair, brown eyes, ordinary and yet... extraordinarily sexual. "But as you are the last to arrive, we should go inside, yes? Attend to business?"

And as he turned back to Grayson and formally bowed his head, I questioned what custom I was unfamiliar with, and why Grayson hadn't already explained it to me.

CHAPTER 34

Noa

THE PLANS CHANGED FOR the Gathering: Mace remained outside. I took my place in the receiving line beside Fallon, while Grayson continued to hold my hand. I could feel his tension the way I felt my own. He knew what he'd done and said to me last night. Knew he'd left before I awakened. I'd been more open and honest with him than anyone I'd ever known, even my mother. And he'd turned my concern into gullibility and abandoned me.

I wanted to be angry. But he needed the harmless, vapid girl in her grown-up clothes because everyone knew about the Lady in the Lake. And the nymphs, the vampires, the other wolves—they came today, not to see the girl marked by the Alpha of Sentinel Falls. But the *faille* who might have broken the sky.

Perhaps even now, as Grayson's chest rose evenly and his features seemed relaxed, more enemies waited.

Our enemies.

I tightened my fingers on his with an offer of support. He accepted with a slight dip of his head. And we both smiled at Julien because the vampire was the first to pass through the receiving line. No other vampires were in his delegation. Perhaps his ability to disappear at will was protection enough.

Next in line was Anson Salas, the Alpha of Carmag—tall, handsome, with striking red-gold hair brushing his shoulders. He wore fine leather and a black shirt, which I thought must be some Alpha uniform because they all wore similar clothes. He was an ally, although when I looked at him, I was certain his pack's interests were the priority. He smiled at Fallon. She smiled back, and I wondered what the connection was. If it was casual, or serious enough that she'd leave the Alpha of Sentinel Falls for the Alpha of Carmag.

"Anson." Grayson had noticed, too, since his dry amusement drew the Carmag's attention. "If you're done ogling my second, I'd like you to meet Noa Bishop."

Anson offered a gentleman's head tip. "A pleasure. I've been curious, but you've been hiding out."

"Hardly your concern," Grayson murmured. "Unless you're here to poach my females?"

Anson's laugh held amusement and not irritation. He winked at me, introduced his guard, and after a moment, they entered the meeting room. Through the open door, I noticed the oak-paneled walls. No windows, only chandeliers for light. An oval conference table with chairs gleamed in the center of the room. Identifying flags directed the seating. Glasses and sparkling water waited, along with folders, an assortment of pens and writing pads.

Next in the receiving line was a young girl, sixteen, possibly seventeen. The straight black hair, alabaster skin, and dark eyes added to the youthful innocence.

"Autumn Paige, witches," she said with a girlish voice that didn't match the chill against my skin—a breeze from an open door? But she nodded and passed by before I could decide, and my attention slid to the next man in line.

Lec Rus. The *Alpen*.

While he was not the alpha who had taken Laura, he was the one who sent his wolves to force Leo off a deserted road. To hunt Levi, and chase me from Seattle. Use a headless Callum to defile Leo's home.

For that alone, for daring to come today and stand in front of me with that smug *wolf* arrogance, I held his stony gaze.

And then I smiled.

Slowly, as if I *had* broken the sky.

As if I was there to collect the retribution Lec Rus owed me.

He snarled. Wolf energy slammed against me.

"Enough," Grayson warned.

But the Alpen couldn't halt his sneer. "We came in peace, and you meet us with a weapon at your side."

"I'm no more a weapon than your presence here is peaceful." I wanted Lec Rus to understand I wasn't the frightened girl he'd chased from Seattle. I held his gaze—a dangerous challenge to a dominant wolf—and he flexed his shoulders with the same rolling movement I was sure he made right before he killed.

Grayson sent a silent command through the pressure on my hand and the wicked twitch of his rune. I turned my head, relenting. Lec Rus could win this round.

He moved away. I focused on the scents of honeysuckle and peppermint floating from the nymphs waiting in line. Nia smiled, introducing her assistant, a meadow nymph in green—Ashina.

Then the doors closed with a thud of finality. The emissaries took their seats while their assistants sat in chairs backed against the wall. Fallon sat next to me. She kept her attention on the participants, while I watched the shadows that shouldn't be there, given the direction of the light.

I had no time to consider it, though, because the Gathering was called to order and arguments erupted—so much for the pre-planning. Emissaries leaned forward, pounded fists hard enough to jolt water in the glasses, swearing with words I'd never heard before. Nia was concerned about the water flow in rivers controlled by the Alpen. Fish were dying. The lack of food forced nymphs to flee from ancestral homes, with no recompense for their trouble.

Lec Rus was forceful in his denials. He claimed unexplained landslides in the north changed the water courses, something Sentinel Falls had caused because they allowed humans to mine in the area.

Grayson denied that accusation, pointing out that the land-slides originated in Cariboo territory and the Alpen should get his facts right before making accusations.

Carmag raised concerns over trade routes, cut off by sim-ilar landslides, while Julien crossed his arms and leaned back, amused by the circular arguments. Although, when the Carmag demanded confirmation about trade issues vampires had with the Cariboo, Julien admitted to similar problems.

"Vampires have no wish to disrupt pack loyalties," he added. "But the responsibility to monitor Cariboo belongs to the wolves. And yet, how many Gatherings have they refused to attend with nothing done?"

The turmoil became a physical pressure in the room that ached behind my eyes. My skin tingled. The runes on my arm squirmed, and I forced the sensations down with the heat from Albert that still lingered in my palms. Boredom persisted, though. I curled, then flexed my fingers, realizing the more I played with the heat, the easier it was to move.

I became the moon and heat was my tide. I entertained myself by pushing, pulling, until Fallon shifted her weight. When she glanced at the air conditioning vents set high in the wall, at the small white ribbon fluttering in the air flow, I wondered if she felt a difference. If I might be pulling heat from her... without touching her.

I locked my hands together, pressed them between my knees. As the arguing continued, I felt untethered. My gaze bounced from the walls to the overhead lights, then to the table, the worried nymphs, the vampire lounging as if amused. I moved on to the witch, sitting with her back straight, folded hands on the table. Everything about her seemed frozen—other than her dark, swirling eyes.

She rocked forward, then backward, her lips parting to reveal a seam of white foam. My gaze darted, jumped to the moving shadows. They continued to flex and gather, stronger than what I'd noticed before—could no one else see them?

The chandeliers flickered.

Pressure in the room bulged.

Carmag's alpha rose to his feet, knocking a glass that spilled water everywhere. His voice was odd when he said, "What's the witch doing?"

Then Lec Rus's snarl slammed like a fist to my throat as he said, "What's the fucking *faille* doing?"

Whatever I was doing, it was the *faille* part of me that thrashed with urgency. Grayson lunged to his feet, his chair skidding backward, tipping. As it crashed, a woman screamed. I turned toward the sound, frantic when I saw Nia sprawled on the floor with her blue gown tangled in the chair legs. Blood bubbled from her lips. Over her, a shadow crouched, then wavered.

The witch cried out. She fell forward, black hair fanning.
And the shadows became wolves, ripping, tearing.
Killing.

CHAPTER 35

Noa

THE ALPHAS—ALPEN AND CARMAG—HAD already shifted. So had their guards. Beside me, Fallon was no longer sitting in the chair. She was in wolf form, taking down the wolf that leapt toward Grayson.

"Julien," he roared as he gripped my arms. "Get her the hell out of here."

I shook my head, my lips forming the word, "No," unsure if anyone heard me. Blood and gore coated the floor, broken chairs. Crumpled flags littered the table. The noise clanged like dull cymbals. The trembling in my hands matched that in my legs and, turning, I gagged, hand to my mouth, stumbling back as the vampire wrapped hard arms around me.

"Don't puke on my shoes," he warned before black smoke swirled. Then I lost my breath beneath the force of wind, feeling weightless until we stumbled into the middle of sunlight and screams. More chaos as the streets filled with fighting wolves.

I could not tell friend from foe. Would not know who was approaching me, and I gripped Julien's arm for stability. Or perhaps to keep him from disappearing again without me. The fabric in his jacket was soft, but I felt rock-hard strength beneath—a vampire, and I was clinging like a child to a nightmare because he was my best option. He could get me back inside where my friends were fighting.

Maybe I could help.

"No way," he snorted before I could ask. "The precise order was to get you the hell out of there. The wolf will be fine. I won't be, if you are harmed."

Mace was in the distance; for whatever reason, he hadn't shifted into his golden wolf yet. But I realized he'd brought in reinforcements, and fighting wolves filled the streets. Not innocents, thank the gods.

"Noa," he shouted, pointing toward the far end of town, toward Leo's vet clinic. But there—I saw a disheveled woman leading a dazed man. Miranda. And Albert.

My breath caught, and I flashed to Nia, lying dead in a pool of blood, her beautiful long-fingered hands splattered with red while her gown slowly darkened.

"Julien—how many can you take at one time?" I had to scream over the din, one hand shielding my eyes from rising dust. "Like... transport to safety?"

He'd already noticed where I'd stared. "Two trips," he said. "If they'll trust me."

Then it was dark shadows and swirling wind—and I was in front of Miranda. "Trust me," I shouted, telling her I'd go first, then she and Albert would follow.

"To Leo's vet clinic," I added, hoping she knew about the passage to Azul. She nodded, and within seconds, we stood in the forest. I held Albert's left arm while Miranda supported him on the right; he kept asking, "Mira, where are we going?"

She kept murmuring, "Home, dear heart."

We hurried past the tree where the Green Man once left me rusted wolf traps to use against Stewart. This far from Sentinel

Falls, the only sounds came from our ragged breathing, Albert's voice, and the crunching of twigs beneath our feet. The shuffling of leaves. Heat flowed from Albert into my hand, but I refused to let go of his arm, let him fall. To do so would mean never getting him back up, not in Miranda's exhausted state. She was Hattie's age. It was a miracle she'd come this far, and I cried out when I felt the trembling resistance of the magic, then pushed through into the passageway.

The chill shocked me. While darting moths and luminescent vines lit the obsidian, water dripped from cones of ice. Or perhaps it was my over sensitized awareness, noticing every nuance. Minutes crept like hours. Miranda slipped once, while Albert struggled over the uneven, wet stones. I hoped their strength would be enough to get them to Azul. Once there, they could rest, and I could alert the men, have them help those in Sentinel Falls.

They already know, Noa. Through the pack bonds.

Which I did not have. I chided myself for not thinking, for being helpless without a wolf. All the reasons why I was more a liability than an asset. What fighting I could do was weak compared to the wolves. I had no way to communicate, or react to any strategy, and the sting in my throat twisted when I thought of Grayson. Fallon. Mace.

I wished for a way to reach out and know they were safe. I couldn't shut down the image of Fallon in midair, taking on a wolf still part shadow—had the shadows come from the witch? I'd first noticed them hovering around her. Then she'd seemed caught in a trance. Until she fell forward. The shadows disappeared, revealing the wolves. The enemy.

But who would dare attack during the Gathering? When all the species were there? It was a call for all-out war, when the witches had no strong interest in the Selkirk territories.

And why did I see the shadows when no one else did?

As burning as those questions were, they would wait until another day. Once the wounded were tended, the frightened calmed. Thank the gods Levi was the Pied Piper, leading so many children away—although the bitter taste in my mouth was cold and sharp, filled with a need for retribution.

My resistance to Grayson's bargain died when Nia died. When other innocents died. I wanted to learn how to use whatever I was—monster or savior—and I nurtured that ember, the anger. Drew strength from it. Felt the dark inside me expand as if breathing.

And then I stepped through the end of the passage with Albert heavy at my side and Miranda shaking from the exertion—only to have the bitterness turn into the taste of ashes.

Because Azul was burning.

CHAPTER 36

Noa

THE BEAUTIFUL TOWN, a sanctuary for wolves who deserved peace and security. Grayson's secret kept for so many years. The hidden azure lake shimmering in the sun. Overflowing gardens. Red umbrellas at the outdoor café... everything disintegrated beneath the ripping, stampeding creatures.

Creatures like those who stormed through the gray vertical slit weeks ago, scuttling, corrupted.

Crab-like nymphs swarmed toward a woman in a flowing yellow dress. They caught the hem, clawed upward even as she shifted into her wolf—too late.

The swarm overwhelmed her, and I screamed as I ran, tripped, fell face down in the dirt.

No time, Noa.

But I knew movement drew the creatures. Fresh prey. If I could lure them toward me, away from her...

Pushing upward, I waved my arms, jerked forward. The swarm turned as one, the chitinous clicking drying the saliva in my throat. I veered around trees, trapping the creatures in the tangled underbrush, smiling at the frenzied thrashing. Then another sound.

From a distance, high-pitched screams, adding to the cacophony. I burst through the trees to see the girls fighting—my posse, too young to shift, but determined. Arrows flew toward three tusked creatures closing in, but Fallon's training had the girls holding their ground and fighting as a group.

I changed direction, racing toward my house and the weapon inside. The door dented the wall as I burst through, whipped the bow and arrows from the rack. Instinct kicked in, pulsed with my heartbeat. I restrung the bow, not daring to think beyond each step. I snatched up the second quiver of arrows Fallon had given me; the first was already over my shoulder. The leather I hated now became an asset—it would slow the creatures down if they got to me.

When I sighted the first target, I let the arrow fly; the shaft bowed, arcing through the air before connecting with a wet *thwap*. So many screams. Grunts and shouting voices. I needed to close them out, not listen, not see the gray-haired men wielding poles because they were too frail to shift into wolves. Not worry about the women, shepherding frightened children into boats and desperately rowing toward the center of the lake—no monsters there. Not yet.

I took aim at the tusked pigs. Shot. Ran. My fingers were numb. The sounds became a white noise. The reek of gore thickened the air.

Around me, vicious tearing snarls as wolves raced toward the fight—the men of Azul—those able to shift. My blood thrummed with the blood-lust the way I imagined their *wolf* blood thrummed. Exhilaration burned, a drug in my veins. I was a wild creature, refusing to be tamed. Racing free as I'd never raced... never been free...

I danced with a graceful violence. Killing. I craved more. Found targets and killed more. My body dampened with heated sweat. Or blood. I wasn't sure.

But as I drew closer to Leo's clinic, the need to weep nearly broke me.

A wheelchair, tipped on its side beside a body on the grass, the discarded blanket turning into black rust.

Halwyn...

Don't think, Noa.

I screamed Leo's name, running, panting.

A gray form charged from the side and I spun, bow ready, arrow nocked, jerking up at the last instant when the wolf did a quick tuck-and-roll—then he was up again, yipping, circling, asking me to follow.

Levi.

I ran, lungs heaving, following Levi's wolf the way I'd followed the black wolf through the meadow. Thoughts dashed past, overflowing with memories... Grayson... how he'd looked in firelight. The sound of his voice. *Convince me...*

And I hadn't convinced him. Couldn't.

A sob choked on the realization. I'd failed, and the subsequent cost of this day would be too much. The challenge hadn't been to the Alpha of Sentinel Falls.

The challenge had been to every species in the Selkirks. To every emissary at the Gathering.

With this death and destruction.

And what I thought of next was the hate in the Alpen's voice when he'd asked, "What's the fucking *faille* doing?"

Had I been interacting with the witch somehow?

See it see it see it...

Don't think don't think don't think!

My feet pounded against the ground. Each enraging impact gored through my knees. I focused on the pain. On the energy surging through me.

Heat rose from my toes through my legs, and I thought of the Green Man, the King of the Forest—did he see this carnage? The willful destruction of the sanctuary Grayson created?

Useless thoughts as my quiver emptied. I threw it aside and pulled the second into place.

Fighting rose and fell like ocean waves. The number of tusked beasts churning up the bloody field diminished, while the dead lay with arrows or wooden poles speared through their bodies, pinning them to the ground until the meadow looked like an ancient battlefield.

But ahead, shafts of golden light shimmered through the grass, still wet with dew—like pink sunlight through the rabbit's ear.

Please, let it be dew. Please let the rabbit be alive.

A grunting, hairy boar broke through the shrubbery, knocking me to the ground. We rolled. Dirt was gritty in my mouth as I twisted to my back. Stiff-elbowed, I fought against the lunging weight, the slashing hooves. The leather held, but the pig's wiry pelt stank of rot, and the snapping, drooling jaws jabbed inches from my face; I gagged on the thick, salty slather that fell into my mouth.

My thoughts hurtled toward the darkness, to the *faille* part of me that knew how to drain the life-force from an enemy... and my wrestling fingers sank into a body that turned into shriveling, putrid flesh.

The creature jerked.

The burn in my fingertips increased, but without pain. The more the heat flowed, the more invincible I felt.

I couldn't turn it off, stop it.

Then Levi's wolf was there, leaping through the air. Tearing what was left of the creature into flapping, bloody strips—leaving it like pink laundry scattered on the shrubbery to dry.

I pushed to my feet, caught in a nightmare with eyes wide open. Hearing the monster inside me... a rasping whisper above the turbulent sound.

So close I could feel the hot breath.

See me. Become me.

And whatever freak or weapon or danger that Grayson wanted—I was already there. Red haze distorted my vision. The black lake inside me surged upward with a volcanic force, flooding my throat, heaving through my heart until I thought it would stop pumping.

What the-gods-hell was *I?*

Had I drawn these creatures today? Killed these wolves, the others... Halwyn...

The idea gouged until I had nothing left except the realization that I was the monster. The blood spilled this day was on my hands, and I would never wash it off. Never absolve myself if I'd done this.

Levi's wolf yipped, but I shook my head, bent over, hands on my knees. No more running. No more refusing to see what a *faille* was, why I never should have come back here. Better to be ripped apart on this bloody field beside Halwyn... who had more honor than I had.

He deserved better than what I'd given him—what someone broken brought to a pack. Death. Destruction. No matter all the pretty stories in my grandfather's books, the tales of the old kings and queens and their bloody rivalries.

If this was what a *faille* was... what a *faille* did... then I deserved to be shunned and killed.

I deserved to be broken into all those tiny pieces, scattered in the wind.

"*Noa!*" Catrina limped toward me, clutching her arm.

At the sight of her, the pink streak in her blood-stained hair, the smears of dirt on her face... something snapped back into place. I straightened. Levi's wolf yipped, then dashed off in a different direction. He'd been leading me here, wanting me to help her the way I'd helped him. Helped Laura.

Because whatever else I was, I could also heal broken wolves.

"Come on." I wrapped an arm around her waist. "Let's get you to the clinic."

We hobbled across the muddy distance. I told her to look away when we passed the wheelchair, the blanket. The door hung on broken hinges, but the air inside the clinic held a stinging disinfectant scent. Nothing foul hid there, and the first exam room was bright and clean... normal. I urged her on the padded table. "Let me see your arm."

She stifled a groan, peeled her fingers back.

"It's not that bad," I murmured, sounding like Grayson when he'd lied about my worm wounds.

"A pig got me," she said through gritted teeth. "I got it back."

Her shudder jerked, while the lingering horror added a stark pathos to her face, and I said, "I haven't gotten used to the noise yet."

"They smell like a rotten pumpkin." She breathed in when I probed the edges of the wound.

"That got to me, too." I went to the small sink, washing my hands first, then filling a kidney-shaped bowl with water. I found sterile pads and arranged the items on a metal tray, moved it closer to the table. I took my time, letting her see what I was doing. Calming through a lack of panicked haste.

"It's okay to be scared," I said as I washed the blood from her skin. "I felt like that the first time I saw a nymph, and I can't count how many times since then. But what I learned is that it's okay to feel scared and hate what you have to do. Because then you remember why you're doing it, and that's the good part. Knowing there's a reason."

"Like you." She clutched my hand. "You are good, Noa. Don't... just don't... I asked Laura for books. I told her it was a school project, but I wanted to read about the queens because people say they became *failles*."

"I read Laura's books too," I admitted. "But those things happened thousands of years ago. And maybe the stories aren't accurate."

Catrina looked away, chewed on her lip while I cleaned the rough gouge on her arm. "That's what Laura said. But... people say bad things when they don't know what they're talking about. And if you've heard some of them..."

I tossed a bloodied pad and ripped open a new package, dipped the gauze into fresh water.

"I wanted you to know," she continued, "that I wish I was like you. Brave enough not to pee my pants when the pigs charged. Because that's what I did. I couldn't stop the pee, and it was so warm when it got into my shoe, I wanted to throw up. Then I ran into the lake and drenched myself so no one would know."

She shivered; I hadn't realized her jeans were wet.

"I threw up in front of Grayson," I said, unfolding a blanket and settling it across her lap. "His wolf killed a rabbit in front of me, and I couldn't handle it. Then I threw up on Mace's back. And an hour ago, I almost threw up on a vampire's shoes. But that wasn't the worst of it. When I was sick with worm poison..."

Let her see how flawed you are, Noa.

"The alpha had to help me in the bathroom."

Her lips twitched. "He listened to you pee?"

The laugh rose easily as I washed more blood from her arm. "Worse than that. He stood there and watched. Then had to…"

"Ugh. Maybe I'm not so bad."

"No, sweetheart. You aren't so bad."

The supply drawer was empty, and I said, "What size scrubs do you wear? I need bandages for your arm, and you need something dry. I'm going to leave you alone, but I'll be right back."

She tugged at her braid, the pink stripe in her hair still vivid. "Small. And I'll be okay alone."

I paused in the doorway. "Minutes, Catrina. I'll leave the door open so you can hear me."

She tossed a package of gauze, missing my head by a foot. "You're worse than my mom."

Maybe, but I hurried down the short hall, sorting through the shelves and drawers, looking for what I wanted and thinking about Leo. What he'd do. Where he was. If he was alive. I thought I'd sense the loss if he wasn't. The same with Laura, Hattie. Oscar. The list I'd made, all the wolves I cared about.

And then, like an insect buzzing around my ear, I felt the threat an instant before Catrina screamed.

My heart shifted in my chest.

I snatched up a scalpel, the only weapon I could find. Skidded down the hall and burst through the door I'd left open so Catrina could hear me, feel safe. She was on the floor, and I launched toward the hairy, grunting pig pinning her there.

The blood pooling on the floor, slippery and warm—that blood had to belong to the pig. I refused to let it belong to Catrina. Not to the girl who wanted to be like me.

It had to be the pig because I was slashing and slashing at the ugly gray body. Screaming. Teetering on the edge of a precipice, with the abyss yawning beneath me.

But the thing in that dark *faille* place was no longer hiding. It breached like a monster from the ocean's depths, heaving through me as I slashed downward, ripped upward. Again and again while hot blood spurted and coated and ruined my soul. The tenuous grip I had on myself.

Or who I used to be.

Grayson found me like that, a feral creature, my braided hair sticky and red. My teeth bared. Choked sounds coming from between my thinned lips. I wondered why he was there, stopping what had to be done. Even while I realized something about me wasn't right.

His hand closed around mine despite my struggle to kill what was already clearly dead. A creature who defiled what was left of my world. Who didn't deserve to live.

But... in that moment... Grayson was there. He was in the darkness with me, feeling the hate, the violence. The emptiness. Did he realize what I'd become? A derelict creature? The useless weapon he wanted to create?

For the space of a breath, I hated him. Then I pitied him for believing in hope when there was no hope inside me.

"Noa."

Through the dark, I heard his voice, a tether back to him, glowing like a thousand stars before the dawn. Blazing like the beacon fires, flicking one by one, leading me back to him.

"Leo's here," he said. "Catrina's alive, but he can't help her if you don't move."

My hand spasmed. The scalpel was slippery against my heated fingers.

"I'm taking you away. Don't fight me."

"Not Julien." With my thoughts muddled, I thought of the vampire sweeping me away in dark smoke and wind. Removing the catalyst.

"No, not Julien." Grayson took the scalpel from my hand, then gathered me in his arms, rocked back before rising to his feet. He was naked. I frowned at his inky-black alpha tattoo, then down at my clothes covered in tufts and muck.

"I killed it."

"I know."

I released the tight hold I kept on myself. Stared at Catrina while a fist wrapped around my heart. She was breathing. She'd defended herself with the metal tray I'd used, holding it like a shield between her and the tusked creature.

Leo bent over her; I couldn't watch.

Grayson turned away. I let him take me where he wished. Let him shoulder open the door to my house—which was un-touched. Let him carry me upstairs and into the bathroom.

As he stripped away my bloody leathers, I wanted to ask him who had survived in Sentinel Falls. Who was at fault.

He'd always been willing to take my anger. Tell me what was real. Not real.

But I remained silent as the bath filled and steam fogged the mirror so I would not have to see myself.

CHAPTER 37

Noa

IT DIDN'T SEEM POSSIBLE that, three nights ago, wolves stood beside this lake and celebrated the Night of the Beacons.

Or that two months ago, I'd thought I could get in, get out, and be five miles down the road before anyone knew I was here.

They knew now.

I tipped my head and stared at the sky. It surprised me, how quickly the days changed. Lengthened. Gone was the stench of death. That, too, surprised me. I thought the putrid scents would stain my lungs and I'd never be free.

Not far away, a woman sobbed while a boy—perhaps no older than ten—gripped his father's bow. They stood side-by-side at the lake's edge where a boat waited. Six boats by my count, lined in a row, still tethered to the land and bobbing like cradles rocking the dead.

So few, some had said, thanking the gods.

Too many, others growled as I'd passed. Walking in my leathers, fist gripping my bow, hair in the heavy braid I hated.

One of the alpha's inner circle. The *faille*. I'd shut down the murmured insults that filtered toward me, walled off the glares of suspicion.

I was no fool. I recognized the danger I posed to them. The threat they were to me. The threat I was to myself. But wasn't

I like the queens of old? I did things wolves could not do; saw things they couldn't see. I was the myth. *Their* fairytale. The one they used to make the children behave.

The wolf rune on my wrist twitched. I flicked my hand, as if I could toss that twitch away.

No hope, though. The rune solidified a bargain made. A promise embedded in my skin. Perhaps a warning. It would remain until Grayson cut through it. Drew blood for our ending.

But maybe now he saw the necessity.

The risk.

I faced the breeze. The late spring warmth had filled with the scents of growing things, opening buds. The promise of long, lazy summer days. Grayson built Azul because he treasured those days—torn apart now—and I could not shake the conviction that Mosbach was right. I was the catalyst. And it was also true, what he'd said, about the rabbit.

It wasn't the first cut.

It was the scream when the ripping began.

Twilight lingered. The murmur of voices mingled with the cicadas, chirping. The ceremony would soon begin, and the idea weighed like a frigid shroud. I'd been unable to say no. My heart had been too broken to deny Halwyn this last honor.

I rubbed at my bony shoulder; the curve was more prominent now than when I'd been ill with worm poison. What weight I'd gained, I'd lost. Perhaps it was a consequence of turning feral. Or at least as feral as I could be without a wolf.

During my slashing spree, I'd bent the scalpel, melted the handle, although the heat hadn't touched my skin.

What I'd left of the pig was unidentifiable. In my rage, I'd dragged the body from Catrina and kept slicing, slashing. Watching the gore and blood like I was creating a photograph by Edward Weston—gods, that life was so long ago. I'd been the girl in the forest. The girl who dreamed. Who saw the world in color, and yet admired the art in black and white.

And what was I now? How could I heal silent wolves, then steal the energy and use it to destroy? Was I even intending to heal? Or exploiting the helpless?

Around me, the gardens were neat again. Children laughed beneath the trees, caught in another game of tag, too young to appreciate the reality of death.

How quickly they could return to normal. How blessed they were in their lives.

But murmured comments drifted in the breeze; I could no longer ignore the voices, harsh, grieving. Laura once said wolves were two creatures in one—the wolf was emotional, suspicious, while the man made the moral judgments.

And the wolves had judged me. Because now they had proof of what a *faille* could do—beyond easing silent wolves like Halwyn. I could do things far worse.

Even my posse turned away, refusing to make eye contact. The pink was gone from their hair, including Catrina's hair. How could I fight it? When wolves would believe what they wanted to believe?

"Noa."

I breathed in when he said my name. Looking at Grayson, I saw the strain that tightened the creases around his eyes. He wore black. His hair ruffled in the breeze. A muscle feathered in his jaw.

But I knew the hours, days, nights... they hadn't been easy on him.

"The light is fading. I'll need you soon."

My fingers tightened on the bow. Fires flickered along the lakeshore; I hadn't noticed. I'd been lost in thought. But flames reflected on the water, creating wavering crimson ribbons—fingers reaching over ripples for the boats. One last hope that love could hold on. Delay the inevitable. The need to let go.

I looked away. "I know what to do."

His weight shifted. We hadn't talked about what happened. I hoped he didn't want to talk now. But he said, "I thought you'd want to know. Nia and Ashina were the only casualties at the Gathering, other than the enemy. And the witch. We're looking into her coven."

"Did she spell the wolves?"

"We think so. Kept them shadowed until she died. Whoever sent them burned off the pack marks. And since the Alpen killed all survivors, we have no one to question."

I nodded, numbed by what he continued to say.

"The creatures who attacked here—we don't know how they discovered Azul. Got through the wards."

"I drew them."

"I don't accept that."

His mark on my wrist warmed, then faded, and I regretted the loss, despite how I'd felt earlier. About endings. But my emotions were complicated and I wouldn't work through them today, in front of him. Perhaps I could unravel how I felt later, in the quiet of the forest, with no one around to watch.

Grayson stepped toward me. "It never goes away, the grief. The debt owed to the dead by living."

I looked toward the lake again, considering the debts I owed. If I ought to ask for absolution.

But Grayson was the Alpha of Sentinel Falls, hard and commanding. The gathered crowd had fallen into silence, listening to our conversation, and I was thinking, *no pity no pity no pity*.

He studied my face for a long heartbeat. Behind us, the women and girls walked along the water's edge, tossing flowers toward the boats. Those that landed on the water floated like flower petals thrown for a wedding.

But what I saw looked more like splashes of blood.

"We need to talk," Grayson said. "But it's time."

For the rite to begin.

I took my place behind Halwyn. His body was at rest in the boat. Someone had dressed him in clean clothes, perhaps a favorite shirt because the flannel revealed signs of wear. A blanket covered his missing lower legs; he could have been sleeping.

Fallon stood a few feet to my left; in the boat she guarded, the woman attacked by the chitinous mass looked untouched, wrapped in a flowered dress with her hands cradling a teddy bear. Fallon had explained it earlier. At the moment of death, most wolves returned to human form—with exceptions. Callum hadn't because of his missing head. Then she'd looked at my expression and turned the conversation toward what I'd be required to do.

The young boy stood to Fallon's left. The bow was shaking in his hand, the tip dragging on the ground as he sobbed. With a nod toward Grayson, Anson Salas—the Alpha of Carmag—stepped up and put his large hands on the boy's shoulder. He bent his head and murmured several words, then took the bow, stood beside the boy and nocked the arrow.

I could not look at the others who formed the line. Each of us dipped the arrows into waiting fires. Readied for the first step in the rite.

"We honor our warriors. Our departed friends. Those we loved." Grayson's voice held the strength and authority of the Alpha of Sentinel Falls. Each word carried to the gathered wolves. "We come tonight to send them on their last journey."

The crowd murmured words of sorrow, hope.

Honor that twisted in my throat.

I aimed the arrow toward the sky, the flames guttering like candlelight.

"One to light the way," the Alpha of Sentinel Falls said as six flaming arrows arched into the night, splashing in near unison beyond the now drifting, untethered boats. Yards from the shore.

"One to break the bond." Arrows arched again, streaking through the night, sinking this time into each boat's wake. A flash of orange catching on the ripples before winking out, breaking the symbolic tether to the shore... to life... to any mate bond that might exist. Allowing the living to be free.

"One to sanctify the dead," Grayson intoned.

The bowstring slid from my fingers as if I'd plucked a harp string, sending one last note into the night. Arrows etched flaming arches through the dark before landing in the boats. Ruby smoke puffed, then swirled upward. Water lapped against the shore, rhythmic. The boy had turned into Anson's hard body, his arms wrapped around the Alpha of Carmag's waist. I wondered if Grayson had granted Anson the honor of comfort, since he'd had to officiate. Or if Grayson felt the pack would not be receptive to him, comforting a boy who'd lost a father.

Because he'd protected the *faille*. Giving her a pack mark. Bringing her into their midst.

Six pyres burned on the starry lake because of what I might have done, and I turned away when Grayson approached.

"In the morning, Noa," he said. "We can talk."

"Alpha." Anson Salas stood with several men in a flanking position. "It can't wait until morning. Surely you know that, how your pack is reacting. We all see it. Let her come with me—"

Grayson's snarl was pure menace. "She stays here."

"Don't be a fool, man." Anson had stiffened. "I can protect her. You can't."

Each alpha braced, alarming me. They were ready to break the taut truce over something that couldn't wait until tomorrow—something they knew—but I did not. Even Fallon and Mace; they stood beside Grayson, and behind them, another row of wolves.

I stared at the bow in my hand, at the fires reflecting on the lake beneath a glowing moon.

It never goes away, the grief. The debt owed by living.

I could see the fierce determination on Grayson's face, the tanned skin pulled taut over bones that had sharpened in the last few days. This *Wolf* of Sentinel Falls, the man who had laughed at the Lady of the Lake and bargained with her over an ancient, immeasurably valuable artifact. For me. And as I looked into his bi-colored eyes, I wondered which part of him battled harder for hope—the man or the wolf.

Then I wondered if I'd ever know.

But maybe never knowing was what I deserved.

Because a spark had turned into disaster.

Because magic was a soft stroke against my skin.

And because Grayson held a hope that I could not allow myself to destroy.

I turned, following the magic, what felt clean and shining. Behind me, voices rose and fell. My throat tightened. I would not say goodbye after the goodbyes already said this night.

Those that were painfully final and far more important than mine would be.

"Noa," Catrina said, her voice wavering. "You can't."

I wouldn't explain about the emptiness inside me, beyond the black abyss. I wouldn't give myself a second chance to hurt her. Or Grayson. Leo. Hattie. All the others on my list.

So I lied, and said, "I'll be right back."

"No, you won't." Tears pooled in her eyes. "You're leaving us."

I glanced toward the forest, the spaces between the trees. Light shimmered with the green of spring. With wreathes of ivy and new, sprouting grass. The magic felt familiar, the tang of metal.

A soft tug in my chest—what I'd felt before, when I'd tipped my chin to the alpha and told his wolf, *no more being strong for me.*

"Noa."

I glanced at Grayson, his powerful body. He'd moved with a stealth I hadn't noticed, as if afraid of startling me. My voice was hoarse. "How can you keep going? After this?"

"Because what's at stake is worth more than one setback," he said. "And I have to believe this evil isn't insurmountable. That we each have a role to play. Because I want to look at my children someday and tell them I did everything I could to protect their world."

I shuddered at the sincerity in his voice... at the thought of children.

My voice broke as I whispered, "And I won't tell my children that I destroyed your world, Grayson. Or grieve at graves for the lives that were lost. This is the debt I owe."

He shook his head. "No. You owe no debt. We owe the debt to you."

I smiled sadly. "Show no pity, remember?"

His mouth tightened; I knew he'd heard me before, hoped he would understand now. Looking up at his beautiful face, I said, "I wish I'd convinced you. That night. Before all this happened. When the beacons burned."

He took a jerky step forward. "You still can."

My turn to shake my head. I couldn't speak. Instead, I pressed my hand to my lips when his wolf shimmered—a shadow beside him—two, when it could only possibly be one. But such was the curse of a *faille*, going where she didn't belong. The wolf was as real as he'd been that night in the firelight... when I'd crossed the line. I sank my fingers in the wiry pelt, felt the shifting muscles, the warmth of breath against my skin. Emotion welled. "Take care of him, wolf..." I whispered. "Promise me."

The wolf growled.

Grayson's eyes locked on mine, and what crossed his face burned into my soul.

I stumbled back a step.

Do it now, Noa. Either stay, or walk away.

I turned.

And let the Green Man's magic take me, tug me through the veil.

CHAPTER 38

Grayson

LEO WAITED IN NOA'S house. He sat stiffly in a chair with Hattie hovering behind him. Oscar rocked at her side, foot-to-foot, the way he'd once sorted fishing lures. His restlessness slammed into me, as if Noa's leaving drained the light from the sky. The life from the silent wolves. All those she'd helped.

Rage crackled like black lighting across my skin. I fisted my hands to keep the claws from extending. The *wolf* craved more violence. He wanted the steaming heat of blood, the shaking pallor of men who knew they were about to die. The scent of terror. And I would not deny him. Not even the rite had calmed the rage. It blackened my heart with a need for vengeance.

During the attack at the Gathering, I'd destroyed wolf after wolf who never stood a chance against me. I did what I did best, without a hint of compassion toward the enemy, knowing it was my *fucking fault* that a traitor had infiltrated the pack. Perhaps more than one. And Noa paid the price.

After Callum—after Julien's gods-damned warning—I should have anticipated. Few enemies got past me, in one piece, at least. The enemy who betrayed the Gathering breathed the same air I did. He lived close enough to know the details needed for a dual attack. And those details would betray him.

His life afterward would not last long.

I passed the empty wall rack where Noa kept her weapon, the table with her camera, aiming toward the kitchen instead of the living room with the tall windows that overlooked the lake. Muffled voices dropped into silence; I knew they watched me—Hattie, Oscar, Leo—and I shoved it down, the roaring in my head that hadn't stopped from the moment Noa said, *"Promise me."*

"She's coming, right?" Hattie looked past me toward the open door where Anson stormed in, followed by an angry Mace and Fallon.

I shook my head and dragged a bottle of cognac from the cupboard while my wolf threatened to take control. He'd been howling, clawing behind my chest as if I didn't know his pain, the hollowness. We'd both heard the thunder of Noa's heart, watched her fight as if she still didn't understand her strength. Saying her goodbyes.

"You let her go." Anson gripped my shoulder to spin me around. Mace growled, stepping forward, his body braced. Fallon's face was pale. She still held her bow, but set it aside and moved in.

"You're in Noa's house, Anson Salas," she said. "Show some damn respect."

She had no fear of him, even though he was the Alpha of Carmag, a threat in his own right.

Anson said, "I've a right to ask."

"Not with that tone."

Her eyes were cold; Anson went rigid. I fought the impulse to intervene. Fallon wasn't one to back down, and Anson was no stranger to killing. We'd fought more enemies together than I could count. And each other occasionally.

"I offered a solution." Although Anson spoke to me, his gaze hadn't left Fallon's face, and whatever simmered between them needed a blood-letting soon, before it got out of control. I'd have to talk to her at some point. But I was incapable of doing it now.

"You offered an impossible solution," I said coldly.

"And you're fecking reckless."

Anson's canines punched down before he controlled the fight-urge. We both understood the turmoil shredding Sentinel Falls. Attacking the Gathering was bad enough, a failure on our part that demanded decades of atonement. But Azul—*fucking* damn hell.

Azul was a crushed dream. Everything we'd worked for over the years—the secrecy, the safe haven—all of it, destroyed within an hour. And more wolves than I expected blamed Noa Bishop.

"You think letting her leave was a solution and not another fecking postponement?" Anson's skepticism rippled through the room. "Listen to your *pack*, man, if you can't listen to me. They're *telling* you what they see."

I focused on the cognac. The glasses.

"He's right, Gray," Fallon said. "The pack is restless. They don't know what to think."

"They'll think what I tell them to think," I snarled, even though I knew pack members decided for themselves. They might base that decision on what I said, but also on what they heard and saw, measuring current against past experience. I couldn't—and I wouldn't—dictate.

Coerced cooperation went underground and festered into rebellion. I'd watched it happen before, and I understood why I had to address the pack. Soon, while memories were fresh and before rumors got out of hand. Before that damn fucking Mosbach turned it into a blood-filled shit-storm worse than it already was. At least I'd have the chance to kill him—if he proved to be the traitor.

Fallon swept at her hair, at the few blonde wisps that tumbled free during the rite. Her face remained colorless. Anson's jaw hadn't relaxed. Mace stood, eyes narrowed on Fallon as if he, too, wondered about her relationship with the Alpha of Carmag.

Hattie broke the silence. "If she's not here, the wolves will think she's guilty."

"Mosbach will twist it," Fallon added. "Downplay how Noa fought for those girls. The warning in Sentinel Falls. He'll use her against you."

I turned away from their arguments. Hattie and Fallon saw reasons, the way Anson did, when I knew danger would follow Noa no matter where she went. Unless she went where the King of the Forest wanted her. On the other side of his magic. He'd been protecting her since she arrived, and I had to believe he was still protecting her. Even when I hated it. Even when I'd stood on the upper floor of the ancient watchtower, staring at the dawn breaking over the horizon and begging whatever gods existed for another solution.

Anson angled his head, a fellow predator looking for weakness. I would use whatever weapons I had, no matter the fallout. Sending Noa away was one such weapon. One that could be turned back on me.

I poured an exact measure of cognac into two crystal glasses and held one out to Leo. The other was for me, to get us both through what I had to say. Two years ago, I'd been the deciding voice in his decision to leave Noa alone. Leo had accepted the necessity, agreed with faking his death if it would protect his granddaughter. The only solution, I'd said.

I wondered what he'd say if he knew the truth.

We'd talked about Noa so many times over those years. I'd had chance after chance to explain reasons I hadn't quite believed. A total fuckup. I'd refused to consider fate as anything other than what I controlled. Another part of me had laughed at the idea.

Then she showed up.

And when she rolled in the mud with that defiance in her eyes... the night had shuddered.

Leo gripped the glass with hands that shook. "She couldn't stay?"

"I'm sorry, Leo," I said as calmly as I could. "Wolves saw her at the Gathering. They saw her fighting in Azul, the things she could do." I swallowed a mouthful of cognac that could not fill the emptiness. "I don't doubt Anson's abilities, but the packs know about her now. The vampires, the witches. Beyond the rumors. They want her for the same reasons I want her, and they won't stop hunting her."

Leo's eyes had dimmed. Hattie curved her hands against his bent shoulders, and I wasn't sure if she was supporting him or hanging on. Alcohol burned my throat. What I had left to say would crush them, and I couldn't bring myself to do it.

Not yet.

"Grayson." Hattie's voice choked. "Where is she?"

"Safe."

It wasn't enough. But it was all I would offer.

"You're blind, man." Anson helped himself to the cognac. I'd brought in a bottle for Noa because she liked the taste, and she hadn't discovered it yet. She wouldn't now.

No pity, she'd said, realizing the risk before I could allow myself to see it. Pity would have given Mosbach—or some other elder intent on power—the chance to say I pitied the enemy before the dead were honored.

Because she'd always believed she was the enemy. That what she lacked made her damaged beyond repair.

During the rite, I'd watched her lift the bow, fire arrows steady and true, and knew that with each arrow, she confirmed the decision I'd always known she would make.

From the day I met her, when I realized she had the courage of the wolf.

She would put the pack first. Put me first.

I walked to the windows and stared at the darkened lake. Looking for answers or someone worth killing. It didn't matter. Neither one would bring her back. The wolves had all gone home, back to their houses to grieve in private. Only the boat skeletons remained, sinking low, drifting while guttering flames turned rippling water into pale orange ribbons. My fingers clenched as I raised the cognac, felt the heat on my lips. Tasted... her. The way she'd tasted when I'd kissed her. The night Mosbach sent everything to hell.

"You know something." Anson stood beside me, staring out at the black night the way I stared.

"I know the enemy," I said. The attacking wolves had burned off their pack marks, making their pack affiliations unidentifiable. As insurance, the Alpen killed all survivors. Despite those efforts, some secrets could not be hidden. Not from someone like me.

Anson knew what I meant. "You found one alive."

I nodded. A werewolf with a mutilated pack mark was without defenses. His pack bond was wide open to any alpha who probed his mind, and for me, the man had been nothing more than a butterfly pinned to the ground. Mace kept the prisoner alive for the two days I needed. I'd relished the time. I could have granted mercy. The man knew he was dying. But I'd wanted the suffering. To hear the screams. The begging. Push him to the edge, then bring him back again. And during those hours, whatever humanity I'd had left disappeared beneath the memory of Noa's face, her terror when I'd dragged her from that pig. Away from Catrina. Leo.

For that one thing... there'd been no mercy.

I'd clawed through memory after memory without pity, hunting until I found the information I wanted.

I wasn't proud of it, but I'd do it again in a heartbeat and still feel nothing.

"The witch at the Gathering," I said. "She worked for the Alpen. Her spell shadowed the wolves—mercenaries bought and paid for, men without loyalty. Allowed them to slip past security unseen."

"Witches don't like wolves," Anson argued. "Why would she do it?"

"She looked young," Fallon pointed out. "Maybe she left her coven. Needed protection."

"If they're resorting to mercenaries, the strength of their fighters must be low." Mace crossed his arms, already working out the weakness in his enemy and how to exploit it. Fallon had gone quiet, her thoughts shielded from me. But also from Anson—another wrinkle in the problem, if what I suspected was true.

If so, what would she do? And how reliable an ally was he, if he only wanted Fallon?

But it was Leo who needed my honesty. Noa was *his*. I knew his heart was breaking.

"She warned us," I said to him. "She fought for us. But she had to leave. We have a traitor in the pack. Maybe more than one."

I shocked everyone but Mace and Fallon, who had known as long as I'd known.

"The Alpen knew Noa would be at the Gathering. Rus wants her, wants a *faille*. And then he found out about Azul and Laura, and it was too big a prize to let go. Getting both of them. They split the attack, taking the chance that surprise would be enough, then get away before we could react."

"What about those creatures?" Anson demanded.

I held his gaze. "We haven't worked that out yet."

Hattie's face had blanched. "Where is she, Grayson?"

"With the Green Man. I asked him to take her. Hide her where no one can find her."

"Not even you?" Leo asked.

I turned to hold his stricken gaze. "Especially not by me."

I knew of no other way to protect her. I'd had to let her turn toward the passage that opened. One keyed to her energy and no one else.

"You trust that old man too much." Anson's knuckles whitened as he dragged the cognac to his lips. "The King of the Forest is senile. He tried to repair the wards around Carmag. It was a damn mess. Had me repairing them for months."

Mace shifted his weight. "She melted a scalpel. Obliterated a pig twice her size. She can't control what's emerging."

I tightened my jaw, held the cognac to my lips.

"If she's in trouble..." Fallon's voice was hoarse. "You won't be able to find her."

Rage weakened my knees. Noa had always been... *there*. The abyss. The endless sky. Wolf and not wolf. I'd prepared myself.

Knew that once she was with the King of the Forest, I'd be cut off from her thoughts.

I'd hoped the wolf rune would remain strong enough to sense her. But even that tether snapped when she disappeared, and the resulting silence felt like a cut that still bled.

"Coming back has to be her choice." What I wanted, for Noa to have a choice.

Mace didn't agree. "We need you both. You know that."

"Didn't you hear what she said?" I turned on my second, barely holding back the snarl. "She called it *my* world. *Our world*. Not hers. I won't destroy her over this."

"But she's alone." Hattie's whisper trembled. "She has no one left."

"I know."

Futility shifted like unsteady ground. They didn't know—how could they? They hadn't heard what I'd heard. Felt what I felt. But when I'd found Noa, buried in the ruined pig, I knew she believed she was feral. And as Alpha, I'd be the one who destroyed her.

How in hell was I supposed to tell them that?

When she was a *faille*. And I was...

The thought made me stiffen. I hadn't been able to talk to Noa, explain. I knew she wasn't feral, and even if she was, I'd never hurt her. I'd be in that fucking darkness with her. My fucking *brand* was on her skin—I'd promised my life in that mark. But she refused to see me. Refused everyone.

I could have ordered Laura, as her alpha. Forced her to open the door. I could have ordered Leo to give Noa whatever drug she needed. Calm her long enough for a conversation.

I wouldn't do that to her, destroy the fragile control she held so valiantly through the rite.

The strength she'd had, standing there. Asking me why I held on to hope.

I hoped because I had no choice. And I wasn't holding on to the hope she thought I held, what any of them thought.

I held on to the hope that leaving would save her.

Because *I was the fucking reason* why she couldn't stay.

Fate was the fucking reason.

The shit-show that had started eons ago.

Tears ran down Hattie's cheeks. She held Leo's shoulders. Oscar rocked from left to right. His hands were fisted. Anson's gaze hadn't left Fallon's face, while Mace stared with the cold determination he always displayed when preparing for war.

"You can't ignore the coincidence," Anson said. "She shows up in the Selkirks at the same time we're invaded by creatures from the north."

I wasn't *ignoring* anything. I was fighting like hell against it.

"Noa left to protect those she loves." And I hoped they believed the lie. "She knows what she's capable of doing, and she hates herself for it."

"You were teaching her," Leo argued. "She was accepting it."

"I'm sorry Leo. But after Halwyn... she knew how the pack was reacting. If I'd forced her to stay tonight, she'd try to run tomorrow." And if she ran when I couldn't control where she went, she really would be lost. All I could do was make sure the Green Man was waiting to take her to safety. Beyond my reach.

Beyond *anyone's* reach.

"The Alpen will hunt her," Fallon said. "She isn't safe. Even with the King of the Forest. If these creatures could find a passage to Azul, they can break through anywhere."

"Then we hunt first," Mace countered. "Avenge Azul. Sentinel Falls. Make it safe."

"What's the next move?" the Alpha of Carmag asked. He stood beside me as I turned to face them—Mace, Fallon. Leo, Hattie, Oscar.

My rage simmered, but it was controllable, and would soon find a target.

"Learn who the traitor is," I said. "And we kill him."

CHAPTER 39

Noa

THE PASSAGE I ENTERED was unlike any I'd experienced since learning of their existence.

Most passages were shadowy and blue, illuminated by the bi-oluminescent creatures and plants that covered the jutting walls. The stone was familiar—obsidian—and the light was bright. I followed a path that seemed blessed by the Green Man, because everywhere, I saw the King of the Forest. I saw it in the green of the moss. The green of spring grass, and the darker forest green of ivy, twisting around tree trunks.

For the space of a heartbeat, I wondered at the oddity of trees growing in a sunlit cave. Then the doubt drifted. Rain-bow-colored mist from the waterfall's veil dampened the air. The falls spilled over rocks, gurgling into a pool where frogs croaked from between the lily pads. When tiny, wispy sprites emerged from the foliage, I laughed at their many colors, at the way they swirled and danced. I wanted to join them, extend my arms, wait for the tickle of their wings as they glided across my palms... and a shudder passed through me at the recognition.

I was in my nightmare, the one I'd had months ago, with my feet sinking into the mud that flowed up my body, into my mouth. Grayson had been there to pull me out. But he wasn't *here*, and when the passage behind me closed, I stumbled in a circle, blind panic roaring through me when I saw Metis standing there.

"You've finally come," she said. "Noa Bishop, consort to the Dread Lord."

THE END OF BOOK ONE
BOOK TWO
THE GIRL IN THE FOREST
There is a history of kings and queens.
Alphas and *failles*.
And a catalyst is burning.

ABOUT THE AUTHOR

SUE WILDER FIRST DISCOVERED the power of storytelling as a child living in California, when she got caught sneaking into a neighborhood orchard and starting a grapefruit war. She managed to absolve her cohorts from guilt and has since moderated her behavior. She now writes Contemporary Romance and Paranormal Fantasy Romance - stories that keep her up late at night, filled with laughs, tears, and characters who hang around long after the books reach "The End."

When she isn't writing, you'll find her listening to jazz, enjoying red wine and watching the sunsets.

She lives in the Pacific Northwest with her husband and a yellow lab named Maxine.

For more information, visit suewilderwrites.com
Cover Design: Regina Wamba, ReginaWamba.com
Connect with her through:
Sue Wilder Writes on Facebook, Instagram
Join Sue Wilder's Wild Women reader group on Facebook

Follow

Sue Wilder on Amazon, Goodreads and BookBub

Add

Sue Wilder books to your "want to read" on Goodreads

Other books by Sue Wilder

The Man Wars Series—Contemporary Romance

Dare Me

Ex Me

With Me Series—contemporary Romance

Risk

Scandal

Reckless

Enforcer's Legacy Series—Paranormal Romance

The Darkness in Dreams

The Fire in Vengeance

The Danger in Justice

The Tears in Midnight

The Memories in Moonlight

The Smoke in Shadows